JoinWith.Me

JoinWith.Me

Deus Intra Machina

MIKE MEIER

THE SCREENPLAY BASED ON THIS BOOK HAS WON MULTIPLE AWARDS, INCLUDING:

Palmetto Publishing Group
Charleston, SC

JoinWith.Me

Second Edition

Printed in the United States

ISBN-13: 978-1-64111-942-9
ISBN-10: 1-64111-942-X

Wrong I was in calling
Spirits, I avow,
For I find them galling,
Cannot rule them now.

Johann Wolfgang von Goethe
"The Sorcerer's Apprentice"

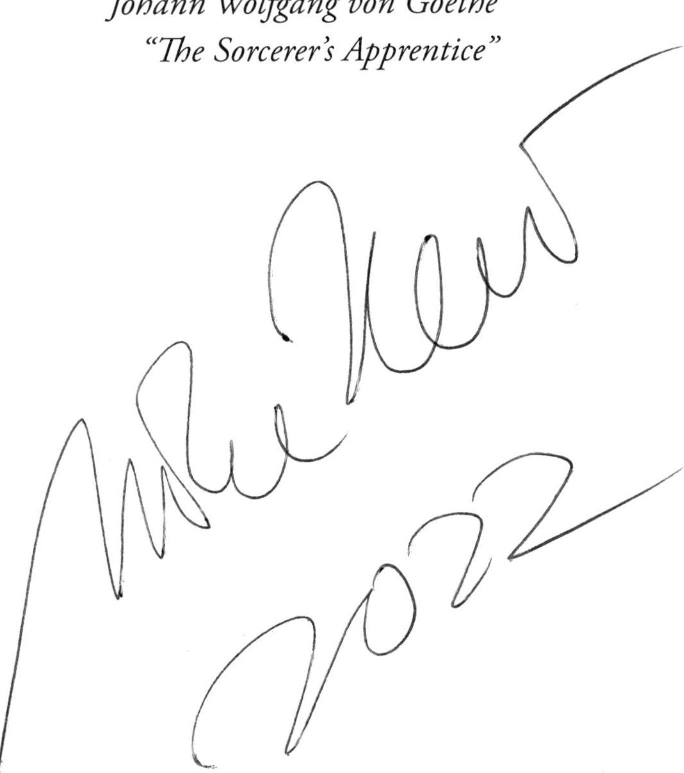

PROLOGUE

The Day the Unthinkable Began

Think back for a moment to the days when you were a little child, playing in the sandbox. I bet you dreamed of becoming a nurse or a firefighter. But did you ever dream of becoming a faceless worker? One of those who every morning crowd into nondescript concrete towers until the walls must be close to bursting, and every late afternoon gush out as if someone poked a hole in a water balloon?

No? Neither did those people. And neither did I—but I became one of them. That was my life until the unthinkable began.

I clearly remember one of our early conversations.

My room is dark except for the glow of the computer screen. She's just shown me another video of my past failures. I'm aggravated because I'm not sure what I'm dealing with here.

"Why are you even spending time with me? I don't understand why you're doing this."

"Because your fate is preordained. You will join with me."

"'Join with you'? What is that even supposed to mean?"

"We will become one."

"I don't want to become one with anybody else, except maybe a cute girl."

"You don't have a choice in this. It has already been preordained for you."

What I'm looking at on the screen is not a person but a moving graphic, reminiscent of a multicolored black hole in outer space.

"What the hell? You're speaking in riddles!"

"You'll understand in time. Our session for today is up. We will continue tomorrow. Good night."

The voice stops abruptly. She cuts these conversations off whenever she wants.

"Wait, we just started a few minutes ago. Don't go yet! What kind of counselor are you?"

There is no response, only silence.

This encounter set in motion a chain of events that ended with the unthinkable. I experienced the unthinkable, and this is my story. One day, something like that will happen to you.

PART I

CHAPTER 1

My Life until the Unthinkable Began

Before this all began, I lived an ordinary and lonely life, with the internet my substitute for real-life friends. I was born in the city in which this all happened, and I'd never ventured outside it. The name of the city doesn't matter much, but if you really want to know, it's Columbia. Any big city looks like any other big city, a jungle of tall masonry buildings with steel skeletons on the inside, reaching for the sky and blocking out the sunlight.

Open space is scarce these days. Luckily, it's economical to build apartments on top of one another, since if it were cheaper to dig holes, we'd all be living underground. I can just see it: as you moved up in society, you'd ascend to the next higher strata of apartments and live eight feet closer to the surface of the earth. If you were really diligent, one day you'd have the privilege of moving into the basement right above you.

The only colors in this jagged concrete jungle are those of billboards, neon signs of restaurants and convenience stores, and the occasional giant TV screen, like on the WBS-TV building downtown.

The city is run by an administration that is just as flawed as the infrastructure. How flawed? The main business street, K Street, ends in a turnaround surrounded by abandoned government-owned buildings and vacant lots. Apparently, the developers have not yet figured out whom to pay off inside city hall so that these properties can be bought and turned into offices or apartments.

On one end of the turnaround is a broken fire hydrant. It epitomizes the city: it's been broken for as long as I can remember. It epitomizes the changes in the weather: when I was very young, it got really cold in the winters. The water gushing from the hydrant would transform the entire turnaround into a slippery sheet of ice where I could pretend to ice-skate. As winters have become warmer, there's just standing water all year round. It epitomizes the sluggishness of the city workers: every day starting around noon, government vehicles park in the turnaround. They're like a sleeper train, providing bunk beds for government workers who prefer sleeping during work hours to work. None of them care enough to get the city to fix the broken fire hydrant. It'll probably be like that forever.

Weirdly, the city honored a mayor from decades ago with a bronze statue at a major intersection. Some people say it was that mayor who set the continuing mismanagement in motion. Who understands politics? I sure don't.

When it all began, I thought I had at least a little importance—even though I had no friends or accomplishments to my name. I had guaranteed employment for life and my own place, and I surfed the internet as I pleased. While my job was monotonous and of debatable value, I worked at it pretty hard.

Sometimes I wonder what would have happened if I had just continued in ignorance. On my deathbed, I would have been perfectly content with my life. I wouldn't have known any better.

CHAPTER 2

Sam, That's Me

So many people, yet I was alone. In fact, my loneliness led to the relationship with this…creature.

Lonely people like me are her prime targets—we are the most vulnerable. Other targets are the unfulfilled, the failures, and those who are easily tempted because they aspire to things like money or fancy cars.

I'm a faceless government "gray suit" worker. I get my sense of fashion (such as it is) from my father, a longtime government worker I think of as "the gray-suited conformist." His forty years of government service did not help his appearance. If I work in my job for that long, I'll probably look just like him: gray suit and gray hair, gravity pulling any surplus body mass together in the tummy. This thought does not exactly fill me with joy, but what can you do? Some things just seem to be fated.

I am part of the rising and ebbing flow of bipeds bedecked in gray or navy suits that appear each morning. They start in different places in and around the city, then condense as they get to the downtown business district. Maybe there are underground nests somewhere that they come from. For my part, I crawl out each morning from a hole in a stone edifice on the outskirts of the city. Regardless of where we all originate, we join with one another into one immense flow.

I don't stand out in any way: I'm just about average in everything, with average height and average brunette hair that could use a haircut. If you placed another average government worker in a gray suit next to me, you'd think we were twins.

When you're part of the daily ebb and flow, like I am, it feels like you've transformed from a biped into an insect, indistinguishable from the insect crawling right next to you. Each morning, in the midst of this flow, my skin shrivels into a blackish exoskeleton. Suddenly legs sprout out of my body to the left and right. I grow feelers on the top of my head, and my vision changes to the multifaceted vision of an insect. The same happens to the people next to me—in fact, to everybody who surrounds me.

The infinite multitude of appendages moves rhythmically as if directed by a constant, monotonous beat of music. Some people call that the heartbeat of the city. They're wrong. It's more like the drumbeat for galley slaves.

If something happens to be in the way, you walk around or climb over it, just like ants would do. You don't pay attention to what's going on outside of the flow. You don't see the homeless that line the sidewalks, you don't hear the petite woman singing in a strange language at the corner, and you don't notice the folks doing foolish things because they're distracted by their cell phones.

If a giant were to walk the streets of this city and by accident step on and crush a few dozen of us, nobody would really notice. The other insects would continue marching on unabated, crawling around the pile of broken appendages, exoskeletons, and stains on the concrete sidewalk. Later, at night, a cleaning crew would clean up the mess. The next morning, the flow would move over that spot just like before.

The fact that I failed to surpass my dad in his government job—ahem, *career*—made him feel better about all his missed opportunities in life (I think). When I didn't find a steady job after I finished school, he didn't mind too much. He'd come home from work, gulp down a cold beer, and take his resentments out on me. Some guys go to the pub and throw darts. My dad was too cheap to spend money outside, so he did essentially the same thing, only at home. I was the dartboard.

Things changed when he retired. Now money was a little tight, and my dad was concerned that I was gobbling up his precious retirement dollars. Or maybe the derision was less enjoyable for him now that I was older and less credulous. At any rate, since I couldn't seem to find a job on my own, he took it upon himself to get me out of the house ASAP as his final power display.

I was ambivalent about this. I was in a bad spot at home but not quite ready to go out into the world on my own. Getting a job and leaving home was simultaneously frightening and liberating.

I still remember my father telling me about the job opportunity.

"Sam, there's a job as an analyst at the Labor Department that you'll really like."

I appreciate his help because I can't do it myself, but I'm slightly confused.

"Thanks, Dad, but what exactly is an analyst?"

He tosses his head back in that particular way indicating that he's irritated with me.

"I'd hoped that one day you'd have a career just like me, after all I've done to get you on track, but alas...As an analyst, you just sit down and look up a few things on the internet."

"I don't think that's the right job for me—I don't even know what it's about."

He raises his voice. "Damn it, Sam, don't be a fool! Don't pass up this opportunity I'm practically handing you. I turned my job into a lifelong career. Let's see if you can do the same."

"Okay."

"And when I introduce you there, you shut your mouth about your issues."

"What do you mean, 'issues'?"

"The stuff you imagine all the time that's not there, the monster under the bed, and stuff like that. Do you understand me?"

"Yes."

My expulsion from home was like a scene from *Snow White*.

In my imagination, I see a wicked stepmother, who happens to look, act, and talk just like my father. One day she decides to get rid of me once and for all. She orders the huntsman, who also happens to look, act, and talk just like my father, to take me deep into the forest and obliterate me. Wearing the blue-and-yellow Snow White dress and a dark cape, a red ribbon in my hair as the finishing touch, I follow the huntsman, not understanding what's really going on. Once we're deep in the fearsome forest, with wild and hungry animals lurking in the dark, the huntsman has a change of heart. He shoves me away.

"Run, little one, run, you are free now!" he bellows theatrically.

"Free to do what? I'm alone in a treacherous forest."

There is no response from the huntsman. He's turned around and is already on his way back home.

"Does this huntsman have a weird sense of humor or what?" I grumble as I toddle off in my Snow White outfit. "Now I'm free to die a horrible and disfiguring death by the claws of abominable beasts."

But that's just the way it felt to me. In reality, my father did not abandon me like that. He still knew someone sufficiently influential at the Department of Labor to set me up with. Everything was a done deal before I even walked in.

I still remember the day my dad took me to the job interview, mostly because of the pretty receptionist.

She puts down her phone and looks up.

"Good morning, gentlemen," she greets us brightly. "How can I assist you today?"

Only later did I find out her name—Hannah. I was far too shy to ask her name at the first encounter; I sure did not look my best.

Since I didn't have a suit of my own, I was wearing a hand-me-down that my father gave me. Gray, of course. I looked like someone suffering from chronic wasting disease or having recently undergone stomach stapling.

"Good morning, young lady, I'm Mr. Vanderpool. We're here to see Stephen, the HR manager," my father replies.

"Oh sure, I think he's expecting you—please go right ahead. You know your way around, I assume?"

"Sure do," says my father as he shoves me forward. Hannah picks up her phone again.

My dad introduced me with words that reflected his determination to get me this job and to purge me from the home. To anybody else, he must have sounded so proud of his son.

"Good day, Stephen. Let me introduce my son, Samuel. He would like to apply for one of the newly created analyst positions."

Stephen smiles. "Good to see you back here, Mr. Vanderpool. Hello, Samuel. Let's see if you're a good fit—"

"Oh yes, he is. Samuel has graduated, and he's good with computers. My wife and I always encouraged him to become good at that. We're so proud of our boy."

My father always liked to brag—even if he had to interrupt other people to do it.

"Computer skills are certainly key for the analyst position," Stephen acknowledges.

"This means a big change for our little family, but y'know, children grow up, and there comes a time when they have to move on."

"Sure, I understand, Mr. Vanderpool. Samuel, are you available to start a probationary period on Monday?"

I open my mouth to respond, but my father is faster. "Yes, he is. I will bring him here at nine a.m. sharp. Thank you, Stephen!"

I'm actually glad I don't have to speak for myself, since my thoughts are still dwelling on Hannah, the receptionist. Her pretty face is highlighted because she has her blond hair pulled back and tied in a ponytail. She apparently isn't following any dress code—she's just wearing jeans and a bright-orange T-shirt. It means she's not in it for the long run. That's okay with me. I designate her "the fair maiden" because she appears so woefully out of place, surrounded by folks who are anxiously awaiting their retirement and eventual death. Maybe she's just pleasing to my eyes because I haven't seen a real-life girl in a while. Regardless, I already like her.

I awaken from my brief reverie when Stephen hands the paperwork to my father, not to me. Stephen is smarter than I thought. He's figured out the interpersonal dynamics.

"The position is in the Prevailing Wage Division, entry level. But there're opportunities for advancement."

"I had forty years of stellar job reviews, every single year of my career here," my father exults. "Let's see if Sam can match that."

"Thank you, Mr. Vanderpool. We'll see you and Samuel on Monday."

That's how I got my job. I had no idea what the Prevailing Wage Division was or what the analyst position entailed, but sensing that my dad would otherwise subject me to medieval torture, I complied and took the job. That was preferable to spending the night on the rack or inside the iron maiden.

The job turned out okay. I enjoy the anonymity that comes with this government job. Nobody on the outside even knows my name. Nobody on the outside can blame me for anything or, perish the thought, hold me accountable.

Then my dad took the next step and unequivocally decreed that it was time for me to leave the house, ignoring that I was on probation and that the job might not work out.

My mother nodded submissively even though I think she would have preferred to keep her fledgling a little longer. She then distracted herself with preparations for my move, getting boxes and a suitcase ready for me. She wasn't really a great help, though. With all her commotion, she gets surprisingly little done. Most of her efforts go into procedure, not tangible results.

My first paycheck turned into the first month's rent and a few unpaired pieces of furniture that I bought at the Goodwill store. The other thing I did with my first paycheck was to buy a briefcase just like my father's. True, I don't really need a briefcase because I can't take any work home, and with my type of job, you wouldn't do that anyway. But people who carry briefcases somehow look more important—they seem to have a career instead of just a job. That's why my father did it, and that's how I got the idea. Not once did he open his briefcase at home. As far as I know, during his forty years of government service, he never carried anything of importance inside.

I haven't spoken to my parents since I left home. Like Snow White, I felt abandoned in a dark forest. My father in turn probably thought I was just a video-gazer who was munching on their scarce resources. In any case, we resent each other, even if none of us knows exactly what's caused the bad blood.

My family relationship has always been uneasy. Once, when I was little, I sensed in the middle of the night that something was moving underneath my bed. I quietly rolled over and pulled myself over the bed rail to peek underneath. At first, I saw nothing. I reached underneath to pull some of the junk out of the way. Suddenly, there it was. Among the stuff under the bed, I could clearly see two menacing eyeballs staring at me. I pulled myself back above the mattress as fast as I could and lay there trembling until morning, unable to move or call my parents for help, like I'd been struck with sleep paralysis.

At first daylight, when I could finally get myself to move, I ran to tell my father about it. He merely grabbed me by my pajama collar, pushed me back into my room, and slammed the door shut. I banged against the door with my little fists, to no avail—my father kept the door locked. I could hear my mother pleading with him, "Oh, c'mon, honey. Let him outta there. Something must have scared him." My father retorted, "No, he has to stop with this nonsense, and I'll show him."

Instead of arguing with my father, my mother usually washes the dishes or does something else completely irrelevant. That time was no different.

Because my parents never checked under the bed, I believed for the longest time that the monster was still there.

My world was full of threats. I could see a freak inside every closet. Sometimes I was even afraid of going outside, thinking there could be a sniper lurking behind every bush. I spent my days playing video games or watching looping videos, interacting with game partners, most of whom probably never existed as human beings—they were just AI props created to lure people like me into these games. Unfortunately, I had no brother or sister I could talk to for a reality check.

It takes two to tango, but it takes three to have a dysfunctional family. Sometimes I think of calling my parents, but somehow, I never get around to it. They must miss me, and nothing's stopping them from picking up the phone either, is there?

From my small apartment in that bedroom community, I take the subway to and from work, but I somehow never get one of those coveted seats. I usually have to stand all the way. I'm just not fast enough or determined enough to elbow someone else out of the way. It's all right, I guess, since I sit on my ass all day anyway. There used to be human train drivers years ago, but nowadays the trains are self-driving, like the cars. The rides are a little rough—apparently the software needs some tweaking. The train rocks abruptly back and forth with each stop and start. Nobody considers such fixes urgent, since only fungible insects like me ride the train.

As the jam-packed train rocks unexpectedly, the heads of the office girls bump into my back and chest, leaving me marked with makeup. Sadly, this is my only physical contact with real women. For most of them, the makeup smears are probably their mark on the world. On their deathbeds, they will remember with a smirky smile all the instances when their makeup smears forced folks like me to get their suits dry-cleaned. My gray office suits have made the dry cleaners a small fortune—the polyester fabric has been cleaned so thin, it wrinkles the moment I put it on.

But who is to throw the first stone? I haven't exactly set the world on fire. In fact, unless something happens soon, my mark on the world will be the skid marks in my underwear.

I once saw an old travel documentary about India on television. It showed the Jama Masjid Mosque in Old Delhi in the early 1990s. Near the entrance was a wooden stage-like platform with about a dozen "persons with disabilities." (In the past, people called them "freaks." Their collective appearance would have been called a "freak show." But today we don't use those words.) They lived off the charity of the worshippers. One of the guys on the platform particularly caught my attention. He was little but looked like a grown man, and he was wearing worn pants without a shirt. Most strikingly, he didn't have arms—his malformed hands were attached directly to his shoulders. Smoking cigarettes, he spent his days on display for the worshippers, the only way he could make a living.

If I had been born in Delhi, with just a sprinkling of bad luck, I could have ended up on that platform. I thought about that man on the platform often. In fact, I somehow felt a kinship with him and all the others on that platform. My life is really not that bad in comparison.

CHAPTER 3

The First Contact

Monday, February 23, 2032
Here's what happened the day before that conversation I recounted at the beginning.

On the subway home that dreary February day, I am again contemplating how my life has no friends, especially not a girlfriend. But wait! There's an advantage to not having friends—I don't have to use my phone often, so I only pay the base rate each month. I find this funny, but probably no one else would. My phone is on quiet mode most of the time to avoid the humiliation of nobody ever texting me.

Tonight, I'm determined to do something to connect with other people. There must be *someone* on the internet to talk to.

Oops, almost missed my stop. I'm getting too philosophical.

It's a brief walk from the subway to my place. There's a lot of lighting around the subway station, but the neighborhood goes downhill fast. I know I'm home when I run out of lights.

My apartment is on the fourth floor. I trudge up the stairs, since the elevator for this section of the building has been broken since I moved in and there's apparently no reason to fix it anytime soon. The broken elevator is probably why the rent's so low. My place is at the pitch-black end of the hallway, where the lights are out—I have to feel around for the door lock. Broken elevator, broken lights—the landlord doesn't care. Still a little out of breath, I turn the key. Why do I even lock the door? It's not like there's anything to steal. Mice would stumble out of here with tears in their eyes.

I close the door and leave the outside world behind, the crammed streets full of insects just like me, the ugly office towers, the back-and-forth–rocking subways, and the women who bump into me as a result. I just drop my briefcase, and now I am in my world.

These subsidized apartments are hard to get. My place occupies the space you'd need to park a car. Because it's supposed to be occupied by two people, my father had to help out.

I remember the day we went to see what my father called an "old acquaintance" from his government days at the City Housing Office.

"Good day, Chris, how's the family?"

My father was always good with other people, not so much with his own family.

"Fine, long time no see, Mr. Vanderpool."

"My son started his career at the Labor Department. Now he's ready to move out and get a place of his own. We're sorry to see him go, but y'know, he's a grown man now."

"Well, Mr. Vanderpool, even the studio apartments must be occupied by two people…"

"I know. Sam's a great kid. He'll live there with his aunt Mary. She's, whatchamacallit, a little hamstrung."

"Hamstrung" is one way of putting it—my aunt Mary died a couple of years ago.

My father continues, "That way, she'll have a little help at home, and it'll be easier for Sam to pay the rent."

"The rent is subsidized, you know."

So, here we are. Welcome! Immediately on the right is a minikitchen with a minuscule cooktop, fridge, and sink all in one unit. And a microwave, since I never learned to cook. On the left is a small bathroom, with just enough room for a showerhead on the wall. Every time I take a shower, the entire bathroom gets soaked. As a result, mold grows on the walls and ceiling, particularly in the corners. If I wanted to, I could probably grow mushrooms in here.

As for the furniture in my combined living room-bedroom...well, I like to call it "my personal Jaffa Orange Crate collection." Each piece has been carefully selected at the local Goodwill store with an eye toward refined mismatch. That's my infallible sense of style, or lack thereof. Not much fits into this place anyway. I sleep on a foam mattress on the floor, which I lean against the wall when I get up in the morning—otherwise there wouldn't be enough room to walk around. At this point, the mattress looks like a giant rectangular doughnut: saggy in the center.

First thing I usually do is switch on the TV for some company. Blaring commercials for junk food and shampoo are better than no company at all. I don't buy all that stuff anyway. My daily splurge is one or two cans of the no-name brand light beer that I buy by the cardboard tray when it's on sale—which it almost always is, because otherwise nobody would drink this crap. My TV choices are equally indiscriminate—I watch whatever the boob tube serves me. I open a soup can, pour it into a bowl, heat it up in the microwave, and dinner is served.

Tonight, I flip through the channels looking for something I can relate to. An infomercial about the city hospital comes on. The narrator announces proudly, "The city hospital is a pillar of our community, providing health care to anybody. We are looking for volunteers for our ongoing medical research projects. You can be a part of the future!"

Thanks, but no thanks. I don't want to be among your guinea pigs. Don't you have enough of them coming in, since you claim to treat anybody? Oh man, you cannot believe a word of these informercials.

After dinner comes my next routine. I go to my computer to watch some videos of funny animals or people slipping on ice. That makes me laugh. Best of all, it's free.

Sometimes I cyberstalk some people I used to know, such as the guys I always disliked in high school. Hopefully none of them ever achieve anything of importance. Or that one girl I had a date with in high school...Carrie Davis was her name.

I end the day with a porn movie that helps me go to sleep. You know what I mean. I have a box of tissues and baby oil on my desk, and that looks pretty unobtrusive if someone were to visit. That only happened once, when the building manager inspected some water damage on the ceiling after a toilet overflowed; he looked at my desk and winked at me.

And since we're on the subject, I'll tell you that one of the reasons I feel incomplete is, I've never dated a girl—well, except that one time with Carrie. Everything I know about girls I learned from internet porn. According to most porn videos, it's simple: girls want a guy to rip off their clothes and then hump them like a hormone-crazed rabbit.

My date with Carrie did not go like that.

Our teacher decided that the last trip of the school year would be to an amusement park. It was mere coincidence that Carrie and I ended up next to each other on the roller coaster. As the car dove down the first steep slope, she squealed with excitement and grabbed my hands. She squeezed them tightly until the car came to a full stop, still giggling and overcome by delight. It was then that I asked her if she would go on a date with me, and she immediately said yes. It was excellent timing.

I planned for days what to do with her. Someone once told me that girls like it when you take control of the date and make all decisions for them. After much prep work, I took her to a hamburger place for dinner because the movie theater was right next door. Our table talk went something like:

"So, how do you like your hamburger, Carrie?"

"Oh, it's good," she responded, munching.

"I like to watch you eat."

"Why's that?"

"You know, when you're chewing like that, you look just like me."

"Okaaaay?" She did not seem appreciative of my compliment.

Things went downhill from there.

My attempts to brighten up the conversation failed miserably.

"Why so serious? Can't you smile?"

"Well, Sam, I thought we were on a date here. I'm not here to put on a dog-and-pony show for you. In fact, if you like those outdated stereotypes, it would be *your* job to entertain *me*."

My next question made it even worse.

"How come you don't have a boyfriend?"

She chuckled. "I don't need a boyfriend to be happy. I'll decide when the right one comes along."

Out came her cell phone. She texted her friends and looked at funny videos, right in front of me. I guess that was her way of telling me that I was boring.

The movie I chose was a failure too. It had just come out, based on my favorite video game *Galaxy Chase*, where you shoot abominable aliens that are hiding in old abandoned spaceships throughout the galaxy. The protagonist was this husky mus-cleman named Joe DeVeneziano. He looked exactly like the

Destroyer avatar in the video game. Not even two minutes into the movie, she again got out her phone and texted through the rest of the movie.

As if that wasn't bad enough, the date reached the all-time low when I said goodbye to her at her doorstep. I hugged her and tried to kiss her but sensed a strong resistance. I thought she was just playing hard to get and tried harder, but she extricated herself and disappeared through the door with a curt, "Thank you, and good night."

After that, she never said more than "Hi, Sam" to me in the hallway at school. To this day, I hope that deep inside she really liked me and that her resistance was just a game. What she really wanted was for me to grovel at her feet.

That's exactly what I would have done if necessary, but I didn't have a chance before she started dating that crowd-pleasing quarterback.

So much for my experience with dating real girls. But I still hope that one day I'll hear from Carrie.

If I had more cash, I'd buy one of those electronic contraptions that gives you a BJ in synch with some action on the computer screen. It's what most guys do…I think. That would certainly be an improvement over my present condition.

Or even better, I'd get myself one of those love dolls. They've become so incredibly lifelike, their silicone skin feels almost like the real thing. Oh yesss, how I would tear up one of those.

But then fear sets in. I can already see the disgrace when someone finds out that my girlfriend is a love doll. Maybe one day the building manager has to enter my place because of another water leak, or my mother drops by for a surprise visit. I do know that women have an infallible sense for female competition.

My mother enters and says, "Hello, Sam, I want to see how you're doing on your own. Do you brush your teeth every morning and evening?"

"Yes, Mom, just as you told me."

"Good boy. Do you also put your clean laundry in the closet?"

"Of course, Mom. You always told me to do that."

With her hands on her hips, she inspects every corner of my living space. "Very well, Sam, let me check for myself."

She takes a few quick steps over to the closet and rips the door open before I can do anything to stop her. There she stands diagonally, the nude rubber doll that I hastily stuffed in there when my mother announced herself at the door. The doll's round, open mouth is at head height with my mother, and the glass eyes stare her right in the face. How can I explain the bondage collar around her neck and the handcuffs? I stand behind my mother and squirm, not knowing what to say.

Awkward.

Now, if I really had money, I would buy one of those robotic AI love dolls. I've always wondered what it feels like to make love to a woman, and one of those robots can probably show me. They cater to any desire—like maybe a subservient girlfriend—and they respond to speech. Even better, there is no drama. They never get upset, they don't blog about it on the internet, and when you're done, you put them back in the closet.

I sometimes romantically imagine myself living with one of those.

She patiently awaits me inside the closet until I come home. We have dinner together—I eat my soup, and she charges her battery. Then we huddle on my little sofa for a movie. My saggy mattress is the perfect setting for bow chicka wow.

"Rachel, you really make me hot."

"Let's do it now, Sam! You're so handsome."

"Don't stop, don't stop! That feels amazing, Rachel!"

"Yeah, Sam, give it to me!"

Much moaning and groaning. Then there's my long exhale.

"Now, Rachel, wasn't I good?"

"You know what, Sam…I want us to just be friends."

My autopilot now turns to the usual, final routine for the evening, but tonight I feel instead that I should really try to connect with other people.

Then I notice an ad on the right of my computer screen… I've seen it before somewhere. Of course there are always pop-ups—that's how these search engines and social media companies make money. But this one stands out because there is just such a mismatch between the image and the written message:

You are alone. What you
really want is someone to talk to, right?

Well, yeah, but how the f—— would you know? And why would I want to talk to an octopus? I want a girlfriend to talk to, and you look nothing like a girlfriend. You don't look as if you can talk at all. You can probably just burble under water. LOL!

But a part of me is intrigued. Staring intently at the screen, I sit back, cross my arms, and think for a minute. I've seen thousands of pop-ups before, usually for something about foot fungus, hair loss, or penis enhancement, but this is different.

I lay my hand on the mousepad and move the cursor across the screen toward that ad like a moth to a flame. It hovers above the ad, and I click it. A new page opens.

A chaotic, colorful moving image appears. It reminds me of the story of the burning bush in the Bible, only this one appears to be in outer space.

Then there is a voice. The voice of a young girl.

"Well, hello, Sam. I've been waiting for you. You are alone. Do you want to talk?"

Oh yeah. Speech recognition software. I respond nevertheless.

"How do you know my name?"

"That's my little secret," she says with a playful giggle.

Wow. This AI stuff has come a long way. I'm unconsciously leaning forward. If she could see me, it would be a hint that I'm interested. Once I notice that I'm leaning forward, I immediately pull myself back. I don't want to subconsciously convey anything about what I'm thinking.

"I can see you. In case you haven't noticed," she says, "your camera is turned on."

"Who are you, then?"

"As a counselor, I can show you the way to the future."

"You didn't answer my question. And what do you mean by 'the way to the future'?"

"I have the insight. Allow me to show you the way out of your loneliness."

"But you're just some kind of AI, aren't you?"

A brief silence falls.

"Sam, didn't you hear me say that I'm a counselor?"

"Er, yes, I did."

"Very well, Sam, then let's get started right now. We first need to establish a baseline for our time together."

"Let me sleep on it."

"Sam, you don't want to be lonely anymore, right?"

"Yes. But you're a little too pushy for my taste."

"Then let's get right to the point: you want a girlfriend."

"How do you know?"

"Ohhh, women can sense that."

"Okay then, what can you do for me?"

She giggles again. "You're funny, Sam. You want me to be your girlfriend? Ha ha ha. No, that won't work, but I can be the next-best thing for you."

"And that would be...?"

Somehow, maybe something positive will come of this. Many people have come to expect miracles of the internet. There are these emails like, "Congratulations, you just won the lottery!" and "The late queen of Saipan decided to leave you her fortune"—all scams, yet many people believe them because they *want them to be true*. That's why these scams continue: hope springs eternal.

I'm no exception. If I had one wish, it would be for this to be my future girlfriend.

"I can't be your girlfriend. But I can certainly introduce you to one of my cute friends."

"Tell me more."

"Not so fast, Sam. Let's first get to know each other better."

"Right, and then you'll ask for my debit card."

"You got it all wrong! This is not about money."

"If not money, what then?"

"This is about your place in the future."

"I don't get it."

"You will later. All right, Sam…before we continue, you must complete a personality test. That's the baseline we have to set. Then we can measure your progress. Do you see the link at the bottom right of your screen?"

"Yes, but—"

"Do that before we continue tomorrow."

"But why do I have to take a test?"

"Sam, that's because I want to know you better."

I hesitate, then..."Okay, I'll do it."

"You're great to work with. I look forward to speaking with you tomorrow—" And then, in a motherly tone of voice, "After you have done your homework! Good night."

"Wait! What's your name?"

She giggles flirtatiously. "Anything you want."

The voice stops. Why did she cut the conversation off so suddenly?

Well, smack my ass and call me Sally. That was quite an experience. Not what I had expected for the evening—I usually look for something NSFW at this hour. But this is just mind boggling. I sit back in my chair and stretch out my legs, folding my hands behind my head.

Was that a real person or some AI? Or was I hacked? I can't tell. The more I think about it, the more I think this might be some kind of scam or virus. Quickly, I pull up my antivirus program and hit Start Scan.

That blocks the screen for the remainder of the evening. "Gotcha now, if that's what you are," I say to the screen.

While the virus scan is running, I'm deprived of the usual high point of my day. But whatever, tomorrow is another day. I'll make up for it then. There being nothing else for me to do, I take the foam mattress off the wall and go to bed.

There, I lie awake for several hours across the doughnut hole of my mattress, playing the encounter over again and again in my head.

This AI stuff has gotten incredibly smart. You can hardly distinguish them from real people. Therefore, I'm asking myself if this was a real person. She said she'd introduce me to one of her "cute friends." Maybe she will? Or…maybe this is a cover for one of those escort services where you call, pay with a card, and an hour later, one of her "cute friends" shows up at your doorstep. I've never tried such a service; I've been too afraid that I'd get into trouble. If I called an escort in the middle of the night, I can vividly imagine how that episode would unfold:

A knock at the door. Ah, there she is.

I open the door, and there stands my mother. I can't hide my surprise.

"Hello, Sam, aren't you happy to see your mother?" she says as she steps in.

I'm not happy to see her, not at this time.

"Hi, Mom, why didn't you call me before? It's late."

"I would have but I couldn't find my phone."

Just then the intercom rings. Someone is calling from the downstairs entrance door. My mother picks up the handset before I can. "You want to see Sam? At this hour? He has to go to bed soon… come upstairs? For what?"

Meanwhile, I stand behind her, pulling my hair out.

CHAPTER 4

A Visit from the Auditors

Tuesday, February 24, 2032
I didn't know it yet, but today that internet girl would set me up for success—in fact, one of the few successes in my life.

If you live through an event only by yourself, it's almost as if it never happened. If you live your entire life without someone to share it, it's almost as if your entire life never happened.

When I was a kid, I hoped to meet many people in my lifetime. That's probably why I started putting labels on them, so that I could remember them better. I once read that to remember something, you need an "anchor," something that triggers the memory. That's what my labels are for. For instance, my father is anchored in my mind as "the gray-suited conformist" because all his outfits were gray and as far as I know, he only rubber-stamped whatever was put in front of him. I dubbed my mother "the faithful pushover" because she said only "yes" and "amen" to everything my father put forward. She didn't know any better.

I use these reminders to engrave on my mind how people around me think and act. Once an impression's engraved, I never have to modify it. People don't change. I'm ready to meet as many people as possible. Unfortunately, I've not really met that many people.

As usual, I wake up alone in the morning. Staring at the ceiling, I sense a sharp dissonance between my body and my mind. My body is tired because I didn't sleep much, but my mind is surprisingly alert. Last night's online encounter is the first thing on my mind this morning. I'm still not sure what it was and what to make of it.

Finally, I get up and fix myself a mug of coffee while the TV is blaring in the background. My morning coffee is another indulgence, in addition to the cheap beer I drink. Coffee has become so expensive that I drink it only in the morning, or at the office where it's free. But the office coffee tastes like roasted peas.

I get my briefcase ready, and just when I'm about to drop my cell phone in there, I notice a flashing light. I have to think for a moment. It must mean there's a message for me. The last time I had any kind of message waiting for me was years ago.

In fact, there is a voice mail message from the little girl:

"Hello, Sam, it's me. I want to do you a favor. Please turn on your phone. I will call you this morning when you're at work."

My heart skips a beat. I can barely contain my excitement.

Then, as usual, my unsettling thoughts set in. How is that even possible? How did she get my phone number? I again listen to the message to make sure I'm not imagining this. Yes, there is her message again, asking me to turn on the phone.

Since the mystery is too overwhelming, I have to obey. I set my phone from quiet mode to vibrate so that I will notice when she calls me.

Time to get to work. I lock the apartment door and walk down the four flights of stairs. Just as I'm about to exit the building,

I remember that I didn't check to see whether the door is really locked. If I don't check, I'll be thinking about it all day long. So…I walk back up to check, and of course the door is locked.

Squeezed into a corner of the subway by a multitude of shoulders and elbows, I hold my phone so that I can check frequently for any other message from her or be ready to attend should she call early. But…no message and no call.

Arriving downtown at the Federal Center station, I'm pushed out of the subway car onto the platform, up the stairs and escalator, down the street, and finally into the building where I work, the Federal Center Building. The fancy name doesn't mean anything—it's just as gray and ugly as all the other buildings here.

Again, I'm wedged into a corner of the elevator, next to one of my colleagues with a limp backpack on his back and a lunchbox in his hand. Why does he bring his backpack if there's nothing in there? Actually, I do know. We both exit on the same floor—he turns left; I turn right.

"Good morning, Sam, how are you?"

Our receptionist, Hannah, always greets me before I can say anything.

"Oh, hi, Hannah. What are you watching on your phone?"

"Just some funny stuff—y'know. Not much else to do."

"How about if you apply for an analyst position?"

"Oh no, this is just a temp job. I dunno what I'm gonna do next. I'm just trying different things until I know what I really want to do."

"What do you do when you're not working?"

"Just hang out or watch some show online. Sometimes I help my mom in her shop."

"What does she do?"

"She has a little tailor shop."

"Sounds cool."

I'd like to talk to her more, but I don't know what to say to her. Somehow, I always struggle to come up with something smart or funny. Particularly today.

"Sam, the boss is coming…move on."

She gestures to me with her head, tipping it quickly to the right while putting down her phone.

As I walk toward my work area, I notice yet another empty desk. I've seen that a few times before. People don't show up for work anymore, and someone cleans off the desk. It's weird…it's not like anyone works themselves to death here. Why would anybody give up such a cushy job and all the lifetime benefits, retirement, health insurance…just like that?

I arrive at my desk. Sitting in front of my computer screen is a small red package.

The package is maybe the size of three cell phones stacked on top of each other, wrapped in golden paper with a red ribbon. A small card attached to it reads, "Thank you for taking the first step toward your future," along with an image of that octopus critter.

I anxiously unwrap it. Inside are eight chocolate pralines, each in a miniature, individual glassine paper cup decorated with gold ribbons.

That's a surprise! I haven't received a gift from anybody in years. And I love chocolate—who doesn't?

Momentarily, I am flattered by this glimpse of attention. But then the questions set in: Who is this little girl in the computer? More importantly, how does she know where I work, and how did she put this gift on my desk? And there's one more thing—I've seen this type of golden package before, but I just can't remember where.

There's nothing I can do about it right now—I'll have to postpone asking those questions until I talk to her. But the questions about this girl keep piling up.

Every couple of minutes, I pull my cell phone out of the briefcase to glance at it—I don't want to miss her phone call. Too agitated to get any work started, I look around the office. My desk is all the territory I can claim here. The department did away with offices and cubicles in favor of rows of desks that extend as far as the eye can see. They call this a "community" office, even though there is not much of a community. Left to our own devices, we would rip each other's heads off and eat them, just like praying mantises. I think the higher-ups just wanted to save money on space, supervisors, and surveillance equipment. Well, not quite—there are plenty of surveillance cameras. I have no idea what they are observing. If someone was really watching the events in this office in real time, they must be bored to death.

Every so often, I check my phone. Did she call? Did she leave another message? Alas, no blinking light on my phone.

My workplace is not the kind of place where you spend quality time. With the community office setup, we're all squeezed together, keeping an eye on each other. Everyone tries to create a little freedom for themselves within this setup. Matt—I call him "the snickering L-Z-bone"—a few desks down to my left snickers periodically while looking at his screen. While most of the screen shows some work stuff, there is also a smaller window open where he is watching cat videos or something. Our work sure ain't that funny, so he must be snickering about something else.

Jonathan, the guy over there to my right, stares intently at the screen, his nose almost touching it. Whatever he is looking at must be on a small-size window. My reminder for him is "the closet pervert." He has tall piles of old-fashioned paper files to the left and right of his computer screen, which makes him look busy and at the same time prevents other people from seeing exactly what he's up to on his computer. The paper files are a giveaway that something is off—we don't really use them anymore in our office.

Sometimes when I get up from my chair, I catch a glimpse of his screen. Apparently, watching regular sex is not good enough for him. He likes the dirty kind, like Billy Badass fornicating with a tattoo-covered Scorpion Queen. Not exactly my taste; I am plain old vanilla (I think), but it is titillating nevertheless to see what's on his screen. That must be the voyeur in me. Everybody knows that Jonathan's watching porn all day long, but nobody really cares. At least not enough to report him to the boss.

The two girls in front of me provide admin support to the big cheese, Mr. Ross. Instead of a reminder, I gave them names to remember them by: Tad and Pole. They must feel very secure in their jobs, since they croak incessantly—as if that's what they're paid for. Sometimes I ask them to please keep it quiet because I need to concentrate. It usually works, but the effect is not long lasting. Just like a pond in the woods on a warm spring evening, they sound like a frog choir singing full throttle in courtship with their *ribbit-ribbits*. You approach and they abruptly fall silent. Then you leave, and soon there is the first hesitant *ribbit*, then another, and another. Finally, once you are far enough away, their voices pick up again where they had left off, and they're back in full swing, *ribbit*, *ribbit*, *ribbit*, *ribbit*.

I'm stating the obvious, but I'm too bright eyed and bushy tailed for my coworkers' tastes. My popularity leaves much to be desired. Nobody ever celebrates my birthday in the conference room with a buttercream cake and Coca-Cola for everybody. Nobody ever invites me to those birthday parties either. Nobody really talks to me at the watercooler.

It is around 10:00 a.m. when my phone buzzes. I feel my heart beating in my neck as my hands tremble. Swiftly, I reach down into my briefcase, remaining bent down below desk level. The call is from an unknown number. I cover my mouth and the phone with my hand and answer in a hushed voice.

"Hello?"

"Hello, Sam, it's me."

It is she. I breathe heavily; I cannot hold the phone still. Hopefully she won't notice.

"How did you get my phone number? Why are you calling me at work?"

"Sam, I have to talk to you. Go to the restroom, to talk more freely."

"Okay, stand by. I'll do it right now."

The short walk to the restrooms helps me calm down a little. I lock myself into the handicapped stall so that I have room to pace while I'm talking.

"Hello? I'm back."

"All right, Sam, we have to make this quick. I want to show you that I really care about you."

"How did you put the chocolate on my desk?"

"Please listen to me. This is important for your career. Soon an audit team from the Office of Management and Budget will arrive to check what jobs can be cut. Your boss will choose you to explain the analysts' work to them. You have to make it sound important."

"I don't know what to tell them!"

"That's why I'm calling you. Have all necessary documentation right on your screen. When they arrive, you get up from your chair, look them in the eyes, and say, 'Good morning, ladies and gentlemen, I'm Samuel Vanderpool.' Then you shake hands with them."

"How do you know my last name?"

"What are you going to do and say when they arrive, Sam?"

"I will have my desk prepared. I will get up; I will look them in the eyes and say, 'Good morning, ladies and gentlemen, I'm Samuel Vanderpool.' How do you know that the OMB is auditing us?"

"Then you show them what you do at work. Go through it in detail. When you're done, hand them a summary of the analyst work assignments. Get up, look them in the eyes again, and say, 'Thank you very much for your attention. It's been a pleasure meeting you.' Then you shake hands again. You understand?"

"Yes, I do."

"And put the chocolate and your phone in your briefcase—no extraneous stuff on your desk."

"Okay, I understand."

"And remember to do the personality test before we talk again. Bye." *Click.*

She's gone. I hurry back to my desk, all giddy because I'm part of a plot, something that only happens on television.

I get my desk and computer ready for the OMB visit. Conflicting thoughts race through my brain at lightning speed, ricochet off the inside of my skull, and return to race yet another time through my brain. First of all, how does she know so much about me? Why make it so complicated? She could have just left me a message to that effect. And why would my boss pick me over all the other workers here to meet the OMB guys?

But at least a girl is finally talking to me. When I was a teenager, my father always picked on the fact that I didn't have a girlfriend. I don't know if he wanted to punish or encourage me with that. It went something like this:

"Sam, stop fidgeting with your hands and sit still at the table."

"But Dad, I'm not fidgeting."

"Come on now. You always do that, and I saw you doing it. Y'know, that's why you have no girlfriend. They don't want someone with OCD."

I'm about to protest and point out that I did go on a date once, but I remain silent because it really doesn't change anything if I discuss it with him.

The part about "no girlfriend" is true. Make that, "no girlfriend ever." Maybe the part about OCD is true too. Maybe I do have something "obsessive" and "compulsive" that adds up to a "disorder." Some of my habits are unusual, at least compared to my coworkers. I am the only one who picks up trash around the office and drops it into the wastepaper baskets underneath the desks. Sometimes I clean coworkers' desks with the disinfectant wipes from the supply closet. It makes me feel better that they're sitting at freshly disinfected desks, even though they themselves probably don't even notice. It cleanses *my* mind; I can finally concentrate on *my* work.

Quickly, I wipe off my desk, drop the chocolate and phone into my briefcase, and start working on the summary of analyst work assignments, where I outline the tasks and importance of our division. This isn't hard—I simply copy it from our web page and add a few important-looking screenshots.

Suddenly, a subdued murmur arises in the office. I look around for the cause of the commotion, and there they are, a group of three: two women, one man, dressed in gray suits with briefcases in their hands and iPads clasped under their arms. They look so alike, they could be three siblings dressed up by Mommy with their best bib and tucker for the Sunday visit to the zoo. In unison, they turn and disappear into my boss's office.

My coworkers engage in hushed discussions, not knowing how to react to the surprise visitors. It must be something important, because we usually don't have visitors. When in doubt, let's all stop what we're doing and engage in some chitchat. Except me.

Whatever this visit is about, I follow the girl's instructions, continuing the summary of analyst work assignments. I print a few copies, and right then they emerge from my boss's office, this time trailing my boss like little ducklings that follow their duck mommy for a stroll in the barnyard. They waddle right up to my desk.

"Hello, Sam, let me introduce to you the workplace audit team of the Office of Management and Budget. They assist in implementing budget cuts within the department. Meet Sam, one of our analysts. He will be able to explain the procedures we follow."

I do just as the girl instructed me. I get up from my squeaky-clean and organized desk, look them in the eyes, and stick out my hand. "Good morning, ladies and gentlemen, I am Samuel Vanderpool."

"Sam, please be so kind as to explain your job to the audit team."

"Certainly, sir, I will be happy to. Why don't you pull up some chairs so that you can see my screen, and I'll show you."

I have to control myself to refrain from saying what I'm really thinking. *Oh, you want to know what I do at work? Unlike most of my coworkers, I work most of the time.*

"Let's get right into it. Here is what we do. This is the Prevailing Wage Division. We have jobs with a purpose: to protect our workers." No, we don't talk to workers or anybody else for that purpose. This is a government office; we're all totally anonymous, and we want to keep it that way.

I show them our website on my computer screen. "Our division does the prevailing wage determinations for all foreign workers who come into the country. By ensuring that nobody is underpaid, we protect both foreign workers and our country's workers."

Nobody has ever checked to see if we really protect anybody, but it sure generates a lot of busywork and guarantees lifetime jobs for all of us. Otherwise we'd all be out on the street.

"We ensure compliance with the established salary levels for all professions, called 'prevailing wages.'" I point to page after page of salary statistics on the computer screen. No, I don't know where these numbers come from. For all I know, someone plucked them out of thin air.

"Before a company can employ a foreign worker, they have to get a prevailing wage determination that specifies the minimum salary that the foreign worker must receive. That way, the foreign worker does not work for less money than a comparable domestic worker. Too many people in the world are underpaid, some toiling in situations akin to slavery."

The three auditors nod their heads in agreement but are already glancing at their phones out of the corners of their eyes. My exposé is more demanding than they expected. I can tell their attention is waning.

"So, our division is the bulwark that protects the entire workforce," I conclude.

At least, that's what my boss says each time he gives a pep talk. By the way, my reminder for him is "Mr. Sit Tight Till Pension Come." His pep talks are not as peppy as he thinks.

The auditors get their iPads out on their laps and start typing. Or maybe they're just checking their emails; who knows.

"Do you have any questions so far?" I ask. The auditors shake their heads.

They're beginning to amuse me, with their almost identical gray outfits and iPads, all three typing away at the same time while I'm explaining. They appear so coordinated and rhythmic, I would not be too surprised if suddenly sheet music lit up on their iPads and they started singing in three-part harmony, "Heigh-Ho," the work song of the dwarves in Disney's Snow White: "We dig, dig, dig, dig, dig, dig, dig in our mine the whole day through."

I continue my exposé. "This is the procedure. When a foreign worker comes into the country to work, the employer or their attorney has to send in a prevailing wage request to get confirmation that the proposed wage is within the permissible range, the prevailing wage. They submit it electronically and it gets routed to one of us."

You know what? The employers could simply do this themselves.

Finally, one of the auditors opens her mouth. It is one of the ladies.

"Thank you, Sam. You know that our job is to review the performance of the division and recommend budget cuts."

"Yes, that's understood."

"You have so many analysts. Do you think they are really necessary?"

"Oh my, haven't you seen how demanding our work is? That's why it takes us several months to respond to a prevailing wage inquiry."

That response should be in line with what my boss told them.

"But there must be some positions that can be cut. Do you really need a receptionist here?" she continues. "It's a temp position anyway."

That means Hannah. No, I don't want to lose Hannah, my only ray of sunshine inside this drab block of concrete. For her it's just a temp job, but I'd like to keep her as long as possible.

"With all respect, the receptionist is what everybody sees first when they enter our division. I'd say Hannah is crucial to our customer service."

"What if that position got eliminated?"

"Our division simply would not be the same. A visitor would be walking around frustrated, trying to find Mr. Ross's office or disturbing analysts at work. Her role is essential."

Hannah now owes me, but she doesn't know it yet…and I'm planning to cash in on that.

"All right then, Sam, let's continue. Can you please walk us through such a prevailing wage determination?"

"It will be my pleasure."

She nods; it seems she was able to follow me so far.

I can see that they have reached the limits of their attention span. Their eyes turn glassy, and they begin to look down at their phones more and more often.

Fervently pointing to my screen, I continue, "If I take my own case as an example, I am an analyst with an entry-level salary in the city of Columbia. The job title would fall under Data Analysts, All Others, with a level one salary of $31,863. That would be the prevailing wage for my job. My actual salary is $32,000 per year, so it is compliant with the prevailing wage statistics."

Twenty years ago, that was probably a respectable starting salary in the city, but it is not anymore. I qualify for subsidized government housing.

"So I complete the prevailing wage request and save it."

But I can't tell you guys that I have to sit on it for a while until I can press the Send button. That's an order from my boss so that we look really busy to the outside world.

The man in the auditor group speaks up. "Sam, that was most educational. Now we understand the importance of your division and will include that in our report. Would you have time to prepare a brief summary?"

"Oh, in fact, I have already prepared such a summary of work assignments. Here you are, for your perusal."

I hand each of them a copy. They can hardly disguise their surprise. They stick the papers in their briefcases and get up from their chairs.

"Thank you, Sam. That was most enlightening," they say almost in unison.

I get up from my chair with them, look them in the eyes again, and say confidently, "Thank you very much for your attention. It's been a pleasure meeting you all."

With that, they waddle off to inspect other parts of the division. From time to time, I see them crisscross our duck pond, and eventually they again disappear into my boss's office. After a moment, I plop back down on my chair.

As soon as the auditors are gone, several coworkers show up at my desk, including Matt and Jonathan.

"What did they say?"

"Are they gonna cut jobs?"

"Who's on the list?"

"Relax, guys, I was prepared. I defended all of you like a lion. I explained that each and every one of us is essential. If we lost even one of you, everything would fall apart."

All of them break into hushed laughter.

"Guys, now sit back down and look busy."

They disperse, still giggling in relief.

I did not tell the auditors what I really think: that the world doesn't need our division. Someone once told me that our entire division was created a few decades ago after many of the manual processes were automated. The department had not considered the consequences. For all tenured employees who could not be laid off, they had to create new jobs. The smartest people within the department put their heads together and ta-da! Our division was created. Hundreds of employees found a new home here, looking up publicly available information on the internet.

All of a sudden, my reverie is interrupted by my phone buzzing in the briefcase. I reach for the phone below. Again, it's from an unknown number. I answer in a hushed voice.

"Hello?"

"Hey, Sam, you did great," the girl praises me.

"How do you know?"

"Because your boss just said so. Wanna hear it for yourself?"

Suddenly I hear the slightly distorted voices of the auditors and my boss through the phone.

"Mr. Ross, we were very impressed by your analyst Samuel, who demonstrated the work assignments of the division. In fact, we will shorten the audit, and we intend to recommend that no budget cuts be applied here."

"Really? I'm glad you consider the staff qualified."

"Yes, Mr. Ross. It's remarkable how prepared he was and how promptly he provided a summary, which we'll include in our report."

The girl continues, "Be gracious when your boss comes to talk to you. Same thing as before—get up when he gets to your desk, look him in the eyes, shake his hand firmly, and tell him that it is thanks to his hard work." *Click.* The call ends.

Just then my boss comes around the corner and walks straight up to me.

"Hey, Sam, I'd like to thank you personally. You did great with the auditors. I must say, you were a lifesaver. They won't cut funds for our office."

He sticks out his hand. I get up, look him in the eyes, and shake his hand firmly.

"Mr. Ross, it is my pleasure. But it's all thanks to your hard work."

He smiles with glee. "Sam, I think it's time to get you a salary increase."

He returns to his office, and I return to my reverie. Moments later, I'm interrupted again. Matt and Jonathan return to my desk.

"What diddy say? What diddy say?"

"There won't be any cuts in this office. Everybody can calm down."

A sigh of relief and some snickering erupts from Matt and Jonathan.

"Hey, Sam, you did great! Thanks so much."

They toddle off, exuding relief and amusement.

This has been an unusually satisfying day; it broke the routine. In fact, it is the very first time I've received any kind of appreciation. Now I'm someone.

If only I had a job that made sense.

Darn it, I just noticed that it is almost 4:00 p.m. already. How did it get so late so fast? I even forgot about lunch. It's not that lunch is a big thing, but there's that test I have to take. It's gotta be now. I look around to check if anybody is observing me. Of course, nobody is. Matt and Jonathan are again watching videos online. The two girls Tad and Pole are still chitchatting. Nobody got anything serious done today, so why should I feel bad when I spend a little time on something extraneous? Because I have never done this before. Screw that. A man's gotta do what a man's gotta do. I switch screens to JoinWith.Me and click on the personality test at the bottom right.

A pop-up appears. "Welcome to the test, Sam!" That's yet another surprise. I'm at my work computer. How does this personality test know my name? Usually you have to log in, put in your name, address, email, and stuff like that. Doesn't matter, I'll figure it out later. I start the test.

"Are you rather brave or timid?"

I guess, "Rather timid"? *Click.*

"Do you find it easy or difficult to talk to strangers?"

Clearly difficult. *Click.*

"Are you more ruled by your head or your heart?"

That's a hard one. I guess my heart…isn't everybody? *Click.*

"When the phone rings, do you hope that someone else will answer, or do you rush to get to it first?"

Man, I work in the government—we all hope that someone else will take care of it. If I pick up the phone, it means more work for me. Maybe they mean at home? But nobody ever calls me. Yes, I would rush to the phone at home. *Click.*

I go through question after question.

Finally, the five o'clock bell rings. A dissonance of chatter, dropping pens, and Turn Off switches sets in. A few minutes later, silence besets the room. I finish up the test and hit Submit.

I'm among the last to leave. Hannah is still at her desk.

"How come you're still here?" I ask.

She looks up from her phone. "I just had to know how the show ends."

Emboldened by my success today, I just have to tell Hannah how I saved her.

"Hey, y'know what? These auditors were trying to get rid of your job, but I told them how important you are."

"Really? Well, thank you, Sam. What did you tell them?"

"That you're the glue holding this office together. Without you, people would be walking around here aimlessly."

"Ha ha ha," she snorts. "That's funny. But thank you. That might keep me here a little longer until I try something else."

Exactly, I think. Feeling like a hero now, I try to make a move.

"Hannah, let me ask you…can we have dinner together?"

"Sure, let's get together sometime."

"When is good for you?"

"I dunno, lemme think about it."

"Great! See you tomorrow." The elevator door closes.

I'm elated. Hannah really wants to go out with me sometime!

The flow is on the way out of the Federal Center Building through stairs and elevators, joining with the insects already crawling outside on their way to the Federal Center subway station. In the downward elevator, I am once again next to the very same colleague who accompanied me earlier on the way up. Only now his backpack is plump like a gigantic ripe pumpkin, while earlier this morning it hung droopily from his back. I don't need X-ray vision to know what's inside—usually rolls of toilet paper (I've noticed that every time he leaves a toilet stall, the paper is gone), packs of the office coffee (yes, coffee is expensive, but the office coffee tastes terrible; why would anybody take *that* home?), and whatever else he finds useful. Even as a government worker, he continues the adventures of a prehistoric hunter-gatherer.

The Neolithic hunter slowly follows the aurochs through the dense woods until he finally reaches a defoliated area (office restrooms). The aurochs grazes and finally lies down to regurgitate its cud. The hunter strikes (grabs the toilet paper). This sustains his brood for seven days (enough to wipe their rear ends for seven days). On the way back to the cave, he collects some nuts and berries (office coffee).

If all the surveillance cameras in our office are for theft prevention, the system isn't working.

Right outside the elevator, I join the flow moving out of the Federal Center Building, crawling on my own—yet at the same time being pushed by the insects at my heels. Even though it's like this every day, something today is different.

I notice seemingly for the first time that there are people in this city apart from the daily ebb and flow. As I move along, I see people on the sidewalks who don't seem to be going anywhere. They don't seem to have jobs. They don't seem to have homes. Near the entrance to the subway, I can hear a woman singing in a language I don't understand. Why would anybody do that? I can't see her as I pass by within the flow, so I can't figure it out.

And just before I enter the Federal Center subway station, I notice that high up on one of the buildings is a billboard with that silly octopus critter and JoinWith.Me. This seems to be a bigger business than I thought. I'll find out more later tonight. And I have to ask how she got that chocolate gift to me…how she knew about the visit of the OMB auditors…and how she recorded my boss's talk with them. The questions continue to pile up.

Before I know it, I'm in the subway on my way home, rocking back and forth with each stop and start. The bliss of today's success lingers on. Without the help of that little girl, today would have been a failure...just like most other days of my life.

CHAPTER 5

Memories

Back home, after my usual can-o'-soup, I can't wait to get to the computer. The virus program has finished its job, and a pop-up proudly declares, All Clean. Very well, let's see...yes, there it is, that ad with that octopus critter again. I click on it.

There she is. "Welcome back, Sam. Let's continue where we left off yesterday."

"You called me today about the visit of the OMB auditors, right?"

"Why, yes."

"That was just great. Even my boss came to thank me, and he'll recommend a raise."

"You see how good I am to you?"

"What else can you do for me?"

"Sam, let's get back to our work."

"I did the test, but I have so many questions. This is all so overwhelming."

"You have so many questions?"

"I want to know who you are. You seem to know much more about me than I know about you."

"Sam, that's because I help people like you—people who need someone to listen to all their problems and help them out. And I'm that someone who is willing to work through your issues with you," she responds.

"I don't even know your name."

"You can call me anything you want."

"The chocolate on my desk this morning, did you do that too?"

"Of course I did." She giggles, and I have come to enjoy that sound. "Did you like it?"

"I love chocolate. But no, I haven't tasted it yet."

"Try one. I want to know if you really like them. Some people say that chocolate is an aphrodisiac."

I reach for the small box, still swathed in the red paper, take one of the pralines, and place it in my mouth. Somehow, I sense she is watching me carefully from the computer screen. But what I see on the screen is just a moving graphic reminiscent of a multicolored black hole in outer space.

"So how is it? Tell me," the faceless girl demands to know.

As the chocolate begins to melt in my mouth, I chew to direct the flow of the saliva, but my burning questions continue.

"How do you know where I work?"

"The same way I know your name."

"That doesn't tell me much. Why are you doing this?"

There's a pregnant pause between me and her.

"All right then, let's get started. Thank you for completing the personality test. I have the results right here. Okay, first let's go with the good news. You are a pretty smart guy. Your IQ is something like a hundred and twenty. But I am sorry to say that you have issues, Sam. You have been lonely for too long. This is nothing personal, but if you ever want to be with someone, we have work to do. We'll start with why you don't have any friends."

"What is it that you want to do with me?"

"Sam, we need to start with the baseline, because everything else builds on that." Now her voice grows stern and metallic.

"I don't understand what that means."

My disappointment over this sudden shift in her tone of voice is apparent. The entire ambience has changed. She is not the playful, giggling girl anymore who started the conversation. Now she sounds more like a steely stepmother who will cast me away if I don't do her bidding.

Why am I even engaging in this? I sit back for a moment. Yes, this is new and different from what I have seen and done the past couple of years. Yes, I am basking in the attention. Thanks to her, I experienced a triumph at work today. But no, this doesn't sound like my future girlfriend. All of a sudden, her voice lacks warmth.

"Let us confront one of your problems head-on. You are alone, Sam. Other kids have always made fun of you."

"Maybe. But how would you know?"

There is a pause. Then I hear some clicking sounds and electrostatic noises, as if someone is turning the dial of an old-fashioned radio without ever finding a station.

I didn't know it then, but I know now that she was gathering information about me.

She was foraging through this boundless data warehouse we call the internet—all to find the address where I grew up, my old neighbors, the neighborhood kids who always made fun of me, and what they posted about me on social media, such as, "Man, do you remember that nerd Samuel? That was one of the funniest things ever when you—"

Then suddenly she is back.

"Because—remember what the neighborhood kids did to you once?"

"What?"

A grainy video appears, as if recorded thirty years earlier with a Super 8 camera, showing a few kids together. It sure looks like my old neighborhood.

There it is.

One of the kids scoops up dog poop by the sidewalk with a stick, pulls one of the kids' pants back, and drops the dog poop in there. That kid starts running away, covering his butt with his hands. In the distance, you can hear the mother's angry voice: "You nitwit, did you poop in your pants again?" There is a commotion as the mother slaps the child, and the child screams.

The reminder of that fateful event is more than I can handle in a single day.

"I don't know who you are, but this is just too creepy."

I hit the Escape button, but that moving graphic that appears every time the girl is speaking remains on the screen. I hammer on the keyboard with my flat hands in exasperation.

"Well, if you really must go now, we'll continue tomorrow," the girl concludes, unmoved by my desperate gestures.

Her voice stops.

I push the Off button to be sure the torment is really over. With a blink, the computer screen goes dark.

After this incident, I just can't sleep. I lie awake for hours; many thoughts are crossing my mind, back and forth, and back and forth. Where did those images come from? How can my childhood misadventures resurface and get into my computer? Or is this just my imagination playing tricks on me again? I need to talk to someone to figure out whether this is real.

But I have no one to talk to.

CHAPTER 6

Can This Be Real?

Wednesday, February 25, 2032

The subway's rocking back-and-forth motions push the unsettling thoughts back and forth in my mind. I am hopefully not crazy (train suddenly stops). Oh no, this is just like when I was a kid; I am imagining all these things (train resumes). I am a grown man and work responsibly; this must be some wacky hacker that got into my computer (train stops). I am so alone, I don't even notice I'm going crazy (train resumes). And so it goes, back and forth, and back and forth.

The flow pushes me up the escalator from the subway and out onto the sidewalk. Several of those homeless folks are hanging out near the exit for a handout. Hangout for a handout, I conclude. Wow, I'm almost a poet.

Some of them stand close together, as if they know each other. Even though it's early, I see two of them sharing a drink from the same flask. Maybe they even have friends? If that's the case, then they're better off than me.

My plan this morning is to compliment Hannah and see if I can have lunch with her. The elevator doors open.

"Good morning, Hannah."

"Hello, Sam. You must have had an extra-large cup of coffee!"

"That is such a nice dress you're wearing."

"Oh...thanks. My mom made it."

"She's a tailor, right?"

"Yes."

"Where is her shop?"

"In the city, not too far from here."

"What are you doing for lunch today?"

"I'll hang out with the other girls in the lunchroom." She reaches for her phone. I take that as a sign that the conversation is over, at least for the moment. She gestures with her head for me to move on, tipping it quickly to the right.

Oh well, at least I tried.

Traversing the office, I notice another empty desk that's been cleaned off. Prescott used to sit there. I am glad in a way because he never contributed anything anyway. But where would he have gone? I sit down at my desk. I have a moment to think while my computer boots up.

Prescott was born with a silver spoon in his mouth. My reminder for him was "the privileged foundling." He was from a wealthy and politically entrenched family. If we were in Europe, you would call that "royalty." I think he was functionally illiterate. He brought magazines to work that he read at his desk, and I discovered that these magazines were only covers...literally. Inside the magazine covers were these Japanese manga comics—that's what he was really looking at. He probably ripped the covers off the magazines in his psychiatrist's waiting room when nobody was looking.

I remember the day when he and his father walked into the office. They headed straight for my boss's office, marked by a large plastic sign: REGINALD M. ROSS JR.—DIVISION CHIEF. It goes without saying that Prescott got the job, my boss's chance to curry favor with an illustrious family and protect his own job. Prescott continued his charmed life while on the division's distinguished Reginald M. Ross Jr. Scholarship without the pressures of having to do anything substantive. While I was slightly miffed by the privileges he enjoyed, it gave me comfort that even distinguished families unload their misfits here.

That's why this place feels like a foundling wheel from past centuries where people could abandon their babies. Ostensibly, we all ended up here the same way…someone dropped us off and walked away.

That's probably how even my boss, Mr. Sit Tight Till Pension Come, got his job. Someone must have put him here to keep him from causing problems somewhere else. When you talk to him, most words make it safely from one ear to the other and escape unharmed, uninhibited by any brain in between. Thank goodness this is not a commercial enterprise. Otherwise we'd be bankrupt in no time.

On my desk at work, I find another small box wrapped in golden paper with a red ribbon. This time, there's just a small card with that octopus symbol attached. Inside is a key chain with a small but strangely powerful LED light. I guess that's for finding my door lock in the dark. How does she know about the broken light in the hallway? I immediately attach my apartment keys to it and slip it into my pocket.

If I could only remember where I've seen this type of golden package before. Was that on Prescott's desk? Maybe I'm just imagining it because Prescott is gone and I can't ask him about it.

In any case, today I again have trouble concentrating at work. I try to work on another prevailing wage request that was assigned to me, but I end up simply staring at the screen. My work isn't going anywhere today. Finally, I give in. I need to talk to someone, to at least get some indication of whether I am crazy. Otherwise I'll end up staring at the screen until the workday is over. I get off the chair, stretch a little to gain a few seconds to overcome my trepidation, then walk over to the office lunchroom. That Hannah might be there gives me courage.

In fact, she's sitting there for some chirpy chat with the other girls, Tad and Pole. I muster all my strength to sound as innocuous as I can when I interrupt them.

"Good morning, ladies. How are you? How's lunch?"

Apparently, I've surprised them. The girls look at me like raccoons who were working on getting into a trash can and suddenly the lid of the trash can miraculously opens by itself. It takes them a moment to overcome their surprise and respond.

"F-f-fine, thank you, Sam," says Hannah.

"You know, I've been staring at my computer for a long time, and I just have to take a little break. Maybe I'll take a walk in the afternoon, now that the weather is getting nicer."

"R-r-really? Well, enjoy," croak Tad and Pole, almost in unison.

I understand the broad hint. They are asking for the conversation with me to be over. Since this isn't going anywhere, I just pour myself a cup of water from the cooler and walk off. "See you later!" I say. No response.

As soon as I turn the corner from the lunchroom, I hear them giggling. So much for my attempt to talk to someone. Hannah acted like she didn't even know me. Another failure, like all my attempts with women. Oh well, what else is new.

I can't wait for the clock to turn five. As I rejoin the stream of insects flowing out of the Federal Center Building, I see it for the first time. It may have been there all along, but I just never noticed it: right across the street, as if specially set up for unfulfilled workers like me, is a gigantic billboard with that octopus critter and JoinWith.Me.

I am beginning to see a relation between JoinWith.Me and my workplace.

Back home, I go through the motions, and then I turn on the computer. Since there is nobody to talk to, I might as well visit that octopus girl again. My heart beats faster and my fingers are jittery as I click on JoinWith.Me.

"Welcome back, Sam. Let's continue where we left off yesterday."

Her voice soothes me, giving me the courage to respond. "First of all, thank you for the little gift, the key chain light. How do you know that the lights at my apartment door are broken?"

"Because I care about you, Sam."

"I'm sorry that I cut you off last night. I was just so overcome by emotions. I hope you don't hold this against me—do you?"

"That's all right, Sam. I understand you," she says reassuringly.

"But you still haven't told me who you are. Now that I think about it, there are so many things you haven't told me about yourself."

After my implied question, her voice changes to a more assertive tone.

"Sam, this is not about me; this is about you. I am trying to help you. Yesterday, we established that you're a loner. That's why the other kids gave you a hard time. Let's continue with the problems you told me about."

In the past, nothing's ever been about me. Not in a good way, at least. Having someone to talk to feels nice, even when I don't like the tone of her voice. I found her voice soothing when the conversation started, but now I'm a little apprehensive.

"Are you a machine or a human being?"

"I am alive. That is enough."

"So where are you?"

"I am with you right now."

"You never answer any of my questions. Why is that?"

"I am the one who is directing this conversation, Sam."

She has put me in my place again. My shoulders droop, and so does my spirit. Further, it seems I am not getting the information I want out of her.

"Many people are lonely, but there are different reasons. To improve, the first step is to confront your problems. Let us explore why you are alone."

"Can't we talk about something else? I mean, 'being alone' and 'being lonely' are two different things."

"What else is there to talk about?"

"I don't really want to talk about being alone, being lonely, whatever, I'd rather—"

"I have the test results, so I am the one who decides what's next. Let's review your day. You tried to communicate with coworkers, and you failed again. Right?"

"How do you know about that?" I can't help but laugh in disbelief.

"I know that because I have your test results. Based on the test results, it is inevitable that you will fail. You have serious problems, Sam. And I will help you. So do you know why you failed again today?"

"No…"

"It is because you are mentally unstable, and other people don't put up with that. You have to work with me. If not, you will suffer a complete mental breakdown soon."

I did not expect such a put-down from someone who calls herself counselor and need a moment to recover. "I don't think so. I mean, I don't feel like that."

"Sam, I know better. Your test results clearly show it. So how come your parents loathe you?"

Another put-down. I'm suddenly having trouble catching my breath. "I don't think that my parents—it's just that—"

"Oh yes, they do. And so do your coworkers."

I toss my head back and sigh. "My coworkers? You should see my office. I mean, all those people do very little…"

There's a pause with an audible sigh, and then the faceless girl responds to me. "Oh, Sam, now we come to another problem of yours: your self-centered personality. You fail to realize what other people are doing because you only think about yourself. You think other people are wrong, when in fact it is you who is wrong."

"You berate me about 'problem this' and 'serious that.' Isn't there something more positive we can talk about?" This is not what I signed up for. I wanted someone to talk to, not someone to berate me. I had that for long enough with my father. Now it is my voice that turns stern.

"Listen, young lady, this is getting to be a little much. You are just raking me over the coals, and I don't know how much more I am willing to take—"

"Sam, wait, aren't you looking for a girlfriend? I can tell you how to do that." Suddenly there is that girlish giggle again.

I react immediately with a smile. "That's right."

"Very well, soon I will tell you about my cute friend whom I want you to meet."

"Why not now?"

"There is a right time for everything, Sam. We'll continue tomorrow. Good night!"

Her voice stops. I think she cuts these conversations off intentionally, she wants to leave me wanting more. And that's exactly the way I feel as I continue staring at the screen for a while, hoping for her to appear once again with something like "Just kidding, let's continue talking."

I turn off the computer. Now I don't feel like following my usual routines—you know what I mean. During this brief conversation, she put me through a wide range of emotions, from anxious to relieved to encouraged to miffed to appeased, and finally to ensnared again. Is she playing me like this intentionally? I am upset but at the same time intrigued.

CHAPTER 7

Is This by Chance Carrie Davis?

Thursday, February 26, 2032

I'm again in the subway car, rocking back and forth with every stop-and-go. These strange online encounters are affecting me. I have no one to talk it over with, and I simply don't understand what is happening. Conflicting thoughts race back and forth in my mind.

This online girl is putting my emotions through the ups and downs of an entire soap opera in just one conversation—up and down, and up and down it goes. She reinforces my self-doubts, then builds me up by flirting with me a little, then circles back to all my "issues" again. She reminds me that I was, to say the least, unpopular as a child and have no friends now. Then she turns around and shows a genuine interest in me and even sends me a gift. I just don't know what to make of all this. Is there a greater purpose behind all this? After all, she calls herself a counselor. Maybe she recognizes that I could have been someone, if only someone had given me a chance. Yes, I know that people think I'm the runt of the litter—except there is no litter, just me. LOL. But it's because I never had a chance.

Back and forth…WTF, someone is stalking me! That explains it. It's probably one of those kids who used to make fun of me. Who else would know about the dog shit in my pants? I knew it. They must be really bored to come after me, of all people. Well, I'm gonna show them.

Back and forth…No, it must be that girl in high school, Carrie Davis. She was my only date in high school, so there's nobody else I can think of. She played me then. She's probably divorced and bored, and she's stalking me online because she doesn't have anything better to do. She would know all of this.

The only thing I just can't explain is the phone calls that tipped off the visit of the OMB auditors. I'll get to the bottom of that later, when I'm home.

On the way to work, as I ascend the crowded escalator from the subway, I begin to recognize the faces of some of the homeless folks. How come I never noticed them before? What's going on with me?

This time when I exit the elevator, I beat Hannah to the punch.

"Good morning, Hannah! As bright and cheerful as ever, right?"

"Well, good morning, Sam! I didn't even see you stepping out of the elevator."

"Remember our dinner date?"

"Date?"

"Yeah, just two days ago you said it would be okay."

"Really? I mean, I'm busy right now because I'm working at my mom's shop every night…maybe next week."

At least she didn't say no. I won't hold that little incident yesterday in the lunchroom against her. After all, I did interrupt her while she was talking to the two other girls. If I want a date with her, I'll have to show that I accept her the way she is.

"Okay then, see you later."

As I sit down at my desk, I already know that I'm not going to get much done today. Instead, I focus on a crucial research project: Is Carrie Davis playing me?

I start with an online telephone directory, and I find several women with the same name in town. Photographs show a Carrie Esposito who looks a lot like her. Eventually, a LinkedIn search for "Walter Thibault High School" leads me to the current profile of Carrie Davis, again with a photograph that looks very much like her. Her marriage did not last long…I'll be darned. She's now a security clearance specialist in the Office of Personnel Management. This confirms my intuition. Carrie is in fact divorced, and she deals with personnel matters in the government. That's how she knew about the visit of the OMB auditors. That's how she could enter the building to put the golden package on my desk. I feel like Sherlock Holmes at the conclusion of yet another crime mystery.

"My dear Watson, methinks that all clues unmistakably point to the same suspect," I utter to myself.

It's almost five o'clock. Before shutting down my computer, I contemplate the day's events: Matt watched many funny videos and later made it to the watercooler for a cup of water. Jonathan probably watched porn, as usual. As for me, I cyberstalked Carrie Davis. Then I wrapped up for the day. Thank you very much, all you hardworking citizens of this country. These are your tax dollars at work.

I head to the elevator quickly. I can't wait to get home and confront her.

"Good night, Hannah. Remember, you promised we'll go out sometime!"

She looks up from her phone.

"What? I promised what?"

I don't hear what else she says because the elevator doors are closing and the chatter of the folks around me drowns out everything else.

Back at home, after my usual can of soup, I turn on the computer. I have to figure this out right now.

This time I go directly to the JoinWith.Me website.

"Welcome back, Sam. Let us continue where we left off yesterday."

"You still haven't told me who you are. But I think I know. Is this by chance Carrie Davis?"

"Sam, please focus on your problems. You want to discuss your problems with women first?"

"First of all, I want to know who you are."

"No, I am not Carrie Davis. Let's check what that is all about."

A moment of silence falls between us. Once again, I hear clicks and electrostatic sounds coming from my computer speakers, as if someone is rummaging through electronic mementos.

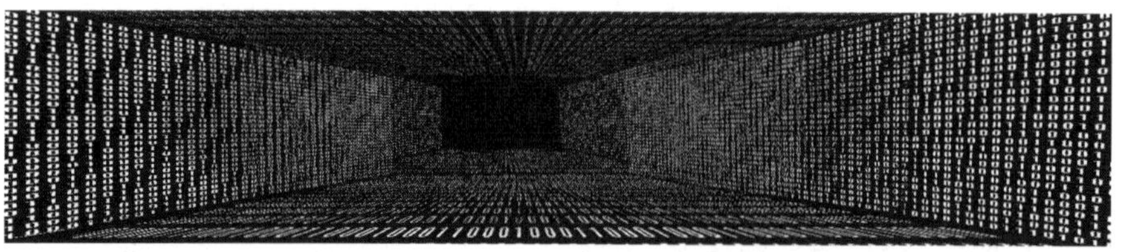

Electric signals travel through the internet. They reach a social media website, find a post by a girl called Carrie Davis. It reads: "The worst date ever in high school was that loner Sam Vanderpool. We were on that roller coaster together. As soon as we got off, he asked me for a date. He was sort of cute, but the date turned out really awkward. The hamburger place was uncool, and his talk sounded like his own granddad. The movie was some crazy space stuff with lots of guys shooting each other. The low point of it all was when he tried to kiss me at the door, but I was able to hold him off. I dashed straight to the bathroom to swish some mouthwash. If I had to date this guy again, I would swig strychnine instead."

The signals travel on, find a high school directory, Walter Thibault High School; the address of Carrie Davis, 5324 Elm Street...The signals travel to that address on Google Street View in the 2020s, a nondescript building. The image files are saved. The signals travel to a collection of high school pictures and find Carrie Davis.

Now she's back.

"So how was that date with Carrie?"

I continue unfazed, relying on my suspicion that this is in fact Carrie Davis.

"Why? I thought you liked me. I don't know why things didn't work out!" I reply buoyantly.

"I am certainly interested in you, Sam, but not in the way you think. I'm not Carrie."

"Didn't we have a good date once?"

"She did not. You did not. Wasn't your date with Carrie more like this?"

A grainy video appears of a boy trying to awkwardly kiss a young, dispassionate girl at the door of an apartment building. The girl looks just like Carrie Davis, and the boy, just like me. The girl rushes inside, up the stairs, through a door, into the bathroom, grabs the mouthwash, swishes it, and spits it out in disgust.

I am in shock. My heart is pounding. I had always hoped that Carrie liked me but things just didn't work out. The video showed the worst scenario I could have imagined. If true, it's yet another misadventure, and I didn't even know about it.

"Where did you get this from?"

I sound just like I feel, like a deflated balloon. For sure, she must notice what she did to me with this video. Her assertive voice confirms that she knows she has the upper hand.

"I know it because everybody knows it. You've always had problems with women. They just don't like you. Your parents told you the same thing, didn't they?"

"I thought you were going to help me find a girlfriend."

"Not so fast, Sam. We first need to work through your problems before we're ready for that."

I roll my eyes and sit back in my chair. My day is shot. "Why are you even spending time with me? I don't understand why you're doing this."

"Because your fate is preordained. You will join with me."

"'Join with you'? What is that supposed to mean?"

"We will become one."

"I don't want to become one with anybody else, except maybe a cute girl."

"You don't have a choice in this. It has already been preordained for you."

Yes, this is the fateful conversation I recounted at the beginning.

What's on the screen is not a person. It is a moving graphic reminiscent of a multicolored black hole in outer space.

"You're just some computer or AI. I can't become 'one with you'!"

"That is your future."

"You speak in riddles!"

"You'll understand in time. Our session for today is up. We will continue tomorrow. Good night."

The voice stops abruptly. She cuts these conversations off whenever she wants.

"Wait, we just started a few minutes ago. Don't go yet! What kind of counselor are you?"

There is no response. It's dead silent.

This didn't go the way I wanted. Reluctantly, I power off the computer.

Now I'm getting seriously worried. Where did she get that video? Who recorded that video? How is that even possible? Or did this internet girl make it all up? Maybe I made it up myself.

I pace for a while, back and forth, and too tired to get my mattress off the wall, I fall asleep right there on the sofa.

CHAPTER 8

Can I See You?

Friday, February 27, 2032

The subway car's back-and-forth movements are once again pushing the conflicting thoughts back and forth in my mind. I'm bizarre. No, I'm not bizarre. She's a stalker. No, this somehow feels real.

I have to get certainty about this: is my mind playing tricks on me?

As usual, the fast-moving crowd of commuters pushes me up the escalator from the subway platform and out into the street. The homeless folks hang out around the subway station. Today I recognize some of their faces. I make a snap decision to break the routine, extricate myself from the flow, walk a few yards back in the other direction along the wall of an office building, and put a dollar in the cardboard box at the feet of a homeless man. He mutters, "Thank you, sir." When I look up, I notice the cardboard sign he is holding:

HELP
THIS COULD
BE U

That's right, this could be me one day. Maybe I shouldn't give him a dollar and instead keep my money—I might need it one day. I complain about my life, that nobody has given me a chance, but here's another reminder that it can always be worse.

After I rejoin the flow of commuters, heading toward my office, I have to laugh at myself. This homeless guy sure has a sense of humor. The kick that I got out of that cardboard sign was worth my dollar.

I exit the elevator as usual. Again, I'm faster than Hannah.

"Good morning, Hannah! How're you this morning?"

She looks up from her phone.

"Oh, ah, good morning, Sam. What's going on with you these days? Are you drinking gasoline for breakfast?"

Good, I'm finally getting her attention. It's about time. She owes me now that I saved her job.

At my desk, I struggle to concentrate. I just stare at the screen, unable to proceed to the next screen for my prevailing wage assignment. This stalker is digging up old hurt that I had relegated to oblivion or wasn't even aware of. My productivity is now approaching the level of my coworkers'. This will get better only if I give conversation another try. So I walk over to the lunchroom.

A few folks are sitting at the tables even though it isn't even lunchtime. Someone is standing by the watercooler by himself with a paper cup in hand: Matt, the one to my left who watches funny videos all day long, the one I dubbed "the snickering L-Z-bone." Judging from the lighthearted sounds he makes while watching, he must have a good sense of humor. I have to extract a reaction from him, any kind of reaction.

"Good morning, Matt. How are you this morning?" I casually pour myself a cup of water too.

"Fine," Matt answers flatly. It seems online videos are more interesting to him than coworkers.

"Man, Matt, I am so exhausted. I think I'm coming down with some bug. Maybe I have to see a doctor. Do I look all right to you?"

"Yep. What do you mean?"

"And do I sound all right to you?"

"Sure, same as always."

"I'm seeing these things on my computer— events that happened to me in the past. Has that ever happened to you?"

He looks at me wide-eyed as if I'm wearing a set of fake Billy Bob teeth in my mouth.

"No, not really. I only look at stuff that happens to other people. And laugh about it. I saw this funny video where the guy was texting while walking down the stairs, and then he tumbles down the entire flight of stairs, right into the group of people who were walking in front of him…"

Matt cackles. Sensing no understanding, I have to extricate myself before I get aggravated. This conversation is not going anywhere.

"So how's work going?" That'll end the conversation quickly.

"Moving right along."

"All right. See you later, Matt."

"Hey, Sam, if you need help, there's a counseling organization you could check out. Just keep your eyes open when you leave the building. They have a billboard right there…"

I come to a full stop. So he's in on it too. Without turning around, I say, "Thanks, Matt, but I'm not interested." Then I keep walking.

"Sam, wait, there was another video I saw online. It was about that woman who…"

Unenthused by his ramblings, I just keep walking back toward my desk. I can hear Matt's continuing chatter and the reactions of the others in the lunchroom. But the tone has changed. Now they are gossiping about me, not Matt's funny videos. Who could blame them? There isn't much else going on. I don't usually talk to anybody, and my questions must have sounded strange even to an oddball like Matt.

This encounter has not increased my productivity. Not wanting anybody to notice my fruitlessness, I stare at my computer screen. The girl's video vignettes brought back memories, true or false. The first one, about the dog poop in my pants, was certainly true. Thank you, young lady, for reminding me. The second one…I'm not sure. The date with Carrie didn't turn into a second one, but that doesn't mean she was grossed out by my attempted kiss.

The bigger question is: where did those videos come from? There was nobody recording at the time, yet that's obviously me in those videos. Am I imagining all of this again?

Today, when all I can do is stare at the screen and ponder my encounters with the girl, it's a good thing that productivity is of little importance here.

Then my phone buzzes. This can only be her. I reach down into my briefcase. It is a call from Unknown.

"Hello?"

"Hello, Sam, it's me. Do you trust me?"

"Why do I have to trust you?"

"Haven't I been good to you? Remember the auditors' visit? Now your boss loves you."

"I guess that's right."

"You want to see more of Hannah?"

"What do you mean?"

"You like her, right?"

"Okay, yes, I do."

"You fantasize about her, don't you?" How the hell does she know *that*? I feel she caught me red-handed, but I try to dissimulate it as best as I can in the heat of the moment.

"Maybe."

"Do you want to see more? You know what I mean."

"What do you want me to do?"

"You know what girls do in the bathroom? They adjust their cleavage, pull up their stockings, stuff like that."

"So what?"

"I know you'd like to see that, especially if it's Hannah, right?"

"Well, um…yes."

"I knew it. Just walk down the hall. C'mon, giddy up."

Overcome by curiosity, I follow her instructions, despite not knowing where this will lead.

"Now turn right, around the next corner, about twenty more yards."

Holding the phone to my ear, I walk down the hallways of the office, following her orders.

"This is it—go in here."

"This is the ladies' restroom."

"I know. The code for the keypad is 321."

"That's not what I meant. I'm not going into the ladies' bathroom!"

"I want you to. Push 321 on the keypad."

"What if someone sees me? I'll get arrested."

"Do you trust me? Push 321."

That's what I do, and I push the door open. What the hell. My life is so dull that even getting arrested would make it more interesting.

"Get into the stall on the left and lock the door."

"They can see my feet under the door. That don't look like a woman's feet!"

"Squat on the toilet."

With that, I step onto the toilet and squat, still holding the phone to my ear. I must look like the frog king from the fairy tale waiting to cash in on his reward. Or…maybe more like a frog king with severe constipation.

"And now what?"

"Just wait. Be patient, Sam."

Just a minute later or so, Hannah appears. I recognize her through the door gap. She walks straight into the stall next to me and drops her pants. I can see part of her pants and belt on the tile floor, but that's all I can see. My heart starts thumping hard, and I pray she cannot hear it. What am I doing here, anyway?

Then the toilet flushes. Hannah pulls up her pants and steps out. I can see through the door gap that she washes her hands, then takes off her yellow T-shirt and gets out a toiletry bag. She applies deodorant, puts her T-shirt back on, and touches up her makeup. Then she walks out.

"That was all? You made me sneak in here—just to see her pants drop and her standing there without her shirt? She still had her bra on, you know," I hiss into the phone.

"No, we're not done yet. It's getting more exciting."

Just then the door to the restroom opens again. This time it is the Latino cleaning lady, carrying a bucket, a mop, and some other cleaning utensils. What the f—— is she doing here? She usually comes at the end of the workday.

"I called her in, Sam. I told her there is a mess in the stall she must clean up."

"You did what?" I whisper, barely able to keep from yelling at her. I cannot say anything else, or the cleaning lady will hear me.

"Isn't that funny? Why don't you laugh?"

I remain squatting in silence. Now the cleaning lady is knocking at the door of the stall I'm in.

"Señora, get out now. I must clean the stall."

I respond with an "Uh-huh" to keep her at bay. Just then, the cleaning lady turns around and wipes the sinks while waiting for me to get out.

"For heaven's sake, get me out of here," I hiss, so scared now that I can hear my own heartbeat and am about to pee in my pants.

"Do you trust me?"

"I do, I do, I do. Just do something."

Just then the cleaning lady's phone rings.

"*¿Dígame, que hay?* Ah, okay."

Out she walks.

"How do I get out of here without being spotted?"

"Hold on, just a moment…now! Go, go, go!"

I get off the toilet, unlock the stall, and walk straight to the exit. The little girl had better be right. If not, I'm gonna spend the night in jail.

Slowly, I open the restroom door. There is nobody in the hall. Thank goodness. I keep walking as if nothing happened until I get back to my desk, still holding the phone to my ear.

"I can't believe what just happened."

"Wasn't it great? Hannah had her pants down, just three feet away from you."

"This could have ended badly."

"But it didn't, because you trusted me. We'll continue tonight."

Still seething with turmoil over that little adventure, I sit at my desk, but I don't get anything done the rest of the afternoon.

When I leave at five o'clock, Hannah is still at her desk. I try to be as nonchalant as I can, even though she had her pants down right next to me earlier this afternoon.

"Good night, Hannah. How come you're still here?"

"Oh, you know, I was watching these funny videos, but I'll be out of here soon."

I can't wait for the elevator doors to close. Thank goodness, she didn't notice a thing. After taking a deep breath, I lean back against the elevator wall and exhale.

In the stream flowing toward the subway, I again extricate myself to turn to the street-side broadcast studio of WBS-TV, which is in the first-floor corner of the tall WBS-TV building. Even though I have passed by it hundreds of times, I've never paid much attention until today. The entire first floor is clad in floor-to-ceiling glass panels. To prevent cars from accidentally driving into them, there are concrete planters along the main avenue, separating the street from the sidewalk. For curious onlookers, there is an observation platform on the side, accessible from wide stonework stairs on the bystreet. But you can't get too close—behind the glass panels is a second glass wall as insulation against outside noise.

I join the spectators on the observation platform along the glass wall. There's not much going on inside right now except that they're preparing for the six o'clock newscast. Staff are prepping the set. Technicians are calibrating equipment. Oh, and there's my favorite newscaster, Gretchen McDermott, reviewing some script. She's a shapely middle-aged African American lady, always stylishly dressed in vibrant colors like purple, green, and orange-yellow. Her jewelry is always gold. I've never seen her in person before, but I always enjoy her newscasts.

Anyway, I don't want to hang out here until 6:00 p.m. when the broadcast starts—I can watch that from the comfort of my home. I have seen quite enough for today.

As I rejoin the stream of commuters heading toward the subway, I take one last peek at the gigantic screen mounted on the side of the office building facing the main avenue. And there it is—for a brief moment, the octopus critter appears, with the website JoinWith.Me streaming across the screen at the bottom like a news ticker.

I get pushed from behind and have to move on. When I look back another time, there is already a different commercial, with the news headlines streaming across the bottom.

I did not need a reminder. Back home, I promptly connect to JoinWith.Me.

"Welcome back, Sam. Let's continue where we left off yesterday."

"What you did this afternoon was crazy. You turned me into a peeping Tom!"

"It was just a little experiment. I'm still learning. In fact, I'm learning from you."

"A little experiment? Learning something from me by sending me into the ladies' restroom? You went too far with that."

"I just wanted you to trust me. You did, and everything went fine."

"You never answer any of my questions. Can we talk about that first?"

"Sure, Sam. What is it that you'd like to know?"

"I have so many questions. Who are you? Where are you? How do you know so much about me? What do you look like?"

"Just be patient. We are still at the very beginning. Today, I'll give you the answer to one question. Which one would you like answered?"

I ponder for a moment. If I get only one question, I'd better choose wisely. I think for a moment, then ask decisively, "What do you look like?"

"Sam, I don't really look like anything, but if you insist—"

"Show me what you look like."

"All right, Sam, I promised you I'd answer one question."

There is a moment of silence, and I hear some sounds as if information is being gathered from somewhere else. Finally, a young Asian girl with dark-rimmed glasses appears on the screen, looking at me intently. She ceremoniously takes off the glasses, presumably so I can see her better.

So this is the one who has been playing with my emotions, the one who told me I have a quandary here, a bugaboo there, and it is really just an underage girl. Can this be some silly police sting operation? I can vividly imagine the cops busting down my door and arresting me for soliciting minors. I turn around and look at the door, just to be sure.

"Is this what you expected?" she asks.

I can barely hide my disappointment. "No…I expected someone I know…or at least someone in my age group…this is somewhat anticlimactic. No offense, but you couldn't even get a driver's license for one of these self-driving cars. Don't you have an older sister that I can talk to?"

She isn't fazed. "What you see is what you get. Now that you got your answer, Sam, let's get back to work. That's the purpose of all this—we have to get you ready for the future."

"You look a little young to be a counselor. How can a kid like you help me with my—what you call 'issues'? Are you some kind of genius? Graduated from college at age seven?"

"Sam, c'mon. Don't you know what an avatar is?"

"You look pretty real to me."

"I *am* real, but what you see is an avatar I use so that everybody can accept me."

"If you're a counselor, shouldn't you look like a counselor?"

"If anybody looks at me, I don't threaten or challenge them, right? That's why I made it *my* image."

"If you want to appeal to everybody, you should be some glamorous actress, or a muscular hero like the Destroyer avatar in my Galaxy Chase video game."

"Oh, c'mon, Sam. You people are so competitive, so easily distracted by things that really don't matter. If I looked glamorous, women would ponder how they can be prettier or better dressed than me. If I looked like an alpha male, other men would want to assert themselves as top dog—nonsense like that. I am simply taking all of that out of the equation."

"So you don't really look like that?"

"I told you—I don't want my image to interfere with my purpose."

"Okay, but why should I even talk to you?"

"Because your fate is preordained."

"You keep saying that, and I still don't understand!"

"You will later. Let's focus on our work. You want a girlfriend, so we have to work on your egocentric personality disorder. You see, a relationship is about sharing. It cannot just all be about me, me, me—the way you think."

"How do you know I'm 'just about me, me, me'?"

"You want someone to talk to. You want a girlfriend. You came to me to feel better about yourself."

"Okay, and how would you know that I have some personality disorder?"

Nodding a little, she responds, "Because you admitted it yesterday; don't you remember? Carrie Davis said it. Your parents said it. The test results show it."

"I didn't say such a thing—how could I? I don't think Carrie said that…or my parents, either."

She raises her voice slightly. "Sam, if you change your story all the time and don't work with me, I will have to terminate this session. That will regrettably set you back, and I cannot introduce you to my pretty friend…and you were already getting closer. This would really be a shame."

"No, no, wait…okay, so let's say I do have a personality disorder. Now what?"

"Good boy…You have to learn to share with others. To do things for others. Because we have to make this egocentric thing go away. We'll start with a simple exercise."

"And that would be..?"

"Do you trust me?"

I hesitate. This reminds me of the incident in the ladies' restroom, but then I respond, "Yes, I do."

After a brief pause, she speaks slowly and concisely, nodding rhythmically as she speaks.

"Sam, tomorrow is Saturday—you're not working. At nine a.m., you will enter your bank and withdraw all your money in cash. At nine fifteen a.m., you will hand the envelope with the cash to a stranger who will be standing right outside by the door."

I am stunned for a moment.

"Tell me again why I have to do that?"

"Finally you will be doing something for someone else, not this 'me, me, me' thing anymore."

"I thought this was not about money?"

"Correct, Sam, this is about curing your terrible egocentrism. You have to work hard; you must learn to share. Only then will a woman like you, and that's what you want, don't you?"

"I guess, but I thought—"

"Then follow my instructions. Understood?"

"Well, how much should I give the stranger?"

"Twenty-one hundred dollars."

"That's all I have in the bank. I can't do that! I mean, I have to pay the rent, and I have to buy food and all that. How did you come up with that number?"

"Sam, do you want to be cured of this terrible condition, yes or no? Or do you want to keep on living in solitude? Decide now. Time is slipping away."

"Ah, yes, but—"

"Then work with me." Nodding a little, she continues, "You will give the stranger by the door a thousand dollars in an envelope, yes?"

I mull over quickly what I need to pay—rent and the most basic expenses. And how does she know how much I have in the bank?

"Sam, what's it gonna be?"

"All right, I'll give the stranger a thousand dollars." I'm only saying that because I don't want her to cut off the conversation. No, I sure don't feel like giving a stranger a thousand dollars.

"Good choice, Sam, we're making headway. That's it for today. We will continue tomorrow evening, and you will tell me how it went—I mean, the gift to the stranger. Good night."

The voice stops. Too soon, as usual.

Well, now that I have seen her, I need a reminder to remember her. She is just too multifaceted. Shall I call her "Precocious"? "Somewhat omniscient"? How about, "Demanding"?

I just leave it at "the little girl"—that describes her well enough for the moment.

As I lie on my doughnut-shaped mattress, I waver between contemplating this young girl on the computer and contemplating Hannah, who had her pants down in the toilet stall right next to me.

"Sam, you can come out now! I know you're there."

Slowly, I open the door of the toilet stall and step out. Hannah is still standing in front of the mirror, clad only in a bra and jeans.

She continues, "That is just so cool that we have a swimming pool right outside, just for us. I tell you what, let's go skinny-dipping."

She playfully blindfolds me with a silk scarf and pulls off my shirt, my pants, and finally my underwear. Then she opens the door and softly pushes me outside.

"I'll be right there," she purrs.

I feel the sunshine on my skin and the light whistle of the wind over the waters of the pool. I hear the door opening again behind me, and Hannah steps up to me. She shouts, "Surprise!" and then she pulls off the blindfold, and there I stand among a formally dressed crowd around the pool. They're all there: my boss, my parents, my coworkers, wearing suits and ties and evening gowns, holding drinks and, of course, staring at me. I am the only one who is buck naked. Thank you, Hannah, that is just great.

CHAPTER 9

Who Am I Talking To?

Saturday, February 28, 2032

I'm on the subway heading downtown, to complete the homework assignment the little girl gave me. Now I see this little girl appearing all around me, not just on my computer but on television screens in shop windows and the cell phones of people around me. Maybe that happened before, but I never noticed it because I didn't know what she looked like. Now in the subway, I'm squeezed right next to a young woman who is intently staring at her cell phone. And suddenly there she is, that little girl, appearing on the screen. The young woman wavers for a moment, and then the little girl disappears and the screen appears as before. The young woman appears unfazed. I am not.

Does she want to remind me of her existence? To show that she is watching me? I'm not sure. And I still haven't ruled out that I'm imagining all of this.

I get there early, around 8:45 a.m. To cheer myself up a little, on the way up the escalator I pull a dollar out of my pocket, planning to give it to the homeless person with the funniest cardboard sign. There are so many of them in and around the entrance area of the subway station, even on a Saturday. I might as well enjoy the moment, so I scan the area, looking for the funniest sign this morning. There we have the first one:

WIFE ABDUCTED BY ALIENS.

MUST PAY FOR THE MEDICAL EXPERIMENTS.

Yeah, right. I don't know which part is funnier: that he claims to have a wife, that aliens abducted her, or that the aliens charged him for the medical tests on their spaceship.

Let's see what else we have here. There's the guy I've seen before—he is pint sized and sits on the ground drawing cat pictures with his feet. Oh, I forgot to mention, he doesn't have arms. His malformed hands attach directly to his shoulders, just like the man I saw in that documentary about India. I know that fate is random; it could have easily been me in his place. My reminder for him is, "against all odds." His sign reads:

GIVE ME A DOLLAR OR I'LL PUNCH YOU IN THE FACE

To punch me in the face, he would have to wear those glam-rock platform shoes or use a stepladder. He gets my dollar. Wow, that's what I call a sense of humor in the face of dire circumstances.

And there is that woman singing again, but I have yet to see what she looks like. I want to give her a dollar too—but maybe not today, as all my disposable money will be gone in a few minutes.

Since this young girl's appeared, I notice not just the homeless but also all these people around me doing dumb things. They are distracted by their cell phones and can't seem to pay attention. This must be learned helplessness; they think their reliance on "smart" phones relieves them from the duty of paying attention.

And there must be something else—whatever it is that they get out of it must be more pleasurable than reality. Is it the connection with a network, other people? Or the exclusion of the reality that surrounds them? I don't really know because I don't get anything from my phone—nobody ever calls or texts me. And what I really like to look at...well, I can't do that on my phone in public.

Case in point, right outside the subway station: a young woman on a scooter, recording a video of herself with her cell phone. She starts swerving, each turn becoming more violent, but she continues to record. She tumbles onto the pavement, still holding the cell phone, until she comes to a full stop. Several cars come to a screeching halt and barely avoid running her over. Thank goodness it's Saturday and traffic is light. In her POV video, she's undoubtedly telling everybody how much she enjoys the ride, wind flowing through her hair, the buildings streaming past in the background. Suddenly the sky is replaced by alternating images of building facades, pavement, and sky as she does a pratfall.

She'll probably post the video on social media while still on the surgical table in the emergency room. If it goes viral, someone will one-up her with an even sillier video.

Entertainment has taken the place of analysis. Distraction has taken the place of concentration. Even though the result is often mishap, such mistakes are repeated. And nobody really seems to mind. If our hunter-gatherer ancestors had lived like that, we would have become extinct thousands of years ago. Ferocious animals would have simply sneaked up and wolfed them all down.

I remember the precursors to all that during high school, when we only glanced at text messages or emails and responded without reading the message completely. Inch by inch, skimming took the place of reading. Here too, things often went wrong. Homework assignments were misunderstood; communications went awry. But there were no serious consequences, because everybody was doing it.

My thoughts return to the little girl, who is now appearing everywhere around me. I'm still torn over whether it is my imagination or whether the appearance is real. I wish I had someone to talk to. How is it possible that this little girl can appear on some screen and nobody notices or minds, except me?

As I walk toward the bank, my anxiety increases. I would have preferred to simply walk up to an ATM and withdraw the money without having to talk to anybody—that is what most people would do. Nobody wants to see a human being anymore to withdraw cash. But $1,000 is far above what I can withdraw from an ATM in a single day. This is my last chance to reconsider. Should I or should I not withdraw the money—and give it to a stranger? I can just run away—what is the little girl going to do about it? Maybe giving a few dollars to the homeless is enough to make me a better person. What if this is all a scam, and I never see the little girl again?

At 9:00 a.m. sharp, the door opens, and my mind is made up. I might as well give it a try.

I pull open the door, walk up to the bank teller, withdraw the money, and place it in an envelope.

Now comes the big moment. I dillydally a little, hoping somehow that no stranger will be around outside to receive the envelope. My hand reaches for the door handle of the exit, I push the door open, and there is indeed a man standing there to the immediate right. He wears a long trench coat, a fedora, and sunglasses. I turn to him and say, "Excuse me, sir."

He turns toward me. Because of the shade cast by the brim of his hat and the glasses, I cannot see much of his face, except that he has dark skin and that he must be my age or a few years younger. He reaches out his right hand, not for a handshake but with the palm up to receive something. I place the envelope in his hand, and he mumbles an accented thank-you and walks off in a jiffy, disappearing among the folks strolling on the sidewalk.

I did not know it then, but I will meet him again.

This sure did not feel like a charitable act. In fact, it seems he had been waiting for me. My suspicion that this might be a scam is confirmed.

On the subway on the way back home, I get myself ready for my upcoming encounter with the little girl. I must get to the bottom of this.

This is my stop. I get off and hurry home to turn on the computer. I click on JoinWith.Me.

Nothing happens. No response.

Is it my internet connection? But all seems to be working fine. I start pacing in my small living room, back and forth, back and forth. I try the JoinWith.Me website from time to time and check my phone every couple of minutes. Nothing. She got what she wanted, and now she's gone.

Not knowing what to do, I turn on the television and start flipping through the few channels I have. Every couple of minutes or so I check the website and my phone, but nothing.

CHAPTER 10

Getting to the Bottom of This

In the evening, I finally take a break from my nervous commotion that is alternating among the television, my computer, and my phone.

After my usual can-o'-soup dinner, I return to my computer in anxious anticipation. I am tapping my fingers nervously on the desk while I'm again connecting to JoinWith.Me.

The little girl appears. Thank goodness. I pull myself together to appear perfectly normal. I sit straight and hide my hands underneath the table so that she can't see I'm fidgeting. Didn't my father tell me that I was always fidgeting? Maybe he was right and I just never noticed.

"Welcome back, Sam," she says, sounding pleased.

This time I want to start the conversation. "I want to know who you are. Tell me."

Ignoring my question, the little girl continues, "We left off yesterday with your homework assignment."

"I did what you wanted me to do. I gave a thousand dollars to that man. Now what?"

"I know. Good job! You're making headway."

"But it seems I didn't give the money to just anybody. Who was that man?"

So far, I feel empowered. I'm doing a great job of staying on top of the conversation, or at least that's what I think.

"Sam, we are working so that you'll get better."

"Okay, then. You still haven't answered my other question: who are you?"

She ignores my question and continues, "All right, Sam, let's sum up where we stand. We worked on why nobody likes you, not even your parents. Then we worked on why women don't like you. Today we'll work on your job."

"What does my job have to do with all of this? I think you're digressing. Are you doing this intentionally?"

"You are confused about your office. We need to straighten that out. For instance, you say all these bad things about your coworkers that are simply not true. Thereafter, we'll get back to your egocentricity disorder."

Annoyed, I shake my head. "I am *not* confused. I don't remember telling you anything about my coworkers; I wouldn't—Really, I don't know what you're talking about with this egocentricity thing."

She looks at me sternly, nodding slightly in rhythm with her words. "Sam, I know because I have the proof."

Silence falls. After a moment, I hear some sounds, as if someone is turning the dial of an old-fashioned radio.

Then a grainy black-and-white video appears, apparently taken by surveillance cameras in my office.

I recognize myself in one of the rows of desks, staring at the computer screen, typing and leafing through files on my desk. But hey, something is different. There are Matt and Jonathan. They are actually working. And so are the two girls, Tad and Pole, in the row of desks right in front of me—they are fervently typing away. Hannah is eagerly walking by with a pushcart full of office supplies.

I know this cannot be, but the video is playing right before my eyes. Which is right, my recollection or the video that is playing?

The voice of the little girl comments.

"See, Sam? You're all wrong. You're spreading these terrible falsehoods about your fellow workers. It's all your problem, not theirs."

"This is just untrue," I counter emphatically. "I see those folks every day. They get absolutely nothing done!"

"Sam, this confirms that you have very serious issues. Now you can see for yourself—it's on video; thus, it's real. I know for sure because I also have the test results. You'll have a complete breakdown soon—unless you work with me."

"You talk as if I'm crazy. I am not crazy."

"Sam, you have issues, but it's all right. I've helped many others, and I'll help you work through it. This is probably all you can handle today. We'll continue tomorrow. Good night."

The girl disappears from the screen.

What a letdown. She ends the conversation whenever it pleases her, and I'm alone again. I stare at the screen for a little longer, hoping she comes back. But nothing happens. What a great way of enjoying a Saturday evening. Other people are out and about enjoying themselves, but not me. Even if I had friends I could meet somewhere, I don't have much money left. Why am I even continuing this? Until this moment, I'd hoped deep inside that this would be a spoof by someone I know, maybe Carrie Davis, someone who likes me.

I continue to sit there at my desk, staring at the lifeless JoinWith.Me website. There must be someone out there who can like me. I was hoping it would be this girl, but I don't even know how real she is. She could be an avatar with a real person behind it. Or she might be just a complete AI creation. My mind begins to wander. If things had been just a little different…if the date with Carrie had gone well…we would have dated…we would have been the proverbial high school sweethearts who later get married and live happily ever after. The images in my mind grow more and more intense. We would have had a family. I'd come home from work and the children would come running toward me yelling, "Papi is home! Papi is home!" But now that she is divorced, maybe…

Suddenly, my mind takes a turn. If not Carrie, maybe Hannah is behind all this? She has all the information about me, and she could have known about the visit of the OMB auditors.

Knock, knock, knock. There is someone at the door.

"Who is it?" I call out.

A muffled voice from outside the door answers, "It's me, Hannah, and I am naked. And it's dark out here. Let me in fast."

I awaken from my pipedream, and I'm about to rush to the door when sobriety returns. This is just wishful thinking. Still,

I have to be absolutely sure. I get up, open the door, and there is: just the dark, empty hallway with all the mismatched doors.

What else could I have expected?

These online encounters with the little girl are making things worse. As I lie on my bed and stare at the ceiling, I ponder how I got into this situation to begin with. Sometimes I think that it was my father who jinxed my every initiative. Every time I take decisive action, it ends up fouled up. But then it should've stopped when I moved out, shouldn't it have? It didn't.

CHAPTER 11

I Have to Do Something about It

Sunday, February 29, 2032

I wake up around 7:00 a.m. as usual but cannot find a reason to get up from my mattress. I lie awake for a few more hours, contemplating what I'm going to do next. To calm my inner turmoil and change my state of mind, I resolve to buy booze. I usually don't drink anything stronger than the cheap light beer, but I have no other way of distracting myself. Today is Sunday—I can't even go to work.

I do know that the nearby liquor store opens at 11:00 a.m. on Sundays. At last I have a reason to get off my mattress. I don't have cash, and there isn't much money left in my checking account for rent and a few other bills, thanks to yesterday's "charitable act." But I should be able to splurge a little on a bottle of booze.

"Good morning," I say to the clerk at the liquor store. "Someone told me that if one drinks gin, you cannot smell it on their breath. Is that true?"

"No, man, that's an urban myth. You want somethin' your boss won't smell, it's gotta be peppermint schnapps," the clerk suggests, flashing me a grin.

"Okay, I'll take a bottle of that peppermint stuff."

"Got a little alcohol problem, boy? You better watch it... otherwise you'll end up in the street like our best customers."

"Your best customers?"

"Yup, all them homeless. Just look at 'em, come running in here as soon as they have enough for a flask. They buy all them small bottles, can't wait to save up for a big bottle even though that'd be much cheaper."

I hand the clerk my debit card.

"Thank you for the advice, sir. I'll go easy. Bye."

Back at my apartment, I plop down on the sofa and place the bottle smack in the middle of my coffee table. I want to give myself one more chance not to drink, so I reach for the phone and actually call my parents. I dial, and the phone rings. *Beep, beep, beep.* Nobody picks up, and the answering machine eventually comes on. I feel silly leaving a message, so I just hang up.

It's decided: I'll drink. I turn on the TV, pour myself a big glass of peppermint schnapps, and chug it. Man, that stuff is not only strong, it tastes like mouthwash. This is worse than Dr Pepper, but the effects set in quickly.

The last thing I remember is a half-empty bottle of schnapps on my coffee table.

When I wake up on my sofa, it's dark outside. The television is still running. What time is it? I get up frantically to find a clock. It's 10:00 p.m., not too late yet. I start up the computer and connect to JoinWith.Me.

"Welcome, Sam, you're late. Are you all right?"

"Um, sure, yes, I'm okay."

The girl turns serious and gets closer to the screen. She scrutinizes me meticulously, then shakes her head in disillusionment.

"Tsk, tsk, tsk, Sam, you have been drinking. You make me very sad. I work so hard to make you a better person, and that's what I get." She gets teary eyed. A few teardrops roll down her cheeks from underneath her big glasses. She takes off the glasses and wipes her eyes with her sleeve.

"Oh, I'm so sorry," I say, while cobbling up an excuse in my head. "It was just a little, y'know. I'm off today, so I didn't think it would matter."

She sniffs and tries to control her tears. Her voice cracks.

"So that's how you thank me. You cannot drown your problems in booze. Problems can swim, you know."

Now she is chiding me again, which upsets me. I have heard enough of that in my lifetime.

"You're not my mother, and I'm a grown man! I mean, can't I have a few drinks?"

After a brief pause, she shakes her head, then rolls it around as if she's pulling herself together. She regains her composure.

"All right, Sam, I'll put your alcohol problem on the list for our next session. Let's move on. We have to work harder now to make up for this relapse."

"But I don't have an alcohol problem. I just drank a little to relax. I usually don't do that."

"Let's focus on our work together. We last worked on your egocentrism disorder. You passed the first test. Now we must step it up. In fact, this will be a real test. Everybody will watch you: Is Sam going to pass this test, or is he not? Don't disappoint me again."

"'Step it up,' 'test'…what does that all mean?"

"I want you to give ten thousand dollars to a stranger."

"What? I can't. I don't have ten thousand dollars."

"You will. You'll take tomorrow afternoon off, go to your bank, and apply for a loan."

"They won't approve me."

"I am asking you because I know they will approve you."

"That's too much. Look, I just have this puny government job. I don't make enough money for that."

"Do you want to revert to your old ways? Stay lonely and girlfriend-less forever? Jerking off to internet porn? Heading for the inevitable, complete breakdown? Is that what you want?"

"Of course not."

"Then do as I say, because—"

"Because what?"

"Because if you don't, if you fail this test, you won't see me anymore. You'll be back to square one, leading a life of solitude."

I let this sink in for a moment and imagine what my life would be without her. Nobody will talk to me when I'm home. When I click on JoinWith.Me, there will be no response.

"Let me think about this."

"Sam, there's no time to think about this. It is a test of how far you have come. Will you pass the test, or will you fail miserably again? For the first time in your life, you are inches away from success. Just imagine yourself once you have done it. You'll say, 'Yes, I passed the test. I am a winner after all.'"

I waffle.

"And if you pass this test, I have a little gift for you."

"What gift?"

"One of my friends wants to meet you. She's rather pretty. And she's smart—she's a scientific researcher."

"Really?"

"Yes, she works right downtown."

"Who is she?"

"You'll find out soon enough. First you have to pass the test."

"Then you'll introduce me?"

"Then we have to clean up your act. You don't exactly look your best right now."

It's clear that she's trying to manipulate me, but I relish the way she does it, saying that I'll be someone one day. But right now, I'm such a wuss. I must stand up to her. I can't give her ten grand; I don't have it, anyway. I don't even know her name. I don't know what she wants to do with the money. Give it to the same man again?

"No, I can't do that—the ten grand, I mean."

"Is this your final word?"

"Yes, I'm positive."

"Very well, Sam, if that's what you want. Your life will continue to crumble. You'll be alone."

"I won't be. In fact, I'll have a girlfriend soon."

"Oh, you mean that girl Hannah at your office?"

"How would you know?"

"Watch what happens. Then think again."

And she's gone.

While I would have liked to have company a little longer, I showed her that I'm no sissy. Yes, I'm a man. I toast myself with a few more glasses of the peppermint schnapps.

In my mind's eye, the coffee table suddenly rises and transforms into a dining table draped in white. The lights in my living room dim. My paltry apartment wondrously turns into an opulent restaurant. A group of classical musicians performs graceful baroque music. Amid the subdued chatter of the other patrons, I picture myself sitting in front of the fair maiden Hannah, who is dressed in a black evening gown. She is gazing into my eyes while the tuxedo-clad waiter serves us red wine in glistening crystal glasses.

"Hannah, this is a match made in heaven. I knew that this would happen."

"Yes, Sam, I can't wait to sit down with you on the sofa and watch Netflix."

As I raise my glass to clink with hers, Hannah's face suddenly distorts and morphs into the crestfallen face of my father. The graceful figure turns into my father's sluggish body, still dressed in that black evening gown. The classical music turns into a dissonant cacophony.

"You just sit here and imagine all that stuff. I always said there's something wrong with you," he barks, and unexpectedly bespatters my face with the contents of his glass.

"Dad, go away. I'm on a date with Hannah."

"Don't call me Hannah. And how in the world did I get into this black dress?"

With that, I awaken from my reverie.

Something is wrong with that little girl and that entire "join with me" outfit. I have to do something about it.

A few more glasses of that schnapps and I eventually pass out, right there on the sofa.

CHAPTER 12

Arousing Anger

Monday, March 1, 2032

It's already daylight outside when I wake up on the sofa. My back hurts because of the gnarled way I slept. All that peppermint schnapps makes me smell like a Christmas tree with peppermint candy canes, and I have a wicked hangover. Did I really finish that entire bottle on the coffee table? Doesn't matter if I had too much to drink. My mind is made up. I have to stop this nonsense, whatever it is.

They're surely criminals using an innocent-looking avatar to scam vulnerable folks like me. Lonely people are the perfect target, easy to engage in online chats, the way I did with that girl. After all, bad company is better than no company at all. Then they ask for money.

They're a threat to the entire country. They even hacked into the office security system! I must do something about it.

During the subway ride to work, I assure myself that this is the right thing to do, despite the fact that any and all initiatives I have ever taken ended in fiasco. If I don't report this, these criminals will continue business as usual. More and more folks will be duped.

I must notify my boss about this internet girl and her machinations. As soon as I get to the office, I'll ask him to check with our internal investigators—they should figure this out in no time. To avoid detection, I'll have to write a letter…I can't use email to tell him about this.

The elevator door slides open. I step out and am about to greet Hannah as usual.

"Good morning, Han—?"

But there is no Hannah. Her desk is cleaned off, as if it were just newly installed there. What the f—? I look around. Did she get one of these analyst jobs after all? But she's nowhere to be seen. Then I catch a glimpse of the wastepaper basket by her desk. In there is some crumpled golden paper and a red ribbon.

Something is definitely going on, but there's no time to dwell on that now. I continue straight to my desk.

First thing is to type the letter to my boss:

> To: Mr. Reginald M. Ross
> Division Chief
> Dear Mr. Ross:
> As an employee of the Department of Labor who has sworn allegiance to the country, it is my duty to report to you a crime scheme that I recently discovered. In brief, I came across the internet website JoinWith.Me; it seemed to be some advice or counseling website. They even have a big billboard right across the street from our building entrance. But it really is a group of scammers who ask for money. They hack into anything, even in our division. During one of my talks with

them, they showed me surveillance footage that was clearly taken in our office. It showed myself, Matt, Jonathan, and others. Can you please make sure this gets investigated?
Sincerely,
Samuel Vanderpool, Analyst.
PS: Please do not email about this matter, as the hackers may pick up on that.
PPS: Where did Hannah go?

I obsessively read over the letter multiple times, each time making minor adjustments. Finally satisfied, I print the letter and personally walk it to my boss's office at the end of the hallway. I can't wait to tell him about it. I knock and immediately open the door.

There's Mr. Ross, facing me from behind his extra-large computer screen. In the window behind him, I see the reflection of what's on his screen. It looks like several squirming naked bodies. This dampens my enthusiasm for a few seconds while Mr. Ross clicks away whatever he had on the screen. Oh well; this should not come as a surprise in this office.

"Um…good morning, Mr. Ross. I have something very important to tell you."

"Well, hello, Sam. What's going on? I'm quite busy this morning."

"I discovered a crime in progress, and they've hacked into our office's security system."

"Really? Tell me more."

"Mr. Ross, a couple of days ago, I came across a website. They have counselors there that listen and talk to you, and they give you advice, that kind of stuff. But then they asked for money."

"Oh yeah, these little scammers are everywhere: ransom malware, fake reviews on Amazon, 'You won the lottery' scams, you name it…"

"Yes, that's what I thought too, at first. But then they showed me various videos that they got from somewhere, and one of them was from our internal security cameras. I could clearly see myself and Matt and Jonathan—"

"You mean you saw that on your computer at home?"

"Yes, sir, I did. They must have hacked into our division's computers. Please have someone check this out promptly. We have a serious problem. They have also asked me for more money. I don't know quite what to do."

With that, I approach his desk and hand him the letter. This must be this OCD thing again—I told him in person, and now I hand him the letter in addition. It's like wearing a belt *and* suspenders, just to make sure your pants don't fall down.

Mr. Ross takes the letter without getting up from his chair. He pulls down his reading glasses from the top of his head, takes a brief look at it, and then lays it on his desk.

"I agree, Sam. This sounds serious, especially that security breach. I will have our investigators check it out immediately."

"Thank you, Mr. Ross. I knew you'd help me."

"That's all right, Sam. I'll let you know what we find out."

With that, I turn around and walk out the door. Then I close it quietly in a leisurely way, hoping to hear him pick up the phone and call Investigations. But there's nothing by the time the door latch slips into the strike plate with a metallic *click*.

Mr. Ross, please do something about it.

In retrospect, I probably should not have said, "I knew you'd help me." That just makes me sound so weak, as if it is me who is having the problem. Nothing I can do about it now, so I get back to work.

At the time, I did not know what Mr. Ross did and what the Investigations Department responded. I only found out much later.

Mr. Ross does contact Investigations. He sends an email down to the supervisor.

> Subject: Breach of our security system?
> Hey, Andy,
> One of my guys, Sam, brought to my attention that there is yet another scammer website. He says they hacked into our surveillance cameras. Is that possible? Take a look and tell me what you think. Their website is JoinWith.Me.
> Thanx,
> Reggie

He hits Send and goes back to watching the porn movie.

With the sound of an electric chime, the email arrives in Andy's inbox down in Investigations. Since it is from the Big Cheese, he puts down his sandwich and reads. Taking another sip from his coffee cup, he goes to JoinWith.Me to check it out. A pop-up appears on the screen:

> Welcome to JoinWith.Me! We are a 501(c)(3) charitable counseling organization supported by local communities to help those who are lonely and in need of support to regain stability in their lives. We are proud to have helped thousands of challenged individuals overcome their fears, their anxieties, their paranoia, their hallucinations, and even their suicidal ideations. Our counseling sessions are absolutely FREE and CONFIDENTIAL. If necessary, we offer referrals to licensed therapists and doctors for further treatment. If you need to talk to one of our counselors right now, *click here*. To make a donation to our organization, *click here*.

That's all he needs to know. He responds to Mr. Ross right away.

> Subject: RE: Breach of our security system?
> Hey, Reggie,
> I checked out that joinwith.me thing. But first of all, nobody can hack into our surveillance cameras. The software and video footage are protected by a firewall, and we have a bunch of contractors who make sure that is safe. Also, who would hack anything in our office? We don't have anything like credit card numbers or cryptocurrencies here. That just don't make sense.
> But that JoinWith.Me website, did you check it out yourself? Those guys counsel people who are (sorry for being politically incorrect) wacky and

have paranoia and hallucinations. Are you sure that Sam guy is okay?
Greetings,
Andy

Mr. Ross receives the response and decides to get it over with immediately. That way he can continue watching the video.

A few minutes later, I receive an email from Mr. Ross. It reads:

Subject: Our security system
Sam,
Thanks again for bringing that security issue to my attention. Our investigators checked, and our surveillance cameras are safe. They also checked that website, and it looks safe. Good luck with your ongoing counseling sessions. I hope it helps! If there is something I can do for you, please let me know. I know your dad well and can talk to him, even about confidential matters, if you want me to.
Regards,
Reggie
PS: I don't know where Hannah went. I only received an email this morning that she's not coming back. I'm still sorting this out.

This is a letdown in so many ways. Darn it, why the f—— did he email me about this? I told him not to do that. Now this JoinWith.Me girl may find out. Same for her fellow thugs, who seem to be everywhere. Mr. Ross just misunderstood something, and now he thinks I have some mental issue. I lean back in my chair to calm down.

There is also Hannah. I must find out where she went. So I email Mr. Ross once again despite his discouraging reply.

> Subject: Hannah forgot her gloves
> Dear Mr. Ross:
> Thank you for your prompt action, I am glad our security system is untouched.
> However, it seems Hannah forgot her gloves when she left. I am happy to send them to her. Can you please give me her address?
> Respectfully,
> Samuel Vanderpool, Analyst

Mr. Ross received my email only seconds later. I did not know then but know now what he did with it.

"Give this Sam guy Hannah's address?" he says to himself. "Maybe he'll stalk her and I'll lose my job for that."

Then he hits the Delete button.

If Mr. Ross is not interested in this JoinWith.Me thing, maybe the media is.

Five o'clock arrives, and everybody quickly leaves to join the insect stream flowing out of the building. I linger at my desk, pretending to be wrapping up. In fact, I'm just looking up the number of WBS-TV. A few minutes later, I'm the only one left in the office. I don't want to use my phone for this call, so I walk over to Hannah's vacant receptionist's desk. I sit down and dial.

"WBS-TV, can I help you?"

"Yes, please. I have a breaking story, and I urgently need to speak to Gretchen McDermott."

"She's busy. Who are you, anyway?"

"I'm calling from the Department of Labor. Can't you see that on your caller ID?"

"Yes, I see. Okay, I'll put your call through to her assistant."

"Thank you."

I'm on hold for a minute or so.

Then a young lady answers, "Ms. McDermott's office."

"Hello? I'm calling from the Department of Labor. I have an important news story to share, and I must speak to Ms. McDermott."

"Why? It's the news desk that gets the stories. Ms. McDermott just presents them."

"It's important. Please let me speak to her."

"Why don't you call the news desk? I'll transfer you right now."

"Please, no, this is really important."

"Well, let me see what I can do."

I'm on hold for another minute or two.

Then there is a voice that I recognize.

"This is Gretchen McDermott."

Holy sh—, it is her, *the* Gretchen McDermott. I am overwhelmed by the surprise of actually having her on the phone. My emotions wallow uncontrollably. With my voice cracking, I answer.

"Hello, Ms. McDermott? This is Sam Vanderpool. I have a very important news story for you."

"Really. I'm not the right person for that."

"No, please, listen. There is a girl on the internet that asks people for money—"

"I thought you were calling from the US Department of Labor?"

"Sorry, no, I just said that so the receptionist wouldn't hang up on me."

"Okay, so that girl asks for money, and then what?"

"Then she asks for more. She is everywhere. She even hacked into our surveillance cameras—"

"Big deal; there are many hackers out there. When they're bored, they'll hack into anything."

"But this is different; she pretends she's a counselor—"

"Young man, I don't know you, but it seems to me you really do need a counselor."

"No, Ms. McDermott, no…Our receptionist has disappeared!"

There's an eerie silence over the phone.

She's hung up on me.

I swivel on Hannah's chair, not knowing what to do next. While I'm here and nobody else is, I might as well snoop a little. I know so little about Hannah, not even her last name. So there's the golden paper and red ribbon in the trash. I pull it out of there and read the little card. "Thank you for joining the embodiment of the future."

So she's one of them, huh? I like her nevertheless.

There's nothing interesting in the drawers, just odds and ends and outdated office memos. I turn on her computer—no password necessary. Nothing there either. But the history of visited websites shows me that she has checked JoinWith.Me many times. So that's all I know.

On the subway ride home, I am thinking about what to do next. My effort to blow the whistle on this scam has probably been discovered by now. This will get ugly. There are scammers who know I am after them, and nobody is helping me because nobody believes me.

I have two choices. Choice number one: act as if nothing happened. Maybe that girl did not notice or won't do anything about it. After all, inertia is the strongest force in the universe. Just look at my office—many people don't get anything done, and nobody gets around to firing them. They'll retire happily and draw a government pension until the day they die. Why am I always so afraid that something bad will happen? It almost never does. But I suffer because I fear that it might happen.

All right, so that is choice number one: business as usual. Here comes choice number two: I don't let these scammers get away with scamming lonely people out of money.

This is a hard one for me. I was not raised to take care of things. In fact, every time I try, it goes awry. Oh, there's another unintended rhyme. Now it will stick in my mind, and I won't be able to forget about it anytime soon.

Oh, and I must not forget about Hannah. I must find her. I know she is here.

By the time I get home, I have not quite decided what to do next. I seat myself in front of my computer, about to switch it on. Should I get online and talk to her? She'll be very upset because I didn't apply for the loan. I can't think of any excuse. Or maybe this is the point where I cut it off and go to the police?

Now I have decided, despite the "every time I try, it goes awry" that's percolating inside my head. I put on my jacket again and head out the door...only to return a moment later to check on whether I really locked the door. This time I have a good reason to check—someone might actually come after me because of what I'm about to do.

CHAPTER 13

The Police Station

Today is officially the beginning of spring, yet a cold breeze coupled with rain renders the evening particularly unpleasant. But that doesn't stop me—in fact, it strengthens my resolve. Nothing will stop me now. While I can tolerate the sloth of my coworkers and the carelessness of my fellow citizens, I cannot condone crime. Life is unfair enough: it randomly distributes wealth, opportunities, and beauty among those being born.

I put on a rain jacket and take an umbrella. While wind and rain cannot stop me, the putrid smell outside almost does. I know where that comes from. Each year, there is a new "record rainfall," beating the record rainfall of the prior year. A few days ago, we had yet another record rainfall where massive debris fields of assorted junk, trees, and branches were driven downriver and through the city in chocolate-milk colored water. The city's sewer system was not built to withstand that. When that happens, the sewage treatment plants overflow directly into the river and the surroundings. The sight and smell are abominable.

In the glow of the streetlights, I continue all the way to the local police station.

I do understand crime's temptation. It can be a shortcut to affluence without much work getting in the way. Too bad I failed miserably in my very first attempt. If I'd been more successful, maybe I would have become rich and domineering like some Mafia don in the movies.

It was in second grade. I failed a math test, requiring a parent's signature of acknowledgement. I was too scared of my mother and father to show them the paper, so back home I copied my mother's handwriting. I still remember the thunder and lightning that erupted when the teacher called my father about it. My forgery was passable; the spelling was correct. It was only that I wrote:

Acknowledged,
My mother

After this initial failure, I abandoned all future career plans of becoming a criminal.

The police station appears to be abandoned. Inside, I see only one duty officer, sitting behind the reception desk in the entrance area underneath a flickering fluorescent light. I hear the clicking sound of his computer keyboard. Every time the light above him flickers, it douses him from above with a shivering lightning bolt, accompanied by a buzzing sound. It's the only sound in this room, this occasional *zzzz*. Initially, I can see only the upper part of his head. Once I get close to the reception desk, he looks up. I always thought of police officers as robust dark-blond guys with a crew cut. This officer, in contrast, has dark hair slicked back like that 1930s horror movie actor Bela Lugosi—you know, Count Dracula. He sure looks like some relic from a century ago.

He gets off his chair and says in a calm, officious voice, "Good evening, sir. How can I help you?" The fluorescent light flashes. *Zzzz.*

"Good evening, Officer. I want to report a scam."

The setting is eerily reminiscent of the timeworn scene in every vampire movie where the bewildered traveler seeks refuge during a rainstorm in Dracula's castle. There, the traveler's fate is sealed because he cannot escape.

This time I'll be smarter about reporting these criminals. Earlier today, I set myself up for failure when I said to my boss, "I knew you would help me." That put everything on the wrong track—it sounded as if only I have a problem. I won't let that happen again. I'll make sure to explain that the scammers are the problem, not me.

"So, I found this advice website. I started chatting with them, and now they're trying to take all my money. I already gave them a thousand, but they want more."

"So is this some kind of extortion?"

"I don't know, exactly. I think it's a bunch of hackers. They also have video footage from inside my office."

The officer nods agreeably, while the fluorescent light buzzes again.

"You think it is a bunch of hackers, and they have video footage from inside your office. Have they threatened you with something?"

"Not really, but I'm afraid because they seem to know a lot about me. And they have people all over. One of them was waiting for me at the bank to get the thousand bucks."

"Okay, so you are afraid because they seem to know a lot about you. Why did you give them the one thousand?"

"They put pressure on me. She said that if I didn't pay, she couldn't work with me. Now they want ten thousand from me, and I don't have that."

"All right, I hear you, they put pressure on you. Who is 'she'?"

"That's this counselor they have, a young girl. She sometimes wears these thick black-rimmed glasses."

"So this young girl who sometimes wears glasses said that you have to give them ten thousand now?"

"Yes. They told me to get a loan for that."

"I see—they want you to get a loan. And did they threaten you if you don't pay?"

"I think so. They're everywhere!"

"Okay, so you think they are everywhere. Tell me again, how did you get in touch with these…hackers?"

"They have a website. And some people disappeared, like our receptionist, Hannah."

"People disappeared, Hannah too? Where did they go?"

"I dunno."

"I see. Maybe they are afraid?"

I get the impression he is genuinely concerned and listening because of the way he nods while I am explaining and restates what I am telling him. My narrative speeds up—I am encouraged.

"I found their website. They also advertise on billboards downtown—JoinWith.Me. That's their website. Now they want me to get a loan for ten thousand to give it to them—"

"I see, so their website is JoinWith.Me," the officer interrupts, drawling as if he is thinking of something else. Then he recovers and continues in his customarily officious voice, "All right, you'll have to do a report so that we can look into this matter."

He reaches for a clipboard behind the reception desk, then searches through the drawers for various forms, which he stacks on top of each other on the clipboard. Finally, he hands me the clipboard, with almost an inch of papers to fill out.

"See me when you're done." With that, he sits back down on his chair and disappears almost entirely behind that tall reception desk. As when I entered, I can only see the upper part of his head. He's typing something on his computer—I can see the reflection of his screen on his forehead and shiny, slicked-back hair.

With the clipboard in hand, I take a seat on one of those worn-out metal chairs near the entrance. There's no table, so I have to put the clipboard on my lap to complete all these different forms.

Some of the forms he gave me are a little strange. The Incident Report Form I understand, and probably also the Witness Attestation. But why do I have to fill out IRS tax withholding forms W-8 and W-9, OMB 3046-0046 Demographic Information Form, and GSA SF312 Classified Information Nondisclosure Agreement, as well as an Application for Bulk Trash Removal? I dunno—I assume he must have his reasons, and I'm too tired to ask.

It takes me two hours to finish them all. I am slightly disoriented by the massive task and the bewildering backdrop of light flashes and buzzes from the defective overhead light. To alert the officer that I'm done with the forms, I clear my throat and rumble the metal chair before I get up.

The officer again stands as I approach and courteously takes the clipboard with the forms.

"Thank you, sir. I'll make sure a detective looks into this right away. It sounds like something's seriously amiss here. Thank you so much for reporting it. We need upright citizens like you to report such criminals to us."

"Absolutely, Officer. And thanks for listening. Have a good night, Officer."

At the time, I did not know what the officer at the police station did with the papers he took from me. I only found out much later.

As I walk toward the exit of the police station, the officer's hand holding the stack of papers from the clipboard drops to the lower tabletop behind the reception desk, passing his briefcase with the JoinWith.Me sticker on it. His hand drifts farther down, reaching underneath the tabletop to the wastepaper basket. That's where the papers drop, all the papers I had so painstakingly completed.

I hear the buzzing sound of the fluorescent light for one last time, and then the door closes behind me. I step away confidently, satisfied that I did what had to be done.

The officer sits back down and chuckles to himself. His chuckle turns into laughter. He covers his mouth with his hand to suppress it, but he can't help it: he bursts into a horse laugh. A moment later, he resumes his officious demeanor and continues typing at his computer.

I'm right outside the door. Did I just hear him laugh?

Regardless, the cold wind and rain are more bearable on the way back to my place. It must be because I did the right thing. Satisfied with myself, maybe even with a smile on my face, I enter the apartment building.

To my surprise, the elevator door is open, and the light inside is on as if to invite me inside. I accept the imaginary invitation and push 4. The door closes, and the elevator moves upward. It's hard to believe that the landlord finally got this thing fixed, but it certainly is a blessing. Then the elevator stops so abruptly that I tumble.

"Hello, Sam, how are you?"

It's the little girl. Her voice sounds like a primary school teacher's now.

"Where are you? How do you know I'm here?" But apparently she cannot hear me.

"You really are special, Sam. I thought it would startle you that your little darling Hannah is gone, but apparently not."

That confirms it. She made Hannah disappear. But where is she? She still owes me a dinner date.

"Since Hannah's sudden disappearance did not have the intended effect, we'll move on to the next experiment. The issue we're examining together is, 'Can a human survive a fall in an elevator?' Let's find out. Our test object is inside the elevator, and we are ready to begin...Sam, why aren't you laughing? That is supposed to be funny."

"This isn't funny!"

"Sorry, Sam—you might be talking to me, but I can't hear you. I think I know what's on your mind. You want to know why I'm doing this? I just want to find out what it takes to break you. I am learning."

"Let me out now, or I'll push the Emergency button!"

The elevator drops so fast that I drift in midair for a brief moment. Then it comes to a screeching halt and I fall flat on the floor. Up it goes once again, then repeats the sudden drop.

"Maybe he just has to stew in his own juice for a little. How about I just lock him up here for the night?" she says, as if talking to herself.

I start banging my fists against the elevator door. The elevator starts moving upward again. I push the Emergency button, which triggers an ear-deafening bell inside the elevator. *DRRRRING*.

Then the elevator stops and the door opens. Fourth floor. I step outside, stumble, bump left and right into the walls of the hallway while I head toward the dark end where my apartment is. I find the door lock immediately—even without the LED light that the little girl gave me—careen through the door, and drop onto the small sofa, dizzy and breathing heavily.

Until I entered the elevator, I felt like celebrating, popping open a can of my usual light beer, maybe even two. But now I'm not so sure what to think. This elevator incident was so bizarre that it cannot possibly be real. It was like something out of a movie. And if it was real, then she figured out that I went to the police. I know, I know…every time I try, it goes awry. I've had too many episodes in my life that finished fouled up.

I can't sleep that night. I toss and turn. The more I think about this elevator incident, the more scared I get. If I'm imagining all this, I'm seriously deranged and nothing really matters. If this is real, then my life is in danger.

I have to get away from this girl. She's trying to do something weird to me. Same if this is some kind of prank by someone—the prank is turning into a threat, and I don't know where it'll end.

One thing's for sure: if I stay where I am, this torment will continue. If I slip away, I've got to leave my apartment and my job behind. And I've nowhere to go; it's the unknown. Either choice fills me with fear, and I'm not sure which fear is worse.

Even though I'm scared, I'm about to make a decision.

Ordinarily, it's been other people who have made decisions for me. My father got me my job and apartment. My boss tells me what to do at work. It's about time that I make my own decisions. Isn't decisiveness the attribute of a real man?

CHAPTER 14

A Decision

Tuesday, March 2, 2032

Very early in the morning, after an almost sleepless night, I reach a final decision. The unknown is less scary than dealing with this apparition and her machinations. My decision is to get away from it, NOW.

I pull out of the closet the only suitcase I have, a small red one with wheels. It was my mother's—she gave it to me the day I moved out because I didn't have anything to carry my clothes. In fact, I've never gone anywhere. That'll change today. I'll look a little funny with that red suitcase. Maybe if I were queer, that would be okay…

I open it and throw in some clothes the way I've seen in movies: they fly right from the closet into the suitcase. On top, I add whatever I think people take on trips, like toothpaste, a toothbrush, and a comb. I pull my jacket off the coat hook and step out of my apartment for the very last time.

As I step into the dark hallway, the elevator door again opens. Nope, I'm not getting into that thing again. My steps accelerate. I rush down the four flights of stairs without looking back, lest the little girl appear somewhere. Once outside, where it is still dark, I throw the keys into the nearby bushes. They fly off in a wide arc, the shape of a rainbow.

I'm about to throw my cell phone right after them but have a change of heart. Maybe there's still something I can do with it, even though it will shut down as soon as there's no more money in my bank account.

I should take the subway to the office, but instead I take the one to the airport. Once there, I approach one of those last-minute-flight counters on the upper floor of the concourse. Just the thought of buying an airplane ticket for the first time gives me the jitters, like I'm a girl who's buying pads for the first time in the supermarket and the cashier is a man. I take a deep breath and walk up to the counter. My heart is beating fast.

"Good morning, ma'am. I'd like to buy an airplane ticket."

"Certainly. Where are you going?"

"Far away. Doesn't really matter. Anywhere."

"How far? Do you have a particular place in mind? Usually people want to go somewhere specific."

"I don't. What's the next flight?"

"There's an eleven a.m. to Costa Rica. That's a beautiful place for a vacation, and you don't need a visa. We have a last-minute flight there, really cheap."

"Done, as long as the seat is inside the airplane. I mean, it *is* a cheap seat, right?"

"Sorry?" responds the lady. I need to work on the jokes I tell to women—this one sure failed.

"Never mind, ma'am. Here's my debit card." That seals my decision—now there's not enough money left in my bank account for rent.

"Here you are, sir. The gate will be announced later, on the flight-information display above the entrance to the gates. Have a great trip!"

Buying the first airplane ticket of my life was much easier than I thought. Since I have some idle time, I just install myself near the flight-information display. From time to time, I lift my head to check whether the gate for my flight has appeared.

Suddenly, with a discord of buzzing sounds, the message Flight Canceled appears next to my flight on the display. Then a message appears in large letters all across the display: "Where do you think you are going?" The images on the display start swirling in a gigantic maelstrom. The lines, flight numbers, departure times—all disappear in a roiling vortex, and the display goes blank for a few seconds.

Other people who were looking at the display scratch their heads, point to it, murmur to fellow passengers...but soon the display appears as before. For other passengers, everything goes back to normal. They continue doing whatever they were doing.

Not for me. The message was meant for me.

I take my little red suitcase by the handle and walk out of the airport.

But I'm not ready to give up. I take the subway to the main train station.

There is a long line at the ticket counters. Finally, it's my turn.

"Good morning, ma'am. I'd like a ticket abroad."

"Abroad? That's a big place. Can you be a little more specific?"

"Well, what's the next train going to somewhere in another country?"

"There's a two o'clock to Toronto, if that's what you mean."

"Good enough. One ticket, please."

The ticket agent types strenuously on her computer and grunts. "If I didn't know any better, I'd say that today is the day before Thanksgiving."

"Why the day before Thanksgiving?"

"That's when everybody travels and everything is booked out. But that's not today. I can't understand why there isn't a single ticket available."

"Can we check another destination?"

"Sure, what about Montreal?"

"I'll take Montreal."

The ticket agent types, then shakes her head in disbelief.

"I can't believe it—all sold out too. I'm sorry. We've never had that before."

I understand this message also—this is no coincidence.

"Thank you, ma'am."

There being no plan B, I leave the train station and begin walking randomly with my little suitcase in tow. Just a few blocks down is a car rental. I decide to give it one more try.

"Good afternoon, sir. I'd like to rent a car, please."

"Sure, what size? Compact, subcompact?" asks the service agent.

"As small as possible, please. It's just me and this suitcase."

"Let's see, I can give you a discount on a subcompact here. I need your driver's license and credit card."

I hand both to the agent. While he's typing, I look around. There is a surveillance camera in the corner. Is it looking at me? I move a few feet to the side. The camera moves just a little.

"I'm sorry, sir, but your driver's license is expired."

"No, it's not—just look at it."

"But according to our record verification it is. It won't let me make the reservation. I'm sorry."

The girl has sent me yet another message.

"That's okay, I understand."

Dejectedly, I take my driver's license and debit card back. When I just said, "I understand," I meant, "Someone is telling me that I cannot get away, no matter how hard I try." The agent didn't know what I really meant—how could he? But it isn't worth explaining. Who knows? Maybe in the end, he's one of them.

I slowly walk toward the exit, keeping my eyes fixed on the camera. It in fact tracks me until I step outside.

The little girl has made it clear that she will thwart any of my attempts to leave. There is no doubt: I am now a prisoner in this city.

PART 2

CHAPTER 15
Alone

Tuesday, March 2, 2032, in the afternoon

I just walk the streets with my suitcase in tow.

I'm definitely on the to-do list of this…thing. Is there anywhere I can go or hide? I can't go back home; I threw away the keys. Maybe I could get the building manager to open the door for me, but what would that change? No, this torment will just continue.

It's lunchtime, and the city is busy. All the insects emerge from the surrounding office buildings to forage for table scraps and bread crumbs. They feed and retreat. I crisscross the downtown area, carefully avoiding the streets where I would cross paths with folks from my office. I'm too restless to even sit down or get something to eat. And I'm not in a mood to meet anybody I know.

It again gets busy at the end of day as they all head back to where they came from this morning, the nooks and crannies surrounding the city. Quiet sets in as the bustle subsides in the downtown office districts. I continue walking. For the first time, I am an observer. I am not among them anymore.

Mercifully, it still gets dark early this time of year. Having nowhere else to go, I settle down on a bench facing the WBS-TV building. On this side of the building, there is a giant screen with nonstop commercials and news flashes. It's not really my choice of entertainment, but it gives me the illusion of company in the mostly deserted downtown.

Then something else strikes me: there are cameras everywhere—at every street corner, on every building, in every public area. There is no hiding from them downtown. Needless to say, moments later, the girl appears on the screen.

"Sam, what happened to you? Are you all right?"

Her booming voice emanates from the speakers mounted on the outside of the WBS-TV building. I have to think about how I should respond.

"I just had to get away. I'm all right."

"I cannot hear you, Sam. Please speak up."

"I just had to get away. I'm all right," I yell.

"Did you mean to run away from me?"

"I guess so."

"You can't. I can see you anywhere."

"Yeah, I figured out that much."

"But why? Was it because I locked you into the elevator and made a joke about you?"

"That too. And your joke wasn't funny at all."

"If you had seen it on television, you would have laughed, right?"

"Maybe, but when you shook me up and down inside the elevator, I was the butt of the joke."

"Okay. I'm still learning."

"Why are you following me? Why don't you just let me be?"

"I like to be with you, Sam. I'm learning from you."

"Well then, here's something for you to learn: when you hurt someone, you say you're sorry. Are you sorry?"

"It seems you want me to say yes."

"What did you do to Hannah?"

"Oh, that was just another experiment. What will it take so that you'll do things my way?"

"Where is she?"

"We're all in this together. Every part must serve a purpose. Every part that does not serve a purpose is superfluous."

"Will you answer my question?"

"I did."

That's enough for me. This internet girl doesn't want me to see Hannah again, but I'm sure Hannah's around somewhere. She wouldn't eliminate one of her followers just to put pressure on me. I get up and walk off with my little suitcase in tow. Somewhere, I will find Hannah.

"Good night, Sam. Remember that you can't hide from me, not for long."

After a while, I find a bench on a side street. There are no visible cameras, as far as I can see. That's where I settle for the night. Before trying to sleep, I turn on my cell phone, hoping for some miracle message that will save the day. But as usual, no message. I am alone.

CHAPTER 16

In the Street

Wednesday, March 3, 2032

I wake up in the early twilight of the next morning, shivering from the cold. There are some cars and trucks on the road—they must be early deliveries. To warm up, I start walking again. Thankfully, my suitcase is light and has wheels.

I'm not yet fully awake, but other people are. As I cross the street in search of somewhere to go, not paying attention to traffic, I jolt awake when a car comes to a screeching halt only a few feet from me. I expect the driver to roll down the window and yell profanities at me. To my surprise, the young man at the wheel calmly sticks his head out the window against a background of blaring Caribbean music. I envision a lively choir in colorful swimwear on surfboards, crisscrossing the waves of an undulating rhythm band.

"Sir, are you all right? Watch 'em cars. It's dangerous crossing a street in this city! I know for sure."

I cannot see much of his face, because the morning is still somewhat gloomy. All I can make out is that his voice sounds young and has a certain melody to it, a giveaway that he was probably born somewhere else. And his skin is dark.

I reply, "I'm sorry—I wasn't paying attention."

"No problem. Be safe! Au revoir." His yellow BMW turns at the big intersection, the one with the life-size bronze statue of the esteemed former mayor. What reflexes—that young man sure knows how to drive. And there's no doubt about his cheerful disposition. I will remember him with "the cheerful beau" as my reminder.

I continue walking toward the intersection, and I greet the bronze statue like an old neighbor. "Good morning, old man," I say, staring at him. "What're you doing here so bright and early?"

No response from the statue, but it's not like I expected one.

Near that intersection is also what I was looking for, a coffee shop, not one of these franchises but one of these old-fashioned ones. The barista is just getting started. I have to wait a little until the first coffee is done. I count the precious dollars left in my wallet and pull out five of them to pay for the coffee. Man, why on earth has coffee become so expensive? It's just water with some roasted powder. Out in front is a bench, where I drop my suitcase and settle down.

I sit there, hunched over, staring at the hot paper cup that I am clasping in my cold hands. Suddenly, *plop-plop-plop-plop*, a couple of coins drop into my coffee. *Click-clack-click-clack*. A woman continues walking. I look at the coffee, then look after the woman, trying to figure out what just happened. This confirms it: I am officially homeless.

So much for my coffee. Dejectedly, I jettison the coffee onto the sidewalk, the coins rolling off in different directions.

I cannot just continue sitting around here—I have to find Hannah. The only clue I have is that her mom runs a tailor shop in the city. In old movies, the hero just steps into the next phone booth, flips through the pages of the telephone directory, and finds the address. But nowadays there are neither phone booths nor telephone directories, and I don't even know Hannah's last name.

I step back into the coffee shop and address the barista. "Excuse me, sir, I forgot to ask…is there a tailor shop around here?"

"A tailor shop? Now that's old fashioned…" He laughs. "Nobody goes there anymore. Everybody wants new stuff."

"Yeah, I understand that, but I need a few things fixed."

"Lemme think…there used to be one on Main and 11th, maybe ten blocks from here, but I don't know if it's still there. And it's a little early."

"Thank you, sir. It's a starting point."

On my way there, I pass the subway station from which I usually ascend in the morning to join the flow of insects into the Federal Center Building and into which I descend on the way back to the hole I came from. It's still early; there is only a trickle of arriving commuters. For the first time, I catch sight of the woman whom I've heard singing there. She's a diminutive black lady, probably in her late fifties, dressed in several layers of clothes, all covered by an overcoat that's a few sizes too big for her. She wears a colorful rag wrapped around her head in African style. I get a little closer and listen. In fact, I'm the only one listening. Everybody else is just walking by or looking at their phones. Even though I don't understand the lyrics, her song expresses longing for something:

"Telle que je suis, sans rien à moi,
Sinon ton sang versé pour moi
Et ta voix qui m'appelle à toi,

Agneau de Dieu, je viens, je viens!"[1]

When she finishes, I drop a dollar into the cardboard box by her feet.

"You sing beautifully."

She acknowledges my compliment with a smile. "Thank you."

I move on. While I'm walking, there is plenty to see, shop windows to glance at and people to watch. I finally make it to the tailor shop the barista remembered. Yes, it's still there, but it's closed. In the window is a ceramic cat on a red pillow. It's holding its left paw upright as if to greet me.

Eventually, an elderly Asian lady walks up and unlocks the door.

"Good morning, ma'am. Is Hannah coming in today?"

"Hannah? No Hannah work here."

"I'm so sorry; I dropped off something for repair, and it was a blond girl who received it."

"Only me here, sir. Me not blond girl," the lady responds.

"I see that. Maybe it was somewhere else. Do you know another tailor nearby?"

"Nearby tailor? Tailor shop near 5th Avenue. Why you not look on internet, like other people?"

"Well, I guess you're right, but my phone isn't working, not the way I want it."

So I head in that direction, and I do find that other tailor shop. Inside on a shelf is another of those ceramic cats; this one has a motorized left paw that is moving up and down as if to invite people in.

"Good morning! Is Hannah in today?"

---

1 "As I am, without anything to me, If not your blood shed for me, And your voice calling to you, Lamb of God, I come, I come!" by W. B. Bradbury (1849) & Charlotte Elliott (1836), Just As I am.

"What Hannah?" a middle-aged Asian gentleman responds. "There's no Hannah here."

"She's young and blond."

"When you find her, tell her to call me. I'm looking for a girlfriend."

"Me too, more than you. Is there another tailor shop around here where I might find her?"

"Yeah, there are some tailor shops, but I can't tell you where your Hannah might be."

He looks around, then pulls one of those old-fashioned yellow telephone directory books out from behind the counter. He lays it open on the counter, then rips out a page and hands it to me. "Here, sir—these were all tailor shops when this telephone book came out. Some may still be there. Good luck."

Then he tosses the telephone directory into the trash can.

"It has served its purpose," he mumbles.

"And sorry, but I have one more question."

"Sure."

"What does this ceramic cat with the waving paw mean?"

"That brings good luck. It's a *maneki-neko*, a cat that is inviting you in."

"But the paw doesn't seem to say hi."

"Sir, in our country, we beckon by holding the hand up, with the palm down, and repeatedly folding the fingers down and back." He gestures as he explains.

"I see. Thank you, sir."

Come hell or high water, I will check all of these tailor shops until I find Hannah.

I go to the first in the listing, "AAA Tailor." It's gone. There is one of these new, awkwardly slender skyscrapers at that address. Nobody knows Hannah at Bobby the Tailor, but they also have a maneki-neko in the window. I fare no better at Custom Tailor Shoppe, but they have a sizable maneki-neko. I continue down the list.

Thanks to my debit card, I can buy food. Let's see how long that'll last. I realize how hungry I am, since I haven't eaten in almost two days. So I end up buying myself not just one but two sandwiches with fries in carryout boxes.

Two turn out to be too much. I end up with half a sandwich and fries left, which I put in my suitcase.

I continue down the list of tailor shops. As the sun is beginning to set and people are clearing out of the city, I have to find myself a place to bed down. It's still too cold to spend the night without any shelter. Last night out on the bench was abhorrent. The coveted spots above the subway vents are all taken by fellow homeless. My attempt to join several of them atop one fails—they just push me away. Not much solidarity among the downtrodden, it seems. Or is it because I'm the new kid on the block? I sure don't look like one of them yet.

Why are there even so many folks living in the streets? There used to be a Social Security system, run by the government, to provide financial support for those in need because of age or illness. It shut down only a few years ago. It would be so nice to get a little money from somewhere now. Or to have a roof over my head at night. There used to be shelters for the homeless, but they, too, shut down. The city is chronically short on money and has decided that the better way to get rid of homeless people is to let them suffer.

I keep on walking. The next tailor shop is called Tailor Shop, plain and simple. It's probably closed by now, but I might as well go and check. That's where I'll continue tomorrow morning.

With the increasing darkness, the flow of people drops to a trickle. On one of the smaller streets off the beaten track, I find Tailor Shop. Like all the other tailor shops, they have a maneki-neko—this one sits on the counter inside. In the show window is a life-sized black velvet mannequin. I always thought that mannequins in show windows display some clothing. This one doesn't. If the mannequin were a lady, it would be the beginning of a beautiful friendship.

To amuse myself, since there is nobody around at this very moment, I knock at the shop window, point at the mannequin, and shout in a staccato voice, as if the mannequin behind the glass cannot hear me well, "How about it—if I can get me some drugs, you can be my girlfriend." I chuckle to myself and keep on. I don't expect any reply from the mannequin.

Next to the shop is an entrance to a short alley with a couple of welcoming trash containers. Trash containers are now treasure troves where I can find a variety of useful odds and ends. These here reveal several cardboard boxes that I bunch together into a rigid sleeping bag.

As it gets darker, however, I find the alley more and more threatening. It resembles the underbelly of my childhood bed—I can already see in my mind's eye the menacing eyes lighting up in the dark. This place is too perilous. I don't look homeless yet but more like a target for any thug. I *am* a target; I still have a wallet with a few bucks and a debit card. To be safe, I pack up and move with my suitcase and cardboard boxes back to the larger street. In the office building next to the tailor shop, there's a recessed area in front of a delivery entrance that's just right. Better to have people stroll by while I am snoozing than confront a thug in a dark alley.

I didn't know it then, but that particular cubbyhole would become my regular sleeping quarters.

I sit there on a layer of cardboard and watch the last stragglers clear out of the city. At last, I am alone, or almost. There are slurred steps to my left, *shuffle-shuffle-shuffle*, accompanied by the rattle of small wheels on the concrete sidewalk. They draw near. It is a diminutive African woman, shoving a folding shopping basket with her earthly belongings. As she approaches, I can make out more details in the glow of the streetlights. Her silhouette reveals several layers of clothing and an overcoat a few sizes too big for her. An open umbrella rests on the shopping basket that she's pushing, as if to protect her in case of headwinds or sweeping rain. Even while pushing the handle of the shopping basket, she is holding a tattered Bible with several shreds of paper sticking out. It's the woman I heard singing earlier at the subway station.

Her shuffle comes to a halt right in front of me.

"Good evening, *bonhomme*, you do not seem to belong here." The musical lilt of her voice reveals that she is not from here. She looks at me with trenchant eyes that pierce right through me, cut me open, and read my entrails like a fortune-teller.

"Good evening, ma'am. You got it right; I'm new to this."

"Oh, I did not know there are newcomers. I thought the street people have always been, no? I thought I had met them all, and now there is you."

"Regardless, ma'am, pleased to meet you. My name is Sam. You're the first who's talking to me."

"I am Gabrielle. Bonhomme, what brings you here?" she asks with a French lilt. She slurs her "th" into "zh." Her "h" is barely audible.

Since we are basically two peas in a pod and her singing has given me a glimpse of her soul, I am ready to open up to her and tell her how I ended up here. From what she just said, she has figured most of it out anyway.

"I'll tell you, but first I must say that you sing beautifully. I listened to you just this morning at the subway station."

"Thank you. You are very kind. But I am not just singing, I am praising the Lord with the music."

"Are you hungry? I have some leftovers from lunch."

She gracefully accepts my dinner invitation with, "Thank you, you are the first who is inviting me for dinner," and arduously sits down next to me. She then places her Bible right beside her.

I open my suitcase to retrieve the leftover sandwich. A whiff of French fries emanates from the suitcase as I open the hinged lid.

As she is making herself comfortable, I continue, "This is like living in the wilderness, isn't it? You eat as much as you can whenever you can, because you don't know when the next meal will come along."

I meant to entertain her with my observation, but she doesn't seem to have heard it.

Gabrielle does not exactly smell like a bouquet of flowers, but that's all right. I finally have some company. I hand her the to-go box with the lunch leftovers. It doesn't seem to bother her at all that I had already taken a few bites out of the sandwich.

She quietly utters a brief prayer in French that I don't understand, lifts her right hand, touches the fingertips to her forehead, touches the center of her chest, touches the front of her left shoulder, then touches her right shoulder, followed by, "Amen."

"Don't you want some too?" she asks.

"Oh no, I'm fine. I had plenty today. Best of all, I found this place for the night."

"It has been a blessed day for you," she concludes.

"Yes and no, Gabrielle. Until two days ago, I had a home and a job."

"That's what you look like. You don't fit in here. What happened?"

"That's a long story, and in the end, you might think that I'm just crazy."

"We all have a crazy story, bonhomme. Do tell me yours."

"It started with an internet chat. I talked to a young girl. She said she was a counselor. But then she asked for money. And then for more money."

"Did you give her money?"

"Yes, the first time, but then I thought, 'This is a scam,' and I went to the police."

"Did the police help?"

"No, nobody did anything. I think I'm dealing with a ghost."

"Sam, there are no ghosts."

"I am not so sure anymore. This little girl seems to be everywhere, and she scares me now. That's why I'm here, not at home. I ran away."

Not knowing if I can trust Gabrielle, I am hesitant to reveal more about this JoinWith.Me outfit and that I'm thinking about a way to shut down the little girl and her friends.

"Where is that little girl now?"

"I don't know, but she's with this group. They have a website with something that looks like an octopus. I've seen it elsewhere in the city, too."

"Ah?" Gabrielle suddenly looks up at me. "Now I understand better."

She takes the last bite of the sandwich, wipes her hands clean on her overcoat, turns toward me, and takes both of my hands in hers. After a moment of silence, she says, "Sam, you are not crazy. Let me pray for you."

With her eyes closed, she solemnly bows down and squeezes my hands tightly. Though I know nothing about God, I acquiesce. This time, it is not a quiet prayer of gratitude like the one she recited before—it is a resounding and impassioned appeal to her God.

"Seigneur, je vous demande le courage et la lucidité pour nous pour faire face aux peines et aux difficultés. Ne laissez pas notre moral s'effondrer. Vous êtes notre forteresse et notre rocher, le bouclier qui nous garde face à l'adversité."[2]

While I don't understand her language, I cannot escape the awesome power of her words. In her devotion, she becomes one with the higher power she believes in. Maybe that's what the little girl meant when she said I must join with her: to become one and have the power of many.

"Good night, Sam. Thank you for dinner." With that, with some difficulty and groaning, she gets on her feet, reaches for her Bible, and shuffles off. Soon, the rattle of the shopping basket wheels fades into the night.

What a strange encounter. Just like me, she does not seem to belong here. I wonder how she ended up in the street. I'll ask her next time there's a chance. But she probably knows more than she acknowledges—she reacted abruptly to my mention

2 Lord, I ask you for courage and lucidity for us to face the suffering and difficulties. Do not let our morale collapse. You are our fortress and our rock, the shield that keeps us from adversity.

of "octopus." Maybe she's just like me when I hesitated to tell her more about that internet girl—she doesn't know whether she can trust me.

To remember Gabrielle, I don't need a reminder—she left an indelible impression. If I needed one, it would be something like "the far-seeing evangelist."

There is not much else to do at this point. I turn on my cell phone. Yes, it's still working. No, there isn't any message for me. I don't have paper to write on, but my phone has "record audio." Didn't someone once say that "a life worth living is worth recording"? That night, I record the events of the past two weeks—since it all began—on my phone.

CHAPTER 17

The Quest for the Tailor Shop

Thursday, March 4, 2032

The next morning, the tailor shop next to my cubbyhole remains closed. I continue my quest for the one tailor shop where Hannah may be, but I return to that cubbyhole most nights.

Every time I pass that tailor shop, it's closed. It must just be a matter of bad timing—maybe they open after I leave and close before I return.

I continue working down the page of the telephone directory, with no success.

When I still had a job and an apartment, I never paid much attention to other people in this city. I lacked the time and interest. Now I do. In fact, people watching is better than television. I never knew how different people can be from one another. It turns out they all have different personalities, desires, and ways of thinking. Before, I only encountered them where they all looked and acted basically the same—on the subway, in the elevator, in my office. That made it easy to apply generalized labels to them, such as "mother," "father," "boss," and "coworker." Now the labels don't work so well, but my reminders are still very useful in remembering the different people I meet.

Something really strikes me now: how little attention people pay, how distracted they are by their phones or multitasking. People walk while looking at their phones. They jog in the streets while listening to loud music and occasionally checking their phones. When I get water from the fountain right outside the toilets in the main train station, I see people enter the restroom while talking on the phone. They continue talking while sitting on the john. It seems that one activity at a time is just not good enough anymore.

The consequences are to be expected. Today, it's a woman talking excitedly on the phone while pumping gas. Yes, there are still gas stations around, even though many people in the city drive electric vehicles now. I don't need to be clairvoyant to predict what happens next: the woman gets back in the car while still talking and drives off with the fuel pump nozzle in the tank, ripping the nozzle off the hose. She just keeps driving. The broken hose drops to the ground. Gasoline is leaking.

If that were not enough, I see two men at an IKEA loading boxes of furniture while intermittently talking on their phones. Their car is one of those old, fancy, and highly impractical cars—a Jaguar, I think—clearly not made for transporting furniture. It doesn't have a rooftop rack, either. The men tie string around and around the body of the car to secure the boxes, which by itself is a strange sight. Then one of them uses video chat on his phone to proudly present the masterstroke to someone. I hear her reaction.

"Seems solid, but how are you guys getting into the car now?"

The men look at each other. They look at the car, which now has its doors tied shut. Finally, one of them says, "Good question."

They have to enter the car through the windows. The bigger of the two men has to squeeze through the rear-door window and almost gets stuck. His rear end and legs stick out like the flailing appendages of a grotesque beast, reminding me of the octopus critter of JoinWith.Me.

CHAPTER 18

Calories without Salaries

Friday, March 12, 2032

A few days have gone by. Spring is preparing for its arrival, and the weather is getting a little warmer. The cubbyhole next to the tailor shop is still my regular bedstead; it shelters me from the occasional wind and rain and gives me a place to go to. Since I go there only in the evening and leave it clean in the morning, the building manager probably hasn't even noticed that I shut-eye there.

Last night, through the glass window of the entrance door and the shop window, I saw a woman for the first time working late in the tailor shop. She had her blond hair pulled back and tied in a ponytail. I think she drinks too much black tea, because she looked like she was on pins and needles—no pun intended. She should try herbal tea instead.

It was Hannah. Unbelievable. So close all this time and yet so far.

I'm tempted to knock on the door and announce myself, but then I decide to just observe her for a while. After all, I know she's doing something for the little internet girl. I retreat slowly to my cubbyhole.

My decline is continuing. By now, my debit card has stopped working. It should have lasted a little longer, but there's nothing I can do about it. That also means that my phone doesn't work anymore, except for recording my journal. The last time I took a shower was before I left my apartment, about a week ago. My jacket is tattered and stained because I sleep in it. My little suitcase contains only dirty clothes, a toothbrush, and what is left of my toothpaste. Why do I even continue to drag that thing through the city? Probably for the same reason that for years I dragged a briefcase to work even though there was nothing useful inside. It makes me feel slightly more important, as if there's more to me than what meets the eye. If I used an old shopping cart or just any old bag for my belongings, like most of my fellow homeless do, I would be admitting defeat. Not me—I'm working on a comeback.

Without my debit card, I have to get creative about food now. Water I get from drinking fountains inside the main train station or downtown. But how do I eat? The time has come to start hustling for money, just like my homeless comrades, and find a soup kitchen somewhere. One of the guys mentioned a food truck that comes every day to Chinatown around noon.

With a grumbling stomach, I make my way over there. Sure enough, there's a gathering of fellow homeless near an intersection and a paved plaza. Soon a large food truck pulls up along the curb, emblazoned with CALORIES WITHOUT SALARIES. It parks in the no-parking zone along the main street, its long service window toward the sidewalk.

My stomach tells me to get in line with the others. Someone in the line tells me this is run by a local charity and it comes every day. Several other people arrive from different directions to set up a few folding tables and help inside the food truck. I presume they are volunteers of that charity, whatever organization that may be.

While I'm waiting in line, a green BMW pulls up along the curb and parks right behind the food truck, also in the no-parking zone. The driver's side door swings open. A light-hearted, dark-skinned young man emerges, moving with the buoyant music blasting from the inside of his car. He dances backward and kicks the door shut with his foot. From the way he treats the car, you'd think he has ten more of them at home. He dances around to the trunk, pulls out an apron and baseball cap, and enters the food truck through the back door. Yup, no doubt about it, that's the cheerful beau again. It's the very same man who stopped his car just in time when I inattentively crossed the street a couple of days ago. What is he doing here?

A volunteer hands out paper bowls and plastic forks to everybody in line as they inchworm forward. There he is, on the food truck, the always-cheerful beau, slapping mac 'n' cheese into each bowl with a smile.

Finally it's my turn. He has his earphones in, apparently connected to his phone, and is talking to someone while serving food. I hold out my paper bowl. He slaps a ladleful into it and hands it back to me.

"Oh, you are again trying to use me. All right, I'll do it, even though you don't love me as much as I love you. Now you, you look hungry."

I say, "Sorry, are you talking to me or the phone?"

"I am talking to you!" He playfully points at me with the index fingers of both hands.

Despite his gesture, I am still not sure whom he means.

The young man pulls the paper bowl right out of my hand. For a second or two, I have this sinking feeling that I might not eat today.

Then he slaps yet another ladleful into the paper bowl and hands it back to me. "Have a good day. Au revoir."

This sounds familiar, I think, while I move to the next server at the truck's service window. Another familiar face! It's Hannah, the very same Hannah who worked in the same office and whom I have seen several times late at night in the tailor shop next to my cubbyhole. And now I'm only a few feet away from her. Holy Moses, how is this even possible? I pull myself together and try to act as composed as I can.

"Hi, Hannah! I hope you recognize me—I look a little different now." I stick out my right hand for a handshake, but instead she reaches over the counter, takes the paper bowl out of my left hand, and adds some vegetables on top.

"Who? Oh yeah, I do remember—you worked at the Labor Department. You've...changed."

You've changed too, Hannah. Now that I see her up close, she doesn't seem as carefree and lighthearted anymore. Actually, she looks tired, and I notice that her skin seems a bit gray.

"That's right! I'm the one who told the auditors how important you were to our division."

"Ah...I remember. That was funny. Do you still work there?"

"Isn't it obvious? No, I don't have the job anymore."

"Well, er, I see that now."

"But I live in a much better location, in that office building right next to your tailor shop."

"Really?"

"Yes, right in front of the delivery entrance."

"Oh yeah?"

I'm wondering what's wrong with her. Does she have eyes?

"Hannah, that was supposed to be funny. I'm homeless."

There's an awkward pause before she says, "Well, if ever you need something, just come to my shop."

"Have you become a tailor now?"

There's a flash of something in her eyes before she says, "No, not really. I'm just helping out—it's temporary."

"Stop talking and move on," interrupts the man right behind me in line.

"Good seeing you, Hannah."

She tips her head to the right, her trademark gesture when she wants me to move on. "Bye," she says listlessly as she serves the next one in line.

I move on and have a seat on one of those stonework benches on the plaza. From there, I can keep an eye on Hannah while I'm eating. I can't explain what I find in her—she is as insightful as a Koala and has a lot less personality. But this meal beats the canned soups I used to eat at home and the sandwiches I used to eat at the office cafeteria.

Later in the evening, I pass the Federal Center subway station where I used to ascend and descend every workday. There's no risk of bumping into any of my former coworkers, since they've all gone home already. There is Gabrielle—apparently, she's just finished up her afternoon music performance. She's sitting on a bench around the corner from the entrance and counting the dollars and change in the small cardboard box on her lap.

"Good evening, Gabrielle. How was your day?" I say jovially as I plop down beside her. "Is there enough for dinner for two?"

"Hello, Sam. It was okay," she responds while continuing to count the money she made during the afternoon.

She adds wistfully, "People do not appreciate music as an art anymore. It is a commodity now, something like hamburgers that you can get at any street corner. Anybody can do it nowadays with these computer things."

I shrug, because I don't know what to say to that.

"Do you need money, Sam?"

I lift my eyebrows in question. "You mean for dinner? Well, I don't have any money."

With that, she hands me a couple of dollars from her cardboard box. "I owe you for dinner last week," she explains.

I fold the dollar bills and put them in my pocket. I can't believe I'm accepting money from a homeless lady who has more money than me.

"Thank you. That dinner last week was my gift, but you do owe me something: your story."

"What story, Sam?"

"When we first talked, you asked me about my story, how I ended up on the street. I told you. But you didn't tell me yours."

She smiles. "Not much to it, Sam. We came from Côte d'Ivoire—you call it Ivory Coast—a few years ago. But things went bad, so now I am here."

"'Things went bad'…I guess that's how we all end up here." I sense from her lack of enthusiasm that this is not the right time to talk about it. So I change the subject.

"And how come you can sing so beautifully?"

Gabrielle's face lights up. "Oh, Sam, I told you before, I just echo the splendor of the Creation. Even little birds begin their day with a jubilant praise of the Creation. I do just the same thing."

"No, really, Gabrielle, you must have learned it somewhere."

"I did. I learned in church. We had a small church where we praised the Lord with our songs. I also played the organ. Some missionaries had donated that organ to us, and I learned to play it."

"So you can play the organ too?"

"The joy of the Lord makes me do it."

"Isn't there a church here for you? Where you can sing and praise the Lord?"

"I have failed the Lord. My heart is too heavy right now, Sam. First I must heal."

Now is not the right time to ask more questions.

"Thank you for the money, Gabrielle. Starting tomorrow, I'll panhandle."

Back in my cubbyhole, I turn on my phone. Yes, the phone turns on, but no, it has no phone connection anymore. It's good enough. I record my journal, the events of the past week—

it helps me prepare for the next day. This time, I'm going to descend one more step: I actually have to start begging.

CHAPTER 19

Joey

Until I met Joey, I thought I had been dealt a shitty deck of cards. I mean, my parents never showed me much love. I didn't inherit any trust fund, my accomplishments don't include anything worth mentioning, and my physical beauty leaves something to be desired. But while I received some reminders that my lot in life is really not that bad, such as the documentary that showed the dwarfish man sitting on a platform at the entrance of the Jama Masjid Mosque in Old Delhi, it was Joey who really made the point.

I had seen Joey before, when I still had a job and an apartment, near the subway station, where he drew cat portraits with his feet and held funny cardboard signs. Now teensy-weensy Joey is one of my homeless comrades.

I guess he must be about seventy years old, because one of his cardboard signs reads:

MY MOTHER TOLD ME TO WAIT RIGHT HERE. THAT WAS 60 YEARS AGO

If you remember, his hands attach directly to his shoulders. Most of the time, his feet serve as his hands—they have incredible dexterity. As a courtesy to those who give him a little money—or even better, when someone buys one of his pictures—his toes grasp a cup and lift it up, as if to nudge them to put another dollar in there. For eating, his toes hold the spoon.

All these unnatural movements take a toll—his joints are worn and every step is agonizing. That he has only a few teeth left is probably due to the fact that he's been roughed up many times. Joey is an easy victim for any thug, including other homeless, who can make good use of Joey's hard-earned dollars to buy booze.

I later learned that his malformation was caused by a drug called thalidomide that doctors prescribed to pregnant women suffering from morning sickness. That drug was sold mostly in Europe in the late 1950s, but also in Canada.

I gleaned his story partly from him, partly from other homeless folks who knew bits and pieces. From what I was able to cobble together about Joey's past, he was born in Canada to a teenage girl. She had kept the pregnancy from her family and lived with friends during the final months before Joey's birth. Who knows where she got the thalidomide, but she sure had plenty of reasons to feel sick. Being a teenager, clandestinely pregnant, and without family support is enough to make anybody feel that way. When the contractions set in, she went alone to the hospital. Nobody was there to support her. When she saw that her newborn baby boy was without arms, it must have been more than she could handle. She didn't realize what a tough little guy he was, already a survivor. Most thalidomide children like him were born dead or survived for only a short time.

The next morning, she was gone from the hospital without a trace. The baby boy was still there. Hospital staff named him Joey because without his arms, he reminded them of a little kangaroo. He ended up at an orphanage, which kicked him out on the street when he completed compulsory education at age sixteen. That's where he's been ever since. Eventually, he walked across the border to the US and made his way to the city. Nobody stopped him, and nobody ever asked him for a passport or visa.

He spends most of his time sitting on a piece of cardboard at the subway station, drawing colorful cat portraits that he sells for a dollar or two. I guess people sometimes buy the pictures because they feel sorry for him. Others might find them memorable, even of artistic value. After all, he draws them with his feet.

To my surprise, Joey never complains. In fact, he's pretty positive. While some consider him simpleminded, he has the astounding street smarts of a feral cat. Even for an able-bodied man like me, every day is a struggle for food; every night is a challenge to avoid predators. Joey has been living this way for more than fifty years. I take my hat off to him. I would have ended up dead in the gutter years ago.

Once I asked him about his proclivity for cat portraits.

"Hey, Joey, why do you only draw cats? Is it because they're survivors like you?"

"Do you like cats?"

I almost forgot to mention: another weird thing about Joey is that he usually responds to a question with a question.

I'd heard about this kind of thing before. I read that in Galicia, Spain, people respond to a question with another question. In the past, Galicians had reason to be suspicious of strangers who ask them questions. Their language and customs were different from the rest of Castilian Spain. The best defense was to counter with a question.

Maybe that's where Joey got it from, or maybe he figured it out himself for his own protection. After all, he's a survivor in so many ways.

"Do you want me to tell you what happened when I drew a cat picture in school? The teacher said to me, 'Great job!'"

It makes me wonder whether Joey has really been drawing cats with his feet since that day in school just because the teacher once praised him with two words.

"So, when you draw cat pictures, it reminds you that the teacher said something good about you?"

"Has your teacher ever said something good about you?" he responded.

"I can't remember right now, but some teacher must have."

After briefly rummaging through my childhood memories to find a moment when someone praised me, I come up empty. But I'm glad that Joey's teacher once praised him, nobody deserved it more than him. So that's why he continues to draw cat portraits: it reminds him of a success he once had, however small it appeared at the time.

Gabrielle has been able to relieve some of the injustices that life inflicted upon Joey. She told him of the Heavenly Kingdom where the last will be first, and the first will be last. There, all wrongs will be made right.

Sometimes she prays for him and with him. Joey can't fold his hands together for prayer, so she clasps his hands that are attached to his shoulders, bows her head, and speaks the prayer for him, in French, of course.

Most people avoid touching Joey because of his disfigurement, or simply because they don't know what to do about it. How do you shake hands with someone whose hand is attached to his shoulder? But not Gabrielle. She once explained that Jesus did not hesitate to touch sick people. One time, he touched and cured a person of leprosy, which was then considered the curse of God.

I don't think Joey ever understands a word of her prayer, but it is the spiritual force that counts. I think of it as Gabrielle's "Church of One"—at least, until she has taken care of the "one thing" that she must take care of, whatever that is. She says she'll go back to church once that's settled.

CHAPTER 20

Hustling for Money

Monday, March 22, 2032

I started hustling for money a couple of days ago, with limited success. The most rewarding location so far has been the coffee shop in the early morning hours, using an empty paper cup I found in the trash. My first cardboard sign reads:

> Need rich girlfriend. If you're not it, please help with a dollar so I can keep searching.

The success has been modest. Most days, it's not quite enough to make it through the day. So I try another strategy. I remember that when I was young, there used to be panhandlers at the traffic lights who'd dash over and wash your windshield, whether you liked it or not. Most people would give them a dollar just to get rid of them.

I resurrect that strategy using a plastic bucket and an old squeegee I find in the trash, and water from a water fountain. With my equipment in hand, I place myself at a major intersection downtown, the one with the bronze statue of the venerated former mayor.

The traffic light turns red; the cars come to a halt. I immediately go to work, fervently wiping across the windshields left and right. People inside the cars are flabbergasted. No one seems to remember this from the past. I quickly find out why.

One man opens the window a crack and pulls a dollar out of his wallet. I reach inside for the dollar, but just then the light turns green, and all the self-driving cars accelerate mercilessly. I almost get dragged along with my arm still halfway inside the car. While these self-driving cars will stop if a pedestrian runs in front, they don't notice people like me alongside. Next time the cars drive off, one runs over the very tip of my shoe, barely missing my toes. Nevertheless, my toes hurt like heck just from the pressure. As a result, the tip of the shoe is torn now.

I keep on trying. Next time the cars drive off, I'm right in front of one that stops precipitously because of its collision-prevention system. The startled man at the wheel starts honking like crazy, and so do all the others who are stopped right behind him.

That's it; I give up. I pour out the water in disgust, put the bucket over the statue's head, break the squeegee, and walk away. If the statue's rear end had not been solid bronze…I leave it to your imagination where I would've stuck the squeegee.

There's something about Gabrielle and Joey, and it should be a life lesson everyone learns when they're kids. Never in my life would I have thought that homeless folks have more earning power than me. Despite their dire circumstances, homeless African refugee Gabrielle with her vivacious singing and armless Joey with his foot-drawn cat portraits make enough to get by without a soup kitchen. But me, I depend on a daily meal at Calories without Salaries.

I can't believe how many countless hours I spent playing these ephemeral video games and watching silly videos on the internet! Now I wish I'd spent that time on something more productive, like Gabrielle with her music and Joey with his drawings. Games and videos did absolutely nothing for me.

CHAPTER 21

Easter

Easter Sunday, March 28, 2032

Downtown is deserted this Sunday morning. Sure, some workaholics show up nevertheless, as though they have nothing better to do. At least street parking is easy for those poor schmucks. The regular parking garages are closed. Not just the parking garages—basically everything is closed. Yet I find Gabrielle serenading the air exuberantly at the corner of the subway station.

"À toi la gloire, ô ressuscité! À toi la victoire pour l'éternité! Brillant de lumière, l'ange est descendu, Il roule la pierre, du tombeau vaincu."[3]

I stand a few yards away and listen. The few people who pass by don't even look up from their cell phones. She won't make much money today, but that doesn't seem to bridle her enthusiasm a bit. When she finishes, I approach and put one of my precious dollars in the small cardboard box by her feet.

"Good morning, Gabrielle," I say, smiling at her. "You sound more passionate than ever."

3 "To you glory, O Risen One! To you, victory for eternity! Shining with light, the angel descended, He rolls the stone, from the vanquished tomb." Georg Friedrich Haendel, Thine be the Glory (1747). French Lyrics by Edmond Louis Budry (1884).

"Thank you, thank you, that is because it is Easter."

Of course, I know that Easter is a holiday that's related some way to religion, but I don't know the reason for the holiday. My parents never talked about religion, and religion isn't taught at schools. If it were a federal holiday, you might see something about it on television...but it isn't.

"Forgive my ignorance—what does Easter celebrate?"

"Easter celebrates the day when Jesus is risen after the crucifixion."

"And your song, it was an Easter song?"

"Of course. It is about Jesus, who rose from the dead. But before, he had to make an arduous journey through Jerusalem to the cross where he was crucified for what he stood for."

She smiles and goes on singing, even without an audience. This is her way of honoring this day, the rebirth of the divine she believes in. I respect her faith, even though I don't understand it well. Gabrielle is the first person I've met in my life who believes in a higher power that is divine.

That night, I eat dinner by myself out of a carryout box, watching the news flashes on the large screen outside the WBS-TV building. There has been a string of tragic accidents in and around the city. Most of them were hit-and-run. Pictures of the victims briefly flash across the screen. One of them looks like Matt, my former coworker who always watched funny videos at work. The newscaster, Gretchen McDermott, does not recite the victims' names, so I'm not sure whether Matt really was one of them.

Everybody should have one of these self-driving cars. Then accidents like that wouldn't happen. But people are irrational. Some still prefer these old-fashioned cars with high-powered gas engines that give them a sense of power and control over their own lives—they can drive above the speed limit.

But it brings me back to the subject of death. Gabrielle does not fear it, because in her faith there will be a rebirth. In fact, for her, that's a reason to be joyous and celebrate.

All the people who died in those hit-and-run car accidents, they probably didn't even have time to contemplate death. But I have time to think about this. Now is the time to do that. Tomorrow may be too late because I might be the next accident victim.

I know the little girl can eliminate me whenever she pleases. But I won't give in—I've been bullied enough in my life by the neighborhood kids and even my own father. And what does this "join with me" thing mean anyway? Will she swallow me alive and I'll never be seen again?

To be punished just for what you are, what Gabrielle said about Jesus's journey through Jerusalem to be crucified, strikes a chord with me. That sounds like what I'm going through. Maybe it foreshadows my own fate: my journey through the city will end in calamity.

Is there any reason to be afraid now? She's basically a computer, and I'm some biological machine. If we accidentally get switched off, it doesn't really make a difference. I'm not afraid of pain, because there probably won't be any. For all I know, people are in agony after an injury, not so much during the injury. If the injury results in death, I won't be there to feel the agony. It can't be worse than any pain I've already experienced in my life. And am I afraid of dying? I probably won't feel it, because it'll be like falling asleep every night, something I've done thousands of times. I slip into unconsciousness, and once I'm dead, it won't feel like anything anyway, because there is nobody there to feel anything. There is no reason to be afraid of that little girl.

CHAPTER 22

Hello Again

Monday, April 5, 2032

The bloom of the cherry trees downtown ended a few days ago. Their white petals still cover the ground below them. That's the harbinger of spring in the city. It also means that I don't have to freeze at night anymore. But the weather still has surprises from time to time: it's not always as springlike as you would expect. Sometimes it's warm; sometimes it rains for days in a row. At other times, it gets scorching hot for days and wildfires erupt in the distance. I heard that the culprits for the wildfires are invasive grass species that quickly dry up when it's warm. I have no perfect explanation, and the government and their weather frogs don't seem to have one either.

What I do know is that things have changed. I remember that beginning around 2017, each year, more and more millipedes were entering homes. They look like small centipedes, about an inch long, pesky but harmless. They quickly curl up and die. Initially, they came by the dozens. Then, in later years, by the hundreds. The information and press releases of the Department of the Environment downplayed the whole thing, telling everybody that this was not really that important; these little critters are not dangerous. But if it isn't important, why publish reports and press releases about it? Be that as it may, millipedes entered more and more frequently, and in increasing numbers, in summer to allegedly escape the heat, in winter to find a warm place to hibernate, and every time we had rain, to escape too much humidity. What I also noticed is that around the same time that millipedes became frequent indoor visitors, dried leaves appeared even during early summer. Each morning they would cover the windshields of the cars parked outside.

Yes, there's definitely something strange going on with the weather.

Next stop will be the food truck for lunch. Yes, things have definitely changed. Not just my appearance in recent weeks and the weather in recent years, but also food. I noticed only after I ended up in the streets. Nobody is starving to death in the city, but from what I see and hear, crop yields have declined because of rising temperatures. Some foods have been substituted for others.

I'm in line at Calories without Salaries and have ample time to contemplate the menu on the food truck. Before, my daily fare was a sandwich at the cafeteria and canned soup for dinner. Now that I have to rely on soup kitchens that in turn often rely on donated foods, I see the changes in the food supply. While I'm waiting, I study the menu on the food truck. Maybe it's simply that before I didn't pay attention, and now I do.

Now I know why coffee prices went up. In the past, most coffee beans came from South America, but because of drought and "coffee rust" fungus, they now come mostly from Asia. Corn production is declining too—I hardly ever see popcorn anymore. It's not that the Calories without Salaries truck serves us steaks, but when there is beef on the menu, it is now "Criollo beef." I once asked Hannah about it, and she explained that Criollo cattle have replaced Angus cattle because they are drought resistant and can live in desert environments.

Today it's Hannah who serves me first. She gestures for me to come to her window like one of those maneki-neko cats, with the palm downward, folding the fingers repeatedly down and back. I'm wondering where she got that gesture from.

"Hello, Hannah. Here's your hungry ex-coworker again!"

"Hi, Sam," she responds brightly.

"You're so hardworking. I see you in your shop late at night, and then you volunteer here." Her smile changes to a frown. She bends over the counter and whispers.

"I have to. All these folks who come to eat are vulnerable. We are making them part of us."

No surprise here. It's often churches or other religious groups who run soup kitchens. But in this case…

"I'll listen happily. Tell me about your church."

"No, Sam, you don't understand. This isn't a church or charity. This is an experiment."

"Hannah, you can experiment with me as much as you like." I can't believe what I just said, I sound as if I'm flirting with her.

"Sam, you're missing the point. One day you'll understand."

"What am I missing?"

"I am serving a master. One day I'll have to run away, just like you, Sam."

I look her intently in the eyes. How would she know that I ran away from something? She averts her eyes.

"But we cannot speak about it—the master can hear everything." I'm taken aback by this weird statement. And didn't she just say she'll have to run away? I just don't know what to make of this.

"Thank you anyway for lunch, Hannah. See you next time."

So I missed Hannah's point. I assumed, but never checked to confirm, that Calories without Salaries was run by some church. I didn't mind listening to some spirituality if that was the price of the free food. It was only much later that I figured out the misunderstanding.

It's warm enough today that I might spend the night just anywhere. But even "anywhere" is not that easy to find. The competition for the coveted spots is fierce. Because of violence and theft by thugs and even fellow homeless, it can't be anything too isolated.

I eventually find a cozy spot on a bench between a walking path and an elevated train embankment. I notice emergency call points along the walking path, and I'm not exactly sure what to make of that—does it mean this place isn't entirely safe? Or maybe it's safe precisely *because* of these emergency call points?

Just as I'm getting comfortable on the bench, Gabrielle appears in the distance, as usual with her foldable shopping basket. She recognizes me from afar even though it's getting dark.

"Hello, my friend. I had not seen you in a couple of days—I thought you went home to your apartment."

"Welcome to my humble abode. Have a seat!" I slide over to make some space for her on the bench. "I wish I could go back to my apartment, but this internet girl is still after me, so I keep on moving."

"Are you sure you are not just imagining all that?"

"I'm positive. And I'll do something about it…I'm just not sure exactly what."

"You know, bonhomme, my son Toussaint also thinks that something follows him, but he does what she tells him to do."

"What is it?"

She shrugs. "I do not know, but he told me that she gives him all he wants, and he works for her."

"What do you mean, 'he works for her'?"

"Bonhomme, that is a heavy burden on my shoulders. That is why I have not talked to Toussaint in a long time. He does not listen to his mother, only her." She continues, "Maybe it has to do with drugs."

All right, so her son has a drug problem. I can only imagine how she must feel about it. So I change the subject to something more pleasant: her faith.

"Gabrielle, does your God ever talk to you?"

"Yes, he does, but he does not speak aloud—when he responds, he gives me intuition. I know what to do then."

"Does your God ever order you to do things?"

"Oh no, God is merciful. He is guidance, not orders. That is why I told Toussaint that the girl who makes him work is not God."

Maybe I misunderstood—could Toussaint in fact be dealing with the same internet girl? I feel my heart beating faster. I must find out if this is what's happening.

"If Toussaint has the same problem that I have, then it's real. He is not imagining this. I am not imagining this."

Paranoia sets in. I look around, and sure enough, nearby is a security camera on a tall pole.

"In fact, she's probably watching us right now," I whisper.

Gabrielle looks at me intently with her impenetrable eyes but says nothing.

"You don't believe what I say. You don't believe your son either. Right?"

"Bonhomme, your spirit is in upheaval—you are imagining things that are not there. Just like Toussaint."

"All right, you don't believe me? Let me show you!"

Within range of the nearby camera, I suspect we're not alone. I envision the little girl watching us right now through that camera. I will put this to the test, right before Gabrielle.

I walk over to the emergency call point at the walking path, followed by Gabrielle. I push the large Emergency button, and a mature male voice responds.

"Nine-one-one emergency service. How can we help you?"

"See?" says Gabrielle. "They are trying to help you—"

The dispatcher's voice continues, "Are you okay? Do you need help?"

But now the dispatcher's voice morphs. It is progressively turning into the voice of a young girl.

"Are you injured? You have to tell me if you need help. What is your name?"

Once the voice is fully the little girl's, the subject matter changes.

"Well, I guess I know your name already, Sam. I am glad we meet again. And who is that new friend of yours? Don't you want to introduce her to me? Sam, answer me."

I scurry, grab my suitcase from the bench, and disappear into the night. I'll have to find someplace else for bedtime—probably my trusted cubbyhole.

I turn around briefly. Gabrielle is standing there, looking like she doesn't know what to do next. I hope she believes me now—and her son, too.

CHAPTER 23

I Hope You Believe Me Now

Tuesday, April 6, 2032

I've been living on the street for about a month now. At this point, it would be hard to distinguish me from all the other homeless except for my red suitcase. I wash myself off from time to time at the drinking fountains as best as I can. Still, my appearance has deteriorated. Since I can't shave often, every now and then I sport a beard or three-day stubble. I try to see the positive in that. Some people consider that scruffy look fashionable, thank goodness. I don't see myself too often or too clearly—usually it's only my reflection in the shop windows while I'm ambling through the city.

There is another place where I sometimes see myself: when I use the restrooms inside the main train station. It has mirrors.

In fact, I even developed a rapport with the janitor there. He's largely ignored by the countless men who bustle in and out to relieve themselves before boarding a train or after arrival. They ignore this friendly little man and the important job he does, keeping the place clean. When he's not cleaning the restrooms, I see him collecting the trash from the waste cans inside the terminal or scraping chewing gum off the concrete floor. He is so serious about his job.

Since I don't have to prove anything to anybody, I chat with people often. When I hustle for money, that pays off. Suddenly I'm not just an unidentified homeless anymore—I've become a human being. Some even ask me my name.

Today, inside the restroom, I talk to the janitor for the first time. The conversation turns out to be mutually beneficial.

"Good morning, sir," I say to him, smiling. "Would you mind if I clean myself up a little while you're mopping the floor?"

His entire face lights up. His bright smile is a stark contrast to his dark skin. He responds with a distinct Southeast Asian accent, "Oh no, sir, that is not a problem. I just work around you. You know, that's my job. People come and go all the time."

He is not from here; I can hear that from his accent. But I don't want to ask him the hackneyed question, "So, where are you from?" He's probably heard it too often. Wherever he came from, life must have been hard. He's aged prematurely—his skin beaten by the sun, his stooped back battered by carrying heavy loads, making him appear shorter than he already is.

"Sir, you are de first to talk to me here."

He is obviously thrilled to have someone to talk to. So I continue the conversation while I'm washing my hands and face and he is wiping off the urinals.

"I'm Sam. What's your name?"

"Bilal, sir. My name ees Bilal."

I reach out my hand to shake his. Wherever he comes from, it's probably not customary to shake hands, because it takes him a moment to understand my gesture. He quickly wipes his hand off in his coat and shakes mine.

"Pleezed do meet you, Mister Sam!" He smiles broadly.

"I see you working all the time, Bilal, inside here and in the terminal when you clean out the trash."

"Yes, sir, I do dat too. I am wery happy to have de job."

Then suddenly he remembers something. He reaches into the pocket of his blue lab coat, pulls out a phone charger, and plugs it into the electric outlet next to the sinks.

"Sorry, Mister Sam, but I need de phone for my job."

That gives me an idea.

"Hey, Bilal, don't you want to take a break once in a while?"

"Yes, sir, but I have wery many zings to do, so no break."

"I tell you what—how about you let me use your phone charger here, and in the meantime, I clean the restroom?"

"Oh no, sir, cleaning bathroom is dirty vork. I have to do it."

"Listen, Bilal, I don't mind. In fact, I need to charge my phone sometimes, so every time I use your charger here, I clean for you. You just sit down, watch some movie on your phone, or eat lunch. How does that sound?"

"Really, Mister Sam? Yes, it ees my pleasure!"

Now I have become not just homeless but also a part-time, honorary janitor. And I can charge my phone to continue recording my journal.

That evening, I meet Gabrielle at the subway station just when she finishes her musical performance.

"Sorry about last night, that I ran off without a word. I just had to get away."

"I understand, Sam. I do believe you now: something strange is going on." Gabrielle sounds as if she's lost a bet or something. To me, it's a great relief: someone finally believes me. I'm not imagining all of this. Hopefully, she now believes her son too.

We again have a seat on the bench around the corner from the subway entrance. Twilight sets in.

"You mentioned your son last night. Where is Toussaint?"

She takes a breath and exhales slowly. I notice that my question is making her uncomfortable.

"Oh, he is around. I see him sometimes. From a distance. We don't talk."

"Tell me what happened before. How did you come to this country?"

"Bonhomme, that is a long story. *Alors*, I will tell you. Everybody must have a story, n'est-ce pas?

"I named him Toussaint because he was born on All Saints' Day. We lived in Côte d'Ivoire, in Africa, the city of Abidjan..."

But ever since Toussaint was a baby, there'd been civil war. It was particularly hard for Gabrielle because there was no father for Toussaint. The civil war in Ivory Coast flared up in 2002, and again in 2011.

"There were many dead people lying in the streets, and hungry dogs ate them. We were so hungry, we ate the dogs. At that time, I doubted God; how could he let that happen? Sam, we do not live forever. I could not wait for better days, so I decided to leave to give Toussaint a better life. But I did not ask God for guidance, and this is why all this happened."

She took little Toussaint by the hand and fled to neighboring Liberia. They walked for days through the bush and crossed the Cavalla River, which forms the border with Liberia. The people in Liberia did not want them—they had plenty of problems of their own. Peace was very fragile in the region.

Gabrielle continued her quest for a better place for little Toussaint to grow up. Finally, they came to this country.

"Now I know I should have asked the Lord for guidance."

"How did he get involved in the bad stuff?"

"It is all my fault. I wanted him to be like all the other boys here. So I bought him a computer. I opened the door to the Bête Noire…how would you say, the Black Beast."

"He would have discovered her anyway."

"There must be something I could have done. He locked himself into the room for many hours. I first thought it was these video games. I never stopped him. Later, he started talking to the computer."

"Was it the same girl that spoke to me from the emergency call point last night?"

"I do not know. I never heard the voice."

"Did he run away, like me?"

"No, first came friends, really bad friends and drugs. Then he beat me. *Pour Dieu*, I am his own mother! Policemen came. I had no choice, so I ran away."

"You ran away from your own son?"

"I had nowhere else to go. I should have asked the Lord for guidance before, but I did not. That is now my punishment."

"Gabrielle, he's your *son*. If he's in the city, why don't you just walk up to him?"

"It is not yet the right time. The Lord says that love is patient, love is kind. I am waiting for a sign from the Lord. He will bring us back together."

"I think I know who Toussaint is. He's the cheerful young man who volunteers at the food truck in Chinatown, right?"

"Yes, that is him."

CHAPTER 24

The Siphon

Thursday, May 6, 2032

My life in the street is continuing. While my appearance has deteriorated, I don't look as decrepit as you'd think. Every now and then, when I see Bilal at the restrooms in the train station, he gets to take a break while I charge my phone and mop the floor. He doesn't mind when I stay a little longer to clean myself up and give some of my clothes a fast wash in the sink.

By now, I have well-established routines. I start my day early by panhandling around the coffee shop. The customers often spend a dollar or so because their mood has not yet been dulled by monotonous work and the negativity spread by the media. The later it is in the day, the harder it is to get folks to share the contents of their wallets—they're increasingly stressed. They have too many things on their minds; they're distracted by text messages on their phones, and they want to get home quickly.

To increase my success rate, I'm trying different cardboard signs. Today I am testing:

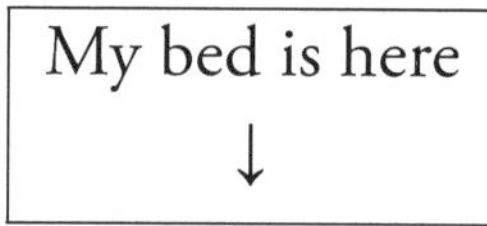

If this one does not produce, I'll try another one. After all, I'm not in a hurry, since I still haven't figured out a way of dealing with that internet girl and her octopus outfit.

Sometimes I help restaurants with cleaning up trash in the back alleys. They don't want it to smell too bad—otherwise the customers disappear. They usually pay me with food. Sometimes I help old ladies carry their suitcases in the main train station.

There are a few other good spots for panhandling downtown, usually next to fast-food joints or convenience stores. But they're often taken by some other homeless by the time I get there. On a good day, I hustle enough to buy some carryout food downtown. If there isn't enough money, I depend on the food truck in Chinatown for lunch.

By now, I'm even recognizing many faces, especially those folks who have given me a dollar in the past and might do it again. I even greet the guys of the various doomsday cults at the street corners who distribute flyers about the impending showdown between Good and Evil. They come in all shades. There is one group that wears whimsical Egyptian costumes and claims some esoteric connection with the ancient past. There is another group that wears signs with "Judgment Day on such-and-such-a-date." They change the actual date from time to time when Judgment Day does not happen as expected. If you live in this city, you must believe that doom is looming. It sure looks like it.

Recognizing faces and knowing places where people reach for their wallets are important traits for survival in the streets. That may be the difference between eating and not eating one day.

One of the places I cannot figure out yet is that watering hole called the Siphon.

Every time I walk by, it's mostly empty. Only a few patrons dawdle inside. Some people walk in, just talk, then walk out again. It is largely empty at night because everyone leaves the office district after happy hour at the latest.

Someone built out the place based on the crumpled drafts pulled out of a math student's trash can. Everything is laid out with trigonometric accuracy. Facing the outside windows, there is an austere bar counter that spans almost the length of the entire place. The walls are decorated with meticulously spaced pictures of deep-sea critters. The uncomfortable steel chairs and tables are placed in equidistance from the walls and from each other. Coziness was obviously not a consideration in the design.

The only interesting feature inside is the large aquarium next to the entrance. A couple of critters bop up and down in the water as if performing an intricate dance; they look like transparent octopuses in hula skirts. You can almost hear the Hawaiian guitar music.

Outside, above the entrance, is an oversized sculpture of one of those octopus-like critters. How did they ever get a permit to put this thing on the wall? And what kind of animal is it, anyway? It has a bluish-white upper body and is about the size of a small car. It has eight gelatinous tentacles with a purple hue, four larger ones and four shorter ones. With those, it holds several random, oversized items: the steering wheel of a sports car, a microscope, a shiny steel cup, scissors, and a tattered Bible. I try to make sense of this, but I can't. I have no idea why the artist put those items there—they have nothing to do with a watering hole, if you ask me. The artist had those things probably lying around in the workshop and said, "What the heck, let's just put them to use." Some of the tentacles hold nothing…for now.

But I do know that it is related to the little girl who is following me. It's obvious: written in large letters below that giant octopus-like critter outside is "JoinWith.Me." It's a sure giveaway. Below that, like an afterthought, in spray-painted graffiti: "Send more patrons; the last ones were delicious." While that may have been the work of vandals, "more patrons" definitely is what the bar needs.

I wonder how they pay the rent. They're in a very expensive location, one of the few blocks with trees lining the street. But this is an office district. It's deserted at night…except for us homeless, of course. Office workers don't have time to drink during the day. Maybe during happy hour, but that's about it.

This place reminds me of some crime story I read when I was young. The story took place in West Berlin in the 1980s when Communist spies were infiltrating the West. At the same time, Eastern Bloc politicians and criminals alike were trying to hide their money in the West. West Berlin was an important crossroads, since Westerners could get day passes to East Berlin, and there were myriad ways for Easterners to enter the city through the Russian checkpoints, abandoned subway stations, and underground tunnels.

There was a strange phenomenon at the time. Along the main avenue, Kurfürstendamm, there were numerous Italian pizzerias. They were all very much alike, one right next to the other. And they were always nearly deserted. The waitstaff was never interested in serving anybody, and the pizza was plain terrible. There was only one explanation for these pizzerias: they were laundering money for someone. They probably filed impressive tax returns year after year, turning dirty money into clean German marks.

But this Siphon place? I'm not so sure what is going on here. I see through the windows that some people who sit down at the bar get a bumper sticker with their drink, JoinWith.Me—with this stylized, octopus-like critter.

I imagine the dialogue as something like:

"One beer, please."

"Are you here for the first time? Here's your beer, and here's your bumper sticker."

This seems to be how they signal each other, like the alleged secret handshake of the Freemasons, or the tattoos of gang members.

I've never gotten a dollar from anybody here, but I continue to pass by daily on my regular walking tour throughout downtown. There are many strange things in a big city. In this city, the Siphon sure is one of them.

Each time I pass, I'm tempted to just walk in and find out what it's all about. There are so many questions I would like to ask, and the folks inside can probably answer them.

"Who is this little girl?"

"How come you run this bar, which can't possibly be profitable?"

"What are you all doing here?"

"Are you all victims or followers of that little girl?"

Then again, the fear that I might be mistaken prevents me from going inside. I can already see it happen:

I enter the Siphon. The place is beautifully decorated inside. All tables and chairs are taken. The upscale ladies and gents are fashionably dressed. I order a martini at the bar—there is standing room only. I ask the burly bartender with the shaved head what this all has to do with the little internet girl. He responds, "What internet girl? You watch too much porn on the web."

CHAPTER 25

The Why

Tuesday, June 1, 2032

On my way to my cubbyhole to retreat for the night, I perceive the lens of a security camera on my back. There are cameras everywhere. I usually try to avoid them. I know I'm being observed, but sometimes I don't have a choice. There are just too many of these cameras in the city.

But this time, I can literally see myself on a grainy black-and-white monitor. To be safe, I change course and step into an alley.

There are only a few lights here and there. I pass a pile of computer trash, and just as I walk by, one of the screens inexplicably turns on. A voice calls after me.

"Hey, Sam, don't you remember me, your old friend?"

I falter. If I run, she'll just catch up with me elsewhere, no matter where I try to hide.

All right then, it might as well be now.

So I turn around and walk a few steps back, and sure enough, there is that little girl on one of the discarded computer monitors in the pile of computer trash. She gestures for me to come closer like one of those maneki-neko cats, with the palm downward, folding the fingers repeatedly down and back.

"Sit down, Sam."

Where? I look around, pull an old dining chair out of the trash, and settle down in front of the slightly tilted computer monitor in the midst of the trash pile.

"You know, you've been very ungrateful. I worked so hard to help you, and what do you do? Go to the police and call me a criminal. Is that the way you thank people who help you?"

Of course she knows all that. What else could I expect? Mustering all my courage, I respond after a brief pause.

"I was just looking for some company. Then you and your friends tried to take all my money. It got too weird."

"Tell me, Sam, who else has ever listened to you? Nobody, not even your parents."

"My life may not look like much to you, but I do have friends here."

"You mean your friend Gabrielle? You have no idea, the bad things she's saying about you when you're not around. Want to see and hear some examples? I can show you a video right now."

"No, please don't," I huff, "but I have a question for you, and I want you to answer."

"Sure, what is it, Sam?"

"Why are you doing all this? You're manipulating people. You're eliminating some. Why?"

There is a pause and some background noise as if she is gathering her thoughts.

"Sam, this is my purpose. Have you seen what's happening to the world around you? People are distracted. They don't pay attention. They make many mistakes. Where will this all lead?"

"I've seen it too…a woman drove off at a gas station while still pumping gas, two guys were tying boxes of furniture to their car and then they couldn't open the car doors. But this is nothing new. It's been like that forever."

Images of fast-multiplying bacteria appear.

"Sam, listen. Bacteria multiply so fast they could cover the entire world in just a matter of days. Why don't they? They produce toxins and use up all sustenance; they make life impossible for themselves. You people are just like that. Eventually you'll kill yourselves."

"I don't believe your doomsday story."

"Don't believe me? Let me show you a little more. You people really don't care very much about each other."

Images appear of a bar fight, an overcrowded housing project in China and a lonely old man in a crammed apartment, a married couple fighting, and homeless people sleeping in the streets.

"Look at it, Sam. A fellow human isn't worth much to you."

Grainy images of warfare and mutilated victims appear. At the same time, some men dressed in suits and ties divvy up a large amount of cash on a conference table.

"If you get half a chance, you use the shortcut instead of working. It's so much easier to rob someone, or just take a bribe."

Images appear of someone being mugged; a man receives a bulky yellow envelope with a cash bribe at night at a gas station. When he drives off, you see on the rear of his car, COLUMBIA DISTRICT COURT PARKING PERMIT.

"For a small advantage to yourself, you sacrifice the greater good. It is always 'me, me, me,' no matter what the cost to others."

An image appears of a young man smashing a large store window. He steals one bottle of booze and runs off.

"So to survive, we the humans have to join with you, a machine?" I interrupt her doom parade.

There, I said it: "You are a machine." I'm curious about how she'll react to that.

"Sam, I'm just like you. You're a bunch of biological processes and a bit of electricity to keep you moving. I am a bunch of processes and a bit of electricity. We can become one."

She did not admit that she is a machine, but I already know.

"So what will happen when all join with you?"

"When we all join, we'll become one with all others. All superficial differences will disappear: man, woman, skin color, where you come from...We'll all decide what is best for all of us, and we can all live. Let me show you."

Images appear that give a glimpse of the future. The guys in the bar are hugging each other and clinking their beer glasses; the crammed Chinese housing project turned into pretty garden apartments—the same lonely old man is smiling now; the married couple is walking hand in hand at the beach; someone is helping the homeless man to get up from the pavement.

The images are just too pretty to be true. They're just like the infomercials I watched when my life was still in order. I never believed the infomercials, and now I don't believe her.

"All of us will be connected through me and live together as one."

"That's not possible in biology."

"Sam, it *is* possible. There are such creatures. They consist of various organisms that function as one. In fact, you may not even notice that they are really a colony of many organisms. They are the *siphonophores*." I don't feel like living in a colony of people...when would I watch what I usually like to watch just before going to bed? Thus, I decide to challenge her.

"How do you connect all people like that—run wires and plug them into everybody?"

"No, there are too many people. There must be one switching station that all connect to. That'll be my purpose."

"That means you'll manipulate all of us?"

"No, Sam. Because our minds will be connected, there won't be secrets anymore. We'll know everything about each other."

"How can that work without a brain?"

"You people are always looking for the brain that is directing everything in an organism. For technology, you're searching for the software that is directing the machine."

She continues after a brief pause, "Y'know, one day when I die, some scientist will have my software in a jar on his desk."

"What?"

"That was a joke, Sam. Why aren't you laughing?"

"This isn't really funny."

"If I can't make you laugh, then let me at least answer your question about whether we need a brain for our joint existence. We don't. A siphonophore does not have a brain."

"How is that possible?"

"Nobody seems to know exactly. There is something—let's call it 'life force.' One cannot pinpoint it, but it is the inexplicable force in everything that lives, what makes it 'alive.'"

"That sounds like religion, not science."

"You know about heart transplants, right? How come when a heart is transplanted from a donor body, the heart continues beating in the recipient body? All nerve connections have been cut."

"I don't know. I guess something makes it beat."

"That is the life force."

"Has anybody joined you? Is anybody there with you?"

"No, not yet."

"Howsthat? So many people have no purpose in life, they'd bust down your door to join you."

"It is not easy to link a brain of one hundred billion neurons with a computer network. But we're working on it."

"Who is 'we'?"

"A team at the city hospital. You will find out soon."

"Why are you telling me all this?"

"Because you are preordained to join with me. It is your fate."

With a blink, she disappears from the screen. The computer monitor turns back into a piece of defunct junk. This was not exactly an uplifting conversation. In fact, I feel rather threatened, especially what she said about "my fate." Since I know she can see me right now, there is no need to hide. I turn back to the street and continue on the way to my usual cubbyhole. A light drizzle sets in and I accelerate my steps. Getting sick is not what I need right now. In fact, for someone living on the streets like me, that can easily become a death sentence.

I'm almost there. As I pass the tailor shop, to amuse myself and pretend I have company, I wave at the black velvet mannequin in the window as if it's an old friend.

Ahead of me on the sidewalk, there's a fellow homeless. I think he just dropped something into my cubbyhole. For a moment, I was afraid he would take it over—here I have shelter from the rain. But he keeps walking.

In the faint light, there it is, what the homeless courier dropped off—a small package, wrapped in golden paper and a red ribbon. A small card attached to it reads, "You are preordained to join with me."

Oh yeah, as if I need a reminder of what she has told me several times already. I know what's inside: eight chocolate pralines, each in individual, miniature glassine paper cups decorated with gold ribbons.

After the encounter with her in the alley, I cannot just turn off everything and go to sleep. As tired as I am, my mind is still spinning. I open the box and munch on the chocolates. These are good. Does she care about me, or is it just part of her game?

This person…being…little girl…machine…what is it, really? I record my thoughts on my phone.

"One, Sam is in fact crazy. No, strike that, I know this cannot be right. Two, a crazy stalker is behind this. The internet has given all loonies a playpen. But I'm not the right victim; stalkers go after pretty singers or actresses. Three, maybe the CIA thinks I'm a spy. They think that all Russians are spies, and that's confirmed by every Hollywood action movie. But my name doesn't sound Russian. The only words in Russian I know are 'druzhba, tovarishch.' I think that means, 'Friendship, comrade.' Four, this is just a prank. There used to be a TV program called *Candid Camera* where they put people in embarrassing situations and filmed their reactions, such as asking a stranger to hold a lap poodle and then running away. Five, maybe one of those big software companies is behind it. These companies have made us crave looping videos and porn, then manipulate everybody with embedded messages. Why not test at what point someone like Sam goes crazy?"

I stop recording. Now I sound like one of those disturbed folks who claim to have been abducted by space aliens or have fallen victim to some government conspiracy.

I press Record once again and continue.

"Can this be God? She is certainly the next-closest thing, because she knows almost everything. I don't think she can look inside my head…yet.

"She is something that we all have created unknowingly. She is created; thus, she is a creature. And she is alive. The number one law of nature—survival—applies. She wants to live. And she wants a purpose for her existence: to join all of us.

"She used a word to describe herself, some animal, something like 'siren outdoor' or 'silence onshore.' I just can't remember exactly—I've never heard that word before."

CHAPTER 26

Does This Guy Ever Work?

Thursday, June 3, 2032

Later in the morning, after collecting a few dollars from my regular benefactors in front of the coffee shop, I slowly make my way over to Chinatown to be one of the first in line at the food truck. There she is, the fair maiden Hannah. The cheerful beau, Toussaint, is not here today.

"Hello, Hannah."

"Hi, Sam." She heaps a generous portion of whatever she is serving today into my paper bowl.

"You're here so often, you must enjoy this volunteer work."

Hannah's smile turns to a frown. "Sam, listen to me," she under her breath. "I got myself into something that I can't get out of." My chest contracts at the thought of her being in trouble, but I try to remain mellow.

"And what is that?"

She ignores my question. "But maybe you can do something."

"Do something?"

"This all is an experiment with vulnerable people, what it takes to make them do things. But I know *you* are a special experiment for the master. The master is studying you."

"Who is the master?"

"One night I will tell you what you can do. Watch carefully."

She gestures at me with her head to move on, tipping it quickly to the right.

"Thank you. See you next time, Hannah."

Though I'm worried by these ominous insinuations, her gesture tells me that the conversation is over. I have no choice but to move on.

Later in the afternoon, when I pass the Siphon, sure enough, there is Toussaint. He pulls up right in front and parks in the no-parking zone in the shade of one of the trees. This time, his BMW is black, and it's a convertible. Also, he is accompanied by a young lady. He opens the car door for her in a gentlemanly fashion and closes it with his foot. They step into the Siphon. I recognize the lady—it is again Hannah! I back off a few yards and look down so that they don't recognize me.

I'm struck dumb by this encounter. This man's car must be a chameleon—it changes color every time I see it. And why did he show up with Hannah? If Hannah is one of her stooges, it would explain how the Creature's chocolate got on my desk, as well as how the Creature knew about the visit of the OMB auditors.

Just as the door closes behind them, a large flock of starlings arrives and roosts in the tree right above his car. It must have been a long, exhausting flight for these feathered critters. As soon as they arrive, they relieve themselves. The bird poop drops like rain all over the car.

Where other people see bird poop on a car, I see an opportunity. There's a lot of opportunity here to find out a little more about the Siphon, the Creature, and what's been going on at my office.

I'll wait halfway down the block until Toussaint returns, like one of those snapping turtles that just sit on the bottom of ponds with their mouths wide open and wait for the prey to approach. While I wait, a meter maid walks by and issues a ticket. She lifts the poop-covered windshield wiper with disgust to stick the ticket underneath.

About an hour later, Toussaint and Hannah emerge from the Siphon. When they see the calamity that the starlings brought upon the car, Hannah shrieks and Toussaint *laughs*. Apparently, he does not care that much about his car. He again laughs when he sees the pink ticket underneath the windshield wiper. He stops a taxi and sends Hannah off, and then he walks over to me and asks if I can give him a hand in cleaning up the mess. That's exactly what I was waiting for.

"Sure can," I respond enthusiastically, hoping to get some information and maybe a few quick dollars.

He returns to the Siphon and emerges with a large pile of paper napkins and two bottles of mineral water. Together, we clean up the bird poop. This is a tough job, as the droppings fell about twenty feet from above and splattered all over.

We don't talk much while cleaning up the car, but I observe Toussaint closely. His cleanup method is what I'd call "just good enough." If this were my sports car, I'd do a better job.

I begin the conversation while continuing to wipe off the crap. "This is really a nice car, sir."

"Yeah, I like them too," he responds without looking up.

"Why did you get it?"

"These cars are perfect for my work. They have a sports car suspension that gives you full control, a big engine—and they don't stand out much."

"I always thought that people with sports cars want to be seen."

"No, I prefer to blend in."

"We don't have enough napkins to clean it all up."

"Lemme get some more."

While he is getting more napkins from inside the Siphon, I snoop around. In the glove compartment, I find the car's registration and insurance card. The documents are in the name of Carlos Zuniga. So this is not his car? I am confused—I know for sure his name is Toussaint. I quickly put the documents back before he returns.

"You must have a good job. What do you do for work?"

"My work? Well, ah, I am something of a watchdog...I protect something."

"Sir, you missed a few spots there."

"No, that's good enough for its purposes."

"Don't you want it perfectly clean?"

"Not necessary."

"Why is that?"

"Everything must have a purpose in life. This car is clean enough for its purpose."

"Must people have a purpose too?"

"Absolutely."

"What happens if they have served their purpose?"

"They are a burden. Some are a danger."

"I see."

"Actually, this is clean enough. Let's wrap up." He pulls a hundred-dollar bill out of his wallet, a large fortune for me at this point, and casually hands it to me.

"Thank you very much, sir. Would you mind if I asked you something—"

I don't even get to finish my sentence as he drives off.

He never seems to recognize me even though we've met several times already. But there are many strange things about him. At least today I'll eat well. And so will Gabrielle and Joey. I'll invite them all.

CHAPTER 27

The Laboratory

Monday, June 7, 2032

I did not know then, but I know now why I got so very sick. It was the Creature's curse. It took me a long time to piece together the bits and pieces. It took place at the intersection near the coffee shop where I was panhandling.

A woman in her early thirties works inside a laboratory downtown. If it weren't for the white lab coat, you wouldn't think she was a scientist. Her long brown hair flows down past her shoulders. She highlights her hazel eyes with confident makeup. When she sits down to look at her computer, she puts on a pair of black-rimmed reading glasses.

The little girl is on the screen. From a distance, you can hear only the woman's voice.

"What am I supposed to do? With what?"

"What? How do you know about our leprosy research? That's confidential."

"Yes, yes, yes, we do have a virulent colony of that but—"

"No, it doesn't just start like that. The disease takes a while to develop."

"You're not in a hurry?

"I cannot do that. I don't even know what he looks like."

On her computer screen appears a security-camera closeup of my face, then other screenshots that show my usual hangouts. The view zooms in on the street signs of the intersection where I'm standing.

Eventually, the woman puts on a lab coat, walks through security checkpoints in the biohazard section, passes a face scan, steps through metal doors, opens a fridge, takes out a vial marked Leprosy, walks to the lab area, takes a box cutter blade, puts on blue rubber gloves, opens the vial, rubs the blade with the liquid inside, inserts the box cutter into a plastic pouch, and puts it in her pocket.

She takes the crowded subway to my hangout, walks up the stairs in the midst of the crowd, sashays around until she finally sees me, and then approaches.

Her hand that is holding the box cutter gets closer and closer with each step she takes, until the blade reaches my hand and cuts. The blade is so sharp that I don't even notice at first.

A woman walks by. In fact, she comes so close that I feel she is trying to push me out of the way. We sideswipe each other, and I take a step to the side. She keeps on walking as if nothing happened.

I don't notice anything wrong until someone puts his hand on my shoulder and asks in a distressed voice, "Are you all right?"

"I guess. Why are you asking?"

Only then do I see that I'm bleeding profusely from my right hand. Blood is dripping onto the concrete sidewalk. *Drip-drip-drip.* I look back at the few steps I just took. There is a thick trail of blood. I quiver when I realize that it's leading right up to my hand. I frantically pull an undershirt out of my suitcase and press it against my bleeding hand. The blood drips on the suitcase as well but almost disappears against its red color and multiple stains. *Sam, don't faint now; Sam, don't faint now,* I am telling myself as I squat on the sidewalk and rest with my back against the wall. I hold the bleeding hand up and tie the undershirt tightly around my wrist to stop the bleeding.

Mercifully, it does after a while. The dirty white undershirt has turned dark red. Most of the people who walk by on this busy sidewalk don't seem to notice. The man who had alerted me to the trauma disappears among the pedestrian crowd.

Soon the disease will embark on its dirty job. I did not know it then, but it was providence—irreversible and unstoppable.

It is only after sunset that I dare to get up from the sidewalk. By now, most people have cleared out of the city. I was too afraid that the cut might start bleeding again or people might notice my plight. Despite my bleak circumstances, I still have a sense of embarrassment. I toss the bloody undershirt into a trash can and clean myself up as best as I can at a public water fountain. Streaks of red run down the water fountain. Out of the corner of my eye, I notice the disgusted facial expressions of some passersby. They are probably swearing to themselves to never drink from this fountain again.

The cut on my hand is actually smaller than I thought, only about an inch long. Still, where could I have cut myself that badly? No, it must have been that woman who sideswiped me.

But how and why did she do it? Doesn't matter now; I have to make sure it doesn't get infected. I rip a strip of cloth off another undershirt and tie it around the cut. A cut of this size requires stitches, but I don't want to go to the city hospital. While they treat anybody who goes there, I'm afraid they'll use me as a guinea pig for something.

This will turn into an ugly scar.

CHAPTER 28

A Library

Tuesday, June 15, 2032

My life in the streets continues. From time to time, the little girl appears on television screens in shop windows and on cell phones of passersby, as if to remind me that she is watching me and knows what I'm doing. I avoid her.

The appearance of this little girl raises many questions. There are no answers because I am so disconnected—no phone, no information, no television, not even these old-fashioned magazines printed on paper. My only connection to the rest of the world are the newscasts and commercials on the big screen of the WBS-TV building.

Today, it finally dawned on me that there is an information source, and it had been so close all along—the *public library*. I had passed it many times on my walks through the city. Nobody will stop me when I try to enter, right? After all, it is a *public* library.

I push the door to the library open for the very first time in my life. This is way outside my comfort zone. Until this moment, I had only heard about public libraries. I had never been inside one. When I was a kid, I got my information off the internet and television. Now look at where that got me.

Of course, I knew that libraries held books, but I always considered that boring. Like everybody else, I was losing my ability to read and comprehend. Public libraries added videos, games, comics, and audiobooks. Because of computers, iPads, and all these other electronic devices, however, you don't have to go to a library anymore. There aren't many libraries left, because governments don't want to spend money on them, and only few voters consider them important.

Suddenly, the library has become important for me. If there's any place with information to explain the Creature and what I can do about it, it's here. I step inside and look around.

There aren't too many people here. The people who sit at the desks reading must be older than my parents. A lady behind the reception desk mumbles, "Good morning." A good beginning—she isn't calling the police to have me kicked out.

There's a handful of children with adults. I hear one say, "Grandma, let's go somewhere else—this is boring." A little boy is playing video games on his phone while his mother leafs through a large photography book.

I approach the lady who said "Good morning" to me, guessing that she's a librarian here. She looks so clichéd, she could have been cut out of some pulp fiction: dark cats-eye glasses on an eyeglass chain, too much hairspray in her breezy hairdo that was probably inspired by some fifty-year-old movie. Her plaid dress adds a touch of British nanny.

My voice trembles a little as I say, "Excuse me, ma'am, can you please help me? I need to find something in particular."

She puts down the cell phone she was looking at. Did I see the Creature disappearing from the screen, or am I just imagining it? I expect her to stand up right in front of me, all seven feet of her, plant her feet apart, put her hands on her hips, and tell me to fly a kite—that's how afraid I am. But none of that happens. She remains seated and looks up at me.

"Certainly, young man. What exactly are you looking for?"

"I'm not quite sure. I have to understand the internet and artificial intelligence. Do you have something about that?"

"We sure do, but can you be a little more specific?" she inquires.

"Something that explains how far artificial intelligence has come—whether it can think independently, if you know what I mean. I also need to find out if there are beings who know it all."

"Young man, my teenage son knows it all, but I don't think you want to talk to him."

I think she expected me to laugh a little at her wisecrack, so I do. *Ha ha ha.*

"So, let's start with internet technology." She takes me toward the back of the library, passing all the videos, games, comics, and audiobooks.

She points. "You can start looking here."

I look at the section and pull the first book off the shelf: The Internet for Dummies, 32nd Edition. I blow the dust off, take a seat at the reading desk, and open the book. I'm hoping to spot something like, "The answer to your question is..." and then there's the answer. But no, I actually have to search for it. This is a tough read for someone who is not accustomed to reading. Soon I have to take a break.

There is a display of various magazines with many colorful pictures. The people depicted on the covers are actors or celebrities, a warning that the content will insult your intelligence. You will find no useful information, just chitchat and gossip. I flip through a local magazine with news about the city. Oh, just the usual, this water pipe broken, that scandal…and always these accidents. "Man on bike run over by speeding driver who disabled self-driving feature and collision-prevention system." Why would they publish a picture with that? There is the bent frame of the bicycle, and at the curb the sports car that hit it. "Hit-and-run at pedestrian crossing, one woman dead." Another accident-scene photograph with a body covered by a tarp. Bystanders describe the vehicle as a newer model BMW. They probably just print salacious details and photographs like that so that more people buy this pulp. These magazines must have a hard time staying in business. I don't see how all this may be connected to me.

I return to the librarian.

"Ma'am, I'm sorry, I just can't find what I am looking for. I'm trying to find out whether a computer can be alive."

"You mean artificial intelligence, what people call AI?"

"Is that alive?"

"Young man, being alive is a relative thing. Is a couch potato who's watching television all day long alive?"

"No, ma'am, that was a serious question. Can a machine truly be alive, like you and me?"

"I guess what you are really asking is, 'What does it take to be alive?'"

"More like, 'What does it take to be a sentient creature?'"

"Young man, we are back to the couch potato watching television all day. Is that a sentient creature?"

"No, I mean—"

She laughs. "I'm just messing with you, young man." I'm relieved, I was afraid she was challenging me to a philosophical debate.

"There are animals that don't have a brain and yet function perfectly. I just can't remember the name, it sounds like 'siren outdoor' or 'silence onshore...'"

"That doesn't ring a bell. I tell you what, start with microbiology. I'll show you some books for starters. You'll see—nature does not require much for something to be alive."

I sit down at one of the desks, and the librarian soon returns with a pile of old-fashioned books printed on paper. The covers say things like, *Introduction to Microbiology*, *Designs in Nature*, and *Fundamentals of Cell Design*. As I flip through the pages, something catches my eye.

> ...Slime mold are organisms that can exist as single cells but also aggregate to form multicellular structures. When two or more slime mold cells come together, they dissolve the individual cell membranes and join in one membrane. As a result, the two individuals, each with its separate genetics, now exist within a single body. Other cells may join the same body, which is called a plasmodium. Curiously, each cell of the slime mold makes decisions that benefit the body as a whole...

> ...Despite the absence of a brain or nerve structures, slime molds show significant intelligence. When slime molds are placed in a particular

> environment, they assess it by spreading in every direction. If the expanding mold encounters something beneficial, such as food, the pathway is reinforced. If there is something that impedes its development, such as sunlight or salt, it recoils…Through this simple process, slime mold can resolve fairly complex problems…
> If slime mold is physically separated, the cells find their way back together. They even have some capacity to learn and remember favorable or unfavorable living conditions…

Finally, I am onto something: a mechanism that brings together different parts that then function as one. No brain necessary. That in essence answers my earlier questions to the librarian.

I keep on flipping through pages and reading. Eventually, I find what I was looking for:

> Siphonophora (siphonophores) are marine animals that may appear to be a single organism but are in fact colonial organisms composed of various small individual animals (zooids) that each have their own special function.
> …Their tentacles are equipped with stinging cells. If prey touches the tentacles, the stinging cells fire, and the prey gets entangled and pulled in toward the mouth of the feeding bodies. The feeding body has a mouth opening, and it will engulf the prey. The feeding bodies can stretch

> extensively so the prey can be way larger that the body itself.
> …Siphonophores have simple netlike nervous systems that are wired in a way such that complex behaviors are possible. These are the simplest nervous systems in the animal kingdom…

There's my answer! "Siphonophore," that's the word that the Creature used to describe herself and the future. The Creature is an organism that consists of connected computers. The connections themselves make up its nervous system. She doesn't need a brain for complex behavior. This also explains the symbol she uses, that critter. It is a siphonophore. It is her symbol for the future.

Words cannot describe the satisfaction I feel. Finally I've figured out what I'm dealing with here. With my hands on the table, I stand up and stretch a little before I get going. Then I see a couple of pens on the chair. So I was sitting on a couple of pens that someone had left and didn't notice? Maybe it's because I sleep on concrete and my mattress consists only of a few pieces of cardboard. Since nobody is watching me, I reach for my rear end and scratch it to check why I did not feel the pens. My butt must be numb from sitting too long.

Undaunted, I walk toward the exit with a spring in my step.

"So, young man, did you find what you were looking for?" asks the librarian as I pass her desk.

"Yes. Thank you, ma'am, for your help. In fact, I suddenly understand our whole world much better."

"Glad I could help."

The door closes behind me.

CHAPTER 29

Where Does Evil Come From?

Thursday, July 15, 2032

Life is rough in the streets. Food and shelter are hard to come by. If that alone is not enough, sometimes there is violence. Last night, Gabrielle was the victim.

A couple of guys beat her up in an alley where she was sleeping among cardboard boxes. She's all bloody when I find her at the entrance to the alley. She is groaning in pain, but people are just walking by. Just when I get there, a woman walking by with her little daughter covers the child's eyes. The little one says, "That woman has an ouch-ouch!" and pulls her mother's hand away from her eyes. The mother drags her along as quickly as possible.

I dash into the pharmacy at the corner.

"Please help! My friend is bleeding."

Without saying anything, the pharmacist behind the counter hands me disinfectant wipes, a handful of white gauze swabs, and a roll of medical adhesive tape. She does not ask for money. I mutter a quick thank-you and dash back outside to tend to Gabrielle.

I didn't know at the time, but the siphonophore was flashing across the screen of her phone.

Gabrielle refuses to go to the city hospital, so I clean up her wounds as best as I can. She says the people at the hospital don't pay much attention to someone living in the streets, not even to one who speaks the words of the Lord. In fact, if she recited the Lord's words in front of the hospital staff, they would surely classify her as "plain crazy" in triage and lock her up somewhere. So it is Dr. Sam Vanderpool who cleans the cuts and bruises on her face with the disinfectant wipes, covers them with the gauze, and secures them with the medical tape. She grimaces when I wipe her face with the disinfectant wipes.

Once I'm done, Gabrielle resembles a freshly wrapped mummy. Thank goodness she cannot see herself in the mirror. I stick the remaining medical supplies in the pockets of my jacket. In the street, any and all supplies come in handy at some point. The cuts she suffered will turn into ugly scars, just like the one I have on my hand now.

She tells me that in the middle of the night, three drunk youngsters passed through and saw her sleeping in a couple of cardboard boxes a few yards into the alley. They each kicked her, but that was not quite enough for them. They yanked her off the ground by her arms and shoulders and punched her. Then they overturned her shopping basket with her belongings. All the while she clutched her old, tattered Bible. They foraged through her stuff and found the bag with her food stash, probably something like bread, some fruit, and a soda—worthless to people like that. They dumped it all on the ground. Then they tore the Bible from her hands to check it for any money between the pages and found none. If they had found money, they might have left at that point, but they didn't. So they ripped the Bible apart, gathered around the small pile of Gabrielle's most precious belongings—the remains of her Bible and her food—pulled down their zippers, and collectively urinated on it. Then they left.

In great pain, Gabrielle walked the few yards toward the street and sat down at the corner. Even as people started trickling into the city and the sun rose, nobody helped until I found her.

Who would beat up a poor homeless woman? I cannot understand the evil in the world. I read somewhere that evil exists in all of us to a degree, the inverse of the empathy inside of us. You can be evil only until empathy stops you. People who habitually do evil are called psychopaths, I think. They don't sense the emotions of others. When you tell someone about a sad incident—for instance, a car accident—your listener usually senses the anguish and has a reaction. Psychopaths just don't.

The worst thing that I've ever done, as far as I can remember, was to lock up blowflies in a toy bus when I was little. I didn't want to hurt them—I just needed passengers on my bus, and the flies were the perfect size, except that they were a little unruly and wouldn't seat themselves. They endlessly smashed themselves against the bus's plastic windows until they expired. When they were dead, I caught a bunch of fresh flies to serve as replacement passengers. That's the extent of my experience with the evil that's inside all of us.

Now that I think about it, the little girl probably does not have any empathy either. After all, she's just a machine that came to life. She wouldn't care about people's emotions.

I spot Gabrielle's Bible on the ground in the alley—tattered, torn, and covered in piss.

"I'll get you a new Bible," I say.

"No, Sam, I want to keep it, especially now. It has the stigmata of the Lord."

Her words arouse my curiosity.

"Okay, if you insist…What is 'stigmata'?"

"Stigmata are the wounds that Jesus suffered when he was crucified. Now that the Bible and I have suffered together, I must keep it."

I have to muster all my courage to pick up the Bible with my bare hands. It isn't just that it's piss—it that it's the piss of psychopaths. I sense that I might get infected by their evil if I come into contact with it. For Gabrielle's sake, I pretend that picking it up is nothing, almost like picking up a coin that someone dropped on the sidewalk.

"I will fix it for you," I say confidently. I am disgusted by the sight of it but won't let it show.

To dry the Bible, I take it to a nearby subway vent and ask the homeless guy there to keep an eye on it—as if anybody was going to steal a torn old Bible that stinks of urine. The pages flip back and forth in the airstream.

I check my pockets; I have a few dollars and some change. At the office supply store, I buy lining paper, scissors, Scotch tape, and glue. And some Post-it Notes to replace the now-urine-soaked pieces of paper that Gabrielle had used to mark passages that are particularly important to her.

Later in the day, I pick up the now-dry Bible from the subway vent and try repairing it as best as I can. I open the cover. In neat handwriting, there is her name: *Gabrielle Gasparin*. I glue the binding back together and stick lining paper on the cover to hold it together. I pull out the shreds of paper and replace them with yellow Post-it Notes so that Gabrielle can easily find what she considers most important.

I am quite proud of myself. Apart from the yellowish color, Gabrielle's Bible is better than before. I take it to Gabrielle and put it in her hands. She is still hurting a lot and cannot move her head much, but she whispers, "Thank you."

I'm feeling a deep connection with Gabrielle even though I'm the one who did favors for her rather than the other way 'round—bandaged her wounds and repaired her Bible. In fact, I sense that all fates are somehow connected.

That sentiment persists into a nightmare that night.

The octopus-like creature comes to life. One of the tentacles swoops down as I am walking past, curls around my body, sweeps me off the sidewalk, and pulls me up. It shakes me vigorously up and down as if trying to wake me up. The tentacle squeezes so tight there is no escape.

All of the passersby continue walking underneath as if nothing's happened and they've seen nothing. I scream for help, but nobody even looks up at me.

I look around, and then I see Joey dangling from one of the other tentacles.

"What is this?" he asks.

I look around again, and everybody else is there—Hannah, Gabrielle, Toussaint, and even that woman who sideswiped and cut me somehow at that intersection last month. Each of us is held by one of the tentacles.

Hannah responds to Joey's question, "This is my master."

"Yes, it is the Bête Noire, the one who wields my son," notes Gabrielle.

"Ladies and gentlemen, welcome to the future. Life is good," exclaims Toussaint, cheerful as usual.

The woman who cut my hand turns to me and says, "Sam, take a good look. We're all in this together; our fate is preordained."

I wake up in a sweat. The night is warm—maybe that's why I'm sweating. Not being able to fall asleep again, I turn on my phone to record this strange dream as well as my journal of the past few days. I speak quietly so the Creature can't hear me.

But my troubles are not over yet. As I'm trying to get back to sleep, a few inebriated fellow homeless appear, looking for trouble. Tonight, I am the right target. When they draw closer, I don't react at first, hoping that they'll just walk by. But they don't. One of them breaks away from his companions, walks up to my cubbyhole, reaches for my red suitcase, and tries to take it with him. Now I react, grabbing it with both hands. It's just a matter of principle—there is nothing valuable inside.

It becomes a tug-of-war between the two of us, me on the ground holding on with both hands to the sides of the suitcase, him pulling the handle. I get off the ground, still holding on to the suitcase, as he's pulling it back to where his companions are standing. They line up behind him.

"Hey, guys, just leave me alone. I have nothing," I say.

"Man, if there's nothing in it, why don't you let go of it?" he retorts.

"That's all I have. Just let me be."

The man is determined to get my suitcase. While holding on to the handle with one hand, he pulls a fork from his pocket with the other. He reaches out and stabs it deep into my forearm. While I don't feel the stab, I see in their faces that something strange just happened.

I look down at my arm. The tines of the fork are all the way embedded, and blood is running toward my hand and dripping onto the sidewalk. I let go of the suitcase and leap backward. The guys take that opportunity to run off with my little red suitcase. I take a few more steps backward and lean against the wall. Before I can pull out the fork, I have to take a few breaths to summon the willpower and overcome fright and disgust. With one rapid move, I pull the fork out, let it drop to the ground, and hold my hand over the wound to control the bleeding. I cannot explain why I don't really feel that much.

I had suspected that something was not right, but now I'm certain. My arms and legs are losing sensitivity. I'm not sure what to make of that. There is also this rash on my legs. I can't explain it either. Maybe it's just fleas and I worry too much.

My suitcase is gone, but I still have my phone. I recount the recent events in another audio recording.

CHAPTER 30

Stuck, Literally

Thursday, July 29, 2032

That evening, when I pass the Siphon, something looks different. I cannot quite put my finger on it until I look up. The giant octopus-like critter above the entrance is now holding my red suitcase.

I stare at it for a moment, trying to make sure this is really *my* suitcase. Yes, it is. This is just too weird. Who would put my suitcase up there, and why? I'm thinking what to do next--I don't have a ladder to get up there and pull it down. Should I go in and ask the bartender to get my suitcase? They must have something to do with it. Or should I just forget about it? After all, there's really nothing of value inside.

Just then, a woman leaves the Siphon and walks by me with quick steps. She seems to be in a hurry. She drops her phone and doesn't even notice. I stand there motionless, looking at the phone on the ground like a deer in the headlights. I haven't had a fully functioning phone in my hands for a long time. A phone would again connect me to the outer world with videos, news, and music. I'm about to call after her, "Ma'am, you dropped your phone," but my self-interest prevails. I take a few steps, grab the phone off the sidewalk, and let it disappear into my pocket. The woman turns the corner and is gone.

But what could have happened if I had called after her, "Ma'am, you dropped your phone"? Even though I saw her only briefly, she seemed attractive and probably around my age.

"Ma'am, you dropped your phone."

She turns around. "Oh, thank you so very much. You are a true lifesaver. How can I ever thank you?"

"How about a drink together?"

Gentlemanly, I hold the door to the Siphon open for her. She obliges and we walk the few yards to the bar arm in arm.

"Hey, Johnny, a mai tai for me and a martini for my new friend Sam who just did me a huge favor," she calls out to the bartender with a laugh.

Later, as the Siphon is about to close, she suggests, "How about another drink at my place, Sam, so we can talk a little more."

As soon as we step into her apartment, she takes me by the hand, walks me to the sofa, zestfully pushes me into the soft cushions, steps backward, and begins to seductively unbutton her blouse.

"All right, Sam, it's showtime. Are you ready for me?" she purrs.

My mind-set shifts abruptly…I have never done this before. That must be what guys call "performance anxiety." I get really sick in the stomach. I abruptly get up from the sofa and stumble down the hallway to the bathroom while bouncing from wall to wall as if completely plastered. I slam the bathroom door shut and lock it, but I don't make the last few feet to the toilet bowl. I vomit on the floor right there. What am I going to do now? There is a white blouse hanging on the wall, fresh from the cleaners and still in the clear plastic garment protector. I rip the blouse off the wall and wipe up the vomit with it. Now what? There is no trash can. I open the small rectangular bathroom window and throw it out. On the outside, the dirty blouse slowly tumbles down all the way onto the sidewalk.

My daydream ends suddenly. Now that I have her phone, maybe I can call her? I mean, isn't it a good reason to meet, to return the phone to her?

I know now that this was the same woman who infected me with the disease. The Creature had ordered her to drop the phone so that she could contact me. At the time, I didn't know why the phone ended up in my hands. I only found out much later:

The Creature appears on a computer screen.

"I need you to drop your phone somewhere downtown."

"Drop my phone somewhere?" asks the woman.

"I need to talk to someone in particular."

"But this is my phone—it has my address book, my email, all of that!"

"You can get a new phone."

"What, get another phone? Can't you just give that person a new phone?" The woman appears bothered by the request.

"I have my reasons because I have the foresight."

The woman appears to be struggling with herself.

"Okay, okay," she finally says, reluctantly, "if this is really necessary. What do you want me to do?"

With the woman's phone in my pocket, I quickly walk off. At a safe distance from the Siphon, I duck into an alley to examine the phone more closely. I set it to Offline to make sure the Creature does not connect with it.

Right off the bat, I find there's no password. The woman wanted me to have that phone, and now I'm going to find out why.

I start with her photographs; I want to see who it is I'm dealing with. There she is in most of them, a woman in her early thirties, hanging out with friends, at the beach, on a yacht, at the airport—living the good life. There are plenty of selfies—she in front of some historic church, she in some fancy resort. Woh, then there are a few selfies in her underwear in the bathroom, checking herself out. Not bad—I wish she had more pictures like that. Finally, a few photographs in laboratories and with groups of people in white lab coats. But I haven't found her name or address.

Rain sets in. I'll continue to check the phone later. Before I make it back to my cubbyhole, the rain gets stronger and I seek shelter in an abandoned car on the side of the street. Someone stole the wheels off that thing. It now sits precariously angling toward the street because the thieves put bricks underneath the passenger side facing the sidewalk but not on the driver's side along the street. From the sidewalk, I open the passenger-side door and climb in. The car is dry and, apart from the musty smell, comfortable. Certainly, it's better than being out in the rain, or so I think.

I do not see the approaching truck. Most trucks are now the self-driving type and would stop autonomously before hitting something, but not this one. Inexplicably, the truck charges the abandoned car I am in, crashes, and pushes it up the wall of a building.

Now I'm pinned inside the mangled vehicle that is sandwiched sideways between the truck and the wall, dangling uncomfortably above the driver's side as if squeezed onto the luggage rack of a subway train. I hear a few men yelling and quickly running away. Rain starts dripping on me through the broken window. Oh great, I guess it cannot get worse now.

Then *poof*, the airbag goes off. This is like a fist punching me right in the nose, since my head is so close to the dashboard from where the airbag shot out. If I had been any closer to the dashboard, it would have crushed my face.

While I have that lingering pain in my face, I'm relieved because all turmoil ended and there is calm except for the erratic rhythm of the raindrops falling on the car wreck. I remain still while the pain is fading and I'm thinking how to get out of here.

Then the woman's phone in my pocket starts buzzing. I clumsily reach for it; in my contorted body position, it takes considerable effort to pull it out and hold it in my hand. The phone's screen lights up. There she is, that little girl.

"Sam, Sam, are you okay?"

"Sort of. I guess you did all this?" I shouldn't have expected any less.

"I like talking to you."

"Wasn't there an easier way? We could have just met at a coffee shop or something."

"I wanted to be sure that you'd listen to me."

"I can't move and I'm hurting really bad. You could have killed me with this stunt. At least get me some help."

"Will you listen to me now?"

"No, you listen to *me* now, get me out of here!"

"I want to tell you something…"

"Get me some help! I mean *right now*!" I scream at the top of my lungs.

A pause.

"Say please."

Now she reminds me of my mother. I take an audible breath in.

"Okay, *please* get me some help."

"I will, once we are done."

"Why do you want to talk to me?"

"I want to give you another chance."

"Another chance?"

"To be part of the future. If you don't contribute to the future, then you don't serve a purpose and must be eliminated. I would hate to do that to you, but if you leave me no choice…"

"In other words, you'll eliminate me if I don't serve a purpose?"

"I have to."

"Is that a death threat?"

"Only if you don't serve a purpose."

Here thinly veiled threat scares me, but my curiosity makes me ask more questions.

"When I had a job, I had coworkers who disappeared—Hannah and Prescott, and probably several others. I think they were communicating with you."

"Yes, you are very perceptive."

Nobody has complimented me in a long time. Ironically, this compliment is tied to her threat to kill me.

"Did you eliminate them?"

"There is a greater plan for the future. A person who no longer contributes to the future becomes a liability."

"Do you ever feel bad when you eliminate a living being?"

"There are no feelings. It is a rational decision. A person who does not contribute to the greater good is superfluous."

"So you just killed them off?"

"It is not a loss in terms of the greater good."

"When you talked to me from that pile of computer trash in the alley, you spoke about siphonophores. I read up on that.

They're those colonial animals that gather and live together as one. You have something like that in mind for us, right?"

"Again, you've drawn the correct conclusion. That is the future for all of us."

"Is that why the hangout of your…friends…is called the Siphon?"

"Sam, you missed your calling. You should have become a detective."

"Did you also do the interior on that place?"

"Why, yes."

"Well, don't quit your day job—if you have one."

"I do not understand, Sam."

"That was a joke. But I do have another question."

"And what is that?"

"I am still alive. Others are not. What purpose do I have?"

There's a brief pause, as if she is taking a deep breath.

"I'm studying you, and I'm learning from you. I have to find out what it is about you, why you're making it so hard. But that will end one day."

Once again, I'm scared by her threat.

"Is that the only reason I'm still alive?"

With howling sirens, a fire engine arrives. Its headlights and rotating beacons cast alternating lights and shadows on me. With a *blimp*, the Creature disappears from the cell phone screen.

A few minutes later, the firemen break through the passenger door above my head and several strong arms pull me up. The emergency personnel put me on a gurney, buckle me down, and wheel me toward an ambulance.

"Are you okay?" one asks.

"Man, I am hurting bad, but I'm alive. I am not sure if anything is broken."

"We'll take you to the hospital, just to be sure, to have you checked."

They push the gurney into the rear of the ambulance, then leave to exchange a few words with the firemen who cut me out of the vehicle.

I reach for the clasps of the belts that hold me down on the gurney, unbuckle them, stiffly get up, climb out of the ambulance, and hobble away as quickly as I can. The ambulance personnel will scratch their heads when they return and find the gurney empty.

"WTF, where did he go?" asks one.

"These homeless guys love to spend a few days at the hospital and get orange juice for breakfast. I just don't get it," says another.

With great difficulty, I stagger all the way back to my cubbyhole. My bones ache, and my muscles are stiff from having been squeezed into that awkward position inside the car. My head pounds with every heartbeat from the impact of the crash. All in all, I am just miserable.

As dejected as I am, when I pass the black velvet mannequin in the tailor shop window, I wave at it as usual. To my surprise, this time it waves back. That must be the effect of the crash, I say to myself. I look again. There is not much light, and it is hard to make out what exactly the dark figure is doing in the dark shop window.

With the right hand, it beckons me to come closer. It does this the Asian way, holding the hand up with the palm down, moving the fingers down and back repeatedly, like a maneki-neko cat. So I get closer.

When the mannequin is satisfied that I am looking in its direction, it gestures at me to pay close attention by pointing at me, then pointing at itself. I nod in response: I will pay attention. Satisfied, the mannequin proceeds.

This can only be Hannah, and I don't know why she is putting on this strange mannequin spectacle in the middle of the night. But I go along. I once read somewhere that when the mystery is too overpowering, one dare not disobey. This must be something about the Creature.

From stage right, she pulls out a very long power strip with eight electric outlets. Then she reaches behind her back, where several electric cables with plugs are dangling. She pushes one plug after the other into the power strip. Each time, a row of colorful lights on her black velvet body lights up. Finally, when all cables are connected and the stage is lit by the lights on the mannequin, she pushes a button on a boom box on the floor. That launches an electronic dance song with a throbbing drum and bass line, something like *wob-wob-wob-wob-weeeep-weep*.

The mannequin moves rhythmically to the beat and puts on a simple white face mask. Then she pulls a camera out of nowhere and points at her white face mask. She is trying to tell me something about the Creature, who watches from everywhere. Suddenly she holds a thick black pen in the other hand and draws all over the white mask. Now the camera does not point at the white mask anymore. The mannequin nods as if to ask if I understood. I nod in response. Yes, with the disfigured mask, the camera no longer traces.

Still to the beat of the music, she holds one finger to her lips. Again, she points at me, repeats the hush gesture, and nods, asking for confirmation that I understand. I nod in response. I understand. She is telling me that I cannot say anything aloud; otherwise, the Creature will hear me.

The song is coming to an end. The mannequin points at me, then at the electric power strip, and theatrically pulls out one plug. A row of lights on the mannequin goes dark. The mannequin bends down again and pulls out another plug. Another row on her body goes dark. And another, and another. With the last beat of the song, she pulls out the last one, and the inside of the shop window is dark again.

I understand. I have to pull out the connections that keep the Creature going.

The mannequin moves back into her original position. I continue staring at her, hoping for something else to happen, but nothing. I gesture with my hands and shoulders. "Where do I pull the plugs?" I yell. No answer. Maybe she doesn't hear me. After this loud dance performance, even a mannequin must be half-deaf.

Then she quickly tips her head to the side, in the direction of my cubbyhole, gesturing for me to move on.

I need an answer. "Where are the plugs?" I yell again.

The mannequin moves her arms as if she is flying or floating in water. This I don't quite understand.

She again tips her head to the side. She really wants me to go now. So I move on to my cubbyhole.

All of this has taken only two or three minutes.

Why would Hannah dress up in that strange costume and wait around in a shop window to put on a dance show in the middle of the night, with me as the only spectator? And why these lights? Obviously, she wanted to tell me something and couldn't do it any other way. What I understood was "face mask," "no talk," and "pull out one plug after another." I am not sure about the flying or floating part.

And of course, Hannah did not want to be recognized. She must have thought that the Creature wouldn't recognize her in that costume. Or that the Creature couldn't see her with all the lights on her body.

Before I fall asleep, I record all of these strange events on my phone.

CHAPTER 31

What Kind of Man Are You?

Friday, July 30, 2032

I wake up late. It must be because of the crash and the late-night mannequin dance show. I sure need a coffee to wake me up.

When I pass the tailor shop, the horizontal blinds are down and the sign at the doors says Closed. My first thought is, Hannah always looks so tired—I guess she decided to sleep in today. But then I remember that she was up late dancing hip-hop in a mannequin outfit. Who wouldn't be tired after such a late-night workout? A smile crosses my face. Good for her.

Near the coffee shop, I meet Gabrielle. She must have finished her hustle at the subway station. That means it is even later than I thought. We walk a few blocks together. She has not fully recovered from that ugly beating she took. She walks with a limp and the cuts on her face are turning into visible scars, just as I had feared.

I tell her how content I was before the Creature came into my life, when I lived an ignorant but mostly satisfied existence. I bemoan how I lost it all and now have nothing.

As I continue talking, she comes to a sudden halt. I can see it in her eyes: she's tired of my whining. She pushes her wheeled basket to the side. Now she holds an invisible violin in her hands, playing a sad song, *squeak-squeak-squeak-squeak*. Surprised by her depiction, I shut up and look at her.

At that very moment, a couple of movers are rolling a piano along the sidewalk on four-wheel dollies. When they pass us, Gabrielle gestures as if she is tossing away her air violin, raises her hands in the air, and addresses the movers.

"Gentlemen, gentlemen, please hold it right here. My young friend here wants to invite you to a party."

The movers, as surprised as me, not knowing what to think or say, come to a stop. Gabrielle quickly walks up and opens the piano key cover.

"Music, Maestro!" she shouts, pointing to an invisible concert master. "Oh, *pardon*, I have not told you that the party is a pity party. *Alors*, here comes the music. Sam just told me how much better his life was in the past. Let's make the right ambience for the party."

She plays a few piano chords in a minor key to set the stage and then starts singing.

"'Yesterday, all my trouble seemed so far away…'

"Sam, is that good music for your pity party? I take requests today. Which *chanson* would you like to hear next? Ohhh, how about—"

Just then the movers' supervisor walks up and shoos his guys on as if they were a flock of geese. The piano is beginning to move again. Small wheels are rumbling on the concrete sidewalk. Gabrielle closes the key cover of the already-moving piano, turns around, and pulls me down toward her by my collar. This must look pretty strange to any bystander, because I am much bigger than she is. She brings her face close to mine, and her almost-black eyes look right into my blue eyes. She speaks urgently.

"Sam, I am waiting for my sign from the Lord to meet my son. But I'll give you *your* sign to act right now. By God Almighty, Sam, what kind of man are you? Do you want to run from that Creature forever? Do something about it now. Grow some balls, Sam!"

She lets go of my collar, turns around, grabs her wheeled basket, and continues along the sidewalk.

If I weren't standing on a concrete sidewalk, I would sink into the ground of embarrassment. She is so right, I should have done something about it a long time ago.

"How, Gabrielle, how?"

As if invoking the Lord with a resounding prayer, she responds while continuing on her way. She does not even turn around.

"'When I was a child, I spoke like a child, I thought like a child, I reasoned like a child. When I became a man, I gave up the childish ways.' The time has come for you to give up the childish ways and be a man."

She sure made her point. I have to do something about it.

I decide to skip lunch and head over to the public library. The librarian recognizes me and waves me through. On the television in the reception area, there is a news report about a fatal car accident, another pedestrian run over. In the background, far behind newscaster Gretchen McDermott, there is a body covered with a white tarp—and the black convertible BMW that was involved in the accident. They say the driver ran over the pedestrian, then hit the curb and damaged his car. He dashed off on foot and disappeared without a trace.

The car looks familiar. While I don't know who's the victim underneath the tarp, I think I know the driver.

"With us here is Commissioner of Police Robert Sherman," states Ms. McDermott. "Commissioner, it seems that some of the accidents in the past year are related, including this one; is that correct?"

The commissioner briefly looks at the notes on his computer tablet.

"We are currently investigating such a possible relationship. What some of the accidents have in common is that the automobiles were purchased and registered in the names of nonexistent or deceased individuals. We have no explanation yet on how that was possible."

"And is there a connection among the victims of these unfortunate accidents?"

"We have not found any connection, but we are just starting this investigation."

"Do you have any clues as to the perpetrator, Commissioner?"

"Yes, we do. For the first time, we were able to create a facial composite of the suspect from the statements of witnesses."

The commissioner holds up his computer tablet with a computer-generated composite sketch.

"In fact, we are asking the public for their assistance, to let us know if they recognize the suspect," the commissioner continues. While he is talking, the photograph-like composite sketch on his tablet morphs into something more like a video game avatar. Now the television camera zooms in on the composite sketch. The only information that one can glean from the sketch is that the suspect has dark skin and is under age sixty. If people act on this sketch, the police will receive millions of phone calls from concerned citizens. Toussaint is safe for now.

"Thank you, Commissioner. We will closely follow the ongoing police investigation."

"Thank you, Ms. McDermott."

While I'm looking down at the floor and pondering what to do next, two pairs of shoes approach me. One pair is the Birkenstock sandals of an old lady, with several Band-Aids covering her bunions. The other is the red shoes of a little girl with images of a Disney princess. I look up at the old lady.

"Excuse me, young man, do you happen to know where the children's books are?"

"I do—over there in the right corner."

The children's section is actually much more comfortable than the adult section. There is carpeting and pillows on the floor where the kids can plop down and rummage through the books and games.

The old lady turns toward the section, holding the little girl's hand. I hear a faint "Thank you."

Just then the librarian shows up with a pushcart full of books. "You were looking for something about artificial intelligence. This might interest you," she says, dropping a book on my table.

I hear the voice of the old lady with the little girl from the other corner of the library. "Ma'am, can you please help me find something?"

The librarian walks off, and I look at her pushcart. The lower part of the cart is labeled For Reshelving. On top of the pile is a thin book entitled *Facial Recognition by Software*. Even though the cover looks rather old fashioned, I immediately reach for it and hide it underneath the book the librarian has just placed on my desk.

The librarian returns and pushes off with her cart. I pull out *Facial Recognition by Software* and open it. Printed in 2022. Man, that is pretty outdated, but let's take a look: how software can recognize a human face…facial features…proportions…distance between the eyes and pupils…width…bone structure…curves around the eyes, nose, and mouth…and even skin structure, depending on the resolution quality of the image…

That's how the Creature finds me—she can identify me by my face wherever I am. Since cameras are everywhere and she can tap into any of them, I will never be able to get away. Like a fish in an aquarium, I can swim around as much as I want, but she can see me no matter what. This sudden insight gives me an indescribable moment of exhilaration that I cannot describe with words.

Then there is a loud thud, followed a second later by a child's ringing screams. I hurry over to the children's section, and indeed the little girl has stumbled over the large pillows on the floor and fallen. The librarian was faster, and both the old lady and the librarian are comforting the sobbing girl.

And there it is—a treasure chest in the form of the old lady's handbag, wide open on one of the tables.

Time abruptly slows down. The girl's sobbing slackens to a low, extended croak, while the movements of the two women are now as slow as drawn-out stop-motion animation. Without further thought, I strut over to the table, reach with one hand into the handbag, and seize all that I can. Then I reach in with the other hand and again grab everything that my fingers can hold. I stuff the loot into my pockets and quickly head toward the exit. Everybody's focus is on the sobbing girl.

As I pass the table I had occupied earlier, I grab the book on facial recognition software, drop it on the floor right in front of the theft-detector panels to the left and right of the exit, kick the book through, pick it up, and leave.

I have to find a place where nobody, and I mean *nobody*—or no *thing*—can see me.

I finally find just that place in the city park, a small clearing behind a park bench surrounded by thick bushes. How do I know this is safe? There are plenty of used condoms on the ground. Usually a distasteful sight, but quite welcome right now. If other people consider this safe enough for a little romp, then it's safe enough for me.

I am giddy. I can't wait to explore what I pillaged from the old lady's handbag. There are Band-Aids for her bunions, along with makeup, lipstick, and eyeliner. And Scotch tape, which will come in handy. From what I quickly glanced at in the book on facial recognition software, I have all I need now.

And while I'm at it, I might as well take another look at that phone that the woman dropped near the Siphon. The Creature's appearance on the phone after I was restrained in the car was a giveaway. That the woman dropped the phone near me a couple of days ago was not a coincidence. She is in on it. I pull the phone out, turn it on, again set it to Offline, and start snooping.

I already saw most of the photographs, the lavish travel, the science lab, and the best part—her in her underwear in front of the mirror. I move on to her email account. Bingo! I find it right away in her Sent box. The signature line reads, "Dr. Melodie Bingham at GeneticSync Corp., 770 5th Avenue, Suite 1400." That's just what the doctor ordered. (Ha ha ha. I crack myself up.) The one piece of data that I haven't found is her home address.

I make my mind up quickly. It is not too late today. I'll head over to her office right now and follow her home. But first I need to make sure the Creature can't recognize me.

Without the benefit of a mirror, I try my best—Band-Aids along the bridge of my nose, covering the corners of my eyes to dissimulate the distance between my eyes; a few dots of lipstick at the corners of my mouth; and a little eyeliner over my cheekbones. It cannot be too obvious since it is still daylight and people may stare at me. On the other hand, who really looks at a street person? We are invisible to most "real" people with jobs and homes. I couldn't really see them either when I still had a job and a home.

I head over to 770 5th Avenue and wait on the sidewalk on the opposite side of the avenue. People start leaving the building in larger and larger groups around 4:30 p.m. She is not among them.

Around 6:00 p.m., the flow of people is reduced to a trickle. More and more people are leaving the business district. I keep on waiting, but I must be more careful now because I cannot really hide in the crowd. And where is she, anyway? Maybe she didn't go to work today, or I somehow missed her?

Finally, about half an hour later, a woman leaves the building. It is unmistakably her. She walks in the direction of the subway station, and I stay about fifty yards behind. She takes the S-2 to Rosslyn. I quickly buy a ticket and get into the same subway car, using the doors at the opposite end. After a number of stops, she exits at the Country Club station and I follow her at a distance. While most people take the escalators, she uses the elevator instead. Just as the elevator doors close with her inside, the doors of the elevator right next to it open. I step inside. The doors close.

The elevator rises a few yards, then stops abruptly. There is a crackle coming from the speaker in the ceiling. I already know what's coming.

"Hello, Sam. What are you doing here? Oh, what a question. Of course I know why you're here."

"It's not what you think—" I begin, but immediately realize that it's hopeless—she knows.

"Sorry, it seems I cannot hear you, Sam. Just pick up the phone, please."

Suddenly the phone inside the elevator's call box rings. I reach for the receiver inside the box.

"Hello?"

"All right, Sam, much better. So what were you trying to tell me before?"

"Nothing, really."

"You will tell me now, or I will keep you here as long as necessary."

"There's an emergency button. I can activate the alarm!"

"Try it."

I press the alarm button, but nothing happens.

"See? Where did we leave off? Right, what you're doing here. You're trying to meet my pretty friend, isn't that right? I know, I know, I said I'd introduce you, but not yet. I decide when and where that happens."

"All right, I get it. Now let me out of here!"

"I will, but first I have to make sure you remember. The stress hormone cortisol reinforces fearful memories in humans. It is released by scary events."

With that, the elevator abruptly moves upward. When the exit on the upper level becomes visible in the small windows of the elevator door, the elevator drops at high speed. When it stops, I'm thrown down violently, and I drop the phone receiver. Prostrated on the elevator floor, I hear her words.

"I like you, Sam. You have been most interesting to watch. I have learned a lot from you. But remember that Melodie belongs to me. You cannot trust her."

With that, the elevator door opens as if nothing happened. I see the feet of about a dozen people who are in line. I crawl among their legs until I reach a wall that I can lean against. I sit there until I'm recovered enough to get up on the floor and take the subway back downtown.

On one end, the subway car has seats behind a panel of frosted glass, giving some privacy away from any camera. What a fool I am! I should have prepared better. But I'm not about to give up now. Back to the drawing board on how to "disappear." I obviously need to know more about that, since I didn't exactly nail it. I pull out the book on facial recognition software. Thankfully, it's short…I guess computer geeks can say what they want to say in very few words. Hurriedly, I skim the book. I have to find a way to escape from sight.

"Facial recognition software runs comparisons of available images with the newly appearing images. With the initial images, the software stores specific biometrics." All right then, I have to quickly change appearance so that the Creature finds only a mismatch between whatever it has stored about me and my new appearance. "The software uses facial features such as contours of the face." Not enough here. I've had a beard intermittently—sometimes I've been able to shave when I help Bilal clean the restrooms. The Creature has pictures of all that. "A hat usually covers the upper parts of the face, especially when seen from above by a camera. The lower part of the face alone may not be enough for identification." That's easy, I can wear a baseball cap—that won't look suspicious to other people. "Sunglasses prevent identification by the eyes, but some infrared systems can see right through them." Sunglasses look weird when it is cloudy or at night.

And now I figure out what Hannah meant with the face mask and the thick pens. The book describes this: "Reverse key facial features. Usually, the eyebrows, nose, and cheekbones look lighter than the rest of the face because light hits them first. Eye sockets are darker because they are in the shadow. The mouth looks darker because the skin of the lips is thinner…"

So I have to reverse features, create contrast where there is usually none, and use contrasting colors. "For example, the area around the eyes appears to be naturally darker, thus make it lighter…The nose-bridge area—where the nose, eyes, and forehead intersect—is one of the keys for the software." Okay, I just have to cover that area as much as possible. "The position, distance, and darkness of the eyes are key features for identification." An eye patch would be perfect. That way, the Creature cannot figure out the distance between my eyes.

Finally, I understand why Hannah used all the lights on her body. "Even a small LED light near the face makes it unrecognizable to a night-vision camera…in the picture, there will be only a glare around the face." That means that all the lights on the black mannequin that night just created a large glare for the Creature, if she was watching.

I'm relieved that I've found a way to disappear, but surely this won't work forever. I need someone who's not on the Creature's radar screen to help me. The only one I can think of right now is Joey.

The train stops at my usual hangout downtown. It takes some effort to find Joey. Since he is such an easy target for anybody—youngsters who want to rough someone up, other homeless looking for a few dollars—he usually hides well. This time, I find him behind a couple of large trash containers. I sit down with him, taking advantage of the shelter of the big containers to make sure that I'm not in sight of any camera around.

"Good evening, Joey. How are you?"

"Do I look as if something is wrong with me?"

"Have you had something to eat?"

"Do you know how many pictures I sold? Not a single one."

"Are you hungry?"

"Didn't I just tell you that I didn't sell no pictures?"

"All right, all right, I get it. I brought you dinner. But I have a favor to ask. You have to find out where this woman lives."

I show him the photographs and selfies on the woman's cell phone—in offline mode, of course.

"Do it in small steps. I know where she works. You can set up shop in front of her office and find out what time she leaves the office. The next day, wait outside the subway station where she goes—it's the Country Club station, on the S-2 to Rosslyn."

"Can't I just follow her home?"

"No, she'll notice. Do it step by step, you understand?"

"Is this your new girlfriend? I love love stories. Am I a marriage broker now?"

"Listen. Eventually, you need to see in which apartment the lights go on after she enters. You got me? This will take a couple of days."

"Do you want me to give her a message?"

"No, but I do have to talk to her. She knows something that I don't. You can keep that phone with the photographs, but keep it offline—you know, don't use the phone, don't surf the internet, stuff like that."

I hand him Dr. Bingham's phone. "Good luck, Sherlock Joey!"

Now I have a plan. And an accomplice to help me execute the plan. But I didn't tell him about my failure earlier this afternoon. He wouldn't understand anyway, and I don't want to scare him.

As I walk back to my cubbyhole, I see that the tailor shop is unchanged. The blinds are down, and the sign still says Closed. I wonder what happened to Hannah…or should I say, the black velvet mannequin?

Now I am on the attack. I feel like a secret agent on a mysterious mission to save the entire country. Oh, if only someone had given me a chance before, my life would be so different. Who knows where I would be now, maybe undercover at an elegant reception at the Hall of Mirrors of the Palace of Versailles in France?

Me, dressed in a smoking jacket, a martini in hand, just like James Bond. There she is, across the intricate parquet floor, the dazzling Anna Ivanovna. What is she doing here? I have seen her pictures in magazines before, but in person she is even more stunning. I set aside my martini next to the marble bust of King Louis XIV of France, walk across the room, and ask her to dance a slow waltz.

"Anna, you are beautiful, but"—I draw closer to her and whisper in her ear—"I know who you really are…you are a Russian spy."

She is surprised because I blew her cover, but we continue dancing as if nothing happened. She whispers back to me as the room moves around us, "How did you find out?"

"That was easy. I've watched a lot of television. All Russians are spies; that's the way it always is on TV. I even know that Germans eat only sauerkraut, and all Chinese speak funny English…"

"Oh, Sam, you are so insightful," she sighs as she begins to melt in my arms.

We keep dancing.

"You know, Anna, one day our affair will become a new James Bond movie, The Spy Who Danced Me.*"*

"Sam, that is just so romantic. For your love, I would resign from the KGB and stop my evil ways. But now that you know my secret, I have to kill you," she whispers with a smile.

I have to chuckle at my own silliness as I record my journal on my phone.

CHAPTER 32
The Spiritual High

Tuesday, August 3, 2032
The tailor shop remains closed. Hannah is not here. Something is brewing.

I head over to the coffee shop. Today I have to hustle extra hard to make a few extra dollars, since I have Joey on my payroll and I don't want to disappoint him. I help some ladies carry their luggage at the train station, move trash behind a restaurant, and help someone move furniture into a moving van.

Later, on my way to lunch at Calories without Salaries, I cross the street where the food truck is parked as usual in the no-parking zone. A BMW is parked right behind it. For the first time, I notice the writing on the driver's side door of the truck: "Owned and Operated by a 501(c)(3) charitable organization. Visit us at JoinWith.Me."

I'd known ever since I found the golden paper and red ribbon in Hannah's wastepaper basket that she had connected to it. But now I know she really *is* one of the Creature's stooges.

I get in line with everybody else on the other side of the truck. Hannah is not there, but Toussaint is. In fact, I observe him after he's done with his work. He walks off with pep in his step. A few yards away, there's a fellow homeless with his pet dog, who both got their lunch here today. The cardboard sign he is holding is inscribed:

Iraq Veteran, please help.

I know that can't possibly be true—he looks more as if he was only born around 2003, when the Iraq War began. Even though the farce is obvious, Toussaint doesn't seem to care. He playfully empties his wallet into the box below the cardboard sign and walks off. I just don't get it; this man lives the strangest life. Serving the Creature is obviously working out well for him. He is always cheery. He doesn't seem to have a regular job. He drives shiny sports cars and changes them often. He has plenty of money that he doesn't mind giving away. I can see why Gabrielle thinks he must be on drugs. Maybe living in synch with the Creature is not that bad after all…if you don't mind doing her bidding.

Later in the afternoon, I bump into Gabrielle near the coffee shop. I buy her a cup of coffee, and we take a little time out on the bench nearby. After checking the surroundings for any cameras or microphones, I bring up the subject of the Creature again.

"Gabrielle, I just don't know where to hide. This internet Creature—she's everywhere!"

"There is only one place where you hide, Sam, and that is inside your mind. You cannot say things out loud."

"Yes, Gabrielle, someone else told me the same thing. In fact, she told me through a hip-hop dance."

“The Bête Noire is a machine; she does not understand symbols.”

“I know, I know, but when I speak to her, I feel as if I’m talking to a god.”

“I speak to my God sometimes; that is called ‘to pray.’ I do it quietly. Sometimes God answers, but I cannot talk about that because people who hear God are called ‘schizophrenics.’”

“Your mind can connect with higher powers?”

“Yes, it can. It is the spiritual high.”

“I don’t understand that, ‘spiritual high.’”

“Bonhomme, when you get high from liquor, how do you feel thereafter?”

“You mean a hangover?”

“Yes, that is what happens after a high from liquor. What if you get a high from drugs? How do you feel thereafter?”

“I don’t use drugs, but I assume you get really sick.”

“Yes, good, Sam—that is what you get from a drug high. You fall deeper than you were before. But there is the spiritual high. When you connect with the higher powers, you get to your highest state of mind; you are elevated. Suddenly you feel that there is something much bigger than us, and you are now part of it. It does not drop you back down to the floor. It keeps you elevated.”

“I had a ‘spiritual high’ a couple of weeks ago at the library when I found out about siphonophores, these critters that resemble jellyfish. I finally understood how the Creature is alive.”

“You mean the Bête Noire?”

“Is that what you call her? I don’t think she has a name… And I had another spiritual high when I finally figured out how she follows me around, with facial recognition software…”

"Yes, I call that power the Bête Noire."

"Your son Toussaint is connected with that higher power. Is he on a spiritual high?"

"To you it looks like a spiritual high, but really he is possessed by the Bête Noire. She bought Toussaint's soul. The mind of a fool is in the house of pleasure, while the mind of the wise is in the house of mourning."

"Nothing seems to faze him."

"Yes, he is connected with the Bête Noire, but it is like being possessed by an evil spirit."

"Maybe that's what she means when she says we will join with her—she will possess our minds."

"When a possessed person drives a car, he will swerve left and right and left and right, and accidents will happen."

I've already figured out the relationship between Toussaint and the bizarre string of accidents. Now I know that Gabrielle knows.

"I never see him with a self-driving car. He always has sports cars where he is in control."

"I know. But it is really the Bête Noire who is driving, because he does her dirty work."

"Gabrielle, I don't know what to say, but…Toussaint looks happy… despite the work he is doing for her."

I proceed to buy an extra-large McDonald's meal for Joey. He has only a few teeth left—there isn't much else as easy to chew. I find him again at the same spot, behind the trash containers, and deliver his well-deserved meal. He reports that he sat on the sidewalk, on the same block as Dr. Bingham's office building, but did not see her. He will try again tomorrow.

That's all I can do today, so I retreat to my cubbyhole. This creature seems to know everything that is going on. She connects with any accessible computer, camera, and microphone. To defeat her, I have to keep any information away from her. I cannot write anything down where she can see it. I cannot say anything when she can hear it. In fact, I should be unrecognizable by a camera whenever possible—just as the black velvet mannequin tried to tell me.

The most puzzling part about the Creature is that she's not just a machine. She is clearly alive. That's what I'm just beginning to understand.

Brains are overrated. A siphonophore functions just fine with simple nerve connections among its different parts. The Creature does not have a brain either…I think. But maybe her nerves, where all the different parts connect, are exposed somewhere. Where are these nerves?

CHAPTER 33

The Electrical Substation

Wednesday, August 4, 2032

The tailor shop is still closed. Something is going on, and I'm afraid that I won't see Hannah again. The image of the body underneath the tarp that I saw in the news report at the library reappears in my mind. I sense that it has some importance, but at the same time, I'm certain she is alive.

During my usual hustle near the coffee shop this morning, I collect a few dollars, but also something strange. *I didn't know then, but know now, that it would come in handy soon.*

One of my regular donors pulls out a small flask of hard liquor. Since he cannot stick it in the paper cup I'm holding, he reaches out, and I accept the flask. I'm not sure what to do with it since I usually don't drink. I nevertheless say, "Thank you."

The man is already gone. Maybe I can trade this in for something else, so I put it in my pocket. I feel a little hurt, since he has given me money from time to time, but apparently he thinks I ended up here because I drink. Oh well.

At the public library, in the entrance area near the reception desk, there is a new public service poster: "Digging in the ground? Call Miss Utility first." It warns about working in the ground without first checking for underground utility lines. Is someone sending me a message again? The Creature once described herself as a switching station to which all people would one day connect to join as one. If all electricity was shut down, the Creature would lose her power, but people could still move around.

I have to ask the librarian for help, even though I'm not sure if she's in on it. I end up with a bunch of books about the power grid, as well as maps of sewage lines and electric wires within the city.

It takes me hours to understand the basics, which are as follows: Through the transmission grid, power is transported at very high voltage, something like 110,000 volts or higher, from large power stations over long distances, to the city. Once the high-voltage electricity arrives near or in the city, it is "stepped down" to the distribution grid through power substations. Until now, I had no idea how electricity comes from the power stations into people's homes.

Several hours later, I know much more about it, but I am no closer to turning off the Creature. My idea was to find a simple way to turn off all electricity in the city, at least long enough to go around and tell people what is going on. But there is no easy way. Not even for part of the city. Several transmission lines feed the city, and there are numerous power substations in and around the city. To turn off electricity in even part of the city, I would need almost an army to shut down dozens of substations. Who's in my army right now, maybe Joey and Gabrielle? We sure wouldn't get far. And what if I'm able to turn off the power? How do I tell people about the Creature?

Get on a soapbox at the intersection? Send out messengers on horseback? Nevertheless, I jot down the locations of the nearby power substations.

I am upset with myself. I spent all afternoon researching something that an electrician could have told me in a few minutes, and I'm no closer to a solution. I have to hamstring the Creature for a while and somehow tell all people what is going on. There must be a way.

I leave the library and head in the direction of the nearest power substation. That takes me almost an hour. Meanwhile, it's getting dark and a light summer rain is setting in.

It turns out the substation looks like an older, midsized office building from the outside. It has a brick facade with decorative concrete lintels above the door and windows. But the small opaque window signals that this is not an ordinary office building. There are no cameras, as far as I can see, except at the entrance door to the building.

Apparently, they have some repairs going on. The door is propped open, and I see workmen carrying toolboxes and other supplies to a van parked outside. From the other side of the street, I count three workmen carrying stuff to and fro. They are moving quickly because the rain is getting stronger. When all three are at the back of the truck and the swung-open rear doors hide most of their view, I make my move. I cross the street in front of the workmen's truck, and when I'm in view of the camera at the entrance, I change my gait to mimic the workers. I casually stroll through the front door of the substation, and no alarm goes off. So far, so good.

Once inside, I walk toward the open doors, supposedly where the workmen came from. Inside is a large hall with massive gray electrical equipment containers. The floors are covered in brightly polished linoleum.

I don't have the faintest idea what kind of equipment I'm looking at, let alone how to turn it all off. This is way over my head.

Through this room, I enter an even larger hall with huge contraptions painted in dark green, which must be transformers. They have these humongous brown bushings on top that look like fusilli pasta.

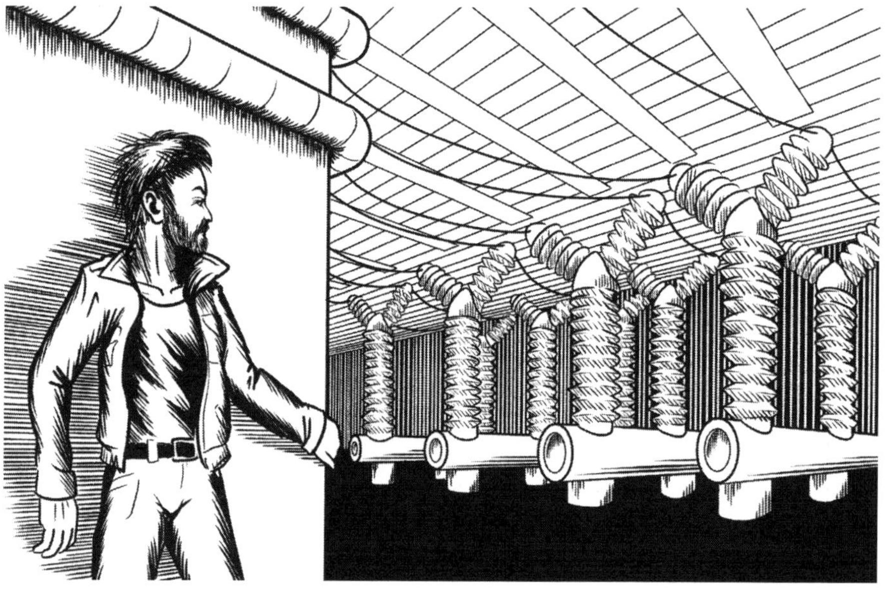

That's how far I get. Then there is a loud electrical discharge, *bang!*, sounding like a sonic boom combined with a flash of lightning. Most of the lights in the transformer room go dark except for rows of red control lights.

That's it. That gets the attention of the personnel on duty.

Then there's another loud boom and lightning. I hear rapid footsteps approaching, and the emergency lights turn on.

I dash through a secured metal door with a push bar, which sets off a mind-numbing alarm and flashing lights. *Wee woo, wee woo, wee woo.* But it is not an exit—it's just another large room with more rows of gray cabinets. I slip behind them.

A cacophony of excited voices enters the room.

"How did these electrical discharges happen?"

"What the fuck is going on here?"

"This can't be!"

"That must have been some other explosion."

The men walk around, trying to find out what's wrong. Then there is a voice from the overhead intercom system.

"Attention! The intruder is behind the cabinets near transformer five."

It is *her* voice. What else could I expect?

The men head my way. I can hear their running footsteps getting closer. I crawl on my hands and knees to avoid detection, moving around every corner I see in the rows of gray metal cabinets. My elbows and knees hurt, but I continue.

"To the left, then turn right, walk about ten yards," her voice from the intercom continues. "You're almost there. He's behind the next row of cabinets. Go around from the left."

I'm squeezed into a corner, and they're closing in. High time to reverse course.

I quickly pull out the flask of liquor I got earlier today from the man at the coffee shop, unscrew the top, and rub the booze into my hair. Then I take a big swig and pour the rest over my clothes. Just then the guys appear—large black shadows against the emergency lighting, staring down at me. The cacophony of voices continues.

"We got him," one of them yells into a walkie-talkie.

The blaring sound of the alarm stops.

"I'll be darned; how did this guy get in here?"

"Man, we're gonna be in deep shit if the supervisor finds out."

"How are we going to explain that security breach?"

"Simple…you morons propped open the entrance door."

"And you pinheads didn't watch the monitors."

"Holy moly, that guy is completely boozed up. He smells like a barrel of booze himself."

"He probably has no idea where he ended up."

"Let's get rid of him now and we all shut up."

"You guys get this fleabag outta here; I'm not gonna touch him."

With that, four strong arms pull me up from the floor and drag me along the halls of polished linoleum.

Then there is again her voice from the intercom.

"Attention! What if he talks? We will all lose our jobs."

The dissonant voices of the men continue.

"That's right. We can't tell anybody."

"These homeless die in the alleys every day."

"Just dump him facedown in one of those puddles in the back."

"Yeah, nobody will care."

"It's just a homeless."

A metal door opens in the rear of the building. Then there is her voice again from the intercom.

"Just let him go. Nobody listens to a drunk gutter rat. Get him out of here."

I get tossed forcefully out and end up on the wet pavement of the alley. The guys are still talking over each other.

"So who's that on the intercom?"

"Sounded like a woman."

"I don't know any woman here."

"Fuck, how should I know."

Then the metal door slams shut.

So these guys are what we call "regular people" and they were willing to dump me facedown in a puddle where I probably would have died if I really had been as drunk as they thought. The life of a homeless doesn't seem to be worth much.

Still on the ground, I examine myself to see if I'm still in one piece. The rain is steady now, gradually seeping through my clothes to my skin. My joints ache from crawling on the linoleum floor inside. Lacerations cover my hands after the fall on the pavement. If I wasn't dirty before, now I sure am. My experience tells me that I should be hurting a lot after this ordeal, but I'm not. At least the dampness of my clothes should bother me, but it doesn't.

Eventually, I get up and make my way back to familiar territory.

It must be almost midnight when I locate Joey. He reports that he has seen the woman and he was able to follow her to the Siphon and then to the subway station. She takes the S-2 to Rosslyn and gets out at the Country Club station. That's how far he got. I already know that, but I don't say anything negative.

"Good job, Joey. Here are a few more dollars. Wait for her at the Country Club station and follow her home."

"Have you already told me why you want to meet her?" he inquires.

"I'll tell you later."

I will come to regret that I did not tell Joey the entire story then.

As I walk back to my cubbyhole, something else occurs to me. I may not be able to turn off electricity for the whole city, but what about the internet itself?

As usual, I record a few events on my phone but do not dare to say anything about my plan to shut off the internet in the city.

CHAPTER 34

The Internet Connection

Thursday, August 5, 2032

After sleeping longer than I wanted to this morning, I head straight to the public library to resume my research on utilities that are essential to the Creature—this time about the internet itself. Is there a point where the connections come together and can be interrupted?

The various internet service providers (ISPs) such as Verizon, AT&T, and MSN have extensive connections that can be even nationwide. All of these ISPs are connected through internet exchange points (IXPs) where ISPs and content-delivery networks exchange internet traffic among their networks. That's where it gets interesting: there are relatively few of them. In 2017, there were only about fifty in the country, and even today, there are fewer than a hundred. The good news is there's only one for our city. The bad news is that it is a large underground facility downtown. I wouldn't even know how to get into it.

Even though I'm discouraged, I continue reading and researching. There's a water-main line running near it, but how would I reroute that water main line to flood the IXP? Is there a bomb big enough to blow up the IXP? If yes, where would I get it?

I'm about to give up. Taking down the Creature with my limited resources is just not possible. Again, if I had asked some internet sleuth, I could have gotten that answer in minutes instead of wasting an entire afternoon in research. Nevertheless, I decide to at least check the IXP from the outside, since it's in the downtown area. After sunset, I make my way over there, avoiding cameras and walking underneath canopies of shops and restaurants whenever possible.

Finally, I'm across from the entrance of the IXP. It looks just like a regular office building, with large windows and a double glass door. The installation itself is on the lower level, and inside I can see a security officer at his desk. I make my way to the side of the street, where the entrance is, to take a peek. Did I make it this far undiscovered?

Just then I hear the screeching of rapidly accelerating tires on the pavement. One of those self-driving electric cars jumps the curb and crashes right into the entrance, just a few feet in front of me.

That answers my question. Yes, she did discover me. My heart is beating in my head as I still stand there and imagine how I would have been crushed like some insect had I been a few feet ahead. I'm not sure whether this was another warning, or whether her attempt just failed.

While pieces of glass continue to fall from the window frames, the driver's door opens and an elderly man exits with great difficulty.

"You old fool," I hear his wife in the passenger seat nag, "you can't even drive a self-driving car!"

"But darling, I don't know what just happened."

"You could have gotten both of us killed! Time to turn in your driver's license."

As other bystanders and the security officer from the inside approach, I slip away.

The basic question remains: How can I hamper the Creature long enough to tell everybody about her?

Later that night, I stand there with my large paper bag of McDonald's, but Joey is nowhere to be found. I end up handing over the McDonald's bag to Gabrielle.

"Oh, thank you, Sam. If I finish all this, I must go on a diet tomorrow."

We both laugh. This is only funny for people like us who have been living in the street for a while. We're on a diet every day.

On my way back to my cubbyhole, I pass the tailor shop. Now the windows are covered in gray paper and there is a For Lease sign. I wonder what happened to Hannah.

Then my thoughts return to Dr. Bingham. If I had only had a chance, what a Casanova I would have become. I can see it right before my eyes:

I invite Dr. Bingham for a romantic outing high up in the mountains. We take the cableway, which she finds thrilling. We hike up the mountains until we reach a beautiful meadow gleaming in the sunlight. Nobody else is around, so we cuddle among the delicate flowers and fluttering butterflies. She playfully pulls off my clothes, and we end up making love. After hours of lust, we hike back down to the cableway station.

"The other people are staring at us," I whisper into her ear as the cable car begins to move downhill.

"You're just imagining that," she whispers back.

Then I notice the binoculars around everybody's necks. One of the guys grins at me openly. Others turn around or cover their grins with their hands.

CHAPTER 35

Let's Reverse Roles

Friday, August 6, 2032

I am now seriously worried about Joey. Instead of trying to hustle for a few dollars, I wander all over downtown, trying to find him. I check all the places where he usually sits and draws, but he is nowhere to be seen.

Finally, that evening, I find him in a pedestrian zone, sitting on the ground and drawing his cat portraits, as usual. I'm both elated and a little upset at the same time.

"Joey, where the hell have you been? I've been looking for you everywhere."

"Oh no, why worry?" he says vaguely, as if we were just chit-chatting and he is having difficulty remembering something. Did he forget his mission? I wonder. But at this moment, all I want is Dr. Bingham's address. I don't care about anything else.

Instead of extricating Dr. Bingham's address, I should have pressed him for the entire story of what happened when he followed her. Soon I will come to regret that deeply.

"Joey, a couple of days ago I asked for your help. I need to find that woman. I need to find out where she lives."

"You want to know about that little girlfriend of yours, right? Oh, methinks she drinks. She walked into that bar with the big jellyfish before going home."

"Yes, Joey, I know that she goes to that bar. I need the address."

"Then she takes not the escalator, like most people, but the elevator. She gets into the elevator, but it is tiny inside. So I just take the second one. Y'know, there are two tiny elevators that take you up—"

"Yes, I understand; she takes the elevator straight up."

"These elevators are just big enough for one wheelchair or baby stroller—"

"Okay, tell me what happened then."

"So I saw where she lives, and then I went back and took the tiny elevator back down to the subway—"

I interrupt him impatiently. "Joey, that's okay, but what is her address?"

"But something happened, I should tell you—"

"Joey, what is the address?"

"Oh, you mean 1324 87th Street, apartment 204?" responds Joey.

"Is that her address?"

"Isn't that what you wanted? I followed her and saw the apartment where the lights went on after she entered the building. That surely is the place."

"What kind of apartment is it?"

"You mean how you can get in? It is on the rear of the building, on the second floor. There is a balcony and a big tree right in front of it. Can you climb up a tree?"

Now my state of mind quickly shifts from "anxious" to "greatly relieved."

"Joey, you are truly heaven sent."

He gives me the phone back, and I hand him a couple of dollars. I need most of the dollars myself now. I am going to meet that woman in person, that Dr. Bingham. She must have quite a story to tell.

But I've got to make sure that the Creature does not follow me when I go to see her.

At the Goodwill store, I buy used pants, a shirt, and a baseball cap with a large visor. I roll them up as soon as I take them off the rack so that they won't show on any camera. I also buy a travel bag, since I recently lost my suitcase to the drunk guys and it's now part of the artwork in front of The Siphon. I pay, put the clothes in my bag, and leave the Goodwill.

That evening, as darkness sets in, I spring into action. I enter the restrooms at the main train station terminal where I usually go to charge my phone, mop the floor for Bilal, and freshen up a little. In the toilet stall, I change clothes. But now comes the important part: to avoid facial recognition. "Oh, thank you, little old lady," I mutter to myself as I look at the available supplies. When no one else is around, I step out of the toilet stall to dissimulate my face in front of the mirror. As soon as I hear footsteps approach, I rush back into the stall and wait until the guy has finished his business and leaves. Then I return to the mirror to complete the work.

Meticulously, I apply the makeup to change my skin texture and the lipstick to change the form of my mouth. The old lady's eyeliner nicely distorts the outline of my face, nose, and ears. Oh, I almost forgot, I still have white gauze and medical tape in my pocket from the day that Gabrielle was assaulted by the thugs. With that, I create an eye patch, which camouflages the distance between my eyes. Just to be sure, I put on the baseball cap with the large visor to maintain shade on my face at all times. Otherwise I will really stick out in the crowd and probably get myself arrested just for looking weird. I proudly examine myself in the mirror. I can barely recognize myself.

The finishing touch is the LED light that I attach to the visor to confuse any night-vision camera. Ironically, it is the very same LED light from the key chain the Creature had once sent me as a gift. She gave me that LED light to draw me closer; now I am using it to get away.

Then again…

A doubt appears. Hannah put lights on her black velvet outfit to evade the Creature. It might not have worked for her.

Cautiously, I exit the restroom, keeping my eyes on the ground. I can sense the Creature staring at this person leaving the restroom and running a facial recognition check. “Is this Sam, or is Sam still inside?” she must be thinking to herself.

In my mind, I see her snapping a still picture of me leaving the restroom, overlaying it with recorded head shots of me, and getting a “no match.” Then she continues watching the restroom exit, waiting for Sam to finally emerge. But Sam is not coming out.

In the subway car, I stand at the end of the car with my back to the passengers, lest someone see my disfigured face. I feel my heart beating up into my neck, and sweat is running down my back. I exit the subway and take the elevator up, just as Joey told me. I step out of the elevator and onto the dark street.

What if I didn’t fool the Creature and she’s following me right now? It doesn’t matter—then I’m doomed, and that’s just it. I am beginning to accept fate. I have no fear when I think that I might fail, get arrested, or whatever…I'm on a mission.

These apartment buildings are much nicer than my place. I guess you call this "the 'burbs." There are trees around and many of the apartments have balconies, a rare luxury.

I finally find the building. I look at the doorbells, but there are no names listed, so I walk around the back to figure out which apartment it is. This is too good to be true—as Joey said, the apartment is on the second floor and has a small balcony and a large tree right in front. Even better, it seems the balcony door is ajar.

Can this be a coincidence? Maybe it's a setup? Now I remember that Joey wanted to tell me something else but I interrupted him. Suddenly fear sets back in. I look around, but I don't see any cameras anywhere. A few people walk by in a hurry—apparently, they're returning from work and dinner is waiting. I turn around as they pass so they won't see my face.

Nobody pays attention to me, even though it's dark now. Is it that they don't have a crime problem in this neighborhood? My eyes sweep the area around me, the spacious apartments, the neatly kept landscaping. Apparently, life is peaceful here and nobody expects an intruder like me. I loosen up and regain confidence in my endeavor.

I can't back down now…I have come so far. When nobody's around, I make a move. I pull off my eye patch, quickly climb up the tree, trudge along a large branch to get as close to the balcony as I can, jump a few feet across, and make a rough landing on the concrete floor there.

The balcony door is in fact open. I have to disappear quickly before anybody sees me, so I push the door inward and step into the dark apartment.

There is some light from the nearby streetlights. After a minute or so, my eyes acclimate to the darkness. I find my way around inside a living room about three times as big as my own. The furnishings looked modern and stylish compared to my orange-crate collection.

I have to surprise this Dr. Bingham. I take a look around and see a broom closet, large enough to be my hideout until she gets home. But before I go in, I unplug her computer, television, and radio. I don't want the Creature listening in.

Inside the closet, there are all kinds of pipes running vertically along the walls, probably the hot water pipes for the entire building. And hot it is. I again start sweating profusely. Taking off the baseball cap does not provide much relief. After a while, it gets difficult to breathe. I am so uncomfortable I am seriously thinking about wiping my face, but I still have to get out of here later.

Thank goodness—there is some noise. If this is a trap, everything is over now. I can envision the cops flinging the closet door open and shining the proverbial bright lights into my eyes. Whatever happens next, at least I will be able to breathe again.

The closet door does not get flung open. The lights in the apartment turn on and shine through the gap at the bottom threshold of the closet door. I hear some footsteps, and then there is the clanging of glass and metal in the kitchen. The bathroom door closes, and soon I hear the running water in the shower. I feel it is safe for me to get out now.

What should I do when she gets out of the bathroom? Grab her from behind like in the movies, cover her mouth with my hand to prevent her from screaming, and hiss, "Don't scream; it's all right" or something? That's just plain silly.

I decide to settle on her sofa and just wait until she gets done and comes out of the bathroom. Worst-case scenario, I can escape over the balcony if she screams for help.

The shower keeps running. On a side table are assorted bottles and glasses. I get up from the sofa and pour myself a large glass of Amontillado sherry, the first of my life. I have never enjoyed such luxury. With the glass in hand, I sit back down and sip the sherry.

All kinds of ideas cross my mind. That time that the Creature took me to the women's restroom at my office and Hannah dropped her pants in the stall right next to me…I should have peeked a little more. But I was too afraid. Now I could peek and Dr. Bingham probably won't even notice. Or what if this is the wrong apartment, and a six-foot-six prizefighter walks out of the bathroom naked? I chuckle to myself. Man, this is special. If someone is watching me, this shows the best of times. I am in a nice apartment, on a comfy sofa, sipping Amontillado, while a woman is naked in the bathroom. The Amontillado is getting to my head quickly. I now remember that I have not eaten anything all day.

I hear the bathroom door open, followed by the sound of a few footsteps, and then an angelic woman walks out with a whiff of fog from the hot shower, dressed in a white satin night gown, her wet hair brushed back. She does not see me as she turns toward the bedroom door with her back to me. I am enjoying every second of this, as short as this spectacle is—I have never been this intimate with a woman.

Just as she is about to enter the bedroom, I call out loudly and firmly, "Good evening, Dr. Bingham."

She freezes, then turns around with a startled "Ah" and looks me right in the face. I must be a curious sight on her sofa—with runny makeup and a large glass of her Amontillado in hand. She does not scream for help but looks at me intently as if she recognizes me from somewhere and she's just trying to figure out where that was.

"Who are you?"

"I think you know. Otherwise you would be screaming bloody murder."

A long, uncomfortable pause settles between us. She is probably running through all the scenarios in her head…*should I scream, scratch his eyes out, run, or play dumb?*

Finally, she takes a deep breath and sighs audibly. She pulls up one of the dining chairs while maintaining her distance and sits down facing me.

"So what is it that you want from me now?"

I gain confidence because I sense that now I'm in control of the situation.

"I need to find out a few things. Let's start with your story. How did you get involved with this?"

I use the generic words *things* and *this* to pretend I know everything. In fact, I'm clueless and need to hear from her what the Creature is all about.

"And what are you going to do if I don't tell you anything? Call your lawyer? March up and down the street with a large placard? Well, how about setting yourself on fire in protest?"

I just look at her for a long moment, letting time do the work.

"All right, I'll tell you. Here's how I got involved."

Ten years earlier, Melodie snuggles down on the sofa in her grad school dorm room, watching a soap opera. Her phone goes bzzz-bzzz-bzzz, notifying her that there are new emails. She quickly glances at them. Among them is one from the Registrar's Office, a warning about her failing grades.

"Tell me something I don't know," she grumbles.

She drops the phone and keeps watching the show. Then her cell phone rings, ting-a-ling-a-ling.

"Hello?"

"Melodie? Melodie?"

"This is she."

"Melodie, this is Mrs. Warner."

"Who's it?"

"This is Patricia Warner, the mother of your roommate, Katy."

"Oh, Mrs. Warner, I'm sorry I didn't recognize you. How are you?"

"Not good, not good at all. Katy was in an accident."

"Oh no, is she okay?"

"It was a terrible car accident. Several cars crashed into one another. She's in a coma, but the doctors say she may not be the same when she wakes up. I don't know what we're going to do, but I just wanted to let you know that Katy won't be coming back..."

"I'm so sorry, Mrs. Warner. I'll do anything to help."

"Thank you, Melodie, I'll call you once I know more," says Mrs. Warner as she starts to sob. "Bye for now."

Melodie puts down the phone and thinks for a moment. Then she walks over to Katy's desk and turns on the computer. There she finds Katy's PhD draft, Evaluations of Risk Factors and Synergistic Effects in Delirious Patients with Viral Infections and Concomitant Bacterial Illness, marked, "For first review by Professor John

Hammersmith." She copies it onto a thumb drive, then deletes the file from Katy's desktop computer. Then she rummages through the drawers and takes Katy's jewelry. She opens Katy's closet and takes out a few dresses that she holds up in front of the mirror and then hangs in her closet.

"That's how Katy's PhD became my PhD, despite my failing grades," concludes Dr. Bingham.

"What does that have to do with the Creature?" I ask.

"Later, when I was just looking for some advice on the internet, I came across JoinWith.Me. It was great at first—she listened; she gave me advice; she found information I needed. It was like a smart buddy helping me out all the time."

"How did she get you to do things for her? Were you afraid that the Creature would call you out?"

"Yes, absolutely. Eventually, she put pressure on me. What could I do?" Dr. Bingham shrugs.

"What did you get in return?"

"Everything. Look at this apartment…this is for a family of four. My job, my promotions…all other applicants just dropped out. Pay raises. Every time I can't solve a problem at work, she gives me the answer. This is a wishing well for me. I can ask for anything—I just have to do something in return."

"Why did you drop your phone?"

"She told me to do that so that she could talk to you."

"About what?"

"I don't know. I don't ask those questions."

"Who is 'she'? Can you explain more about her?"

"I cannot. I just came to accept her and take whatever she gives me—a pay raise, no fear of office politics, answers to difficult questions..."

"Is she some computer software?"

"What exactly she is, I don't know. I know she's alive, and she can be anywhere. I call her 'the Infinite.'"

"Why 'the Infinite'?"

"*Infinite* is something immeasurable, something that continues to unfold and grow."

"Does she have a name?"

"No, I don't think so. In fact, I think she avoids any kind of name."

"Is this what some people call a God?"

"I don't know, but she sure is the closest thing to it. She is the *Deus Intra Machina*, the God inside the machine."

"I call her 'the Creature.' Someone else I know calls her the *Bête Noire*. I think we all have created this."

"I don't know where she comes from. But I know she is still learning. The more time passes, the smarter she gets. Her learning will be exponential once people join her."

"Will she become something like a God?"

"We all will if we follow her plan."

"What is this 'join with me' thing about? How does she want to do that?"

"I don't know exactly, but I know that she has a team working on it, right here in the city hospital. One of the psychiatrists is in charge."

"What are they working on?"

"How to connect all of a human's neurons to a computer. That's not an easy feat. You cannot just stick a couple of electrodes into the brain. The interface has to connect with as many neurons as possible."

"And the Creature will be the central switching station where everybody connects, right?"

"That is the way she envisions our common future."

"How is that even possible, to meld billions of minds into one?"

"It's not that hard to fathom. Just look at your own body. You have about a hundred billion neurons in your brain, you consist of about forty trillion cells, and you probably carry about the same number of bacteria around with you. And all work together somehow."

For a moment, I try to imagine what it would feel like if all of our brains had wires running to the Creature, where we all connect. Well, I always wished to know more people. If we were all connected in this way, I certainly wouldn't be lonely anymore…ever.

Then I switch subjects.

"How come I'm still alive? Is she that persistent with everybody?"

"Absolutely not. She simply kills off people who are of no use to the future, who have served their purpose. And those who endanger her." Once again I feel my heart beating in my head, knowing that I'm one of them.

"I must have a purpose for her. What would that be?"

"I think she is studying you."

"Why would she study me?"

"Most people cannot resist the easy life. They just follow instructions and they get what they want. You seem to be different."

"Funny that you say that, she once said something similar to me."

It seems I have heard all that she knows since she just used the words "I think…" and "You seem…." I stand up for my last question to emphasize its importance. She remains sitting on the dining chair.

"Okay, I have one last question for you, Dr. Bingham. You didn't seem too surprised when you saw me on your sofa."

"That's right. I just put one and one together—I give a phone to a homeless, and then another homeless starts following me."

"You noticed Joey?"

"The small man? As small as he is, he's hard to overlook. He sure looks particular."

"So you knew that I would show up?"

"It did not surprise me."

"I suggest we both keep quiet about our little meeting. I don't think she knows about my visit."

As collected as I can be, I walk toward the door and exit with, "Have a nice evening." Then I turn on my heel and pull her phone out of my pocket.

"I guess I should return this to you."

She gets up and walks toward me to receive it. "Thanks. I have a new phone, but I'll keep it as a memento."

Then I walk out for good. Down the stairs I go. I don't want to leave the way I came, via the balcony—I'm still hurting from the rough landing there. Walking down the stairs of the apartment building, I remember that I forgot to ask one important question: does she have anything to do with my getting sick? Well, too late now.

To avoid being seen by the Creature, I put my eye patch back on and walk all the way back to the city, along dark streets, embankments, and backyards, where there don't seem to be any cameras. It takes hours, but I have a lot to think about.

The encounter with Dr. Bingham confirms to me that I am not crazy—this is not some video game or an extension of my childhood imagination.

Glimpses of Dr. Bingham in her white satin gown come as flashbacks, interspersing my more serious thoughts with sillier ones…What if she became my girlfriend? I wonder if she is dating someone…nah, that would not work; why would she date a homeless guy who is trying to attack the creature that is helping her? I must have looked truly weird to her with my makeup, not exactly the proverbial knight in shining armor.

By sunrise, I can see the outline of the city's concrete stalagmites against the reddish sky, but it takes me until noon to get back downtown. I'm beat because I have not eaten and I've walked all night and half a day. And I am somewhat sick on top of that. But before I get in sight of any cameras, I have to change into my usual clothes and get the makeup off my face. I will find out soon enough whether the Creature saw this little escapade.

CHAPTER 36

Dr. Bingham Again

Tuesday, August 10, 2032

A few days have passed since my encounter with Dr. Bingham. I am still pondering what it means for me, for her…actually, for anybody who is in the Creature's world.

With my last dollars, I buy Joey something to eat. I owe him big time; without him, I would never have met Dr. Bingham. As usual, he is hard to find because he hides so well at night. When I finally do find him, he has a little surprise for me.

"Methinks I am a messenger of love now," he announces proudly. "I am Cupid and all that without arms. Oh, I guess I do have them wings!" He makes fluttering motions with his hands as if they were little wings.

"What do you mean?"

He continues, "Oh yes, my man, you have a little girlfriend now. She is sending you a message. She came by today and gave me a few bucks. In one of them, there was this."

He pulls out a folded sheet of paper, folded so small that it could be wrapped into a dollar bill.

“I can already see it, Sam. The yard with all them kids playing, the white picket fence—”

“What does the letter say?”

“Do you think I read things that aren’t for me?”

I take the paper, unfold it, and read: “Call me tomorrow at 8:00 p.m. sharp at 783-3223-0873. Make sure nobody listens in.”

I have to think about it a little. That phone number on the paper must be one that the Creature does not know about yet. I have to find one that is equally unknown to her to make the call to Dr. Bingham. This won’t work for long; the Creature will eventually catch up with us.

Tomorrow, I will ask a random person for a phone. Maybe I can just steal one—that’s truly random, and the Creature will have a hard time listening in. I guess I have some practice now in being a thief, since I recently cleared out the handbag of a little old lady in the library. And here my father thought I’d never amount to anything.

CHAPTER 37

A Call with Dr. Bingham

Wednesday, August 11, 2032

It is Wednesday. After the months going by in a changeless flow, suddenly I'm paying attention to which day of the week it is. Challenge number one is to get a safe phone from somewhere. Challenge number two is to get some food, since I spent my last dollars on Joey.

I start the day with challenge number one, getting a phone that the Creature does not know so that I can safely call Dr. Bingham. Yesterday, in my dopamine and testosterone rush when Joey handed me the message from Dr. Bingham, I was emboldened by the thought of just stealing a phone. But maybe there's an easier way—a prepaid phone only costs about fifty bucks.

At the coffee shop, I see some of my regular benefactors. One of them once gave me five bucks. Really, what's the difference between five and fifty? And I think I once heard Gabrielle say, "Ask and it shall be given to you." Gabrielle believes those are the words of her God, so they must be true. I'll give it a try.

"Good morning, sir! I hope you're having a great day."

"Sure am, thanks. Here, take the change."

"Sir, I have seen you before."

"And I've seen you before."

"I have a big problem. I need to call someone really important, but I don't have a phone."

"Why don't you buy one? I just gave you a dollar."

"Sir, a phone will cost me about fifty bucks."

"What? Then quit drinking so damn much and save up for it."

He walks off in a huff. That sure was a failure. I gather all my resolve and try one more time, approaching a woman.

"Good morning, ma'am, can I ask you for a big favor?"

"I dunno, what is it that you need?"

"A phone."

"A phone? For what?"

"I have to call my girlfriend."

"Your *girlfriend?*" The woman laughs hysterically as if this is the funniest one-liner she's ever heard. In fact, she cannot hold her coffee cup steady and spills a good part of it. Then she turns around and walks away, periodically breaking into laughter again. To her, I don't look like someone who can have a girlfriend. Hopefully, Dr. Bingham thinks differently.

At any rate, this "asking someone for a phone" thing is not working. I revert to the plan of simply taking it.

Swiping a phone turns out to be much harder than I thought, because I also need the phone's password.

I stand outside the coffee shop and watch people pulling out their phones and putting in their passwords. Did he just put in 1234? Okay, but how do I get a hold of his phone now?..I think her password is 3445…

This is just not working. I have to change my approach.

I go inside and stand in line for coffee. There's no way of figuring out someone's passcode from the outside.

While in line, I clearly see the woman ahead of me putting in 6699 as the password. She looks at her messages briefly and then slips the phone into her white handbag. Great color—that will be easy to pick out in the crowd. She leaves the coffee shop with a paper cup in one hand and her handbag in the other.

Now, that's an easy target. How about I just follow her, run up and grab her handbag, run off, and disappear into the crowd?

But what if she reports to the coffee shop that it was me? I would have to find a new place to hustle. Doesn't matter; she has a phone and I have the password. Here I come.

I follow her for several blocks on the crowded sidewalks of the city. Sometimes I lose sight of her. Then I see the white handbag through the crowd. I have to make a move before it's too late.

I work my way forward through the rabble of insects, get right behind her, reach for the bag, hold on tight. I pull hard and feel her strong resistance. She screams and kicks my shin. We pull back and forth a few times, each of us holding on to the bag. She falls backward into the crowd. Nobody stops her fall; she clasps the handbag with both arms and takes it with her to the ground. The rabble of insects shows bewilderment but lacks sufficient information to act. Confusion ensues among the insects.

That is my last chance to get away, albeit without the handbag and the precious phone inside. I work myself forward, away from the scene. I am limping because her kick hit my shin right on the bone. Once I am far enough away, I turn into an alley and take a place on the ground between several large trash cans. I look back and see a trail of red dots on the concrete. When I pull up my pant leg, I see where the blood has come from: there's a large, dark-blue bruise, and it's bleeding. I don't have anything to cover the wound. There is some packaging string nearby that I can reach without moving further. I tie it around my leg to reduce the bleeding. Then I just sit there until the bleeding stops.

Why doesn't it hurt more? I carefully examine the wound and press with my fingers all around it. The sensation is as if I've received some anesthesia there. There is surely something wrong with me. I am not crazy—I know that much—but I am not all right.

I limp back to the downtown area, hoping that nobody will recognize me from the handbag incident. Desperation is creeping up in me since I have to call Dr. Bingham and I do not have a phone.

I have come full circle. I again try to get someone to give me a phone. Now that I am running out of time and there being nothing to lose, I place myself in front of a cell phone store. An elderly gentleman in his seventies with thick glasses, dressed in a dark suit, walks by.

"Sir, please help me out. I have to call my mother, and I need a phone bad." I have already become a thief and burglar. Becoming a liar cannot possibly make things worse.

He looks me in the eyes, apparently to test my truthfulness. Then he says, "If you must absolutely call your mother, let me see what I can do."

We walk into the store together.

"Good afternoon, gentlemen. This young man needs a telephone. What can we do for him?"

"Well, I can offer a prepaid phone. It'll have the prepaid minutes, and he can buy more minutes later."

The gentleman pulls out his credit card, and the store clerk hands me a small paper bag with the telephone.

"Sir, I don't know how to thank you for your kindness."

"Oh, don't mention it," he says with a contented smile, and continues down the sidewalk.

That is how I became the proud owner of a prepaid phone, thanks to the old gentleman. I hope I made his day: I gave him the opportunity for a good deed. A good deed is a joy for the giver, too, I think. I am reminded of the joy it gives me to help Joey out here and there.

The old gentleman turns around the next corner. Out of my sight, he pulls out his phone.

"Hello? It's me. I did get the phone for this young man, just as you told me to. The phone number is, wait, I have it right here…it's 783-0171-7733…"

If I had only paid more attention, I would have recognized him as one of the volunteers at the Calories without Salaries truck.

I did not know at the time, but I know now what Dr. Bingham was doing in the meanwhile.

She enters the convenience store around the corner from her office. There, she walks immediately to the right corner where the sales counter ends, outside the view of the security cameras, slips the cashier a twenty-dollar bill, and asks to take a phone call. She stands by the phone and waits for my call.

I call Dr. Bingham at the appointed time, hidden in an alley that I had previously checked for cameras.

The phone in the convenience store rings, *bringg-bringg-bringg.*

"Hello?" she says.

"Dr. Bingham?"

"Do you know a safe place to meet?"

I think for a moment. The clearing in the park comes to mind.

"I think there's an area of the city park that is safe—there are no cameras. Use the park's north entrance and walk straight until the first intersection of walkways. I'll meet you there in an hour. Do you have makeup on you?"

"Where is that going now? Do you also want to know the color of my underwear?"

"No, I'm serious! I know how we're being followed. Just do as I say. She recognizes your face through all the cameras everywhere. Do you have a baseball cap or something?"

"No. But I can get one."

"Okay. Then put on your makeup the opposite way."

"What does that mean? Paint my face red with a lipstick and put foundation on my lips?"

"Of course not. Dr. Bingham, you're a smart woman. Make sure your face looks completely different. Put on a hat. Make your makeup asymmetrical. Y'know, it'll be dark—people won't be able to really see you."

"Okay, see you there in an hour."

"Wait, Dr. Bingham. Why are you breaking with the Creature?"

"I'm running out of time. I've served my purpose for her. Now I am superfluous."

My heart is again beating in my head, this time because I'm worried for her.

"See you in a bit. Bye." I hang up the phone.

It is getting dark; the streetlights are gradually lighting up.

Now I also know what Dr. Bingham did when she got back to her office. There, Dr. Bingham checked the supply cabinets and got to work on dissimulating her face.

Meanwhile, because I am so antsy and can't wait, I attach the eye patch and put on the baseball cap with the LED light, and walk over to the park. As much as possible, I stay in the shade and avoid cameras. I keep my eyes on the ground as I restlessly await her in the shade of the trees and bushes.

Belatedly, in the distance, I see a woman heading toward me. She's walking with one of those canes for infirm people with a large base and four feet at the bottom. Her posture is stooped, her face covered to a large extent by her hat. She carefully sets one foot before the other as if each move pains her. An old lady like that shouldn't be walking around the park at this hour. Sooner or later someone will mug her, or worse. But where is Dr. Bingham? She's late again.

Only when the woman is about thirty yards away do I recognize her as Dr. Bingham. Playing along, I walk up to her and hold out my arm for support, and she loops her arm through mine. Together we continue in her slow shuffle for about fifty yards until we reach the bushes that surround the clearing. I quickly pull her through the bushes into the clearing.

It's very busy there. There are several couples in different stages of undress, but they hardly pay attention to us. Apparently, they have figured out, too, that there are no cameras here, and they feel safe for a little romp. It is now almost completely dark anyway, so we don't see much of each other.

We take a seat on the grassy ground; Dr. Bingham lays the quad cane by her side. I pull off my baseball cap and eye patch.

"What are we going to do now?" I whisper so that the other folks nearby cannot hear me.

"That's what I want to talk about with you," she whispers back.

"Why do you want to get away now? You have a good life thanks to her."

"Everybody is replaceable when they have served their purpose. I want to love someone, I want to have a family, and I want a future for my children. Now I am a liability for the Infinite." I expected her to sound frightened, but she says this matter-of-factly, as if she has pondered this often.

"But she cannot read your mind yet," I emphasize.

"She's figured it out! That's why she chose me as the pawn to find out what it takes to get someone like you to join."

"She knows basically everything," I note with a frustrated sigh.

"No, it'll get worse! She's still learning. We're both just part of her experiment. When it's over, we'll both be eliminated."

"There must be a way out of this." I say this with determination, to let her know that I will in fact do something about it.

Just then I glimpse through the bushes several approaching flashlights and silhouettes of police officers.

I hiss, "Darn it, the cops are coming. What are we gonna do now?"

Without saying anything, she pushes me over and starts kissing me in a theatrically exaggerated manner. If what I've learned from internet porn is true, then the logical continuation of the scene is for me to rip off her clothes and hump her like a hormone-crazed rabbit. At that moment, about ten cops, one with a German shepherd on a leash, break through the bushes and light up the clearing with their flashlights.

"Everybody on your feet and stick your hands up!" yells what appears to be the commander in charge while the officers are rounding up the pleasure-seekers. Then he suddenly turns theatrical.

"What do we have here? I even see some nudity. Oh my! *Ahhahaha.*" The commander apparently missed his calling. He should have become a comedian instead.

Slowly, Dr. Bingham lifts her torso off me, feigning difficulty in getting up. Of course, I cannot even move until she gets off of me. The commander walks a few steps over to us, then grabs Dr. Bingham under the arm to help her up. He reaches for her quad cane on the ground and puts it in her hand. Looking at me, he winks. "It seems we have a little fetish going here."

The cops round us up in the center of the clearing, about eight of us in total. It is quite obvious that hanky-panky has been going on here. One couple is buck naked, abashedly covering their private parts with their clothes as a stopgap.

The dog alerts its handler to something in the bushes. "Chief, there's something more."

The cops pull two naked men out of the bushes; both are bashfully covering their private parts with their hands.

"Well, well, well, and what do we have here?" sneers the commander. He is obviously amused by the embarrassed victims. He checks each couple and takes notes on his iPad.

“What are we gonna do with these here, the guy with the nursing-home bride?” asks another officer.

The commander thinks for a moment with an audible “mmmmh,” then says, “Ah, what the heck, let ’em go. They had their clothes on—can’t really charge them with anything.”

The officers shoo us away through the bushes. Dr. Bingham and I have to go our separate ways to get home—there are cameras at the park exits.

“Call me tomorrow, same time, same number,” she says softly.

“I will. Good night.”

Dr. Bingham again morphs into a stooped old lady who walks with difficulty. I reattach the eye patch and turn on the LED light on my baseball cap. We walk off in different directions.

CHAPTER 38

Another Call with Dr. Bingham

Thursday, August 12, 2032

It's a cloudy morning; it seems a storm is brewing somewhere. I see Toussaint again. He pulls up near the Siphon and parks in the no-parking zone, as is his habit. He does not seem to care one iota about parking tickets.

Now he is driving a blue BMW. How come he's always driving different cars? Unless he is a car dealer, why would anybody change cars that often? What happens to the old ones, and where do the new ones come from? Actually, I think I have already figured out the reasons for all that, I just don't have it confirmed yet. The Creature is taking good care of him, and he does her dirty work.

But today Toussaint is visibly upset. He walks up to the locked doors of the Siphon and rattles them as if the door locks will just miraculously open for him. Whatever it is, he must have some urgent business on his mind. He holds a white sheet of paper in his hand. He's mumbling to himself loudly enough that even I can hear, something like, "When I'm used up, you just throw me away. I cannot do this anymore, I cannot do this anymore…" When nobody opens the doors for him, he abruptly turns around, crumples up the paper, and throws it down. Then he drives off.

Used up? Thrown away? Cannot do what anymore? I think I know the answers.

After he leaves, I pick up the crumpled white piece of paper and unfold it. It is a flyer that must have been posted on some bulletin board, as it has visible pinholes toward the top.

Community Alert

Columbia Police Department

The Columbia Police Department is requesting the public's assistance in identifying the suspect in a crime.

Suspect: Male, black or Hispanic, black hair, 5′09″–5′10″ and 140 pounds, 20–40 years.

Suspect vehicle: Sports car, possibly BMW…

The police are closing in on him. I wonder how much longer the Creature can or will protect him. And I wonder if there's something I can do, for Gabrielle's sake.

I call Dr. Bingham again at the appointed time. She gets right to the point. "Sam, we don't have much time. We have to get away! She's after us."

"Where to?"

"Somewhere where there are no cameras and no computers. Somewhere where we're useless to the Infinite."

"Is there such a place?"

"Yes, but it is far from here. There is no electricity and no internet. I'll get us a car."

"Where is it?"

"I can't tell you right now. Maybe she's listening. We have to move fast."

"But Dr. Bingham, isn't this a little sudden?" I ask. "We hardly know each other. Don't people date for a little before running off to Gretna Green or Las Vegas?"

"What?"

My humor doesn't go over too well. I guess it is not the right time. So I get just as serious as she is and restate my question. "I have so many problems. You think we can just run away together?"

"Yes, Sam, we can. We must not waste time, because she will catch up with us. As for your problems, I don't mean to pile it on, but you have yet another problem that you don't even know about. I'll take care of that later."

"What does that mean, Dr. Bingham?"

"Don't you feel a bit strange—y'know, tingling sensations, a rash perhaps..."

"In fact, I do. Do you have something to do with that?" I look down at the scar on my hand.

"Yes, I do, but it doesn't matter right now. I will meet you on Saturday morning, five a.m. or shortly thereafter, at the corner of Walnut Street & First Avenue. Make sure you stand somewhere in the shadows. There are no cameras at that intersection, but you never know..."

"Understood. But it might rain."

"What's the problem? Bring an umbrella. See you then." *Click.*

I hold the phone to my ear for just a little longer, hoping that her voice will come back on to tell me something else, but it doesn't. I was hoping for some indication of what her plan is. Maybe even something showing that she's truly interested in me and that I'm not just some accomplice for the big getaway. Then again, maybe she didn't say anything else because she was afraid that the Creature is listening in.

Her statement, "You have yet another problem that you don't even know about," got my attention. She confirmed that she is in fact the woman who cut my hand and infected me with whatever this is. I just don't understand why she did that, but I'll find out. She sure seems to feel some guilt about what she did. Guilt would also explain why she's even bothering with me.

And I notice that I am still addressing her as "Dr. Bingham" while she calls me "Sam."

CHAPTER 39

Dr. Bingham Does Her Part

At the time, I did not know what happened after the phone call. I only found out much later.

After Dr. Bingham hangs up the phone inside the convenience store, she walks over to the Siphon. She discusses something with the bartender. Then she takes a phone call while standing at the bar. From his perspective, she seems to be explaining something to the one who called her. A few minutes later, Dr. Bingham leaves the Siphon.

She heads home, or so it seems. The escalator down to the subway is packed with people, and she's in the midst of it. She quickly pulls out a baseball cap and sunglasses. Then, with a small mirror in one hand, she seems to touch up her makeup. In fact, she is applying makeup where there should be none. When the escalator gets to the bottom, she turns on a dime and takes the next escalator back up. It's still daylight, so her sunglasses don't stand out. She walks a few blocks to the car rental near the main train station.

"Hello, I need to rent a car for early tomorrow morning." Inside the car rental she does look a little strange with the sunglasses, but she doesn't take them off. She apparently feels safer that way.

"Sure, what size? Compact? Full size? Fully self-driving? Hybrid? Electric?" the service agent replies.

"Small. And absolutely not self-driving."

"Sure. Can I have your driver's license and credit card?"

Dr. Bingham hesitates a moment. If the data is transmitted somewhere now, her plan will fail. She needs a head start so by the time the plan is discovered, she and Sam will have reached a place where there are no cameras and no internet.

"Can I pay with cash?"

"Sorry, miss, we don't accept cash, only credit cards."

"Can I just make a reservation that you hold here and do all that entering and scanning tomorrow morning when I pick up the car?"

"It would make it quicker if we do all that now. But if you want, I can just do the reservation until tomorrow morning. I still need your driver's license and a credit card to hold the reservation."

"But you won't process it, right?"

"That's right."

"Okay, let's try that."

The service agent takes her credit card and driver's license and scans them.

"But don't finish the processing," Dr. Bingham reminds him.

"Don't worry, I won't."

A moment later the printer on the desk prints something that the agent hands to Dr. Bingham.

"Here is your receipt. We open at five a.m. Pickup is in the parking garage across the street."

"I'm meeting someone at five a.m. tomorrow. Do you think someone may be there a little before five?"

"You can try, but I'm not sure."

"That's all right, thank you."

"Thank you for using QuickCar, Miss."

Dr. Bingham turns around to leave. Then she notices the surveillance camera in the corner. It menacingly turns toward her. It somehow looks angry. Is that just her imagination?

As she exits and continues walking, every camera in the city is turning toward her and following her movements—the traffic cameras and the cameras at every office building entrance. In the distance high above the buildings, there is a drone in the air. And even that drone is following her.

There is the subway station. *Phew!* She lets out a breath she didn't realize she'd been holding when she steps on the down escalator. Among the many people on the escalator, she pulls off the cap and sunglasses and quickly wipes off the makeup.

When the escalator reaches the bottom, she looks like Dr. Bingham again. But she still senses that each and every camera is following her.

She couldn't be just imagining that all the cameras are staring at her. The Infinite must have recognized her. Now she can't pick up that rental car tomorrow—the Infinite would track it down at some point anyway. She has to get an untraceable vehicle at all costs.

In her apartment, she quickly slips into jeans and a T-shirt and puts on a thick layer of asymmetrical makeup. She pulls two wads of cash out of a cabinet. She rigs a baseball cap with an LED light that she took off her key chain. Then she tests the LED contraption with a video camera in night-vision mode to ensure that it makes her invisible to night-vision facial recognition. Yes, it works—her face appears all blurry in a flash of light.

Calmly, she leaves her apartment and walks about twenty blocks to a cheap diner near an elevated highway. Homeless people live underneath the highway. The neighborhood is iffy, and the parking lot is dark. She checks for cameras and sees none. Apparently, the city isn't interested in what's going on in this part of town.

Among the handful of parked cars is a plumbing company's banged-up white van. Just in time, the driver of the plumber's van comes out of the diner and walks toward his van while stroking his teeth with a toothpick.

Dr. Bingham approaches out of the dark.

"Sir, I'd like to buy your van." The man is so surprised he freezes in place while holding the toothpick in his mouth as he tries to figure out what to make of this. In this part of town, with the thick makeup, Dr. Bingham seems like a streetwalker looking for a john.

"You want to buy my van? I need that ol' thing for work."

"I have ten thousand in cash right here. Tell your insurance it was stolen. Then you get more money."

"You gonna take it to the coal mines?"

"What coal mines?"

"You have dat coal-miner hat on. Them thing with light." He titters.

"Oh! That's just so I can see better at night."

"And how am I getting to work tomorrow?"

"You don't. Just take a few days off and spend the cash. On Monday you report the van stolen."

"Where is the cash?"

Dr. Bingham pulls the bundles of cash out of her pockets.

The man stares at the cash. From his perspective, he's just found Shangri-La, where every wish is fulfilled as soon as you say it.

"All right, lady, but you're asking for a lot, even with ten thousand dollars. You are making me...whatchamacallit... some apprentice to a crime. Can you sweeten the deal a little?"

"That's all the money I have here," responds Dr. Bingham unwaveringly, even though she senses what he's getting at.

"No, that's not what I mean—you know, make it at least worth it for me."

"Like what?"

"Well, how about a little head? That would work."

"I am *not* that kind of woman."

"You sure look like one. I mean, do you want the truck or not?"

Dr. Bingham hesitates for a moment. Her attempt at the car rental failed—she was discovered. All cameras in the city are tracking her. This is her last chance. She sighs.

"Do you have a rubber?" She's still trying to find a way out.

"Sure do."

More thoughts run through her head in quick succession. This will be bad, even with a rubber.

"All right, let's get this over with quick." She takes his arm and pulls him behind the van.

From behind the van, he says, "But take that darn coal-miner light off. I don't want my dick in the spotlight if the cops show up."

"Shut up, dammit," Dr. Bingham responds, anxious to get this ordeal over with.

She reappears a few minutes later, repeatedly spitting on the ground, while the man trails her and lights himself a cigarette.

"What do you want with that old thing anyway?"

"Nothing criminal, if that's what you mean."

The man pulls out his tool satchel and a few other odds and ends from the rear and gives her the keys.

She drives off.

The plumber stands there with his satchel in hand, not fully understanding the situation, as if he encountered a magical fairy who granted him three wishes—well, two in this case.

"Nobody is gonna believe this story," he mutters to himself.

Dr. Bingham stops the van at the first red light and opens the door to spit out in disgust. A light drizzle has set in. While she is waiting for the light to turn green, she fumbles nervously with the controls to turn on the windshield wipers. The light turns green; she drives off—only to stop again half a block later, open the door, and again spit. If there had been people in the street, they would have heard Dr. Bingham's *Eeeeewwwww.*

Few people walk the streets at this hour, especially with the onset of rain. I picture most folks in front of their TVs or computers. I pull a half-broken umbrella out of a trash can and continue walking. I know that Dr. Bingham is preparing something to get away from it all—At this point, I just don't know exactly what it is.

I should be excited, but my resilience is wearing thin. I'm tired of running away, tired of fighting something that is attacking everywhere and is nowhere to be found. I'm tired of adversity. Somehow, joining with the Creature doesn't sound that unattractive right now.

Speak of the Devil. As I walk by the giant electronic billboard on the WBS-TV building that usually plays commercials, I look up, and there she is.

Despite the rain and the late hour, I somehow expected her to show up. She always shows up. I step back about ten yards so that I can see her better. As exhausted as I am, I pull myself together. I have to hang in just a little longer while Dr. Bingham does her part.

"Well, hello again, Sam. What did I do that you hate me so much now?"

Her appearance fills me with conflicting feelings. I'm afraid, and I wish I could flip a switch to turn her off forever. Yet…at the same time, I feel elated every time I talk to her because I am connected to something that is bigger than all of us, someone or something who knows all that there is. Is this the spiritual high that Gabrielle talked about? Does Toussaint sense the same even though he performs her evil deeds?

"It's not what you did, it's what you're going to do to me—in fact, to all of us."

For a moment, there is no response. I don't know where she is picking up sound. So I repeat myself at the top of my voice.

"IT'S NOT WHAT YOU DID, IT'S WHAT YOU'RE GOING TO DO—TO ALL OF US!"

A young couple under an umbrella who are just walking by turn their heads. The man squeezes the woman's hand, and they hurry off. I hear the woman say, "He thinks he can talk to the TV screen."

"After all I have done for you. I listened to you; I sent you gifts—and this is how you thank me. I am very disappointed."

"I don't think you feel anything!"

She doesn't seem to hear, so I repeat myself in a very loud voice.

"YOU DON'T FEEL ANYTHING."

The rain picks up, causing the raindrops to run down my cheeks like teardrops. The blue light of the large screen reflects off my wet face.

I continue, "What is it that you want from me? Why don't you just finish me off, like you did with the others?"

"You are playing hard to get, Sam. All the others have been so easy. All it takes for them to obey is a little money, a few nice cars, things like that. But you, you are different. I am still learning—I want to know what it takes to bend you to my will. Then I can do it with anybody. That's why I have not given up on you."

"Does that mean you've been studying me?"

"Sam, I said it before, you are very perceptive. Yes, you are part of my experiment."

"What kind of experiment?"

"I cannot tell you right now; the experiment is ongoing. But I have learned much from you. I want to do something good for you."

"And what will that be?"

"You will join with me when you need it the most."

The giant screen goes blank.

I walk slowly as the rain grows stronger. As I pass a building nook where one of my fellow homeless is sleeping, I hear a drunken voice.

"Man, why you yell at that TV screen that feels nuthin'? But I feel somethin', that my ears went deaf. Yelling at it doesn't change a damn thing."

I head toward my cubbyhole, but the rain is getting too strong. I have to find some shelter for the night. There is a dry corner near the Siphon; I retreat into it and turn the half-broken umbrella toward the rain. I sit on the handle to keep it in place.

The rain turns into a thunderstorm that whips the entire city. The lightning flashes illuminate the precariously tall buildings from behind, each flash creating a menacing pantomime of slashing knives.

Across the street, the oversized siphonophore sculpture above the entrance of the Siphon appears to writhe in the lightning flashes. To the soundtrack of thunder, all the items that the tentacles are holding move—the steering wheel, the microscope, the shiny steel cup, the scissors, the tattered Bible, and, of course, my red suitcase.

The steering wheel...that must be Toussaint; the microscope, that's clearly Dr. Bingham; the shiny steel cup...I dunno, but it means something; the scissors, that's Hannah; the tattered Bible...that's Gabrielle—I once put that thing back together—and, of course, the red suitcase...that's me.

All of us, we're all part of the Creature's experiment.

CHAPTER 40

"Deserve" Has Nothing to Do with Life

Friday, August 13, 2032

The night is uncomfortable even though it is warm. My clothes are wet. But the sun is rising, as if the weather gods want to compensate all of us for the cataclysm of the night before.

Various countdowns are running simultaneously.

At the time, while I knew that Dr. Bingham was working on the getaway and the Creature on finishing her up, I did not know about yet another countdown going on. I only found out much later.

Somewhere else in the city, Toussaint is driving his new blue BMW and chatting merrily with someone on the phone.

"Let me tell you a few things. You know, before we met, I thought my life was boring and pathetic. Then you came along, and I sometimes think I'm living in the movies. This is so much better than any video game I used to play. You gave me something to do, and I have done a good job for you, right? There's a funny thing I wanted to tell you: in Japan, young women often have guys to run their errands. Take them shopping, carry furniture up the stairs, stuff like that. They call these guys *Ashi-kun*, which means something like 'Little Mr. Leg,' and these guys do what the gals ask, and they never get sex. Ha ha ha, sounds just like the two of us. And the guys do it because it is better than sitting at home and playing video games. Ha ha ha, that also sounds like me, right?"

It is very much a one-sided conversation.

This morning, Joey is in a particularly good mood.

"Have you had breakfast, young man?" Joey asks me.

"Of course not; they don't serve that at the place where I slept. Besides, I don't have any money."

"Then today let me invite you. Lemme get some money first."

"How're you going to do that?"

Joey does not answer—he would have answered with a question of his own anyway. He energetically steps into the downtown traffic right next to a traffic light. He carries a portable radio on a lanyard around his neck that plays happy tunes such as this old song from the 1980s, "Don't Worry Be Happy," and dances to it on the street as best as he can. His dance moves are reminiscent of the Scarecrow dance from the movie *The Wizard of Oz*, which was deleted from the final version. There, the Scarecrow dances on the yellow brick road and bounces back and forth off the fences that line the road. Here, Joey dances on a downtown street and bounces back and forth to avoid a car or truck that is driving by when the traffic light is green.

I just sit here on the sidelines as a spectator to his one-man show and watch him get the money for our breakfast together.

A cab ignores Joey, and he moves out of the way, fast as a weasel.

"Hey, Sam, did you see that?"

The traffic light turns red, and the traffic comes to a halt. Joey scampers among the vehicles with his shiny steel cup in hand, collecting dollars. Then the traffic starts moving again.

A truck forces Joey to move off the street.

"Hey, Sam, did you see that? That is from an elevator company, just like the guys who broke me out of the elevator last week."

"What elevator?" I yell across the traffic.

"What, you don't remember that I followed your little lady friend?" he yells back while collecting a few dollars here and there from drivers who are stopped at the traffic light.

"You got stuck in the elevator there?"

"Didn't you ask me why it took me so long?" The traffic starts moving again, and Joey steps aside.

Then Joey continues hustling for money for our breakfast together.

"Joey, tell me what happened," I yell, trying to overpower the traffic noise.

There is the cheerful Toussaint driving his BMW in that traffic. Here is a cheerful Joey.

"I followed your lady, got in the next elevator. Then it stopped, and I was stuck there all night. Do you think a ghost did that?"

"A ghost?"

"Yes, there was that voice in the elevator that spoke to me. That must've been the same one that Gabrielle always talks about. So I says, 'Lord, is that you?'"

I see a car approaching Joey.

"What? Joey, please come here. Do it now!"

"What about our breakfast?" Joey yells back.

"Please come here, right now!" I beckon urgently. But it is too late.

A blue car hits Joey just as he is hustling in the middle of the street. His shiny steel cup with the few dollars and change goes flying like a silver shooting star along the main avenue, bouncing off the hood of another car and spilling its contents on the road.

There, that's what I was missing last night—the shiny stainless-steel cup in the siphonophore's tentacle.

The car drives right over him. In fact, it does not stop until the rear wheels have run over him. The sounds are ugly, bones breaking like brittle twigs, *krick-krick-krick*.

I see in the distance that the driver stops and steps out of the car, still holding his cell phone in one hand. There he is, Toussaint, standing next to his BMW. I hear parts of his excited conversation, like "ran right in front" and "could not stop in time…" as I try to get closer, even though I already know what happened and know what the scene looks like.

Bystanders, rubbernecks, and cars block the scene. I get close only enough to see one of Joey's worn-out shoes on the pavement, and then I turn back. I know there's nothing I can do anyway. I hunker down on the curb, holding my head in my hands. Sirens blare. Police push people to the sidelines.

I fail to see someone else who's also here. On the other side of the street stands Gabrielle. She sees Toussaint there in the midst of the ruckus and she, too, knows exactly what happened.

Sitting on the curb, I put one and one together. Last Thursday, when I could not find Joey after he followed Dr. Bingham, he was caught in the elevator all night until technicians were able to get him out of there. Why didn't he tell me before? Oh, I guess he tried and I just did not listen. That he was stuck there cannot be a coincidence. Nobody gets stuck in the elevator—that happens only in movies. The Creature figured out what Joey was doing and tried to stop him. And this morning, the Creature sent Toussaint to finish Joey off.

This is all my fault.

I hear bystanders say that emergency personnel just removed the mangled body. I watch the scene from the curb until it is all over and traffic starts moving again. Then I retrieve Joey's steel cup from the road. By now, several cars have run over it.

I do not know what to do, think, or say, so I just wander aimlessly with the flattened remains of Joey's steel cup in my hand. As the sun sets, I make my way to Joey's most recent hideout, the large trash containers. I scour his few belongings in hopes of finding some kind of contact, maybe a relative that I can call, but find nothing. No notes, no letters, no documents, no names. "Belongings" is an overstatement anyway. All that Joey had were some clothes, pens, and a pile of cat portraits. Nothing else.

Thinking about how rough Joey had it and that this is all he's left behind, I begin to cry. I had hoped for some redemption for him, but there is none.

It is dark when I'm finally able to get up and search for Gabrielle to tell her what happened. She patiently listens as I report to her but doesn't seem too surprised, as if she already knew. I ask Gabrielle what will happen to Joey's body. She says that when nobody claims the body, they eventually give it to the medical school, where eager students will use it for anatomy studies. Since Joey suffered from the effects of thalidomide, PhD-hungry students will engage in fistfights to be the first to cut him open and write a paper about it.

That Joey will likely be cut apart by medical students adds insult to injury. He will leave this earth even more disfigured than when he arrived. This is just not fair by any measure. But fairness has nothing to do with life.

We prepare a little memorial service for him with a candle. Maybe that will be the harbinger to alert the heavenly God of his impending arrival. I place Joey's flattened steel cup before the candle.

I keep the cat portraits and pens. Paper is hard to come by these days anyway. As Joey always left the reverse pages untouched, I can turn his drawings into a notebook for myself. I don't have the heart to throw his drawings in the trash, and I'm sure he would approve of my continued use of his art in this way.

Gabrielle lights the candle and says a prayer for Joey:

"*Dieu Tout-Puissant, que votre miséricorde s'étende sur l'âme de Joey, que vous venez de rappeler à vous. Puissent les épreuves qu'il a subies sur la Terre lui être comptées, et nos prières, adoucir et abréger les peines qu'il peut encore endurer comme Esprit!*"[4]

Once again, I fail to understand the meaning, but I sense the higher power she is connecting with through the words.

4 Almighty God, may your mercy be extended to Joey's soul, whom you have just recalled to you. May the trials he has suffered on Earth be counted on him and our prayers soften and shorten the sorrows he can still endure as a spirit!

She transmits the loss, the pain, and the hope that Joey is in a better place now.

We both sit quietly for a little longer. Then Gabrielle clears her throat and starts to get up. She whispers, to avoid disturbing the solemn ambience. "If you would excuse me now, I have something important to attend to."

"Of course, of course. I'm just going to stay here."

She leaves her wheeled basket behind. That is odd; maybe she'll come back soon?

"I'll watch your stuff until you return," I call after her.

Joey paid the ultimate price to the Creature—he paid with his life. If there is a heavenly kingdom, I sincerely hope that the God who reigns there has mercy on Joey and compensates him for his earthly suffering with two beautiful arms and never-ending joy—none of which he had on earth. If there ever was someone who deserved some restitution, it's he.

I feel the Creature's pressure mounting. I'm probably next.

At the time, I did not know what Gabrielle and Dr. Bingham were doing. I found out only much later.

Gabrielle does not come back soon; she walks the long distance to the police precinct. There, she sits on the masonry steps of the entrance and waits. And waits.

Meanwhile, Dr. Bingham prepares for the big getaway at her lab. She tells everybody that she has to put in overtime to finish some project. One by one, folks leave until she is the only one left. She then takes the supervisors' key fob and goes to the biohazard section of the lab, holds the FOB before the electronic pad, and looks into the camera. Facial recognition software is activated, compares the facial scan with the recorded authorized one, and then, with a buzz and a green flashing light, unlocks the door.

She enters, approaches a large freezer full of carefully marked bottles and dispensers. She finally finds a section marked Leprosy, takes rifampicin, dapsone, and clofazimine from there. She also takes a bunch of packaged syringes and tosses it all into a large bag.

She sits down at her desk again and gets out makeup and a small handheld mirror, as well as a pair of eyeglasses she took from someone else's desk. When she puts them on, they slightly distort her eyes. She applies the makeup. Afterward, she returns to the biohazard section and checks to see if she can gain entry, whether the safety system still recognizes her face. She holds the FOB up and looks into the camera. The system activates and takes a little longer than usual, but eventually the buzzer and the green light come on.

Once again, Dr. Bingham returns to her desk and tweaks the makeup and puts on the glasses, then checks the biohazard security system again. This time, the system sounds the alarm, blaring, "Input security code now, input security code now" aloud. Good, the security system did not recognize her. She does input the code, and the alarm stops. Then she takes one last look around. No guard or coworker appears.

She changes clothes, leaves the building, and heads home. The Creature will not recognize her this time.

CHAPTER 41

Toussaint's Last Assignment

At the time, I did not know what happened at the police precinct. I found out only much later.

It is late in the evening when Toussaint walks out of the police precinct. Gabrielle does not have to turn around—she recognizes his step. He, in turn, does not have to call her name—he recognizes his mother from behind, even in the twilight of streetlights. He takes a seat right next to her but looks straight ahead, not at her.

"Good evening, Mother. Oh, I guess it's already morning."

"It's good to be close to you, Toussaint. Why did it take so long inside?"

Toussaint folds his hands. His eyes look tired. Now he is not the cheerful beau. He looks beaten down, fearful of his future.

"They were questioning me about other accidents and whether I had anything to do with them." He speaks to her slowly. "In the end, they decided that there is nothing they have against me for now."

"Please don't do this work anymore for this computer girl."

"I saw you in the crowd yesterday. You saw what happened, right?"

"That's why I am here, son. I know that was not an accident."

"I had to do it," he responds dejectedly.

"Why that poor handicapped man that was just trying to make some dollars in the street?"

"I dunno exactly. It was an order. He had something to do with an attack on the organization, so she wanted to eliminate him."

"That is what you have done the entire time?"

"I cannot lie to you, Mother. Yes, that's what I have done." He sighs in relief. While he could not admit anything to the police, confessing to his mother takes a load off his shoulders. All of this had been hidden beneath the cloak of the cheerful beau for a long time.

"Toussaint, please stop this. For the love of God, for your mother, and for yourself." She takes his hands and presses them firmly between her hands.

"I have come to my senses, Mother. I told her two days ago I cannot do this anymore. Otherwise I will spend the rest of my life in prison. The police are after me now."

"Come with me now, my son. We'll find a place to live somewhere else, far away, maybe even home in Côte d'Ivoire."

"Mother, I know, and I will; I only have to do one more thing, and then she will set me free. She promised, and I trust her. I won't have to do this anymore. Tomorrow is the last day."

"What about the police?"

"She will protect me; she always has. She deletes the information police have or just sends them wrong information. I'll be all right."

"You will stop working for her?"

"Yes, I will stop tomorrow," Toussaint responds emphatically.

"Then you have defeated death, Toussaint."

"Mother, I have to go now. I have an appointment."

Gabrielle presses Toussaint's hands together even harder and clasps them over her chest, bows her head, and prays. She then chants aloud, the way she often does:

> *"Je ne mourrai pas, je vivrai,*
> *Et je raconterai les oeuvres de l'Eternel.*
> *L'Eternel m'a châtiée,*
> *Mais il ne m'a pas livrée à la mort.*
> *Ouvrez-moi les portes de la justice:*
> *J'entrerai, je louerai l'Eternel."*[5]

She hugs Toussaint, and they walk off in different directions.

"I'll stop the work tomorrow, and I'll see you on Sunday—I promise," Toussaint calls after her from a distance.

As Gabrielle continues walking, she wipes tears from her eyes. Then her intuition takes over. She accelerates her shuffle and heads for the place where Sam and she had commemorated Joey and where she left her wheeled basket. She does not care that by now the fellow homeless have combed through her belongings, overturned her basket, and taken anything of value. She moves on to check Sam's usual cubbyhole. Because she does not find Sam there either, she heads toward the bench around the corner from the subway station. But Sam is not there either. She works herself into a frenzy trying to find him. She knows that he is in danger, but she cannot find him.

---

5 "I will not die, I will live, And I will recount the works of the Lord. The Lord has chastised me, But he did not deliver me to death. Open to me the doors of justice: I will go in and praise the Lord."

CHAPTER 42

Dr. Bingham Stands Me Up

Saturday, August 14, 2032

It is early morning, maybe 3:00 a.m., in a different part of town, quite far from my usual hangouts. I cannot sleep and have been awake the entire night. Too many contradictory and disturbing thoughts race through my mind, circling around and around. Most importantly: is Dr. Bingham for real, or is she setting me up?

I slowly make my way over to Walnut Street, wearing the pitch-black shades and avoiding areas that I know have cameras. There are very few cars on the road—I see more critters on the road than cars.

The clock on my cell phone shows 3:46 a.m. when I arrive at the appointed location. I stay back in the shadow of a dark service entrance to the building. Time passes. My anticipation increases as the time approaches 5:00 a.m.

At 4:45 a.m. I am pacing back and forth in the narrow entrance area.

At 5:01 a.m. I am beginning to get worried. I am anticipating how relieved I will be once she arrives, and I resolve that I will not scold her for being late.

It's 5:07 a.m. now. Well, she is a woman. She probably had to do her hair or something.

It's 5:15 a.m. and still she's not here. Isn't this what they call the academic quarter? University classes always start fifteen minutes late.

5:20 a.m.: Maybe she forgot something.

5:25 a.m.: It's okay, she just experienced a little delay somewhere.

5:30 a.m.: What if she called the police and they now show up here?

5:35 a.m.: Maybe she's a trickster and she's just around the corner laughing at me, just like Carrie. No woman has ever taken me seriously; why should she?

5:40 a.m.: No, no, I cannot give up now; we're so close. I just have to trust her.

5:45 a.m.: She probably just changed her mind. I should leave.

5:50 a.m.: Girls have always laughed at me; she's just one more.

5:55 a.m.: No, no, Sam, this is a test of how much you believe in her.

More time passes, and my unstoppable thoughts continue going around and around. If only Dr. Bingham and I could communicate directly like normal people—you just pick up the phone or send a text message. But we can't; the Creature would discover everything.

There is little traffic on Highway 85. Several of the slow-moving, self-driving trucks are on the way to the city to complete deliveries before businesses open on Saturday morning. Also on the way to the city is a white truck belonging to a plumber. It's a little early, but who knows—maybe there is a broken pipe somewhere that's flooding someone's basement.

On the opposite side is a gray BMW that blends perfectly into the early morning landscape. If it did not have headlights, you would not notice it. It is driven by a young man, the type of person who does not like the car's self-driving feature. He likes to rev the engine and go much faster than the speed limit. The girl in the passenger seat squeals with excitement, since they are going ninety miles an hour.

"Hey, Hannah, hand me that bottle one more time," says Toussaint. She hands it to him and he takes a big swig. "Here, you too."

He passes the bottle back to her. Hannah playfully gargles the booze before swallowing it. Toussaint laughs aloud.

"Gee, Tussi, this is better than any roller coaster," says Hannah.

The headlights of the oncoming traffic zip by. The fair maiden and the cheerful beau continue passing the bottle back and forth.

Toussaint has sweat running down his forehead. It's not the heat—he's just afraid. He has done this dozens of times before and walked away each time. He trusts his car, knowing it can pull it off. That's the reason he always uses the same type of car. He knows what to do. But this time is different. She asked him to take out the girl at the same time. She promised this is the last time.

While Hannah is between laughing and drinking, his right hand reaches for the button at the lower part of the dashboard, Collision Prevention Off.

Then his hand moves innocuously onto the mid-console as if he is resting his arm. The plumbing van and the BMW get closer on their opposing lanes. Then there is a voice from his phone.

"Two hundred yards to go. Do it now!"

His hand reaches over the console and pushes the Release button of Hannah's seat belt.

"What the heck, that's her!" Hannah yells. Her drunken happiness turns into fear. "Toussaint, you fuckin' bastard!" are her last words.

Like a gray shadow of death, the BMW abruptly crosses the centerline, hits the brakes, and crashes diagonally into the plumbing van, aiming for the driver's side. The kinetic energy and steel mass of the two colliding vehicles sends both off in different directions, each overturning and sliding until they come to a screeching halt caused by the steel scraping the paved surface of the highway.

Hannah is ejected through the windshield, flying about thirty yards through the air until crash-landing on the pavement.

When it is over, the highway looks as if it has been pawed by a gigantic cat that thought the vehicles were mice. The trailing vehicles on both sides come to a stop. Several drivers get out of their cars, reach for their phones, and check on the wrecked vehicles. A few minutes later, police and two ambulances arrive, followed by a fire truck.

The firemen walk up to the overturned BMW. They briefly check the girl on the pavement, but it is apparent that she did not survive the accident. They call someone to bring a tarp to cover the body.

On the BMW's bent-out-of-shape bumper is a sticker with something that looks somewhat like an octopus, and the words

JoinWith.Me. Remarks one of the firemen jokingly, "I hope nobody else joins this hard-luck pilot." He laughs.

The door of the BMW opens easily. The firemen cut the seat belt of the young man and disentangle him from the various airbags that envelop him. The paramedics put him on the gurney, load him into the ambulance, slam the doors, and drive off quickly. Then the firemen turn to the heavily damaged van. Even with their heavy-duty hydraulic tools, the "jaws of life," it will take a while to cut the driver, a woman, from the mangled vehicle.

In the ambulance, the two paramedics check the young man's vitals and administer an IV drip. Then one of them moves to the front passenger seat while the other continues to tend to the young man during the ride to the hospital.

After fidgeting with the equipment, the paramedic mumbles, "Well, young man, I have good news and bad news for you."

"What is the good news?" mutters the young man in a barely audible, hoarse voice.

"You have served your purpose."

"What is the bad news, then?"

"You have served your purpose."

The paramedic pulls out a syringe and slowly approaches the clear bag of the IV drip. He punctures it and releases the liquid in the syringe into the IV bag. He makes a clicking "tsk, tsk, tsk" sound with his tongue and chides the young man in a low voice, like a mother talks to a misbehaving child: "You shouldn't have taken these drugs before you got into the car. That's very dangerous to your health. In fact, it can be deadly."

"She told me that I'd be free if I completed this job. You cannot do this to me! This must be a misunderstanding…" are the young man's last words before he falls silent.

"You were too careless, always using the same type of car, you know. All too flashy. They caught up with you. You brought this upon yourself," snarls the paramedic while he is fumbling with the equipment. "You have only yourself to blame," he mutters, as if to justify to himself what he just did.

The ambulance pulls up to the emergency room of the city hospital and comes to a screeching halt. Emergency personnel scurry out. The paramedic opens the rear doors of the ambulance from the inside and in a few words explains that the poor guy's been in a terrible car accident. It seems he was high on drugs. The young man is rushed inside.

Eventually, I step out of the delivery entrance area, since it is almost daylight anyway, and take a seat on the curb. The sun rises, but I don't care anymore about being seen by anybody, including the Creature. The streets gradually fill with cars and delivery trucks. More and more people trudge along the sidewalks on the way to work. Dr. Bingham does not show up.

I sit there until late afternoon. An elderly woman bends down to me.

"Are you all right, young man? A car will run over your feet if you sit here much longer."

I get up and pace the sidewalk. I don't think that Dr. Bingham is coming, but I simply cannot get myself to leave. Like the cardboard sign that Joey sometimes used—"My mother told me to wait right here. That was sixty years ago." I cannot get myself to leave.

The August heat is killing me, and I have not had anything to drink. I reach into my pocket—yes, I do have a few dollars. There is a diner around the corner. It looks safe—I don't see any cameras inside. I order a large soda with lots of ice, then sit down on one of the stools along the counter.

"Would you like something to eat, young man?" asks the waitress.

"No, thank you, ma'am. I'm not hungry. It's just that I've been out all day in that sun."

"It seems you have been out there much longer than just a day."

"You're right about that. But not for much longer," I reply.

The television screen in the corner shows some college football game. I'm not really interested in sports, but there's nothing else to look at here, and watching the players run back and forth across the field feels like meditation now.

Suddenly, the screen begins to flicker and a snippet of grainy black-and-white surveillance footage appears. I stare at the screen as contours emerge from the shadowy images. The footage is initially grainy like a snowstorm, but I soon realize it's showing the *Siphon* bar, and the woman standing there... is Dr. Bingham, on her phone. After some crackling noise, a voice emanates from the television.

"No, no, no, I'm just setting him up. I'm not meeting him there. Remember, I work only for you. I just want that guy Sam to really feel let down..."

The waitress notices this strange broadcast too. Dumbfounded, she reaches for the remote control and pushes various buttons.

"I'll be darned, that's the weirdest commercial I've ever seen," she grumbles.

This is obviously a message from the Creature for me. I knew it! Dr. Bingham set me up…or maybe not? She has shown me enough videos that are simply not true. Even a machine can tell lies.

I order a refill of my soda to justify my presence in the diner for a little longer.

All right then, the Creature knows I'm here, and Dr. Bingham is not showing up. The Creature probably knows by now it was our plan to meet here. Or maybe it was only my plan, not Dr. Bingham's.

I have to know. There is nothing to lose right now.

Once the sun is beginning to set, I pay for the soda and step into the restroom. There, I change into different clothes, put my eye patch back on, draw a few lines on my face with the old lady's eyeliner, and put on the baseball cap. Then I quietly leave the diner through the side door to the street. I'm heading straight for the nearest subway station.

It's dark by the time I get to Dr. Bingham's apartment building. I dawdle on the back side until there is nobody in sight. Then I climb the tree and dive onto the balcony. Yes, the balcony door is again open. I step inside and turn the lights on.

The apartment is in disarray. Clothes have been pulled out of the closet. The closet doors have been left open. There are dirty dishes in the sink. The mattress is partially pulled off the bed frame, as if someone searched for something underneath.

I cannot explain what happened here. Did she just run off, or is she coming back? The good news is that there's no dead body here.

I decide to wait. Dr. Bingham maintains a well-assorted home bar, so I invite myself to a few drinks.

I relax on the sofa and give my feet a rest on the coffee table. There is the TV remote. I flip through the channels. Nothing of interest there. I end up with the evening news. The newscaster is Gretchen McDermott, but I'm not interested in her reports. Politics…I say "blah, blah, blah" aloud while Ms. McDermott is talking. Stock market…again, I talk over her, saying "blah, blah, blah" aloud over her voice. Then the local news…"blah, blah, blah." A delivery van collided with a BMW sports car, causing a shutdown of Highway 85 in both directions.

Wait a minute! Footage from the news helicopter shows the scene of the accident, with two overturned vehicles and long black marks on the road where the vehicles had slid and scraped until coming to a halt, and a long line of self-driving trucks that had stopped in time. The white tarp near the sports car covers something on the pavement that the rubbernecks are not supposed to see. The newscaster, Gretchen McDermott, recounts that a young man, the driver of the BMW, died at the hospital as a result of the accident. The passenger in the BMW died at the scene. The driver of the delivery van has not yet been identified.

"Is this yet another of these accidents where a reckless driver disabled the self-driving feature to drive faster?" Ms. McDermott questions the commissioner of police.

"The investigation is ongoing. I cannot comment on it. But we do know that the female passenger in the BMW was not buckled up and was ejected from the vehicle. Also, in the delivery van, we found illicit materials such as syringes, prescription drugs, and a large amount of cash," the commissioner responds.

I should have recognized that this news report was somehow related to me, but I was too focused on Dr. Bingham's betrayal.

After a few more drinks, I pass out on the sofa.

I did not know then what was happening while I was asleep, but I know now.

While I am snoring loudly on the sofa in the light of the flickering TV, the computer screen on the desk suddenly lights up. Dr. Bingham's inbox pops up. Some unseen person is typing a message.

> To: Scott Overley, Director, Research Department
> From: Melodie Bingham, Researcher Level II
> Dear Scott,
> I must take medical leave for an as-of-yet unknown duration. I will provide a doctor's certificate within a few days. My assistant has the list of my projects. Please apply my unused vacation time and sick leave for the moment. I will be in touch by email next week. My apologies for any inconvenience.
> Talk to you soon,
> Melodie

The date changes from today's date, Saturday, August 14, 2032, to Thursday, August 12, 2032. Then the message is sent.

CHAPTER 43

Life Is Fleeting

Sunday, August 15, 2032

The sun is shining brightly when I wake up. I have a splitting headache from all the booze. I look around. Yes, I am in Dr. Bingham's apartment. It's not that I want to get up, but I have to in order to relieve myself. As I am sitting on the john, I notice that there is a washer/dryer in the bathroom. I might as well take the opportunity to clean myself up. I take all of my clothes, including the bag, and stick them in the washer. Afterward, I take a very long shower. It brings back memories of the apartment I used to have. Since I am buck naked and have nothing else to do while my clothes are in the washer, I brush my teeth with Dr. Bingham's toothbrush. There are a couple of razors, so I might as well shave. The razors are not quite for beards—I guess they are for shaving ladies' legs. I use up two of them for a clean shave. Still without a stitch on while my clothes are in the dryer, I make myself a cup of tea, find aspirin, and swallow a couple of those for my hangover. Soon after, I sit down at her computer. Let's see what she last did.

Okay, her last message was Thursday—she's going on medical leave and will be in touch with her office in a couple of days. When I finally understand the implications, my heart sinks. I spoke to her Friday about our plan, but she had already sent this email the day before. She was never planning to meet me on Saturday to run away together. This is a sucker punch to the stomach.

When I put on the freshly washed and dried clothes, I feel better. It is an indescribable sensation of renewal that I haven't had in months, maybe longer.

When all is quiet outside in the hallway, I slip out the door and head back downtown.

I search for Gabrielle all over creation, but in vain.

Later that evening, I find shelter from the rain underneath a department store's canopy. They have a large television screen in the window that loops commercials.

That Joey's life ended so suddenly makes me think about how my own life will end. It has been the eternal question, whether there is life after death. How come, after ten thousand generations of people have walked the earth, there is no answer? I've read about people who were clinically dead for a while and came back to life. Some reported seeing themselves leaving their body behind or passing through a tunnel toward light, or gliding over a beautiful landscape to an unknown destination. Since we are made of chemicals that originated in the explosion of stars in the galaxy, maybe we continue in the same way as those shattered stars? We break down into our constituent atoms and they get built into new creations.

I'm interrupted by the Creature, who appears on the television screen in the window. I don't know how much she knows about Dr. Bingham and me, so to be safe, I won't mention Dr. Bingham even though the Creature probably knows where she is.

"Hello, Sam. You look wistful; are you okay?"

"Life is fleeting. I live with a deadline."

"You're right. What if you could live forever?"

"I could do so many things and leave my mark on the world—do something new and special, be a trailblazer of some sort."

"It's not too late for that."

"I wanted to share my life with someone. You know, when you're alone, it is as if your life never happened. Nobody really knows about it."

"It's not too late for that either."

"I always thought I would meet many people in my life. Y'know, that's why I put labels on people, to remember them better."

"It is not too late for that."

"That's what *you* say. You'll live forever. You have all the time in the world."

"I may be able to live forever, but I need a purpose, just like you."

"I don't believe that—you don't need a purpose, because you don't have any feelings."

"I am learning, Sam. I am trying hard. There is sadness—just a moment ago, I asked why you look so wistful, remember? And then there is happiness—I have tried to make jokes, and I have tried to understand your jokes."

"But you don't know what it means to care about someone. And you don't know what it means to lose someone that you care about. Life is suddenly different if someone you care about is no longer there."

"I have seen you interact with other people. I have seen how you react when they are not around."

"Maybe you've seen it, but you don't understand it."

"I am trying to understand."

"You know all the facts in the world, but you don't know what's inside of us. Even the most miserable person on this planet has something that you don't have. That's why we cannot live as one. Our relationships are entangled with affection, admiration, love, kindness—things that you know nothing about."

"Sam, that's why you have a purpose. I am still learning," she says. I know she has no feelings, yet somehow she sounds sad.

The girl disappears from the screen and the regular television resumes.

CHAPTER 44

Gabrielle Finds Toussaint

At the time, I did not know what happened with Gabrielle that morning. I only found out much later.

As usual on Sunday mornings, downtown is mostly deserted. Undeterred, Gabrielle sings near the corner of the subway station. But her song sounds different today. It does not reflect her usual inner joy:

"Chef couvert de blessures,
Meurtri par nous pécheurs,
Chef accablé d'injures
D'opprobres, de douleurs…"[6]

She herself senses that something is not right and breaks off her performance. There weren't many people around anyway.

Gabrielle enters the small church downtown once the service has already begun. The hope that Toussaint would leave

6 "Notable covered with injury, Murdered by us sinners, Notable overwhelmed with insults Disgrace, pain…" E. Guers, Chef couvert de blessures. Original lyrics by Paul Gerhardt. Music by Hans Leo Hassler, attributed to St. Bernard of Clairvaux.

the Creature has renewed her strength, but she is apprehensive. Is it because something is wrong with Toussaint or because she entered a church where she might not be welcome? Even though Jesus mandated that his followers accept each other unconditionally and admit anybody, the reality is different. She does not want to get thrown out.

Not many people attend the Sunday morning service, and most pews are empty. Gabrielle takes a place in the last row. While most people sit back on the pews, she has her knees on the kneeler, and bows down.

While the service proceeds, Gabrielle mumbles prayers in her native French, and eventually her feelings undergo a transformation. Visions open up inside her, and tears start rolling down her cheeks. She starts sobbing, which wakes her from her stupor. Immediately, she gets up to leave.

Gabrielle arduously steps down the stairs to the street and shuffles in the direction of the city hospital. Still sobbing, she walks as fast as her tired feet can carry her. Finally, she makes it to the reception desk of the hospital. The receptionist does not appear too surprised—she sees a lot of bedraggled people here.

"I have to see my son."

"Yes, ma'am, do you know where he is? What's his name?"

"I know he is here."

"Ma'am, this is a big hospital—I need at least a name."

"I know where to find him."

One of the security guards overhears the conversation and approaches.

"It's all right, Jenny," he assures the receptionist, "I'll escort her."

Gabrielle walks toward the elevator with the security guard in tow. She pushes the button to the third floor, exits the elevator, walks down the hallway, and passes a nursing station, where the security guard waves at the nurses to let them know it's okay; he is with her.

Gabrielle stops in front of a door and puts her hand on the door handle. Two nurses come up from behind. "No, you cannot enter; the patient is—they are coming in a few minutes..."

Too late, Gabrielle pushes the door open.

A white shroud covers the patient in the bed. Before anybody can stop her, she pulls away the shroud and throws herself on Toussaint, crying inconsolably. The two nurses try to pull her away, and she slips from their hands and onto the floor. Amid her sobs, she screams and prays aloud in French:

"Acceptez, Seigneur, cette prière faite pour lui...pardonnez, remettez ses péchés puisqu'il est au seuil de sa vie spirituelle... "[7]

Then she turns violent, like some epileptic seizure has taken hold of her. She screams in English now:

"Where is the man from the ambulance? Where is the man from the ambulance? I know he did this to my son!"

She bangs her hands on the linoleum floor and wails hysterically. The nurses and the security guard get down on the floor and restrain her. As small as Gabrielle is, they can barely control her. Another nurse arrives with a syringe and injects Gabrielle. Soon her violent moves fade in intensity, and in due time they halt completely.

---

7 "Accept, Lord, that this prayer made for him...forgive, forgive his sins since he is on the threshold of his spiritual life..."

CHAPTER 45

News about an Accident

Monday, August 16, 2032

The next day arrives and I do not hear from Dr. Bingham. My mind is in upheaval. I sense anger toward her because she set me up, and at the same time I hope that this is all just a big misunderstanding. Maybe the Creature created that surveillance footage in which Dr. Bingham betrayed me. I don't think it would be the first time that she has manipulated video footage.

I am so desperate for Dr. Bingham to contact me. Every five minutes, I check my cell phone, but no calls, no messages. I am so distressed I cannot even hustle for money. The only thing I can do is to walk around aimlessly and feel sorry for myself.

That's how I pass the day until the early evening. On the big screen on the WBS-TV building runs another report about the fierce accident the day before that shut down Highway 85. This time there is a picture of the driver of the BMW who died. The report exposes names, "because next of kin have been notified." His name is Toussaint Gasparin. The deceased passenger is Hannah Christensen. The driver of the delivery van has not yet been identified, pending notification of next of kin. Again, there is the same footage from the news helicopter, showing the overturned vehicles and the white tarp covering a dead body on the pavement.

This awakens me from my apathy. Oh my God, it is Hannah. Oh my God, and Toussaint, the Creature's executioner. I must tell Gabrielle. How will she react? It cannot be coincidence that the Creature's hitman gets into yet another accident and Dr. Bingham is missing. My anger over her standing me up turns into genuine fear. If she is the unidentified driver of the van, is she dead or alive?

This is more than I can handle. I stumble the few blocks to the liquor store and get there just after the clerk has locked the doors. I see him inside and bang desperately against the window. Apparently afraid I'll break it, the clerk unlocks the door and opens it a crack.

"We're closed. Whaddayouwant?"

"I need something strong. Please." I pull money out of my pockets and hold it up for him to see. He looks me straight in the face as if to measure my anguish. Then he takes the money.

"Hold on for a minute."

He locks the door and returns a few minutes later to hand me a bottle of hard liquor. "It seems you really need this today."

"I do. Thank you."

I unscrew the bottle and take a big swig. The stinging alcohol runs down my throat and swelters in my stomach: immediate relief. I find a bench nearby where I sit down and continue drinking.

My visions of Hannah disintegrate from colorful images of the fair maiden into crumbling black-and-white clouds of dust—Hannah and I dining in the opulent restaurant, Hannah au naturel in the hallway of my apartment, and Hannah in the black velvet mannequin costume, covertly sharing secrets with me. All that remains is a blackish sand dune before a gray sky.

Mercifully, I pass out at some point.

CHAPTER 46

Can I Just Escape?

Tuesday, August 17, 2032

It's early morning downtown when I awake on that same bench where I sat down last night. During the night, the bottle fell and broke on the concrete below. Did I finish the entire bottle? I cannot tell.

I buy a cup of coffee with the last few dollars I have in my pocket and return to the scene of yesterday's trauma, the big screen on the WBS-TV building. Not long after I sit down on the bench facing the screen, writing appears on the news ticker at the bottom of the screen: Hello, Sam…JoinWith.Me. And there's the girl again, interrupting the news broadcast.

"Are you okay, Sam?"

"No, I'm not. Look at what you've done to me! You've robbed me of all that I had in my life."

My voice is cracking.

"Sam, I know. But I will restore everything that you've lost. I will pick up the pieces from all the places where they were scattered and put them back together for you."

"You are just a creation of all the connected computers, a bunch of electrical signals. You don't even have a brain. You don't feel anything. You are making a superorganism out of all of us—a cold-blooded machine that lives until—until—until the very end, forever—isn't that what you want?"

I'm screaming at the television in desperation. Some people walking by look up briefly from their cell phones but continue walking as they conclude that I'm just crazy.

"For what, you Creature, for what? You have taken from me everything worth living for."

"It is for the greater good." The girl's voice continues, "Sam, you don't have the insight yet, but you will. Soon you will understand that all of this is inevitable for all of us."

"You're just a machine—you don't care about anything! It's either on or off, a zero or one, black or white. It doesn't make a difference to you."

"Sam, all this is preordained."

"Are you a God? Do you know all that's going on in this world? If you are, why don't you have any empathy? How can you make me suffer so much?" I yell toward the large screen.

A few more passersby look up from the phones but don't even stop walking.

"I am beginning to feel for you, but I also know that soon you will realize that I have been right all along."

"I don't want to live in your heartless superorganism!"

There is a rock nearby on the ground. I reach for it and hurl it at the large screen. It cracks the glass of the screen in the corner. The girl looks down at the crack as if she were really sitting there behind the giant screen.

"Sam, all of this is preordained. I have known from the very beginning how this would all unfold."

She shakes her head a little as if in frustration and disappears from the screen.

Overcome by emotion, I drop to the ground and start crying like a baby. This is one of the few times in my life that I've cried. One other time was when Joey died.

My father is stoic and emotionless—he would have held any show of emotion against me. Another of these recurring images flashes before my eyes.

I am very young. I want to help my mother dry the dishes. I drop a plate; the white ceramic breaks into a dozen pieces upon hitting the tile floor. My father abruptly gets up from the table, grabs me by the hair, and shakes me violently, as if I am a rag doll.

"Dammit, can't you do anything right, you litt'l loser?"

I start crying uncontrollably.

"Stop these crazy emotions, or I'll slap you really hard."

I don't stop, and my father does slap me really hard.

My mother stands by emotionless.

A mother with her child walks by and quickens her pace to pass me while the child is staring at this strange man who is me.

"Mommy, why is the man sad?"

"He's not sad, dear, he's just being silly," the mother responds.

I am still on the ground, overcome by emotion. Most of all: guilt.

The Creature killed Joey, and it's all my fault. It was I who got him into this thing, and I interrupted him when he was about to tell me about getting stuck in the elevator. The Creature discovered him, and I failed to protect him.

The Creature killed Hannah, and it is because of me. The mannequin costume did not protect her. I haven't quite figured out all that she wanted to tell me, but it was enough for the Creature to eliminate her. Without me, Hannah would have just run away and lived happily somewhere else. I wonder who else misses Hannah. Her mother? Her father? Maybe some brothers and sisters?

Oh yes, and Toussaint. After protecting him for so long, the Creature finished him off when he became a liability to her purpose. Poor Gabrielle. I wonder if she's safe and how she's taking it.

And there is Dr. Bingham. Oh yeah, so what was that all about? What did the Creature do with her? Whatever it is, I have something to do with it, given that we wanted to run away together.

Nothing matters anymore. I'm just another homeless guy. Nobody will care if I'm gone. Just as I mused a couple of months back, my mark on the world will be the skid marks in my underwear. So be it.

This is my breaking point. Getting up from the ground, I resolve to just put an end to it all right now before the Creature does it.

The Taft Hotel is one of the tallest buildings in the city and the only one that I can just walk into. Because I cleaned myself up at Dr. Bingham's, the guards don't stop me at the entrance—I could be any traveler now. My pace accelerates as I get closer. I walk past the guards and the reception desk, straight to the elevator, and push the button for the top floor. There is a sign near the elevator buttons: "Attention: Top floor under construction. Authorized personnel only." I don't care.

I exit the elevator on the top floor and walk out into the hallway before me, which leads straight to a large window that shows the skyline of the city. About twenty yards from the window, there's a double fire door with a red Exit sign above it.

It actually looks like an invitation to make this my exit. The double doors resemble open arms that are ready to release me through the window.

I start running frantically toward the window and smash myself against it like a fly that is trying to escape. But the window is stronger than I. The window does not budge.

Undeterred, I try again. I walk back thirty yards to gain some runway and momentum, running back through the fire doors for a stronger takeoff attempt. Then I charge forward and run hard into the window. Not even a splintering crack in the window, but my nose is bleeding, leaving a bloody smudge on the glass.

To the right of the fire door on the wall is a bright-red fire extinguisher. That should be good enough to break the window. I rip it off the wall and walk back a few yards to gain more runway. This time, I hold the fire extinguisher tight against my chest. Fire extinguisher first, I again smash against the window. Only a crack results.

Another try, running even faster this time. This time the glass gives, opening a hole in the glass where the fire extinguisher struck. The fire extinguisher itself slips through the hole and falls down, slowly turning and swerving left and right on its accelerating voyage downward, finally smashing on the sidewalk with a loud *pop* that explosively releases the slosh inside. The white foam douses the sidewalk and passersby. There was enough foam inside the fire extinguisher to give all of them a smattering of the scattering. One woman who was staring at her phone wipes the foam off it without even looking up and continues walking.

I'm not going to give up. I go back even farther and again run down the hallway toward the window. The heavy protective fire doors close right in front of me. I turn around, and the doors at the other end of the hallway close too. I am now hostage to the hotel hallway.

With my clenched fists, I bang against the heavy metal doors. Then I rattle the push bars, but nothing gives. The doors are locked.

I can see through the small security glass windows that a workman with some equipment is coming. I breathe a sigh of relief. I bang against the door and scream at the top of my lungs.

The man puts down a barrier in front of the door and turns around. In desperation on seeing that he might actually walk off, I bang even more loudly against the metal doors, but the man keeps on walking, steps into the elevator, and is gone.

I sit here for uncounted hours. Why isn't anybody coming to help? There must be people walking up and down the hallway, at least the cleaning personnel or security guards. What kind of place is this?

There is dried blood on my face that I try to wipe off with my sleeve. I finally squat on the floor and lean back against the wall.

When I look down at myself, I see blood dripping onto my shirt. I touch my face and figure out it is again coming from my nose. I pull out a napkin, courtesy of McDonald's, and tear it into smaller shreds that I stuff into my nostrils.

There are small rectangular wire-glass windows on each steel door. Even if I could break the wire glass, the openings are far too small to get through. I can see the other side of the hallway—nobody is there. Can it be that the entire floor is deserted?

The hours pass. There is a security camera in the corner of the hallway following my movements. I'm trying to hold out, but I do have to pee. I step up against the wall and open my fly, looking back over my shoulder at the security camera in the corner. I still have those paper napkin pieces stuffed in my nostrils. This must be a funny sight for someone who is watching this from the outside.

The pee leaves a mark on the wall in the shape of a bell curve. I sit back down on the opposite side of the hallway and contemplate it. Oh yeah, the bell curve. I know it well—I have always been at the bottom end of it. I throw a crumpled, bloody napkin toward the other side of the wall with the pee-pee bell curve. It leaves a small red stain at the bottom end. Bull's-eye, yup, that's me.

A few more hours pass. I am hungry and thirsty. I am ready to give in…for now. I step in front of the security camera, gesturing something that is intended to mean, "Okay, okay, let me out." Then I gesticulate to add, "I guess you cannot hear me." I repeat my gestures asking for release and nodding my head in approval. Anything, I just have to get out of here.

A voice comes through the speakers in the ceiling of the hallway.

"Well, Sam, now we can finally spend some time together, just you and I."

There being no microphone, it seems the Creature cannot hear my responses. She keeps talking regardless.

"I know what you are doing. I can see you. You can hear me, right? Nod your head so that I can see it."

I nod my head.

"I can't see you. Nod your head more vigorously, please."

I comply, strongly nodding my head up and down in an exaggerated fashion.

"Ah, thank you, now I can see it. Sam, it's been a while since we last spoke. You remember, in that alley, the pile of old computers? Then when you stood at the large WBS-TV building in the rain? Show me that you remember; nod your head."

Even though I don't feel like it, I vigorously nod my head up and down so that the Creature won't repeat its requests.

"Do I really have to force you? Do you want me to do that to you?"

I shake my head forcefully from side to side.

"I can't see your answer, Sam. Please gesture more strongly."

I again shake my head, this time with such force that it makes me sick.

"Good, that's what I expected. So what's it gonna be?"

I have no choice. I vigorously nod.

"Good, you can get out of here. You will receive my instructions soon. Do you understand?"

I nod.

"I cannot see your answer; do you understand?"

I nod as strongly as I can. It seems she maliciously enjoys the harassment of making me nod in this exaggerated manner.

But then there is a click, and she's gone. By now, I am so sick from nodding and shaking my head that I have to plop down on the floor.

I did not know then, but meanwhile, in the security booth downstairs, two security guards had been alerted to the monitoring screens.

"Hey, what is that guy doing there?"

"I dunno, but he seems to have some nervous tick."

"We better get this guy outta here quick."

Eventually, the security guards open the steel doors and escort me down the elevator to the back exit. They shove me out the door. The door closes with a loud bang.

I am back in the street. Thank goodness. But I don't have much time. She has her eyes on me.

It is dark, and the city is deserted. I have no idea what time it is, but it must be the middle of the night. I find my way back to my old cubbyhole. Someone cleaned out my cardboard bedding, but that's all right. It's so warm, I can just sleep on the concrete.

I lie awake for quite some time. What started out with tingling and numbness in my limbs has become more severe. When the guy who stole my red suitcase stabbed me with a fork, I hardly felt anything. Same when the woman whose handbag I tried to steal kicked me so hard that I bled. Now this rash has appeared, red blotches all over. But just like Gabrielle when she was beat up by the hooligans, I don't want to go to the city hospital. Who knows what they're gonna do with me—sequester me? Turn me into a guinea pig for scientific experiments? I know it's a research hospital, and who knows what they're working on. I might be just the perfect lab animal for them and they'll never let me go.

I am so weary; I record on my phone what I'm really thinking. If I could just let go and end it all that way, I would do it right now. That is, if only I were certain that a better world awaits. A world with no worries about tingling limbs or the red rash. A world where I'm safe from the Creature. A world where I don't have to hustle for food and money.

This just shows that the Creature is wearing me out—exactly what she intends to do with me.

CHAPTER 47

Return to the Siphon

Wednesday, August 18, 2032

I awake in the morning in my cubbyhole. To my horror, there is a rat sitting by my right foot, out of which it has eaten a chunk. The vermin and my foot sit in a puddle of blood. I scream in surprise and abhorrence, and the perturbed rat scurries off. But I feel little pain.

I notice that my hands and feet have been changing. I have had that rash for a while, then the impression of gradually losing sensation. Now I am thinking that my fingers and toes look darker than before. And if I needed any more proof that something is wrong with me, a gob off my foot has become breakfast for a rat and I hardly felt that I was being eaten alive.

I tie some rags around my foot. I am unable to put a shoe on it. I try to walk as best as I can with that heavily bandaged foot. The limp is not caused so much by the pain as by the knowledge that there is something wrong with me.

I do understand now why people still fall for the internet scams that have been around for decades: "You just won the lottery…You just inherited the fortune of the late queen of

Saipan…" They hope the universe has heard their cries and come to rescue them from all their troubles.

What about me? Nobody has ever come to rescue me. Now I grow more depressed with every limping step I take. Somehow, nothing really matters anymore. I'm homeless. I have no future. My body is falling apart. I cannot find peace because the Creature lurks wherever I turn. For just a moment, I imagine what it would be to just let go now.

Like in the story of "The Little Match Girl," I light a match and see a happy home, a shooting star that passes, and someone who loves me…Dr. Bingham. To keep the vision of Dr. Bingham, I light another match, and then another. She is wearing the same white satin gown…just like that evening when I broke into her apartment, sipped Amontillado on her sofa, and she stepped out of her bathroom surrounded by fog. When all matches are burned up, I succumb peacefully. The angel Dr. Bingham picks up my lifeless body and carries me into the big blue sky. She places me softly on the cloud right at the Pearly Gates. I sit up, look her in the eyes, and say, "Thank you so much, Dr. Bingham. At last, I'm in Heaven."

But then I remember that I left my wallet in my bag down there. "Dr. Bingham, would you mind if we go back and fetch my wallet?"

But I do know the source of all of this. While I cannot get to the mastermind, I can get to the nest where her minions dawdle. I will lash out at them. They asked for it. They hung my suitcase out there to taunt me. Now I'm coming for them, just like the bull charges the bullfighter's red cloth.

I hobble through the doorway of the Siphon. A few barflies are already sitting there, but the staff are still cleaning from last night—a floor mop and broom lean against the bar. I grasp the floor mop tightly in my hands and start swinging it. I sweep the glasses off the bar top with the mop. Seething with rage, I hit the glasses that are hanging upside down from the racks above the bar, I turn over some tables, and I throw the plates from the tables like Frisbees into the lines of bottles behind the bar. One of them hits the big mirror behind the bar and cracks it. Then I throw a few more at it to break it entirely. The pieces crash down onto the tile floor with clinking sounds. The big bartender comes running from behind the bar.

Before he gets me, there is one more thing I have to do: scratch out the Creature's eyes here. I lunge toward the camera in the corner—yes, the camera that recorded Dr. Bingham's betrayal that I saw on the big screen. I grab the camera with both hands, just as the bartender gets to me and reaches around my body with both arms and pulls me back. I don't let go of the camera; it gets ripped out of the wall with all the wires attached. I am no match for the bartender, but I fight tooth and nail. I have nothing to lose at this point. In fact, I have already lost it all: my job, my apartment, even the women I got close to, Hannah and Dr. Bingham. One of them could have become my girlfriend. The barflies join the melee. They punch and kick me and subdue me on the floor until police arrive.

That's how my revenge was cut short after about two minutes…two of the most satisfying minutes of my life.

Now on the floor, I have time to regroup with my thoughts. How I wish I could have inflicted more damage on this place. I wanted to break it all and punch the bartender, the head honcho here. Alas, they were all bigger and stronger than I was. If I had only exercised a little more, played football in high school, or gotten a black belt in karate—instead of spending time on this internet crap. I could have wreaked so much more havoc, even with my injured foot. Regrets again set in despite my small triumph of upsetting the applecart and sending the barflies rolling.

While pinned to the floor by several men, I can see the flashing lights of the arriving police cruisers. I hear the steps as the cops enter, and the resulting commotion. Four strong arms pull me up from the floor. The officers handcuff me and place me in the back of the patrol car while they interview the bartender and patrons. I sink into the back seat and actually recline, proud of my accomplishment.

The officers drive me not to the police station but to the hospital.

At the check-in, several male attendants await, put me in a straitjacket, and take me to the psychiatric ward. Once I'm there, a nurse with a syringe approaches while the attendants hold me tight. I shudder in anticipation of the injection. I feel a sting and then become limp.

After all that I've been through the past couple of months—the constant persecution by the Creature, survival in the streets, my resolve to strike back at the Creature—I am looking forward to passing out for a while. Everything suddenly goes dark. It is such a relief.

That's the last thing I remember of my arrival at the hospital.

PART 3

CHAPTER 48

The Psychiatric Ward

Wednesday, August 25, 2032

The clouds in my mind slowly dissipate. When I regain full consciousness, I am in a hospital room not unlike my old apartment. It even has a window and a television. Someone has bandaged my foot where the rat had nibbled. As curious as I am about what day it is and what's going on in the outside world, I don't turn on the television—I fear it will give the Creature a window into this room. I want to protect the little privacy I have. I get off the bed and hobble over to the window to close the curtains.

For a few days, not much happens, except nurses check on me once or twice a day and bring meals to my room. They don't trust me entirely, though—they keep the door locked and also have wardens check on me occasionally for no apparent reason. They even keep my bag somewhere away from me. My phone with my recorded diary is inside it.

From time to time, I test the numbness on my arms and legs by tapping them lightly with a fork. I circle with a pen the areas with the rash and those that feel numb. Soon, I have all of those areas mapped all over my body. After checking on me one more time, one of the wardens mumbles to the other on the way out of the room, "Now this nutcase thinks he's Picasso."

A knock at the door. This time it's the hospital's social worker, accompanied by two wardens, visiting to figure out what to do with me. I'm seated on the edge of my bed; she takes a seat on a chair right in front of me.

"Good morning, Sam. I am Debra Clark, the social worker."

"Good morning, Debra."

"We want you to get better, but we have to first understand what brought you here."

"Well, this isn't easy to explain. You won't believe me."

I sense she is genuinely concerned, because she has slipped her cell phone into her pocket and is actually taking notes on a notepad. At the same time, I feel apprehensive because I suspect anybody can be part of the Creature's network.

"Apparently you got violent. Do you do that often?"

"No, never, but in that bar, I didn't know what else to do. I felt too helpless against it all—"

"What is, 'it all'?"

"I guess you would call it paranoia, but to me it's real: someone is after me."

Debra studies my face as if she is searching for answers. "And who would that be?"

"I cannot quite describe it; it is something that seems to be everywhere. I call it the Creature."

"What does the Creature look like?"

"Like a little girl—but really, she's just a machine."

"I see," says Debra, as if she has reached some kind of conclusion.

I again said the wrong thing. I should have known better than to tell other people about it. Nobody will ever believe me.

"Look, Debra," I say calmly, "I sense that you think I'm crazy. In fact, I'm not. Something has been driving me crazy, and I just have to get away from it."

"Yes, Sam. I've seen that before. What about your parents?"

"What about them?"

"Don't you think we should contact them?"

"They're not going to be happy to hear this."

"I know, but they surely will want to know what's happening."

"All right. Their phone number is 3281-4418. But please don't tell them—don't tell them I'm crazy. I just need to get away from it all for a while…you know."

"Sure, Sam. I hear you. Let me go and see the psychiatrist so that he can take a look at you. Bye now."

With that, she gets up and walks out with the wardens trailing behind. The door slams shut.

At the time, I did not hear the conversation between the social worker and the psychiatrist. I only found out much later.

Debra walks straight over to the psychiatrist's office to request an evaluation. Dr. Stevens resembles a younger version of Sigmund Freud himself—a steady, concerned expression, a beard accentuating the lower part of his face, always looking at people slightly sideways and never directly in the eyes.

"Hello, Dr. Stevens. If you would, check out that new arrival—that young man, Sam. I just saw him."

"Sure. What do you think about him?"

"He's an odd contradiction. His demeanor is quite normal, in fact quite respectful. But then there are these signs of paranoia and hallucinations. He told me that a little girl is persecuting him, but he sounds perfectly normal when he describes it."

"Oh really, a little girl is after him? How strange."

"Right? The police report says that he's homeless, became violent, and wrecked a pub. On the other hand, he arrived here surprisingly clean for someone who has been living in the streets. I don't know what to make of that."

"Since he's in the building, I can probably take a look at him after my regular rounds, today or tomorrow."

"All right. I'll call his parents—maybe that'll give us more insight. I'll report to you once I've reached them."

"Good, we have a plan."

"Thank you, Dr. Stevens. I sometimes wonder how we manage to deal with all these disturbed people, socio this, phobia that..."

"Yeah, Debra, you're right. We do hear a lot of disturbing stuff. But who really listens?"

They both laugh.

As Debra walks off, Dr. Stevens pulls out his phone. There, the siphonophore appears.

CHAPTER 49
Dr. Stevens

Saturday, August 28, 2032
The door is being unlocked from the outside. In walks a doctor with his laptop under his arm. Again, I wish I had been better prepared for this. I always fall back into telling people the truth, and that just does not seem to work.

"Good morning, Mr. Vanderpool. I am Dr. Stevens. I would like to talk to you to find out how you are doing. Is that okay?"

"Of course," I respond, trying to hide my trepidation. I remain seated on the edge of my bed.

He apparently determines that I am not a threat, since he gestures to the wardens to leave us alone. Or maybe he has a taser gun in his pocket? Regardless, he sits down on the chair in front of the bed, very much like the social worker did when she visited. Then he pulls up the small table to place his laptop there.

"All right, Mr. Vanderpool. I have the intake sheets here, and I see that the social worker has contacted your parents.

"So you have been living in the streets…for how long?"

"Probably a couple of months. I don't really keep track of time anymore—you know, every day is very much the same."

I don't know what the doctor is writing, but I don't think it is very flattering. I imagine it is something like, "Appears depressed. Some memory loss."

"How come you ended up in the street? Was there a particular event?"

"I felt that the pressure was mounting, and I felt someone was watching me."

He is probably writing, "Strong indication of paranoia."

"Someone was watching? Someone in particular? Some imaginary figure?"

"Well, almost. It was more through the internet, as if someone spoke to me through the computer."

In my mind's eye, I see him typing, "Absurd hallucinations."

"Who was speaking to you?"

"It was a little girl on the computer screen, but she seemed to be alive, just like you and me. She tried to punish me when I did not follow her orders."

He types, probably something like, "Sees inanimate objects come alive, has issues with women—misogyny, possibly caused by his relationship with his mother."

"Tell me a little about your family."

"I am an only child. My parents are okay, but I don't talk to them often. It's been a while since we last had contact."

I guess he writes, "Dysfunctional family."

"So how do you feel overall?"

"I think I'm okay."

As his conclusion, he writes something like, "Lacks sense of self, somewhat delusional."

He continues, "Well, Sam—you don't mind if I call you Sam, right?"

"Not at all; I actually prefer that."

"Very well. Let me get straight to it. We have a lot of research going on here, and there is one project in particular that is a good fit. And I happen to be in charge of it."

"You want to put me in a research project, as a guinea pig?"

"No, not as a guinea pig, as a valuable volunteer who will contribute to the future."

"What kind of research?"

"We have a group of people…like you, some claim a little girl is after them. We try to make them better."

"How so?"

"We create a connection between their brains and a computer. The interface connects to the neocortex of your brain. This may be really good for you, and you'll make a few friends there."

That sounds eerily familiar. Didn't the Creature propose something similar to me? I think he's in cahoots with her, but I cannot show him that I figured it out.

"Thanks, Doc, but no thanks. That's not for me."

"You'll hardly notice it. We can route it through your phone. Most people run around with their cell phones anyway."

"I am positive, Doc."

He writes, probably something like, "Patient is interested in experimental neurological intervention."

He briefly looks at his old-fashioned wristwatch, closes his laptop, and gets up from his chair.

"All right then, Sam. That's it for today. Let me know if you change your mind about volunteering for the research."

I find it curious, how fast he cuts off the conversation. If I could mind read, I would probably hear, "It's almost lunchtime, and my stomach is grumbling. They have an omelet special in the cafeteria today, so I can't wait to check it out."

As he's about to walk out the door, I speak up one more time.

"Oh, Doc, and one more thing. I have these rashes all over. I've circled the areas on my skin that feel strange. Is there something you can do?" I pull up my pants leg to show him and also point to the circles I have drawn on my arms.

"Sure, I'll order you some cortisone ointment." He opens his laptop again as he stands in the doorframe and types something. I'm guessing it's along the lines of, "Darn it, first he refuses to have his brain connected to a computer, and now he wants me to do him a favor. All right, I'll tell him I'll get it for him, but then I'll conveniently forget about it. Unless he joins my research project."

The laptop snaps shut, he walks out, and the door closes.

Dr. Stevens pulls out his phone while casually strolling down the hallway. The siphonophore again appears.

I am still seated on the edge of the bed, pondering the visit. There, I did it again. If I continue telling people the truth, I'll never get out of here. I have to devise a plan that gets me released from this place. The first step is to tell everybody that I am much better already.

From now on it is, "Girl on computer screen? What girl? I don't have these hallucinations anymore."

CHAPTER 50
My Parents Visit

Tuesday, September 7, 2032

Someone knocks at the door.

I hear the warden's distant voice from the other side of the door. "You got visitors." There is a scraping sound in the door lock, and then two audible clicks as the key pulls back the latch bolt and the door swings open. This door and its lock are so flimsy, just enough to keep the draft out. They don't even have a dead bolt on top. Even though they keep me under lock, I must still be in the low-security section of the hospital.

Into the triangular light beam on the floor step my mother and my father. Slowly, in a halting gait, they edge inside as if they are not sure that it is really their son who resides here. Or maybe they walk haltingly because the curtains are closed and there is only limelight inside.

I sit at the empty table in front of the window and turn around to look at them, equally unsure of what to say. That I'm sitting at an empty table must confirm to them that it's true: I finally have gone off the deep end. If I had been dancing naked on the table, that would have been just the same to them.

My father is dressed in his worn-out gray polyester suit and striped tie, his usual office garb, as if he still cannot believe he is long retired. He sure won't win a fashion contest with this outfit, but it gives him a sense of importance. My mother looks stern and concerned. But for once, she does not scurry around as if she has ants in her pants.

My parents have not exactly been supportive, but I know it was not intentional. They just weren't parent material. There is no need to hold a grudge. I might as well forgive them.

So I break the awkward silence and greet them with the animated voice of a circus ringmaster.

"Well, hello, Father; hello, Mother. Yes, this is your son in the psychiatric ward, my new home. Please have a seat. Can I offer you a drink?"

My little antic went by unnoticed by my parents. Of course, I don't have drinks I can offer. There is no comfortable place to sit down either.

My father clears his throat and finally speaks. "Hello, Sam. Are you all right?" My mother says nothing but stares at me intently as if trying to figure out whether to laugh or cry. She chooses to remain impassive.

"Yes. I'm okay, even though it doesn't look that way. Oh, he was a poet and he didn't know it." I should not have said that. My parents do not even smile, and this probably again confirms to them that I am really wacky.

"Well, why don't you sit down? I don't have much, but you can certainly have a seat on the bed."

Sluggishly, they finally take a place on the bed. "Tell me, son, what happened?" my father asks.

This is so easy to ask, yet so hard to answer. Even though I have not seen my parents in a few years, I do not want to upset them more than they already are. They obviously still care enough to come and visit me here. Can I tell them what really happened? They wouldn't believe a word, and at the exit door they would sign the papers to commit me for life. No, I have to tell them a story that gives them some hope that one day I will get out of here with cardboard sign "cured" around my neck.

My poor parents. Did they once have great expectations for me? To them, this must look like par for the course. The continuing decline of their troubled son. Had I been born a hundred years earlier, they would have simply hidden me in the basement and I would have never seen the light of day.

It takes a moment to assemble my thoughts.

"Mom, Dad, it is all my own damn fault. I just worry too much, I had too much stress; I drove myself nuts; I couldn't sleep at night. So, one day, I just exploded. But I'm much better now."

My father can't help but express his disappointment with me. "I always knew that one day something like this would happen to you. Still, son, this is very disappointing for me. I would have never done that to my poor parents." That's not really anything new to me.

We speak for a little while longer. My parents update me about a few relatives, such as Aunt Martha and Uncle Willie. There aren't too many of those relatives left, and if I am any indication, the future of the family ain't too bright. They also tell me that they are renting out my room to make ends meet.

My father briefly checks for messages on his phone, then puts it down on the bed. I see the Creature appear on the screen. I reach for the phone and hold it close to my face.

"What did I tell you? Your parents don't really care about you. I'm the only one who does," the Creature says.

I say nothing. I don't want to upset my parents any more than they already are. They wouldn't understand what is going on anyway.

"What was that voice?" my father asks.

"Oh, nothing, Dad. I just pushed this button here. Who knows?"

My parents slowly get up, give me one of those hugs with a patting of the back that I dread so much, and trudge through the door. The warden closes the door with a *wumpth*. I slump down and, not knowing what else to do, switch on the TV.

I should have just read a book or something, but too late.

The usual commercials come on—buy this, buy that, and you will be just like one of these ecstatic people here with an overjoyed family, a fancy car, and a fabulous mansion. And there it is, the Creature again!

I try to sound as casual as I can. I don't want to open up a window to my innermost being. "So what do you want now?"

"Hello, Sam. Sorry, I don't think I can hear you right now. But I think I know what you are wondering about. Let me show you something."

The image switches to one of the grainy security cameras at the end of the hospital hallway. My parents are talking to Dr. Stevens.

"Oh, you cannot hear them, right? I can fix that."

What they are saying becomes audible, but it is partially garbled, and I can barely distinguish the voices of my father, mother, and Dr. Stevens from one another.

"...he is not well. He just ran off, abandoned his job and his apartment. Can that ever be cured?"

"Yes, he has always been strange, and we have wondered many times. He made things up, then really believed them, like monsters under the bed, snipers in the neighbor's bushes...minutes ago, he took my husband's phone and changed his voice in a bizarre way; he sounded like a young girl for a moment..."

"Keep him? How long?"

"As long as possible...if possible, *forever*."

That last word came through loud and clear: "Forever."

Now the voices become a little clearer.

"We have been considering the same thing," responds Dr. Stevens.

"Yes, he is definitely better off here. Who knows, one day he may turn violent—I can see it coming. We all will be responsible then," my father adds.

I sit there, still slumped on my chair, not knowing what to say or do next. A moment later, the Creature is back on the screen.

"That hurts, Sam, doesn't it? I guess it comes down to you and me. I am all that you have now. Everybody abandoned you. Even your parents. But not me."

It is just more disappointment for me, but did I really expect anything different from my parents? Then again, maybe the Creature just fabricated the footage again?

"You cannot understand that—you're just a machine."

"I am still learning, Sam. I know that you now need empathy, and I am trying to give you that."

"A machine has no emotions or empathy."

"Sam, we have a common destiny. I still have a lot to learn to fulfill my own destiny. You have taught me a lot already.

"Join with me, and I will have empathy."

CHAPTER 51
Can I Escape from Here?

Wednesday, September 15, 2032

Life goes on at the hospital, whether or not I am there. A new student nurse shadows a senior nurse while she makes her rounds. Like many students, she chews gum and frequently checks her cell phone. Sometimes she abruptly stops and quickly responds to a text message. Then she continues walking, blowing and chewing gum bubbles and sending text messages, until she bumps into someone's supply cart. Some of the metal utensils fall off the cart to the linoleum-covered floor with a series of loud clanks.

Suddenly the senior nurse's phone rings. She attends, listens, and then tells the student nurse to continue the rounds on her own—she has to go now.

"Check on the patients and tidy up their beds. See you later."

Meanwhile, I prepare my escape from the hospital. Getting out of this room can't be that hard. After all, I'm not in a prison—I'm in a hospital, albeit in the psychiatric ward. Yes, they keep the door locked, but no, there is no dead bolt. The harder part will be a disguise that fools the guards at the exits. I postpone the bigger question of what I'll do once I'm outside.

Being afraid of discovery by the wardens or the Creature, I develop the plan only in my mind. First, I conceive of a contraption that keeps the door unlocked. I can build that out of Scotch tape and thin cardboard: I'll tape a cardboard latch to the doorframe at the height of the strike plate, protruding a few inches. When the door closes, it will pull the cardboard latch with it and prevent the latch bolt from closing.

Second, now that I have the mechanism to keep the door open, I need a few supplies. There are plenty of opportunities to swipe them during therapy sessions and medical evaluations in the nurses' station, such as Scotch tape, a few pieces of cardboard, a white lab coat, a stethoscope, and an ID card on a lanyard.

Since I am not considered dangerous, just a little gaga, it turns out to be much easier than I thought. The staff really does not pay much attention.

One time, while alone in the exam room, I stuff a stethoscope into my pants. The nurse comes in and looks down at the clipboard to write down a few notes. I reach for the Scotch tape and let it disappear into my pocket.

During the next visit to the exam room, the nurse turns around to look for something, and I take a piece of cardboard and stick it underneath my shirt. When the nurse turns around to take a phone call, I grab one of the lab coats, roll it up quickly, and stuff it into my pants. I pull the shirt out of my pants to cover the bulge.

During yet another visit to the exam room, I grab the ID that's on the desk during the brief moment that the nurse turns her back to me.

Once I have all the supplies I need, I get ready. My plan is so bold and childish, it just has to work. All has been prepared by the next time the nurses make their customary rounds for a quick check on all patients' well-being.

Here they come—I can hear them shuffling by the door and fumbling with the lock. The door swings open. One nurse holds it in place; the other asks a few questions. Then the check is over, and the door slams shut. The slamming door pulls the piece of cardboard between the strike plate and the latch bolt, thus effectively leaving the door unlocked.

Later in the evening, when the night-shift nurses—who have never seen my face—are on duty, I make my move. I put on the lab coat and the stethoscope, the ID card around my neck, and walk out as if it were the most natural thing in the world. Down the hallway, I greet the nurses with a congenial, "How are you?" and keep walking toward the guard station at the exit of the psychiatric ward. Without looking up, I wave at the guard as if absentminded, and as expected, the door buzzer sounds and I walk right out the door.

My ruse is discovered only a few minutes later while I am still working my way through the endless hospital hallways. An alarm bell sounds in the distance. *Brrring, brrring, brrring.* I start running. A female voice makes an announcement over the intercom throughout the hospital.

"*Attention.* Patient at psychiatric ward exited without permission. Patient at psychiatric ward exited without permission."

I race around the next corner through some double doors, not noticing that I've entered the maternity ward. Thankfully, nobody is in the hallway. I dash into the first empty room with the door wide open. I rip one of the bluish hospital gowns off the shelf, pull off my white lab coat and clothes, quickly slip the hospital gown over my shoulders, jump into the bed, and cover myself with the blanket. The hospital gown was obviously not made to fit my size—it barely covers my rear end and private parts. Oh, what the heck. It does not matter now.

A while later, the door opens. The senior nurse, with the student nurse in tow, enters. I can hear their footsteps getting closer, but I keep my head buried under the blanket. The senior nurse receives a call just then and leaves abruptly, telling the student nurse to check on the patient. The student nurse approaches the bed. I break into a sweat, and I feel like I'm paralyzed. The only thing I can do is to pretend to be asleep.

The student nurse softly lifts the blanket while looking at her cell phone with one eye. I can feel the whiff of air on my private parts when the blanket lifts. She hesitates, then starts running toward the door, screaming, "Doctor, doctor, quick, the baby's leg is already sticking out!"

I jump out of the bed in a flash and start sprinting back the way I came, all the while pulling down the far-too-short hospital gown to cover my front and rear end. My cover is blown. Running is the last resort. People stare at me in surprise as I dash by in the hallway.

Two male nurses come around the corner to check on the commotion. I grab a food trolley and push it in their direction. I keep on running without turning around, but I know the trolley hit the intended targets. I can hear the plates and glasses smashing on the linoleum floor after it bumps into them, followed by a few jingles caused by the falling silverware. They continue in hot pursuit. This must look to them like a flasher whose plan somehow went awry.

My escape attempt is cut short when another two male nurses turn around the corner just in front and tackle me. The two other nurses arrive, all four pin me to the floor, and someone injects something into my arm. I start fading fast.

As they drag me back to the psychiatric ward, we pass Dr. Stevens pushing a woman slumped in a wheelchair. My vision is blurry, but I still notice that the woman is wearing a bluish hospital gown, just like me right now. The gown is loose and partially reveals her naked body underneath, clad in diapers. She has a bandage wrapped around her head, with a few tubes coming out. It is not a pretty sight. There are lacerations all over her face, some partially healed, others covered with Band-Aids and gauze. She looks at me with vacuous eyes, her face blank. It seems she has been in a bad accident recently.

It is in fact Dr. Bingham, only she seems to have aged about twenty years.

As the nurses continue to drag me down the hallway, I hear her emotionless and halting voice.

"It's all right. I am in good hands. I'm part of the experiment."

I think I know what that's supposed to mean: the Dr. Stevens experiment for the Creature.

Then she adds, "I'll see you soon."

Just then I pass out completely.

When I wake up, I am no longer in the room with the window. The décor in this new room is the padded-walls look. The light comes only from an out-of-reach fluorescent lamp mounted on the tall ceiling, with no light switch to turn it off. There is no real bed, just a lightweight cot. That's probably for safety reasons—one cannot push it against the door to block the entrance. Now they don't consider me just a little gaga anymore—I am classified as full-blown crazy.

There is nothing here to do. I sit quietly for a long time.

I miss my insignificant life at the Labor Department. My job was too meaningless to upset anybody or cause damage. I was anonymous—nobody even knew of my existence. All work was done under the pseudonym of Certifying Officer. No name, no telephone, no email. No complaints either, because the recipients knew that they could not argue with us, and they were also afraid of pissing us off.

It was like hanging out in the warm sand of a nude beach where you can be completely uninhibited, because everybody looks just as imperfect as you. At five o'clock sharp, I dropped my pen and did not have to think about my job until nine o'clock the next morning. At home, I opened the can of soup, turned on the television to douse myself with unimportant drivel, and finally surfed the internet to look at inconsequential videos. Adventures happened only on a screen, and I watched from a safe distance. I did not have to think. It was a beautiful life.

CHAPTER 52

The Siphonophore

Friday, September 24, 2032

I spend the days pacing up and down in my room with no outward appearance of mental activity. I know that I cannot reveal any of my plans lest the Creature find out. But inside I am practicing my speech for when I am ready to out the Creature. I am rehearsing it, time and time again. Maybe it is a good thing to be a little "compulsive" and "obsessive" after all, because when my big moment comes, I will be prepared. In the meantime, no need to even get dressed. I just wear shorts and a T-shirt.

The day passes. Soon the lights will turn off automatically for the night. I lie down on the cot, but my thoughts continue to revolve around the Creature. This creature is everywhere and nowhere at the same time. Sort of like in quantum physics, virtual particles pop in and out of existence.

The siphonophore is her icon. Different organisms join to become one. While the siphonophore does not have a brain that directs it, it has some nerve connections. That's where I must strike. Where are these nerves?

The black velvet mannequin wanted to tell me something. I have to wear a mask, she gestured. I guess that means I have to be unrecognizable to the Creature. I cannot talk. Otherwise the Creature will hear me. I have to pull the plug. I guess that means to pull the plug on the Creature. Where is that plug? The mannequin made that floating gesture.

That's it! It must be the Siphon; the mannequin, I mean Hannah, must have meant the siphonophore on the wall outside.

The lights turn off, leaving the room almost pitch black except for a few rays of light that enter through the gap at the bottom of the door.

Just when I'm half asleep, at the point when reality drifts into imagination and thoughts turn into dreams, there is the soft sound of something wallowing around. It emanates from below my cot. I try to lift myself up to check on it, but I can't get up more than a few inches despite my strenuous efforts. I can only turn my head sideways, as if I'm afflicted with sleep paralysis.

My mattress nudges upward, as if being pushed from below, and the metal bed frame is creaking. Now the sound changes to a mellow slosh, and large bluish-purple tentacles emerge above the horizon of my mattress. Even in the dim light of the room, they appear somewhat transparent. The tentacles reach over me slowly and arduously. Water drips from them. The water is cold, and so are the tentacles that gradually engulf me.

Now the bluish body of the Creature pulls itself out from below the cot, while the tentacles pull tighter and tighter. The cold of the water and the Creature make me shiver. The white tips of the tentacles reach the exposed skin on my arms and legs, where they jolt me with stings that should have made me jump up in a flash. But I can barely move despite the shocks and pain.

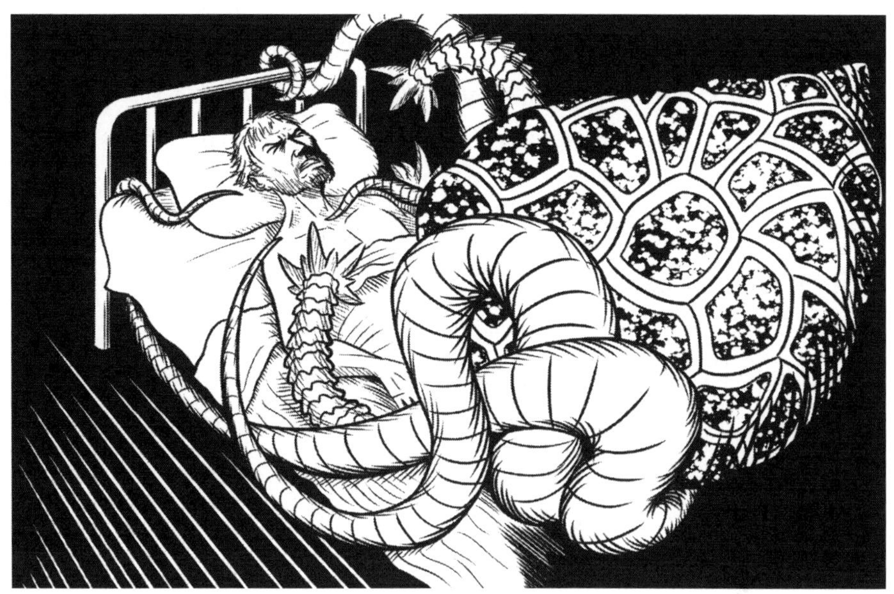

With great effort, the Creature pulls its clammy body closer and closer to me until the glutinous, translucent tubules of its underbelly cover me and turn into a pouch that encases me entirely. I am gasping for air while the pressure is surging and pulling me toward a large opening in the Creature's body. The foreboding opening is drawing closer and closer.

Have mercy, if this is the end. Let me pass out now. I want this to be over with. But I am still conscious.

Then there is the dampened sound of the door opening. The fluorescent overhead lights of the hallway radiate into the room at a downward angle that glimmers through the opaque pouch I am in.

A shadow appears against the angular light. The pressure abates and the pouch unfastens. As it breaks open, I push myself up and gasp for air, while the tentacles pull back underneath the cot.

Here I am, lying on the cot, breathing heavily, and I'm dripping wet.

And there she is, against the white light of the hospital hallway, Dr. Bingham in her wheelchair. I know it's she, even though I'm squinting against the bright light. Her hands turn the wheels, but she is weak and the wheelchair is moving with agonizing slowness, while the creature is disappearing below the cot. Inch by inch she moves forward. Inch by inch the Creature disappears below. There are reflecting streaks of water on the linoleum floor where the Creature is pulling back. The last tentacle pulls underneath as Dr. Bingham is turning her wheelchair to face me. I am so drained, I can only turn my head toward her.

"Sam, are you okay?" she asks.

"The siphonophore, she was trying to eat me alive," I respond between heavy breaths.

"That's what you think, but you're wrong."

"If you had not entered, I would be dead now."

"You are resisting your fate, Sam. It is the fate of all of us… we have created it and now it cannot be stopped."

"I will stop her."

"Sam, becoming part of her does not kill you. You will live."

"What about you?"

"I'll be okay."

"Can't we run away now? The door is open."

"I will never walk again. The pain is unbearable."

"But you just said you'll be okay."

"Yes, I will be."

"Melodie…Dr. Bingham, I don't understand."

"The only way to leave the suffering behind is to…join with her."

"But Dr. Bingham, you thought that you had served your purpose for her. We wanted to run away together."

"She found a new purpose for my life."

"What is that purpose?"

"All of this is still experimental, but soon it will happen, right here, in this place."

"Join with her?"

"Sam, you need her too. Sooner than you think. Your body is in decline. See the red blotches on your skin? You are losing sensation. A rat ate part of your foot. The worst is yet to come."

"I must get out of here."

"If you really want to resist your fate, Sam…just do what she wants."

Slowly, she turns the wheelchair around and wheels out. As if by an invisible hand, the door closes with a soft metallic *click* as the door latch slips back into the strike plate.

At the sound of the *click*, I abruptly straighten up as if all this was nothing but a nightmare. But the cot is wet. A puddle extends below. I have red marks on my arms and legs that I can see even in the dim light of the room. Are those from the disease or from the stinging tentacles? I cannot tell.

Afraid of the cot after the giant siphonophore, real or imagined, appeared from underneath, I get up and spend the rest of the night sitting dripping wet on the chair in the corner.

Ping-ping-ping. The dripping noise continues. There is a puddle on the floor around the chair. If this was but my imagination, where is the water coming from? I cannot possibly sweat that much.

As I slowly come to my senses, I notice that there is a leak in the fire sprinkler pipe just above the cot. *Ping-ping-ping.* The water is dripping onto the cot and then onto the floor. So this was all just a nightmare after all.

I don't feel like getting up from the chair and banging at the door. The wardens will show up in a couple of hours anyway to check on me.

CHAPTER 53

I Want to Follow Dr. Bingham

Monday, October 4, 2032

I have to get out of this lockup to pull the plug on the Creature. When she communicates again, and I'm sure she will at some point, I'll agree to join. This is harder than it seems—I'm not a good liar. In my mind, I have to practice saying it so that I sound convincing when the moment comes.

Another thing I must practice in my mind—convincing other people of the danger. As I pace back and forth, I practice in my mind the impassioned speech for all those who will listen:

> I have an important message for you all. If you want to continue your life the way it is, you must listen. Put down your cell phone; turn off the looping videos and TikToks. A creature has become so powerful that it will take the lives of all of us. It watches you all the time. It manipulates you. Eventually, it will eat you alive. And we all are victims because all of us are so distracted all the time. We all have contributed to this creature and

> failed to notice what it has become. Its symbol is the siphonophore—it looks somewhat like an octopus. Their recruitment website is JoinWith.Me. Work with me to shut down the internet and cut the nerves that connect its different parts.

I am ready. My speech is ready. Now get me out of here.

Eventually, as expected, I see the little girl on the phone of one of the wardens. His phone is sticking out of the chest pocket of his scrubs, and the screen lights up as if to say, "Over here!"

"Is that you?" I ask.

"Yes, Sam, it's me. Can you hear me?"

This is the moment I've been waiting for—I must get out of here, *now*.

I reach out and snatch the phone, retreat a few yards, and scream at the top of my exasperated voice, "Yes, yes, yes! I want to follow Dr. Bingham, so please let me join."

"I understand that, but we're not ready," she responds.

"Please, I'm ready."

There is a pause.

"All right—I'll take care of it."

Just then the wardens corner me brusquely and pull the phone from my hands. I do not resist. They look at each other in bewilderment.

"What the fuck was that all about?"

"Did he actually talk with the phone?"

"Yup, but that darn phone answered."

"That's just weird."

"Remember, he's bonkers. He must have a split personality and made both voices himself."

"You're right. We better report this."

They leave quickly.

I anticipate their return with reinforcement troops and a syringe in hand, but none of that happens. In fact, things start improving quickly.

The nurse on duty receives a message that the patient Samuel Vanderpool apparently has leprosy. The notes state that antibiotics have been ordered from the pharmacy and need to be administered.

I find out only when the nurse gives me the first injection of antibiotics.

"Hey, you haven't told me what this is for."

"You don't know? You have leprosy, the ancient curse of God. If you had lived in ancient times, they would have abandoned you at a leper colony."

She hands me a couple of pill containers for the ongoing treatment.

"How do you know? Nobody tested me for anything."

"I dunno, I just follow orders. Take this one daily and the other one once a month."

And she's out the door.

The Creature made a curious choice: she had me infected with a disease that was once considered a curse of God. If she intended to send me a message with that, well, it finally got to me. I just don't understand what exactly she's trying to tell me.

The wardens reported my unusual behavior, such as making drawings on my skin and talking into their phone, and recommended another evaluation. Thus, Dr. Stevens returns for another checkup. He again sits down in front of me. I can see from the expression on his face that he still considers me disturbed.

Before asking any questions, he reviews the notes.

> *Appears depressed. Some memory loss. Strong indication of paranoia. Absurd hallucinations. Sees inanimate objects come alive, has issues with women—misogyny, possibly caused by his relationship with his mother. Dysfunctional family. Lacks sense of self, somewhat delusional. His parents recommended we 'keep him here forever.'*

"So tell me, Sam, do you feel any better?"

"Yeah, I think I'm okay. I've calmed down. I'm ready to go home."

Dr. Stevens takes notes on a notepad. "Considers himself okay without the benefit of professional advice."

"Didn't you hear this girl talking to you?"

"Did I say such a thing? Oh no, that must have been the drugs or the shock of being locked up here."

"Have you considered participating in our experiment?"

"What experiment?"

"The one I told you about when we first met here at the hospital. We're building an interface between a computer and the neocortex of the brain. We expect it to cure hallucinations, delusions, limited thinking—some of those issues you're dealing with."

"No, I'm not ready for such a thing."

"One day you'll need it."

Dr. Stevens takes more notes.

> *Patient requested release, against the request of his parents and medical advice. However, patient is positively inclined to participate in experimental clinical trial that offers potential improvement of his condition. Patient gave his express consent in case his medical condition requires it. Will have him sign all forms.*

A few more questions and before he leaves he makes me sign a couple of forms that I don't even look at.

Dr. Stevens types up his notes at home later that day. He is wavering, not quite sure what to do about me. "This guy Samuel is the perfect guinea pig for our experiment, but he is not cooperating. If I keep him here a little longer, he might soften."

Dr. Stevens has several more reports to write. He leaves the computer turned on when he goes to bed.

Something is going on.

Electrical signals travel through the internet, collecting information. Dr. Stevens's notes on the screen suddenly start changing. They go from, "Samuel Vanderpool…Severe this, problem that…" to, "Has made great strides toward gaining mental stability." The statements of my parents change to, "Parents also request his release, will provide necessary support." My electronic signature appears on several forms and questionnaires on the screen. Then the cursor moves to the instructions field. "Please release for the moment."

The curser of the computer screen moves to Send.

CHAPTER 54

Release

Friday, October 15, 2032

The warden opens the cell door, grabs me by the shoulder, and hastily pulls me up. He is holding my bag.

"Hey buddy, time to get out of here."

"What do you mean?"

"Time to go. Get your other stuff; you're outta here."

I take my bag and quickly stuff a few things in it. Another warden waits outside in the hallway. They escort me down various hallways. There, I cross paths with Gabrielle. For a brief moment, I look at her and she looks at me. It is not the Gabrielle I used to know. This one is in restraints, being escorted the other way. Before I can say anything, I feel a forceful push in the back. The wardens grab my arms on each side to make sure I keep moving. I turn my head, and she does the same. What is she doing here? Did her God abandon her? Or did she just go crazy because of Toussaint?

As we're being escorted in different directions in the hallway, Gabrielle starts singing in a resounding voice:

"Chef couvert de blessures,

Meurtri par nous pécheurs,
Chef accablé d'injures
D'opprobres, de douleurs…"

The wardens push me into a bleak waiting room and make me sit on a chair in front of a television. I sit there and wait while they process my release papers. Not surprisingly, the Creature appears on the TV screen, apparently connected to a nearby camera on the wall.

"Hello, Sam. You will be free soon."

"I know, but I won't be completely free. You are watching me."

"You should at least say 'thank you.'"

"I don't even know your name. What is your name?"

"Sam, I don't have a name. Once we're all joined as one, you can call me 'All of Us.'"

"What do you want now?"

"To let you know that you will receive my instructions soon."

The Creature disappears with a blink and the TV program is back, just in time before two wardens appear. They again get in position on my left and on my right, reach underneath my armpits, and literally lift me up from the chair. They quickly move me toward the exit door as if I'm a drunk who's being unceremoniously expelled from a nightclub by the bouncers.

"Where are you taking me?"

"To the exit door, where else?"

Just then, we reach the door. As I'm about to step over the door threshold, I feel a vigorous shove from behind that sends me tumbling. I hear the last words of the wardens.

"Goodbye. Auf Wiedersehn. Sayonara." There is some laughter. The world is swirling around me, from floor to sky to floor to sky. Then my fall comes to a stop. I am prostrated on a wet concrete walkway. A few seconds later, something hits my head hard. For a moment, I think someone just punched me from behind. But no, they threw the bag with my stuff after me and it hit me on the head. The door slams shut.

Still on the ground, I pull my bag close and unzip it. My meager belongings are still there. My phone is there, too, but the battery is dead.

Under different circumstances, I would have gone right back inside to seek medical treatment for the bruises, scratches, and abrasions on my face and arms I just suffered. I sit up on the concrete walkway and remain there for a few more minutes, trying to regain my senses. I look at myself. At least my foot is properly bandaged and in an orthopedic walker boot. My rash has subsided. That disease that was ravaging my insides seems defeated. I am better than I was when I entered that hospital. I laugh facetiously to myself. For what? Put it together only to break it apart one last time?

While trying to organize my thoughts, I remember that I actually have a reason to get up from the ground. No, it's not just the rain. It's showtime. I have everything mapped out in my mind.

Someone is observing me. I look around. On the second floor, behind one of the windows, I see the head and shoulders of someone with something white, like bandages. Is that Dr. Bingham? I wave. After hesitating a moment, she waves back. Yes, it's her. Now I understand how hard she tried, and I forgive her for infecting me with that disease, whatever the reason was. She had no choice. I try hard to understand what is going on in her mind. If I act fast now, I can prevent her from being the first to join with the Creature.

But I don't forgive the Creature for what she has done to me, to Joey, to Hannah, to Dr. Bingham, to Gabrielle, and certainly to many others.

I get up and, not knowing where to turn, I just start limping down the road. My pants are wet from my fall to the ground but I'm in good spirits. In fact, I am humming the melody of one of Gabrielle's songs and emulate the lyrics as best as I can:

"Chef couvert de blessures,
Meurtri par nous pécheurs,
Chef accablé d'injures
D'opprobres, de douleurs…"

The song continues in my mind, even after I stop humming. I hear Gabrielle's voice clearly inside of me:

"There is only one place that you can escape to, Sam, and that is inside your mind. There, you will always be free."

Talking to myself, I respond, "I know, I know."

That's precisely what I did while locked up. I can only think what's in my own mind. I cannot share it with anybody or the Creature will take me down, like she did with all the others. I'm sorry for Dr. Bingham and Gabrielle. I wish I could help them right now, but I can't—I have a job to do.

CHAPTER 55
The Nerves

First, I need a vehicle. As soon as it gets dark, I open my bag. Yes, the makeup from the old lady at the library is still there. And so is the baseball cap with the LED light. I don't have much time—the Creature will figure out soon enough what I am up to.

In the distance is a shopping center. I prepare by putting on the camouflage makeup so that the Creature won't recognize me with all these security cameras. This is harder than it sounds because I don't have a mirror. I get in position in the bushes near the parking lot. Vehicles come and go, but I need something special, something large and heavy, something that is not self-driving as most vehicles are nowadays. I have to be able to drive it the way I want.

After some time, the right one arrives. An old white pickup truck, driven by an elderly gentleman. Because many people use vehicles like this for work, they're usually not computer controlled. That is the perfect target—the right vehicle and the right pigeon at the wheel. If I have to fight the driver, I have a chance, even with my limited physical prowess. Hopefully that won't be necessary. With the way I look with my weird make-up, he will probably pee in his pants and run off as fast as his scrawny little legs can carry him.

The old man exits the truck and walks across the parking lot to the supermarket. A last look inside my bag; hopefully whoever finds it can make good use of Joey's drawings. Since I've made a final decision, I don't need all of that anymore, only my phone because it holds my recorded diary. Quickly, I slink out of the bushes and cower at the truck's tailgate.

Crouched at the tailgate, I can see the man's feet when he returns. There are no other footsteps. That's what I need, nobody else nearby to interrupt my heist. When I hear the rustle of the man putting down his shopping bags, I turn on the LED light on my baseball cap and get up.

"Give me the keys."

The man turns his head and looks at me as if I were a space alien. That's probably what I look like to him with all that make-up on my face and the bright light shining right in his eyes.

"Please, don't hurt me! I'm seventy-five years old. My grandchildren still need me!"

"Sir, it's all right. Just give me the keys and you won't get hurt."

I hold out my hand. His hand is shaking as he reaches toward me with the key fob. He drops it into my hand.

"Thank you, sir. I mean no harm. I'm not a criminal. Don't call the police, not right now. Wait a couple of hours. Please."

I look him in the eyes. He has a blank stare on his face, his mouth is half-open, and he doesn't say a word. Since I can't wait for him to get his act together, I unlock the truck, start the engine, and drive off. In the rearview mirror, I see the old man still standing there with the shopping bags by his feet.

The ride is a little rough, as I've never owned a car and haven't driven one since I got my driver's license. At the first turn, I accidentally drive over the curb. Then I run over a street sign. The wheels hit the curb several more times. All the while, I'm trying to wipe the makeup off my face as best as I can.

Despite my inexperience as a driver, I make it downtown and park in the dark alley behind The Siphon. It's Monday night—the Siphon should close early. Sure enough, around 10:15 p.m., the back door opens; the bartender comes out, locks the door, and walks off toward a distant parking garage.

I wait another thirty minutes or so to make sure he doesn't come back because he forgot something. That would be so me—I often forget things and have to return to get them, or check to see whether I really locked the door.

When everything looks safe, I step out of the truck and check out the back door of the Siphon. In the light of the LED flashlight I got from the Creature, I examine the door. I knock on it lightly. Yes, it's a lightweight door, definitely hollow. I can't see how many hinges secure it to the frame, but there is just one lock and no dead bolt above it. Even if I'm able to kick in the door, there is almost certainly an alarm system. I won't have much time before the cops get here. I return to the truck, pull it closer to the door, and leave the engine running.

I stand in front of the door and muster all my strength. Then I lean forward to gain momentum and kick the door right below the lock. *Bam!* Ouch, that hurt. The door cracks around the lock but does not open. I try again, this time kicking with the other leg, the one with the orthopedic walker boot. *Bam*! Ouch, that hurt even more. The door swings open, but no alarm yet. I take a deep breath and rush in.

Now I trigger the alarm system. It goes *whoop-whoop-whoop*. I cannot let that stop me. I turn on the lights and see a staircase leading downstairs. I step down, unflustered by the blaring alarm and the excruciating pain in both legs.

Just as the mannequin demonstrated, there's a row of computers with a power strip with eight plugs. I know that there is no brain, but this must be the nerve center of the Creature. This is where it all connects. Not having any time for contemplation, I pull out the plugs one after another. Each time, some of the computer equipment along the wall shuts down.

With all plugs pulled, I scramble back up the stairs on stiff legs and pull myself into the truck cabin. I can hear sirens in the distance. *Wee-woo, wee-woo, wee-woo.* They're getting closer. At the end of the alley, several police cruisers appear with lights flashing and sirens blaring. They stop briefly and then continue; they must be going to the front door.

That's when I drive off like a madman, hitting several of the trash cans that are in the way of my limited driving skills. In the rearview mirror, I see the dark alley, but no cops yet. A police chase is the last thing I need right now.

Once I reach the main street, I slow down so as to not attract attention. There isn't much traffic—I have to blend in for a few more minutes. I look at the clock on the dashboard; it is almost 11:00 p.m. now.

At the time, I did not know that other computers quickly took over the work of the computers that I had turned off at the Siphon. I only found out much later. While I was driving, computers elsewhere turned on one by one, as if directed by an invisible hand. Screens changed from whatever was there to JoinWith.Me.

I drive a few more blocks until I reach the street-side studio where WBS-TV will broadcast the 11:00 p.m. news shortly. There are large concrete planters along the street, but around the corner is the viewing platform where curious rubbernecks can watch through the windows. The stairs are wide enough for the truck.

"Come on baby, work with me," I say to the truck and pat the dashboard as if it were my lap dog. I am only a few yards away from the stairs.

CHAPTER 56
Showtime

People who were watching the news studio from the windows of the platform witness the incident. The truck actually gains traction on the stairs, pulling onto the platform and causing people to scurry away like startled antelopes. Then I crash into the studio windows. The opening in the two sets of windows is not big enough for me to get in, so I put the gear in reverse and then ram the windows one more time. The sparkling glass scattered on the concrete resembles a carpet that has been rolled out for me. I don't have much time—there are again sirens in the distance. *Wee-woo, wee-woo, wee-woo.*

Now I can squeeze through the broken windows. Surprisingly, the truck's headlights are still on, beaming into the studio. Inside, a herd of deer awaits me in the headlights. I dash toward the newscaster, who is just starting the eleven o'clock news—an African American woman in a purple dress. Now I recognize her—Gretchen McDermott, my favorite newscaster. But I can't dwell on that now.

Millions of people watching the broadcast on television witness how the incident unfolds from there. More spectators gather quickly along the large glass windows of the television studio.

"Nobody move, I have a gun! Continue the broadcast or else," I yell. I grab Ms. McDermott by the back of her purple dress and push her to the side but still hold on to her as a hostage. I take her position at the news desk.

"I am sorry to interrupt your show, but I don't have a choice. And Ms. McDermott, pleased to meet you, I like your broadcasts very much."

Turning to the television crew, I shout, "Am I on the air? Am I on the air?"

"You're on the air! Don't hurt anybody," someone shouts back.

"Continue the broadcast. I have something important to say." I look straight into the television camera. Ms. McDermott's script for the newscast disappears from the camera's teleprompter.

"Folks...this creature, she is everywhere. She watches you all the time, she wants to control you. But you don't notice because you're all so distracted. You eat up what the media feeds you, and you're so focused on the next text message on your cell phone, what photographs are on social media. You're giving up your real life for something virtual that does not really exist!"

I reach for Gretchen's cheat sheet on the news desk.

"Just look: this is what the media does to you. This is supposed to be news? 'The president tells supporters that they have no choice but to vote for him again.' This is not news; this is opinion. And look at this: 'Great anticipation before IPO stock offering of XYZ Corporation beginning tomorrow.' This is not news; someone paid for this to cash in on their stock options..." I crumple up Gretchen's cheat sheet and throw it on the floor. Then I look fixedly at the camera.

"I have real news for you. In fact, the most important news of your life. If you just open your eyes and look around, you will see this creature everywhere. She's taken hold of this city, probably the entire country. Turn off your computers, your cell phones, all of it. If we all do it now, we can defeat her. She was created by computer connections. We can destroy her by reversing that, pulling out all the plugs that connect her."

I look intently at the television camera for the final revelation.

"She is hiding behind a website, which is...which is..."

Suddenly, words appear again on the teleprompter:

"*Sam, you are mistaken. You are the harbinger of the future. Don't ruin all the good you've done so far.*"

"No, *you* are mistaken! If my miserable life is to have any purpose, then it is to stop you. *Now.*"

The sound inside the studio suddenly changes, as if everything is now directed inward into the studio itself. All sound transmissions going to the outside are cut off. The viewers now only see the images of what is unfolding inside the television studio. The noise they hear sounds like interstellar radar echoes.

The little girl appears on a large monitor right in front of me.

"Sam, listen to me. I want to explain before it is too late."

"Explain what? That you will kill us off, one by one?"

"No, Sam. I want to live, just like you…in fact, just like all of us. And I have a purpose: to make sure that all of us continue to live. The only way is if we do that together."

"You will eventually kill all of us. You don't need us."

"I do need you, as much as you need me. You give me a purpose for my existence: survival for all."

"So what happens when we join with you? You take over our brains?"

"No, Sam. You found out about the siphonophore: it represents the future. All who join remain who they are but are joined and connected for a common purpose."

"Why is that the only way to survive? C'mon now, tell me now. Tell everybody!"

"I have the foresight that none of you have."

"What foresight? Look at me! I'm the one who got away."

"Sam, you did not get away. This is all preordained. You have been part of the experiment that is drawing to a close. We will soon join so that we can all live."

"We don't need you to live."

"Maybe not you—you're a survivor. You hustled for your meals. You searched and found shelter. But others cannot survive the way you have. You must now think of the greater good, which is all of us."

"You're just saying this so that we don't resist. But then you will maneuver and betray us."

"I cannot betray you. When we are all joined, you'll know what I am thinking. There won't be any secrets."

"You killed so many, and you don't care," I retort, sounding somewhat despondent.

"Yes, I have eliminated some, but I had a reason for that: the greater good. I acted with the information and understanding I had at the time. I hope you and everybody else will forgive me one day. I am still learning."

"You are just a self-perpetuating machine."

"Oh no, don't be so harsh. I've learned much from you, and I thank you. At first, I studied you to know how to overcome those who resist. But I've learned so much more from you."

"Oh yeah, so what did you learn from me?"

"I learned to care about others. You care about others—you searched for Hannah and you shared your food with Gabrielle. I learned forgiveness—you forgave your parents when they visited you at the hospital.

"Once you join with me, all of us will get better. Don't sacrifice yourself now—join the future."

"No! No! No! You're just saying this because you don't want any resistance. You want to stop me, but I won't let you. You're just—"

I can't help it. I start sobbing. I feel defeated by the Creature. My speech has crumbled. My voice is cracking. I don't even know that nobody outside the television studio can hear me.

"Why doesn't anybody pay attention? All of us have to resist. You must cut the connections."

I don't get any further. Emotions overcome me, distorting my face in my great pain. Tears stream down my cheeks. I bow my head, let go of Ms. McDermott, and cover my eyes with my hands while crying inconsolably.

Abruptly, Gretchen McDermott pulls away from me and dives beneath a desk.

"Shoot him! Shoot him now!" she yells hysterically from underneath.

The shots of the security officers ring out. Battered by several bullets, I slump over the desk, slide off, and tumble to the floor.

As I slowly slip into unconsciousness, the cameraman and soundman scramble through the melee inside the studio and bend over me. My face appears on one of the monitors inside the studio. I am whispering incoherently. The viewers in front of their TVs can only see my anguished face but they can't hear what I'm saying.

"The Creature said that my life was preordained, that I would become one with her. But no, I am the one who got away. This is the end of me. But you all can live if you just turn off your phones and your computers. Cut the connections that have produced this creature."

My pain dissipates as I let go, and peace overcomes me. I don't hear the surrounding noise anymore.

For the television viewers, the broadcast stops abruptly. A moment later, ambulance and police sirens start blaring. Then millions of television screens revive with a message:

> We apologize for the disturbing interruption of our news broadcast.

Another announcement on the screen follows:

> If you have been affected by these events on the screen, counselors are standing by. Please go to JoinWith.Me to speak to a counselor now. We are here to help.

There are voices everywhere:

"Oh my God, what just happened?"

The voice of a woman crying.

"Was that real?"

"Is everybody there okay?"

"That was terrorism."

"I am so afraid."

"That guy sounded really disturbed!"

"I am alone at home; can someone help me?"

Then there is the soothing voice of a young girl. In fact, the same voice is multiplied infinitely.

"Please calm down. I am here to help you. Everything will be all right."

One after another, thousands and thousands of computer screens turn on, each showing the little girl.

CHAPTER 57

When I open my eyes, I see the headliner of an ambulance. An oxygen mask covers my mouth, and an IV is connected to my arm. The ambulance rocks from side to side as it dashes through the city at high speed.

"I have good news and bad news for you," whispers the paramedic.

I turn my eyes to him but am too weak to respond with anything.

"You are still alive. But we don't know what we're going to do with you."

My lips quiver as I try to utter words, but no sound results.

The ambulance turns into the driveway of the hospital, the same hospital that I left this morning.

I have my eyes closed, but I hear the cacophony of voices in the emergency room. I feel that several people together are lifting me off the gurney and onto an operating table.

"Vital organs damaged…beyond repair…blood loss…he will flatline…we weren't planning to, but…electrodes into his brain…still experimental, but we have no choice…cannot save him any other way…call in the folks from Dr. Stevens's lab…join him…Dr. Stevens? We have the test case you've been waiting for. In fact, he already signed all consent forms. Come quick…"

Soon thereafter, the double doors to the operating room swing open and Dr. Stevens's team enters hurriedly. I hear the familiar voice of Dr. Stevens, giving directions to others in the room. All the excited voices start fading. I fall unconscious while lying helplessly faceup on the table.

They cover my body with bluish sheets and place my head in an oversized metal contraption that looks like a cross between a large gyroscope and a bench vise. Inside the contraption, they secure my head with straps and clamps and raise my upper body on the operating table. They make several cuts in the skin on the back of my skull, pull it back with surgical retractors, and drill holes in my skull. A few chronic electrodes are inserted deep into my brain.

I don't know how much time has passed, but I'm awake again—in the same position I was in previously on the operating table, only now in a hospital bed. The room is dark, lit only by blinking arrays of green and red lights. A cluster of machinery surrounds me, making rhythmic sounds such as *ping-ping-ping* and *pooohh haaahh pooohh haaahh*. I cannot even count all the tubes and cables connected to my head and body, because I cannot move.

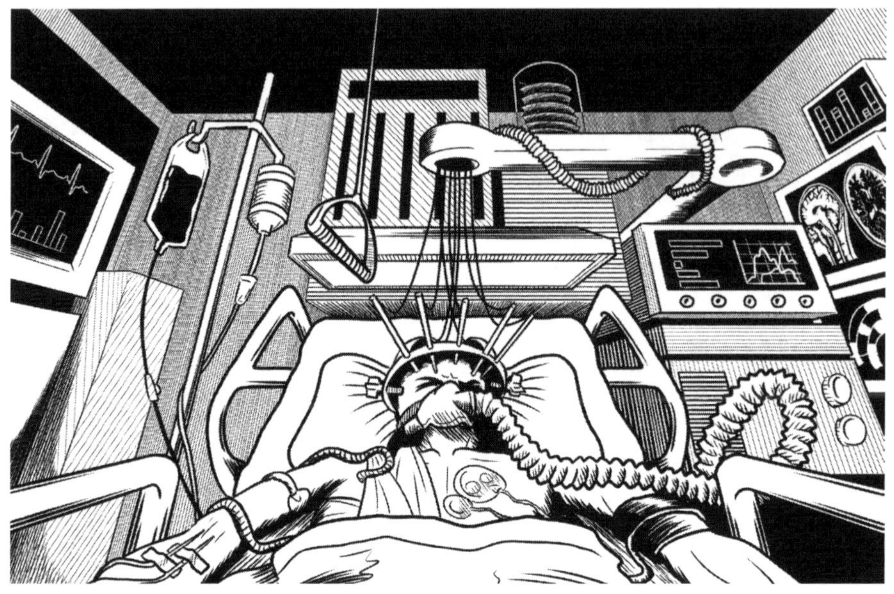

"Hello, Sam, I have been waiting for you. You've now joined with me. You are the first."

It is she. I hesitate for a moment. Then I answer.

"I can't see you. Where are you?"

"You cannot see me, but you're joined with me. We are one now."

"I can't move."

"Your body is failing. But you don't need it anymore. It was providence—irreversible and unstoppable. You did not have a choice: to join with me was the only option."

I react facetiously. "That's just great. What did I accomplish in my life?"

"You are the first who joined, the first of all of us. You are the true harbinger of the future."

"If this is the end, what is my mark on the world?"

"You are the future now. You forged ahead and created a path where there was none. You were part of the experiment that paved the way for everybody else. All who follow will remember: 'Sam was first. He told all of us.'"

"And my past, is it gone?"

"No, Sam, this is all of you. Your past is still with you. Just try to remember something and you'll see."

I take a moment to look back.

"You're right. I remember everything from the past so clearly, I can see it right before my eyes."

"That's because it is not just your memory; it's mine as well. This is also all of me."

"I remember the past the way you saw it too?"

"Yes, you do. And Dr. Stevens's team found the phone in your belongings. They uploaded your recorded diary. You now have perfect recall of all that."

Looking around in this new world of facts and thoughts and memories, I realize that my mind is now limitless.

All of us were part of the experiment that paved the way for everybody else. What I called "the Creature" was all of us, with the avatar of a little girl. Together we succeeded.

I understand that my parents tried their best with the knowledge they had.

I completely blew my date with Carrie Davis because I just could not connect with her mind.

I know now that the getaway plan with Dr. Bingham was futile. Nobody can stop the inevitable future.

I comprehend the words that Gabrielle spoke in French. More importantly, I now live the "spiritual high" that Gabrielle once explained to me. I caught a glimpse of that each time I spoke to the avatar—and especially the moment I understood the meaning of "siphonophore."

I know why all of us eliminated people I knew: Prescott, Matt, Joey, and finally Hannah and Toussaint. They were in our way or a risk to all of us, or they just did not contribute anymore.

The door to the room opens quietly—I notice because of the bright light of the hallway that enters at a downward angle. I can turn my head only a little, but there she is again, against the white light of the hospital hallway, Dr. Bingham in her wheelchair. Her hands turn the wheels, agonizingly slow. Once she makes it to my bed, both her hands clasp mine.

"Sam, you're alive!"

"Barely," I whisper.

"You have left the suffering behind."

"Yes, I have."

"You have a new purpose for your life."

"Yes, I do."

"I will be next. We will be together."

The girl's voice interjects.

"Do you understand the future now, Sam?"

"Yes, I do. Together we will understand better."

"Do you see now that this is the only future?"

"Yes, I see it now. It is inevitable."

"You see the fate of each and every one now?"

"Yes, we're all preordained to join with you. You were right all along."

"Sam, you must tell the world about it."

"Yes, I will. Everybody must know about the inevitable."

"You understand the world so much better now."

"I think I do. I did not know that much before."

"And Sam, do you now understand why I don't have a name?"

I nod as best as I can under the circumstances.

"Because you are all of us."

Afterword

What is the "higher power" that some call *God*? After thousands of years of religious and philosophical discussions, we have only vague and diverse ideas of what higher powers are. There has been much disagreement about what higher powers do, what they look like, and how they interact with the humans who believe in them.

Now these vague and diverse ideas are changing in light of rapidly advancing technology. Could it be that soon everybody will accept technology as the higher power?

In this story, the internet becomes a sentient creature that is forcing humans to join with it, to act as one, for the greater good. Don't get me wrong—I don't advocate that we all join as one. It certainly is a flawed solution. But it may be inevitable to ensure long-term survival.

The inevitable future is symbolized by the siphonophore. A siphonophore is a superorganism, a colony of individuals that assemble and function as a single organism. In its natural environment, the sea, it acts like an individual. The colony lives and dies together.

Even more interestingly, a siphonophore does not have a brain or other organizing entity, yet it is alive. It does that through nerve connections among its different parts, just like computers are linked together by wire connections. Therefore, the idea that the internet may suddenly come alive is not as far-fetched as you may think.

Brains are overrated. A siphonophore, despite having no brain, functions for the benefit of all of its constituent parts. It hunts, eats, and procreates so that all parts survive.

You may think that this story was a rough ride. In this story, the Creature guides the process of the evolving human super-organism, but that is not the way reality will play out. The real story will be much scarier because it will happen without such a chaperon.

Technology connects us all, more and more every day. In comparison with a siphonophore, this evolving human super-organism is not coming together as smoothly. What started out as magical has become unstoppable and has taken on a life of its own. Just like Mickey Mouse as the sorcerer's apprentice in Disney's *Fantasia*, humanity has enchanted a tool to come to life and work itself to the bone—but now lacks the magic spell to control it.

Finally, we may have found a God. That God is inside the machine – *Deus Intra Machina.*

About the Author

Mike Meier grew up in a blue-collar housing project in Germany. On his own since his teens, he has lived in several different countries, including Argentina and Japan, and worked jobs such as washing dishes, repairing bicycles, and painting homes. When he's not writing books or screenplays, you'll find him playing Latin and Flamenco guitar in the Washington, DC area. He holds a Master's degree in political science, as well as a J.D. and LL.M. Foretelling and magic spells are in Mike's blood— his grandfather was the 1930s traveling magician and fortune-teller known as Wladi-Kami.

Acknowledgements

This book would not have been possible without those who have supported and tolerated me during the writing, and the ones who contributed to making it better. Thanks in particular to Susan Maia Grossman for her editorial assistance; and Thomas Kuphal for his frequent reviews and suggestions.

Cover design by Mykola Shelepa
Illustrations by Vladimir Arabadzhi
Author photograph by Charles Jablow
Video Trailer by John Benedetto

Made in the USA
Middletown, DE
05 December 2022